KNIGHTS OF THE ALLIANCE

STEFANIE CHU

CANARI PUBLISHING

KNIGHTS OF THE ALLIANCE

First Edition: October 2021

Second Edition: May 2022

ISBN: 978-1-7377125-0-3 (paperback)

ISBN 978-1-7377125-1-0 (hardcover)

Cover by *Booksmith Designs*

Map by *Janas Art Fantasy Illustration*

To family & friends who light my fire.

And the people who choose to challenge their fate
and let imagination take the reins.

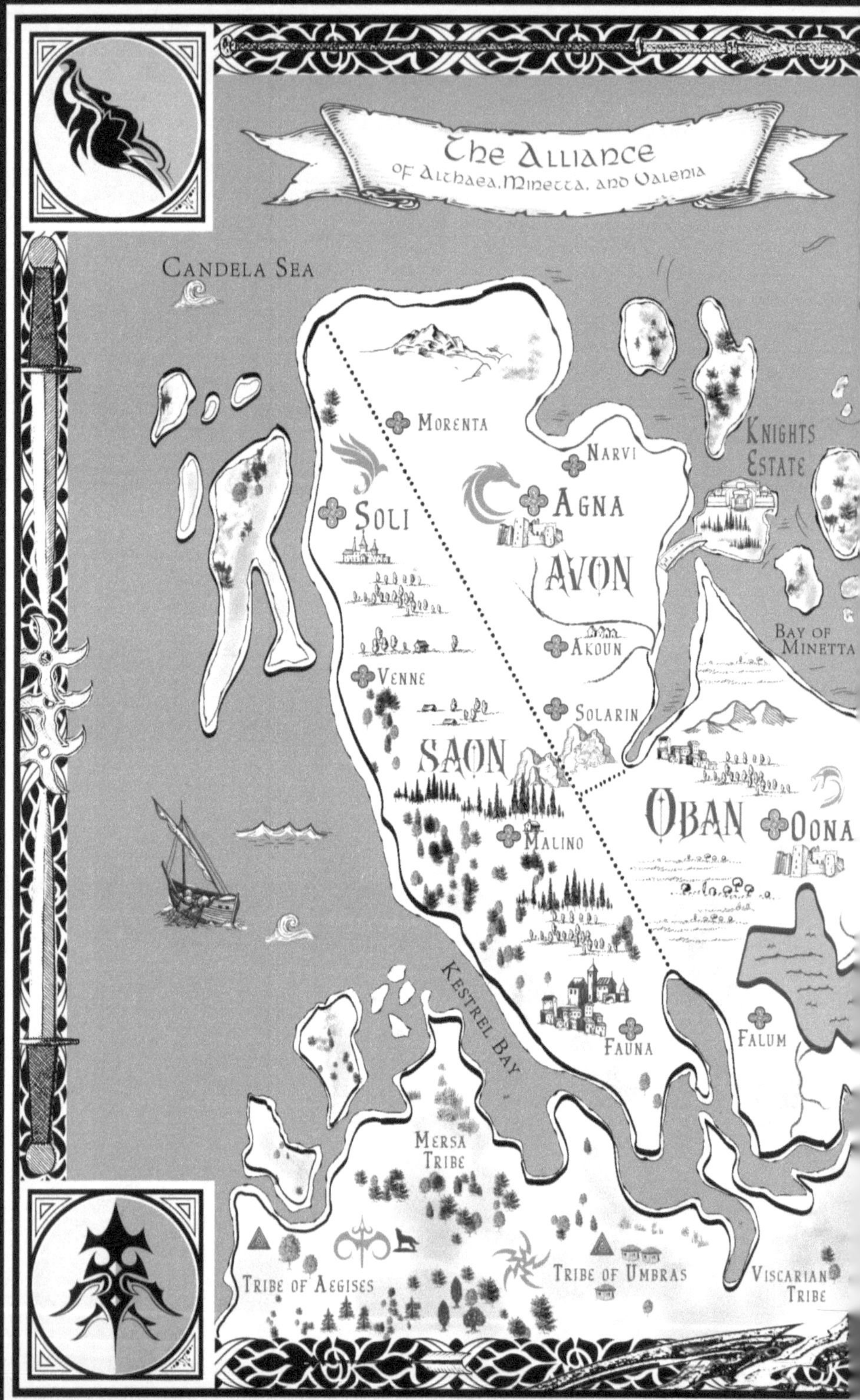
The Alliance
of Althaea, Minetta, and Valenia
CANDELA SEA
MORENTA
NARVI
SOLI
AGNA
AVON
KNIGHTS ESTATE
AKOUN
BAY OF MINETTA
VENNE
SOLARIN
SAON
OBAN
OONA
MALINO
KESTREL BAY
FAUNA
FALUM
MERSA TRIBE
TRIBE OF AEGISES
TRIBE OF UMBRAS
VISCARIAN TRIBE

ALTHAEAN SEA
ALTHACITY
ALTHA HILLS
ALLETE
ELEGEN
EVALEEN
KISHNIN
EKVELT
NAMANI
DESDEMONA
RHEA
YOUNTILLA RIVER
ALTHAEA MAIN
NANAKA
ENDINE
ALTHAEA MAIN
NAIAD
GANMALI
OLINA
GULF OF ORIS
OPHALLEN
LAKE URABE
AXILLAIRE
XERAN
TRIBE OF CELTAS
BELLIGMN TRIBE
ZLAN TRIBE
ALYSSI
THE HEARTH
TRIBE OF PARAGONS
N
W
E
S

THE ALLIANCE

Empire of
ALTHAEA

Councilors
ADDER & SUZAN

ALTHAEA MAIN
Leader: Gaven

AXILLAIRE
Leader: Yoah

EVALEEN
Leader: Landon

ALTHA HILLS
Leader: High Priest

NANAKA
Leader: Noire

OPHALLEN
Leader: Cole

PROLOGUE

A dozen fighters stood below the ashen sky, weapons bristling as they surrounded a lone warrior. The man and his spear were dripping with blood, but the soldiers circling him knew that the blood was not his own.

I wrinkled my nose. Seeing crimson trickle down his blade brought my attention back to the rancid stench that had paved the boulder field. Even with my mask, the smell was nauseating. It reminded me of how many had fallen during this battle. I couldn't let their efforts be in vain.

A chilly wind snatched at their cloaks of authority and set their assorted banners snapping like spinnakers in a gale. This alliance of soldiers fought under various insignia, their competing flags telling a story of their own. They were not a single army, but a unified force from different empires and regions.

And I was the man who had gathered them all together to crush the rebellion led by the gory warrior. This was the endgame.

In my hand, I held a silver spear I rarely used. I could fight if I had to, but strategizing was my forte. And my plan had worked.

The majority of his rebels were crushed or had scattered. Now, he was cornered, alone, facing an entire army. That was not unusual; he was known as the warrior without a partner. But it only made his presence more frightening. It wouldn't surprise me if he took down the dozens of men before him in less than a minute. The soldiers knew as well. Anyone who valued their life wouldn't dare confront the Valiant Tiger.

This proud fighter had no quit in him. He bellowed and jeered, daring any man to come forward and challenge him.

There were no takers.

To face him. To face death. Were they all cowards?

Seeing the crazed look in his eyes, and the way his chest heaved with labored breaths, I was struck by a surprising certainty.

He's gone insane.

A babble of thoughts floated around my head, unheard to anyone but me, tinged in varying degrees of anger and confusion.

The madman thinks he's invincible.

I always knew he was crazed.

The power must've gone to his head. Typical Althaean.

My brow furrowed in concentration as I tried to block out the intrusive chatter. At times, it was mild enough to ignore if I concentrated hard enough. Other times, it was like being locked in a room with a dozen screaming children throwing tantrums. This was the latter.

Between all the sentiments and convictions overwhelming me, two people stood out from the rest: the warrior we had surrounded – cloaked in the finest silver armor and blue cape suitable for the highest ranks – and the seemingly fragile young lady that I brought along with me on this campaign.

What made them different? Their minds were blank. I couldn't hear what they were thinking.

Then, I sensed a change as all those gathered around reacted with surprise, curiosity, and confusion. I soon understood why, as the massed troops parted. The young lady strode forward, toward the open ground that harbored the bloody rebel foe.

As this fearless challenger approached the battleground, the confounded roar of feelings assailed me. Awe. Disbelief. Even shame… For this challenger entering the ring to face the rebel leader was no battle-hardened centurion – no scarred and grizzled myrmidon. She was just a fragile-looking young woman – practically a girl. Not a single one of the fatigued soldiers gaping at this wisp of a thing believed for one moment that she stood a chance.

Except, of course, for me. I didn't know precisely what powers or abilities she possessed, but whatever force she had inside her, I knew it would be terrible to behold. The zeal in her upturned eyes – passionate flares of glowing magenta – told me the same.

Even the heavily muscled rebel, who had proved his lethal prowess a thousand times, looked utterly perplexed at the sight of her. He ripped his spear out from the soldier underneath him and blood splattered onto his polished armor. The bodies that lay around him were like trophies, a prideful display of his strength. But for the girl, the sight of the fallen acted as fuel, making her glare more frightening.

"What is this?" he bellowed. "You miserable cowards send a maiden to do—"

He never finished. Her blood-curdling scream struck like a wave of force as she charged at him with astonishing speed and a sword in hand. He got his spear up just in time to block her first slashing attack.

The sound of their dancing blades echoed through the field, drawing the attention of fighters from both sides. The two of them were locked in combat, so intense that they seemed unaware of the host of bodies surrounding them.

What was going on in their minds? I hadn't a clue. Their

walls were impenetrable; my mental powers were no match for them.

The girl slashed and parried, her assault driven by an immense rage. Their weapons clashed and swiped with such speed it was all a blur. The warrior waved his hand, commanding the ground below them to shatter and erupt. But the girl danced upon the rising rubble, her feet light as wind as she leveraged the fragmented earth to give herself the advantage of the high-ground. She raised her sword to the sky, then struck down with the full force of her body.

The impact of their weapons sent high-pitched waves that caused my neck to tingle, and caused some of the spectators to cower between their arms.

I felt a tug on my arm followed by the warm embrace of my wife's tender hands. I had advised her not to come on this dangerous mission, but she insisted. We had gone on every adventure together after all for decades now. Every battle could use the expertise of a fine healer like her.

"What's going on?" Starlight yelled, covering her flawless face with her arm. Her rose-colored hair, which had always reminded me of thin strands of fairy floss, waved in all directions. I didn't need to see her worried face to discern the distress in her heart.

I stepped in front of my disoriented wife, not wanting her exposed to the peril of this battle any longer. She was a fearless woman, a fighter who carried more courage than my sorry excuse of a warrior. But something profoundly uncommon, not to mention dangerous, was going on. I couldn't explain it. Normally, the outcome was clear and predictable, but what we were witnessing here was far from normal, and the clashing forces of these two combatants threw the rules of the ordinary world into unforeseeable chaos.

Despite my absorption in the battle before me, an awareness pushed forth from the back of my mind. Many soldiers on both sides had been severely injured in the battle that took place earlier.

"Take care of the wounded," I told my wife, reaching into my pocket and handing over a handful of renastōnes to increase her healing capability. She nodded and proceeded to treat bloodied soldiers with the power of kore in the stones.

These probably won't be enough, I heard her think. But even so, I held two stones back, just in case the fight behind me didn't end well.

The warrior attacked and defended with all the mastery and strength of a champion. But the girl, who seemed to be without skill or training, fought with a reckless, murderous fury, fueled by all the demons in Inferna.

Maybe that's why I wasn't surprised when I saw the small ball of fire she caressed in her left palm. She appeared confident now and tossed her sword away as if it were just a bother. The reddish flame she wielded was a rare occurrence and she had absolute control over it.

Although I couldn't read his thoughts, the sudden caution on the warrior's face spoke volumes. It was clear the dynamic had shifted. The girl's elemental control over fire changed everything.

How unusual, I reflected, to see such overwhelming force coming from a commoner who had never seen a battlefield before. Yet, here she was, more than matched to Althaea's greatest warrior.

How... fascinating.

A larger flame erupted from her hand, and she charged straight at the warrior, her voice crying out in a valiant roar. The warrior dodged her fiery attack, darting left and right, blocking her hand with his metallic blue spear, handled with a mastery no other could match. The involuntary fear that erupted in him did not affect his combat skills; they remained the best I have ever seen.

The rest of us kept our distance – it would be unwise to go

near the flames. We could all feel the heat upon our faces, dispelled by the swirling gusts of high winds blowing from the towering mountain in the backdrop. Small balls of fire splashed loose from the girl's hand, like sparks popping from a hot fireplace. They bounced across the ground, erupting in small brushfires in the patches of the tall, dry grass in the boulder field.

For once, I was grateful to be wearing the mask I use to cover my face at all times. Both to conceal the shame of my mutilations, and my very identity, hidden since the cruel punishment of my youthful self. Now, it gave me the advantage of being able to tolerate the heat, and see clearly, while everyone else buried their heads in their shirts.

"Fang, we need to do something!" Shiba caught my attention. He anxiously awaited my command alongside his powerful lieutenant, Neo.

Yes, of course. That was the whole reason I was invited here – to lead this motley alliance of troops from Althaea, Minetta, and Valenia to stop the rebellion.

But frankly, my plan was now obsolete. What we were watching made our petty strategies worthless. Our forces, and those of the enemy, were all enthralled with the epic duel raging before us. We were merely spectators, captivated by the champion warrior trying to curb the astonishing girl and her fiery punches without letting up. Her assault continued, setting pockets of the field on fire every so often. Her hits kept the man at bay, but he was still physically stronger, and might just succeed in wearing her uncanny powers down.

But there was something Shiba and Neo could contribute. They were an odd pair to say the least.

Lord Shiba Zabato was a powerful region leader, a representative of Minetta. He was a sharp-featured man yet handsome in a roguish way, lean as whipcord with all that sting.

His second in command, Neo Xanth, was the strongest brawler of Minetta. Brawlers – I like to think of them as shaved bears – trained and worked hard to turn themselves into massive machines of human muscle. Despite the rigorous training, Neo was a gentle sort of giant, an intelligent, witty, kind, caring fellow who could grab a man around the throat and simply squeeze to pop his head off like a champagne cork.

The two of them were partners sealed by the Paragon's Conduct. It made them twice as dangerous, not to mention the immense reservoir of kore they possessed. Everyone has a bit of spiritual energy, a flame of life. But for some, it was a much deeper pool of strength – the might behind their gift. It took years to develop and control it, and those who were lucky enough to be born with high kore capacity became fighters to be feared.

A patch of grass ignited in front of me. I put it out with a stamp of my foot. Yes, it would be unwise to go near. The possibility of collateral damage was too significant.

"Neo," I said, "can you create a barrier around them?"

"I could generate a ward, like a domed force field, to contain them. But it won't stop them from fighting."

"At least it will confine the damage. Do it."

I turned to Lord Shiba. "Your shadow… Can you hold the Valiant Tiger in place, so she can land a punch?"

"With pleasure." Shiba clapped his hands together, pressed his soles to the ground, and focused intensely on the skirmish in front of him. A dark shadow formed underneath him, seeming to take on a life of its own. The dark, sinister shape quickly slithered into the fight.

As it closed in, Neo slammed his fist on the ground. A pulse of energy vibrated through the earth, creating ripples and bending the air. A transparent dome shimmered into existence, forming a clear barrier that enclosed the two fighters. Shiba's shadow creature made its way inside the area just before the dome was sealed.

Within seconds, the atmosphere cooled down – the heat from the girl's otherworldly flames was contained within the barrier.

Still locked in combat, the fighters were completely oblivious to the force field now trapping them.

As the warrior tried an advance with his spear, the shadow rose and seized his ankles. He strained to break free, but the shadow held his feet like steel shackles. He lost his balance in the struggle and pitched to the ground. Unable to move his legs, he could no longer dodge the girl's fierce strikes.

She showed no restraint. Her arms spread wide as she let the flames erupt, hitting the sides of the dome, causing them to spread over its curved surface until they enveloped the entire dome. As the blasting fire grew stronger, we could no longer see inside. The half globe appeared to be nothing but a giant ball of fire from the outside.

"Fangbane, sir?" Neo said, his voice trembling from the effort of holding the barrier intact. The blaze was pushing hard against it, expanding the heated air. The mounting pressure to contain it strained Neo to his limit. He held fast by force of will, but he was more concerned about what was going on inside.

"They're going to suffocate in there!"

"No, they won't," said Shiba, with his typical humor edged in cruelty. "They'll be roasted alive long before that."

"Hold it steady," I instructed. All around me, a garbling wave of skeptical thoughts started seeping into my subconscious, making me wonder if that was the wisest choice.

"Fang?" Suzan yelled from the other side, challenging my judgment. *I'm not ready to lose two more people.*

I know, my brain answered, even though she wouldn't hear me.

"Hold it," I said again with confidence, having made up my mind. I could sense the fear boiling around me. For all I knew, they were right. Still, Neo held fast. They trusted me. The roaring flames grew deafening, pulsing against the barrier as the heat and pressure continued to climb.

The dome shattered when the weight of the fire overpowered

it. A wave of smoke blew past us. Some tried to cover their faces, and we all tried to not inhale the clouds of smoke and ash. People began to sputter, coughing and choking on the fumes.

Is it over?

There's no way they survived that.

Roasted them like an oven, I'll wager.

Dire and fatal predictions piled up inside my head as the crowd foresaw certain death. Nothing was visible in the thick black smoke.

I knew the crowd was wrong for I sensed a miracle out of what appeared to be a definite tragedy.

And though I still couldn't see anything behind the dark smoke, somehow the thoughts of the two fighters – pain, confusion, bewilderment – broke free, rushing into my mind, proving they were alive. As the smoke thinned, I could make out the two figures kneeling, facing each other with heads bowed, and gasping for breath. They were caked in soot and dirt, but somehow the inferno had not burned them to a crisp as all had expected.

The girl rose to her feet, standing tall, gazing down at the man she had just defeated. She blinked rapidly in a daze, stupefied by the destruction from her fireballs. She blanched, looking at her hands in a panic. Despite the struggle, she showed not a single scratch.

A jumbled trail of her thoughts bubbled to the surface; I experienced her disorientation and uncertainty as if it was happening to me.

I turned my attention to the warrior, who seemed totally wrung out in comparison. His limbs were shaking, and he was covered in cuts and bruises. The only similarity was in their expression of equal confusion. Regaining the ability to read his thoughts put me at ease.

The battle was over. He tried to rise on one knee, but collapsed immediately. The girl gasped seeing him buckle. She took one step forward to help him but retracted just as quickly. Her thoughts told me she was afraid, afraid of the damage she had just caused, and afraid that she was still not in control.

Memories of similar instances played out in her mind.

I read every second of it.

How fascinating. In all my years, I'd never met someone with her… experiences.

So that's why they call you Miss Miracle.

PART I

CHAPTER ONE

Mirari stared at her trembling hands as her lungs struggled for air. Even though her skin appeared normal, she could feel warmth radiating from her palms and fingers.

Why?

It upset her that she couldn't remember... but the unpleasant smell of burnt wood caught her attention.

Was she fighting? Mirari raised her head and noticed wisps of smoke rising from patches of lightly charred grass.

Try as she might, she could not recall what took place only a few seconds – or was it hours? – ago. Even time seemed to have a hole blasted through it. Her warm hands troubled her with a pang of vague guilt. An unsettling memory struggled to take shape, but she pushed it away, unable to confront the feelings now. Nothing made sense. Nearly a dozen people gathered around her, yet none of them showed any unusual concern about the bizarre phenomenon evidenced by the burn marks on the ground. Their focus was intense, but their only interest was the fate of the fallen fighter who lay sprawled several feet away from her.

Her interest in the here and now seemed to fade, and she turned her gaze to soak in the sky alive with purple, orange, gold, and red. As the sun slipped over the distant rocky peaks, a magical glow suffused the desolate acres of the uneven rocky slab that was now littered with the debris of battle. Splintered fallen trees, boulders shattered into pieces, the groaning wounded and silent dead. The grim butcher's bill from the fierce battle that had raged over this broken, bloody ground. And yet, it all unfolded under such magnificent beauty, which went on, unconnected to the puny doings of men.

Peering through her disheveled lilac hair, Mirari gaped at the defeated Althaean fighter. While she was a stranger to those around her, everyone knew her vanquished opponent, the one they called the Valiant Tiger. She knew him, but to her, he was simply Gaven. That was the only way she could ever think of him, and his fate meant more to her than any of the others. Much more.

She watched Gaven strain to stand, most likely injured, but at least alive. That was enough for her now, and she let out a sigh of relief. The sight of him helped bring her back to the present. Although she couldn't recall a single moment of their recent duel, she now remembered he was her mission; the reason she was here in Althaea.

It had been over ten years since they had last been together. Gaven's distinctive blue eyes still held an arresting radiance peering through his black bangs, but his body had matured, large and muscular, magnificently toned, and sharply defined. It was in stark contrast to how Mirari remembered him – scrawny with protruding eyes, always too shy to directly meet another's gaze – as one would expect of a stalwart region leader. Gaven was much more than that – Althaea's greatest fighter, a well-respected warrior who had earned his position among the fiercest competition. But he didn't come without flaws, and no one knew this more than Mirari.

Now, the biggest concern was Gaven's involvement in the uprising. If it were true that he was the leader of this revolt, it would be enough to sentence him to death.

A few of the fighters who had battled against Gaven's rebels quickly surrounded him, kicking Gaven back to the ground, binding his hands behind his back with thick fluorescent straps of energy. One may think such a device to be made of magic or witchcraft, but technology made of hāstals and kore was becoming ever so common, and a favorite to nobles and top fighters.

They all remained fearfully cautious as if he might suddenly spring free and retaliate. But Gaven offered no resistance. He looked spent, tired, and utterly bewildered as if he had just awakened from a dream he could not remember. Mirari could certainly sympathize with his mental disarray.

A man strode up to Gaven, his entire face masked by a silver helmet.

"Question. Are you aware of what you've done?" The man's tone was neutral, almost curious. He carried a shiny silver spear. In contrast to all other weapons that laid on the battlefield, his spear hardly revealed a speck of blood.

Gaven turned his disoriented gaze toward the scattering of blood-smeared fighters that littered the battleground. Healers rushed to their aid, holding those green, egg-shaped renastōnes with veins of gold over the open gashes of the wounded.

Gaven returned his gaze to the masked man in front of him, then his eyes drifted away, back to the ground.

"Would you believe me if I said no?" he muttered.

Mirari wondered if these two had known each other before. She had only met the masked man a few days prior when she was attempting to cross the imperial border from Minetta to Althaea. She'd been stopped by border guards but with the masked man's authority, she was able to pass. They called him

Fangbane, and he was the leader of this armed expedition to capture Gaven.

No one had ever seen his face. No one knew his age or even his real name. His wife, Starlight, was a highly reputed healer. Perhaps she knew Fangbane's secrets – if so, she kept them to herself. Many of these fighters were seeing Fangbane for the first time today. At first, most were skeptical that this unimposing figure with his face hidden had any talent at all. On first impression, he appeared almost bland, a man of a few words. When he did speak, it was almost always horribly sarcastic.

But he had proved brilliant, no one could challenge that now. Fangbane's tactical mastery – his ability to coordinate a team of fighters, his successful strategy to isolate and capture Gaven – had proved his value as an exceptional leader, even if he was no fighter himself. In fact, because his expedition had defeated Gaven, the strongest region leader of Althaea, Fangbane was qualified to become a regional leader himself. Such were the spoils of victory in this world.

Gaven looked to be on the verge of shutting down.

"Nice mask," he said without irony. His voice was almost as shaky as his trembling body. He had heard rumors of the man under the mask, and now he had come face to face with him. "You must be the one they call Fangbane?"

"I am." Fangbane politely reached out his hand. "An honor to meet you, Valiant Tiger." Fangbane kept his hand out, but with Gaven's in confinement, what was he to do? He turned away, ignoring the gesture. Mirari sensed that hidden behind Fangbane's mask was a somber disappointment. But all he said was, "You might be wise to make an ally or two in this situation. I may be the only person who believes you're innocent."

"And why would a featherpit believe me?" Fangbane caught the disdainful tone of prejudice in his voice – not unexpected – he just as well recognized the guilt and confusion overpowering

Gaven. Time was lost to him, memory fogged, details missing... but somehow Gaven knew instinctively that he had done terrible things. The specifics were beyond his recall, but the blood on his hands and clothes came from someone else, and that carried a dark meaning to him. He kept that commanding rigid look, as any leader should in the face of battle, but inside, Fangbane could sense the birth of hysteria. When Gaven looked into the eyes of his fellow Althaeans, all he could see was hate. It wasn't so hard to put the pieces together. Whatever he had done, it was monstrous. Although Fangbane could see the truth, that Gaven was truly ignorant of the crimes he'd committed – without concrete evidence, Fangbane knew others would not.

Mirari stepped into their sight. At that moment, she didn't care about who else was around them. She was happy to see her friend after a whole decade. Yet these disorienting circumstances clouded her sense of procession.

"Gaven, I..." Mirari's choked-up voice wavered. There was so much to say, so much time lost. A little smile lifted the corner of her mouth, but the only words she could manage were, "I'm glad you're okay."

Gaven was unmoved. He stared at her without a hint of recognition. His eyes moved up and down her body, inspecting her unfamiliar features with indifference. He noted she was without armor or any insignia associated with a region. Her figure – healthy with prominent curves, but a body frame unfavorable for a fighter. She wore only a thin tunic that showed off her collar bone, unbearably shabby, and utterly unsuitable for battle. But she did carry a beautifully embellished sword around her waist. Was she a fighter or not? She was dressed neither like a noble, nor a commoner. Typically, the peasants were easy to differentiate from the nobles in Althaea. She was leaning toward neither. Likely Minettan or Valenian.

Then, he noticed the small feather pin on her ponytail, a

decoration used only by Minettans. His confusion quickly turned to disgust. How dare she address an Althaean of high status without honorifics.

"Where are your manners?" Gaven scoffed at her.

"I'm sorry?" Stung, Mirari's gentle smile faded to defiance. She had not expected such a sharp response, especially from him.

"This is not the place for people like you." His eyes locked on her with an intimidating gaze, radiating the pride of a tiger, and reflecting a vain warrior's haughty disposition. He gave her no more than five seconds of attention before turning away dismissively. "You do not belong here. Please remove yourself from our presence."

Mirari stammered to explain herself. "But Gaven... You mistake me. I'm—"

"I don't care what your name is."

"But—"

"You're clearly not a fighter, nor a person of noble standing. I don't see what business I could possibly have with you. So please, leave while I'm still asking politely. If you need directions, go bother someone else."

Her mouth dropped open, dumbfounded at the gall, at the insufferable ego he displayed, despite being a prisoner. A bound captive. His hubris was simply breathtaking. Gaven resumed talking to Fangbane as if she weren't there, but Mirari stood her ground, thinking of a retort to his sharp response. She placed her hands on her hip, ready to yell at him again.

"The least you can do is grant me your attention."

Gaven rolled his eyes and snapped at her again. "Why are you still here?"

"Because I have every right to be." Her voice turned sharp, ready to fight back. "After all I've done for you. How dare you treat me this way."

"Hey now... there's room for all of us." Fangbane joked in an attempt to ease the tension, and it seemed to work as they stopped bickering, though they kept a suspicious gaze on one another.

"She *did* knock you out of your trance, Gaven," Fangbane pointed out. "It wouldn't hurt to thank her."

Thank me? She seethed. Her thoughts came like whiplash and Fangbane had trouble keeping up. *That's all? After all the work it took me to get here? Is he really going to pretend he doesn't remember me? Or is he just that stupid? I wouldn't be surprised. I knew letting him go to Althaea was a bad idea. Typical Gaven. Always on his high horse. To think after all these years I would still consider him my…*

My brother…? Fangbane tried to probe, but other thoughts interfered as she struggled to overcome her pain and anger.

What a headache. He then turned his focus on Gaven's thoughts, hoping for more clarity.

Was she the one who held me down? Impossible. There's no way this Minettan vermin bested me. Her aura is more unstable than a norkfruit tree. But her skin is too fair for a peasant. It almost reminds me of…

Then there was nothing. His emotions were too concealed for Fangbane to probe any further. He found both of their internal mental gymnastics as exhausting as they were puzzling. He returned his focus to the present reality.

"Gaven," he said, "I know all this feels overwhelming. Let's focus on your current circumstances, shall we?"

Gaven pushed his annoyance at the impudent commoner aside and nodded.

"Yes, you're right." He turned to Mirari, and with an air of noble obligation, he said, "Please accept my gratitude for… well, I'm not sure exactly what it is you did for me, do you?"

Mirari lowered her head in an extravagant bow.

"Forgive me, *Your Honor*," she said in a condescending tone. "I'm afraid I am as ignorant as you are."

Gaven sensed that she was mocking him, and yet it felt familiar in a way that he found amusing.

"So, come on and tell me. What's your name?"

Mirari considered telling him more than that but decided to keep it simple for now. She knew she looked nothing like the baby-faced child Gaven had known. She had left that person behind. They were practically strangers, and strangers could only know her by one name.

"Mirari Zanette," she said. "A merchant from Avon." It was a lie, but it was the truth she lived by.

He had to make sure she wasn't the person he felt she was — he needed to confirm she was a stranger. "Mirari, like the Goddess of Miracles?"

"Correct." It put him at some ease.

"Well then, Mirari, I owe you one. Thank you." He threw away the rest of his suspicions and returned to his business with Fangbane. "So, I take it I'm your prisoner."

Fangbane pulled a dagger from his belt.

"Here, turn around." As he cut loose the bonds holding Gaven's hands, he said, "I trust you have come to your senses now. Others may fear you, but I know you are a man of honor. As long as you agree to appear before the Council, you can walk to prison on your own."

The straps shattered like glass and Gaven looked at his free hands. He nodded, surprised at Fangbane's generosity.

"How daring. I have a feeling I'll be seeing you more often."

He got to his feet, still a bit unbalanced, but kept the façade of an indestructible warrior. He didn't know who to turn to — who was a friend, enemy, or friend who had become an enemy. Seeing hundreds wounded brought pity, and the mysteries surrounding what exactly he had done tore him into a state of contrition. Maintaining his dignity, he strode off to the nearest medical tent.

Mirari watched him go, thinking it may be another ten years before they see each other again. She wanted nothing more than to go home and forget this whole event. Salathiel might be waiting for her, a hope she could still cling to.

Regardless of those thoughts, or whatever outcome fate held in store for her, at least she had saved Gaven from harm, and that was her mission. But Mirari's heart ached at the reunion that was not to be.

"That's a shame," Fangbane blurted out.

"What is?" Mirari questioned, looking at him with a creased forehead.

"Why didn't you tell him?"

"What are you talking about?"

"Your real name, *Roselyn Hale.*"

Mirari's face grew pale, her body stiffened, and she was tempted to draw her sword, but she waited for an explanation.

"Easy now," Fangbane said, sensing her antagonistic response. "I won't bite."

"How did you know… *that?*" Mirari demanded.

"Your name? Simple deduction. When I met you at the border you said you were going to Althaea to resolve a personal matter with the Valiant Tiger. But what connection would a Minettan merchant have with an Althaean region leader? Scratch that. You are obviously not a merchant, not if you have a retainer protecting you. Whatever history you have with Gaven, you two must go way back, perhaps as far as children being raised together."

"That doesn't answer anything…" Mirari was dumbfounded as she tried to figure out how he was doing this. She wondered how much more he knew about her, and by extension, about Gaven.

"There are very few things in this world that I don't have knowledge of," Fangbane continued. "Your fiery secret, for example. Then again, everyone here just saw it. That was an impressive duel."

Mirari blinked and looked at her hands again. She had already figured it out from the charred grass, but… *Goddammit.*

She didn't want to accept it was real. Fangbane looked at her intently with interest, watching her panic over the sight of her hands, and reading the same emotion in her mind.

"You saw it?" Mirari asked in a panicked voice. "For sure? It was me?"

"Everyone saw it," Fangbane said. "Well, except Gaven, of course. Just like you, he doesn't remember a second of this battle. Or why it happened, for that matter."

Mirari was wary of the true identity of this masked man, yet somehow she felt that she could trust him. After all, it was only with his help that she had been allowed to cross the border.

At the time, she had no idea who he was, and now she had more questions than answers. No one knew her real name, except her brothers. If Fangbane knew they were childhood friends, then he also knew Gaven was born a Minettan. Such information would overthrow Gaven from his position.

"I respect your wariness," he said. "But there's no need to be alarmed. I did bring you here, after all. Your friend is saved, just as you wanted. A happy outcome for everyone."

"That depends. What will you do to him?"

"Me? Absolutely nothing. This is Althaea's problem. You think they want a Minettan dictating their affairs? They'd have my head."

"Then why did you fight Althaea's battle in the first place? Why bring Minettan troops with you?"

He tried to shrug that off. "They needed help."

"Althaea never accepts help from other empires."

"Normally, they do not, but… perhaps they were desperate to stop Region Leader Gaven. I can think of no other reason the Council would contact me."

"And you jumped at the chance to prove they needed your help."

"Not for personal gain, but only to secure their trust."

"Do you think you've earned their trust?"

"Just as I've earned yours." At his words, Mirari paused to absorb the information. She couldn't read any expression behind that stupid mask. That was the intention of the mask, no doubt, to conceal whether he was being serious or sarcastic. His monotone voice didn't make it any easier for her to gauge his intentions.

"I think my mask is a lovely fashion statement."

"You're a mind reader," she said.

"My wife calls me a 'fortune teller', but, yes. Perceiving thoughts and predicting outcomes aren't that far apart."

"Stay away from my mind," Mirari said as she started backing away.

"Don't you want to see more of my tricks?"

"No!" The last thing Mirari wanted was for him to read any more of her thoughts. She strode away from Fangbane as fast as she could. She had too many secrets, too much about her past that could not be trusted in the mind of a stranger.

Despite the show Mirari had put on, no one seemed to have cared or questioned her fire abilities. Now that Gaven was back to his senses, there was no purpose left for her here. She was ready to slip away in the commotion on the field when she recalled all those who had fallen during the battle. She scanned the field and turned back to Fangbane.

"W—Where's Joachim?" Mirari asked, seeing that he was not in the same spot as she left him.

"Starlight took him to the first tent." Fangbane pointed down the hill in the direction his wife went. Without another word, she trotted down the hill, passing by troops of different empires. Some men were rushing about helping the wounded and clearing the area. Notorious fighters, each carrying a different crest on their cape, bickered among themselves. The future of the empire's relations was unsteady and they kept their gaze locked on the culprit, the rebellious Valiant Tiger.

Few had cared to know Mirari's name, and she liked it that way. She would have no problem leaving the scene unnoticed, and that's exactly what she did. She took her injured friend and left as if she was never a part of this battle.

CHAPTER TWO

Mirari had lived in the small town of Solarin ever since she and Salathiel moved out in search of a more stable life. It was more profitable than a small farm in the sticks. That was good enough for Salathiel's parents, but Salathiel always had bigger ambitions. And Mirari wanted to see more of the world rather than die in a root cellar full of radishes. So when Salathiel left, she went with him.

Solarin was a town known to traffic in imports from all over the empire — official and otherwise. It was a popular stop for travelers and merchants. In comparison to larger towns in Minetta, Solarin was underdeveloped. It lacked the technology and stone-paved roads that larger cities had. It wasn't important to the commoners, and most travelers only stayed a day or two. The lack of development had the advantage of minimal scrutiny from the authorities.

Mirari was a merchant, a reasonably honest one at that, and Salathiel was part of a retinue – a hired guard for those doing business that was sometimes irregular.

Salathiel lived a dangerous life escorting important travelers and guarding their cargo without question. Mirari was quite the opposite. She kept a low profile, only leaving their home for a few hours a day to work in town. She was content to deliver goods from shop to shop, or neighboring towns. She focused on her job and generally avoided speaking to strangers along the way. Generally. But not always.

A month had passed since Mirari returned from Althaea. No one had contacted her since, not even Gaven. She was slightly disappointed as the whole encounter felt like a dream. But it wasn't a dream. She really did see her childhood friend, and he dismissed her as a stranger – her worst fear came true. But upon returning to her empty and dull home, she remembered this was the result of the separate paths they had chosen, and she knew she had to move on.

Mirari was in the market, combing through rows of lined-up fruits arranged underneath a makeshift store at the edge of town. She was picky, looking for ripe peaches, not two drunken louts. But along they came, singing and belching, obnoxious and loud. Not that anyone would tell them to their face. Their spotless white suits with gold trimming stood out from the rest of the people in town – nobles, slumming no doubt, for cheap thrills. They strolled down the street without a care in the world, confident their status would protect them.

The taller drunk noticed an old lady wearing the healing robes native to the celtas of Altha Hills in Althaea. As highborn Minettans, they considered her an unwelcome, and inferior alien presence.

He steered into the old lady's path and roughly checked her with his shoulder. The lady fell forward onto the dirt ground. Her hands and knees would undoubtedly have cuts and scrapes. The howls of the men drew the attention of shopkeepers, but upon seeing that the offenders were aristocrats, they all turned away and pretended to not notice.

"If you're going to live here, at least dress like us." The man laughed. "This flatty forgot what empire she's in."

Althaeans were known to flip between grace and mischief like a flat coin with two different heads. It was a derogatory word, and in this case, it was unwarranted.

Mirari gritted her teeth, watching them. They were the spitting image of her own repulsive birth family. They set her blood to boil. But Mirari worked hard to restrain herself. She knew gaining a reputation for thrashing lowlifes would not help her live the low-profile life she desired. On one hand, there was good reason for her determination to remain obscure and anonymous. On the other hand was her heart – a troublesome thing, always driving her to help others whenever she could.

As she continued picking the fruit, the two nobles – the tall one accompanied by a stout, piggish man – continued walking up the street. Closer and closer to Mirari.

"They shouldn't even be allowed to live here," grumbled the porcine one. He had a gravy stain on his otherwise white garment.

"Or at least they should be segregated," quipped his tall compatriot. "Who wants to walk on the same road after their filthy soles touched it?"

"It's that damnable Althaean rebel. Gravel is it?"

"Gavel, I believe. Calls himself the Valorous Lion, or some such rubbish."

"And the seditious mongrel is actually a region leader. Typical of those flat-faced ruffians," said the stout man. "They respect nothing but violence."

"Savages. And yet, they expect to mix with decent folks, free as they please."

"That rebel renegade stuffed some nonsense into their thick skulls," the flabby friend said. "Suddenly these flat-faces think it's okay to live on our green land, take our resources." He then stopped, lifted one leg, and broke wind, actions as garish as their conversation. The two of them laughed uproariously.

"You're the savages," Mirari mumbled, angered at the reference to Gaven. The men turned on her, amused by her snarky comment. The tall one approached Mirari and began breathing down her neck. His sour breath reeked of cheap booze.

"What did you say, young lady?"

Mirari avoided eye contact with him and continued picking out the fruits from the stall. Salathiel's harsh warnings to stop meddling in other people's matters rang loud in her mind.

The dumpy one squeezed in close now. "He asked you a question, wench."

"Say it again, you two-penny harlot."

Mirari bit back her fury, annoyed because she was more angered by them trash-talking Gaven than herself. She tried to ignore their comments, focusing on the bitter feelings left by her last encounter with the Valiant Tiger several weeks ago. But no matter what happened between her and Gaven, she couldn't stand to hear his name slandered by pompous degenerates.

It wasn't the first time she had heard comments like this. The war that Gaven had allegedly started, the uprising now called the Althaean Siege, had created a discussion over whether or not his actions were justified. A old law forced Althaeans, Minettans, and Valenians to live in their own empire. The reason was for peace, and peace was indeed maintained, as much as it created more division among three empires that were not so different to begin with. Leaders across Minetta and Valenia had abolished this old way of thinking, allowing mixed nationalities to settle in their land over the last few centuries. It was Althaea who refused to move on with the times, and to Gaven, it made no sense. Some argued that omitting Althaea Main's separation policy was an abuse of his power while others praised him for being a forward thinker.

Whether or not Gaven truly led a violent rebellion in support of overturning the Separation Law, his message was clear. The people of Althaea Main were seeking reform. Unity, some called it.

But it was puffed up plutocrats like these two who maintained and encouraged the bigotry. They were the problem, not Gaven.

And now, they were making themselves her problem.

"Keep walking," she said. "You need the exercise."

Instead of taking her sagacious advice, the stout man grabbed Mirari's wrist and pulled her toward him.

"You need a lesson in manners, little tart."

"Let go while you still have your fingers," she said, her words clipped and menacing.

The tall man tapped his rotund pal on his soft, fatty shoulder. "Maybe she likes doing two at a time. I hear these Solarin scrubbers like to—"

But he never finished, because he was screaming after Mirari jammed her knee hard in his notably small package. She yanked her wrist free from the tubby fellow and grasped his, reversing the hold. Her free hand rammed into his elbow.

Twack!

His joint snapped, his arm dangling, dislocated. The first man was now bent double in agony, putting his face in a perfect spot for her to bring her knee up again, this time into his chin.

The man crumpled like a dry stalk of weed. The fat man howled like a stuck pig. She pulled an apple off the cart and shoved it hard into his open mouth.

The thin fellow struggled off the ground, but could only make it to his hands and knees. He looked like a perfectly good bench. She lightly bumped his fat pal, who lost his balance, stumbled backward, and landed on his buddy.

"That lady you shoved has lived in Minetta for thirty years," Mirari growled. "She's one of us. You two, on the other hand, are not welcome in our town anymore. If I see you in Solarin again, ever, I will gut you like a trout. Are we clear?"

When they didn't answer quickly enough, she kicked the fat one hard on the shin.

"OKAY!" he screamed.

But she kicked him one more time. "Just for good luck."

She exhaled and glanced up, noting the awe-struck stares from the people around. She quickly reached in her pocket, handed the stall owner a generous amount of coins, and hurried home. The store owner stared at the two knocked-out trouble-makers, dazed. It wasn't her first time.

As she trudged up a short path to her small cottage on a hill, Mirari spotted a large man with short and spiky silver hair sitting on her doorstep. He was cleaning his nails with the point of his dagger, carefully gliding the blade over his dark skin. He wasn't a giant per se, but certainly huge enough to resemble one. He had legs like tree trunks, a body like a beer barrel, with arms as strong as floor joists, capped with fists like anvils. His feet looked like two concrete blocks and to top it off, a neck-less head, which resembled a small oak wine cask. His massive figure would inspire a strong man to turn around and sprint back down the hill, but Mirari strolled up to him and cleared her throat.

"I'm afraid you are blocking the way to my home," Mirari said, stressing on "my", and looking down at the man sitting on her porch. Neo abandoned his manicure and erupted in his usual grin, baring teeth so huge they belonged in the mouth of a bucking horse. It didn't matter to her that she could never see his eyes behind the tinted shades he never took off; his smile was enough. He stood up and offered to carry her groceries, taking a basket from her hand.

"How you doing, M?" Neo said. "It's been over a month."

Mirari invited him inside and offered him a bottled beer from her cellar. With his massive build, he could barely fit through the narrow door. They had only known each other for a few days during the Althaean Siege, but the affable giant was the only person she got along with during her stay… at least, the last person that was still alive.

Neo was a brawler from the neighboring region of Avon. He was the complete opposite of his lean and grumpy partner, Shiba

Zabato. An odd pair they made, but it wasn't unusual for paragons to take up partners of a different fighting class.

"You live here by yourself?" Neo asked, looking around her humble but clean cottage with some curiosity.

"I do." After a moment, she added, "But I've been considering moving to a different town. Someplace that doesn't remind me of my brother every day."

"Right. I'm sorry." Neo recalled that she mentioned how her eldest brother went missing shortly before the Althaean Siege. He was heartbroken for her, seeing that her brother still had not returned. It wouldn't be her only loss. The dirt had yet to settle around the grave under the tree behind her house.

Mirari opened her bottle and Neo did the same. They sipped in silence for a minute.

"You have an aulōg," Neo broke the silence, gesturing to a black slate hanging outside her door that pulsed in light blue neon. It was the intruder alarm of choice for people in the billionaire class, an ingenious product powered by the energetic charge from hāstals. "Fancy technology for a tiny cottage. Only nobles have those."

"I know someone from the Hale family," Mirari explained, without revealing too much about herself. "He insisted I have one after my brother went missing. You know, in case the same people come for me."

"That's... extreme." Mirari could tell Neo was dumbfounded, afraid to probe any more into her brother's line of business, fearing it may be too personal. Instead, he asked, "You must be someone important to get such a gift. After the head family in Minetta passed away, it's been harder to get their gadgets. Their poor daughter too. There's still a large reward for her whereabouts, assuming she's still alive. What was her name, Rosemary? Rosetta?"

It was an even worse topic to get into. Mirari took a sip of her beer and changed the conversation.

"Yes, poor Rosetta. But what about you, Neo? What are you doing here in Solarin? Surely Fangbane was the one who sent you."

"You can read minds too?" Neo joked.

"Ah, you know about that?"

"Eh." Neo chugged the rest of his beer in a few gulps. "It's no secret. Fangbane jokes about it all the time, but no one believes him. I know it's true. Looks like, so do you."

"Seeing is believing."

"With an ability like that, it's no wonder he's a better tactician than a fighter."

"So, what does he want with me?" Mirari asked in a direct and serious tone. She wasn't used to small talk.

"Lord Fangbane started a project. Calls it the Knights. He's creating a company of men at arms." And women, no doubt. "All kinds. That's his idea. He's recruiting Althaean, Minettan, and Valenian fighters. A mix of combat styles, with no discrimination between any of them. Just the best of every kind – men, women, province, weapon."

"Flatties, featherpits, and swines," Mirari said. "Who is he waging war against now?"

"No one. This force will respond to universal crises. Like the Althaean Siege."

"The Althaean Siege wasn't a universal crisis." Mirari rolled her eyes. It was Althaea's problem, until Fangbane invited Minettans and Valenians to the battle.

"But, Althaea wouldn't have been able to capture the Valiant Tiger without us." He turned to her, adding, "Without you."

"No… You give me way more credit than I deserve, Neo. I'm not a fighter, nor am I about to become one."

"Althaea and Minetta are never at peace. Valenia doesn't have the balls to intervene. We've created this systematic injustice among people who are no different from each other."

"And it's been that way for centuries."

"But what if it doesn't have to be? We share the same sea, same language, and our cultures are intertwined. What if instead of three empires, we were just one?"

"Oh, so you're a believer, huh?" Mirari scoffed, not convinced. "It's impossible. It would require overthrowing region leaders, destroying tribes, and maybe even putting an end to the Council."

"It doesn't have to be that complicated, M. We can keep everything the same, we just need to change how people treat each other. If we work together as fighters, then the regions can work together as people. What we don't need is another Minettan beaten up at an Althaean tavern just because they were born under a different empire. There may be laws prohibiting it, but we need mentors to set the example."

"Easier said than done."

"It is. But, we can try, right? I saw you at the plaza earlier, taking down those drunken fools. Normal people would defend their own kind, but you…? You stood up for an Althaean."

"A woman, sixty years old, Neo. Who cares about her birthplace? No one should treat an old lady like that."

"Exactly."

Stopping a couple of overserved knuckleheads in a small town wasn't the same as course-correcting a whole empire.

"Even if we could change the people, there are political barriers," she said. "For example, we have enough produce to feed half of Althaea, but their barren lands will forever stay infertile. We offer them a tree, and those war-driven oppressors will fight for the whole forest."

"But… we can try, right? We start small, do the things *we can do* first. Remember how we all fought during the war? Me, you, Shiba, Iffy, and a bunch of Althaean brats? We accomplished more than what we ever could have if we'd been divided. That's all there is to it. We proved we can work together. Why not keep it that way?"

"If it's my support you want, you certainly have it. I'm all for unity. But I won't join the team."

"Why not?"

"What you're doing is controversial. Everyone will be watching, and I hate attention."

"Are you telling me you'd rather spend your life hauling goods around town?"

"Frankly, I would. No one pays any attention to me, and that's how I want it. Plus, this all sounds a lot like what Region Leader Gaven just did, and look at how that ended."

Neo couldn't argue with that. It had only been a month since the uprising, and Althaea was still in a state of social unrest. Not everyone took it well, especially the ones with high status, puffed up with Althaean pride.

"The Valiant Tiger. He did something remarkable," Neo said with genuine admiration. "He knew it could cost him his title, but he still did it."

"By the way, where are they at with his trial?"

"It starts in two days. But I won't sugar-coat it, M. I don't think it will end well." Neo glanced at the large frown across her face, not expecting anything less.

She resented being reminded, preferring to push it out of her mind. It wouldn't help to fret over it. There was nothing she could do.

She exhaled, ridding her mind of the thought.

"Besides, what's in it for you? It sounds like you're already on the bandwagon."

"Well, for me, it's not really an option," Neo said, rolling his shoulders back in a gentle shrug. "I go where Shiba goes. And in this case, Shiba doesn't have a choice either."

That was unusual. Region Leader Shiba had always done whatever he wanted. Not for long, if he didn't get his act together.

"The only thing keeping him in office is Fangbane gracefully turning down the offer to replace him as region leader. That, and his connection with Councilor Suzan. The rest of the Council want him removed."

"Fangbane did what?" Mirari was shocked. No sane person would turn down an offer to become a region leader.

"Being a region leader would contradict his mission of unifying the empires. Althaea would never take him seriously if he took the role. Besides, Fangbane isn't much of a fighter. He's all brains, no brawn. It wouldn't be long before someone tried to overthrow him, and he knows it."

"That's quite a gamble."

"Don't worry, I'm just here to deliver the message." Neo pushed himself up from his chair. "But, hey, don't doubt yourself. I know you can fight, and Fangbane thinks so too."

"He's reading the wrong tea leaves."

"You have potential. I can tell you've had training."

"Me? I just grew up in a house with brothers. A girl's gotta hold her own."

"I don't believe you," he said, standing up straight, the movement causing him to release a gassy burp. "Think about giving it a shot, okay? Worst case scenario, you'll end up back here, in this magnificent palace you call home. But, if you never try, this is the only life you'll ever know."

With that, he was gone, leaving Mirari alone with her thoughts.

CHAPTER THREE

A grand, white building commanded acres of manicured open fields in Valenia. Every inch was monitored by attentive guards and secured with defensive hāstal barriers. The purple crystals powered most objects in the vicinity, from the golden gates to the large fountain that sat majestically in front of the main door. Carriages prized out dignitaries who entered the magnificent edifice where liveried staff directed them to a nearly endless flight of stairs.

A trial was ongoing at a place known as the Hearth. History painted the majestic building as the center of peace, but in modern times, it was known as the palace of grand judgment. The Council meeting attended by representatives of three neighboring empires – Althaea, Minetta, and Valenia – proclaimed their orders here. Their next trial involved Region Leader Gaven, who allegedly led the rebellion known as the Althaean Siege.

Seated on the high throne were Suzan and Adder of Althaea, Dareh and Novinha of Minetta, and Tarek of Valenia, all of whom glared down at the impugned agitator and surrounding witnesses. Gaven stood at the center of the court, his hands locked behind his back.

High-profile nobles, region leaders, and extraordinary fighters were permitted to sit in and listen to the proceedings. But this was no ordinary case, and while many wanted to hear the proceedings, few were allowed.

On Althaea's side sat the High Priest of Altha Hills, accompanied by the Bishop and his acolyte.

On Minetta's side sat some of the fighters who had helped Fangbane fight the Althaean Siege: Shiba, Neo, Starlight, and Fangbane himself.

Valenia's side remained empty, as always. Despite the Hearth being established on their land, Valenians couldn't care less about Althaea's problems. They found Althaea and Minetta's constant indictments predictable and a waste of time – a sport to see who could blame the other the most. The Valenians had no taste for such drama.

Powerful as these observers were, all of them were cautious about taking any position that might bring attention to themselves. There was the looming uncertainty about whether Gaven would face execution or be shown mercy. At the very least, no one expected him to keep his title.

There was an endless sea of yelling and finger-pointing. No one on the Council was more vocal than Novinha, a representative of Minetta known for her merciless hostility toward Althaeans. The middle-aged lady came from a long bloodline of fighters who ruled the region of Oban, protectors of the Althaean–Minettan border.

"As a region leader, this sets a bad example for the rest," argued Novinha, pointing her finger at Gaven. He refused to meet her harsh violet eyes.

As the charges against him were read, Gaven was informed that he had killed Iphigenia, a commander of Oban, a young warrior who Novinha treated like family. It devastated her twin sister, Region Leader Nivenda, to the point she resigned. Gaven had destroyed Novinha's family. She had every reason to be angry.

"He no longer carries the honor of a paragon," Novinha reasoned, speaking as a paragon fighter herself. "If we do not at least revoke his status, the world would assume that region leaders can do whatever they want."

"But is it just to punish him if his actions were uncontrollable?" Suzan spoke with the wisdom she had gained from decades of experience. "The Valiant Tiger has no memory of anything that happened during the Althaean Siege." Suzan wanted to remain unbiased, but she would undeniably do everything she could to help her protégé. She believed he had no memory of, nor control over, his treasonous rebellion.

"You claim to have no memory," Novinha addressed Gaven. "But you're aware that the blood of our most talented fighters is on your hands. Are you not... Your Honor? Do I need to say their names for you again?" She delivered the last honorific with spiteful irony.

Gaven kept his head low, not sure of the answer. There was not a speck of memory, not even the feeling of a lucid dream. The things they accused him of planted fake memories in his mind, which he progressively believed to be true. He was willing to accept the punishment for their deaths regardless, not for the guilt or possibility that he slayed his friends, but for the undeniable fact that he could not protect them.

Novinha continued her severe accusations. "Five thousand terrorists across Althaea followed your call to action. They destroyed dozens of towns in your name. Do you, or do you not, advocate for the liberation of the Council's reign?"

"I did not ask them to kill or vandalize," Gaven said. "Not intentionally."

"But you do believe in this cause, correct?"

Gaven paused to consider his choice of words. What was so wrong about people from different empires living together in one place? "People already coexist in Minetta and Valenia. Why should Althaea be the only one running on outdated laws?"

"This is clearly insurrection, an act of terrorism against Althaea, and a rejection of the lawful decisions of the Council."

Dareh stood up to join in. "The Separation Policies are in place for a reason. Althaea is nothing like Minetta or Valenia. You can't expect to go against our long-standing traditions without consequences. The mere fact that you failed to see the repercussions of your actions makes you unqualified to be a region leader."

"Calling it terrorism is a bit extreme, though." It was Tarek who spoke up, unfazed by the accusations against Gaven. "He does have a point. Althaea is behind the times. He's a progressive one, this boy. It's been a while since Althaea appointed a region leader before they're twenty. It's only natural that he has ambitions, and with such youth comes careless mistakes."

He kept his fingers interlaced under the long sleeves of his celta robes, his garments almost as long as his chalky beard. As a representative of Valenia, he had no real stake in what would happen to Gaven, but he did agree with Novinha in one respect.

"Responsible or not, we simply cannot allow him to walk without punishment. The Althaean Siege started in Althaea Main. He is responsible for anything that happens in his territory."

"Fear must be induced among others, or disorder is certain to follow. Clearly, the appropriate punishment is death," Dareh said in his deep, menacing voice. The merciless Minettan couldn't be happier than to see Althaea lose their best fighter.

Suzan objected. "Our empire's defenses and its leadership are largely under the control of Region Leader Gaven. We all have more to lose than to gain if we kill the Valiant Tiger."

"Tell that to the hundreds of victims who no longer have a home or family!" Novinha argued. "These were your citizens Suzan, in your region, Althaea Main. You of all people should understand. You pamper Gaven like a naughty child. He must be put on trial as a man, one who is guilty of grievous crimes."

The debate went on like this for hours into the night before adjourning when the sky was streaked with light purple and dark blue, signaling the approach of dawn.

Starlight kept her eyes glued to the marble floor as she walked out of the chamber. She was normally a cheerful person, but Fangbane could see tears building in his wife's eyes. She tried to hide them behind a curtain of her hair but faulted her pregnancy and its storm of hormones for her loss of emotional control.

"Things aren't looking good for him," Starlight sighed.

Fangbane could not deny it as he gazed out into the open courtyard. He watched the sky fade in purple, and he couldn't help wondering how many more sunsets Gaven would see. He hated to see Gaven's proud legacy end in infamy, but there was nothing he could do. The Council Leaders all had their own ax to grind. Reaching justice wasn't their only concern. There were too many personal issues of power and jealousy fueling this debate. Fangbane was without real influence in this court.

Across the field, he saw a woman's silhouette, a faint orange glow behind her. Fangbane couldn't see her darkened face, but he recognized Mirari's figure. As she began to approach, Fangbane asked his wife to give them some space.

"How is he?" Mirari asked quietly. "I heard the rumors, but..." Fangbane didn't have to use his powers to sense her fear. "I had to see for myself."

Her swollen eyes implied she had been crying for some time. She had every right to be upset. She worked so hard to save his life. All for nothing if he was to be executed.

"Mirari, I don't think you should be here," Fangbane advised, his voice tingling with concern.

"I have a proposal."

Fangbane tilted his head. Her thoughts were of the message Neo had delivered to her. "Let's hear it."

"Why do you want me to join your team?"

"You're a decent fighter."

"If you can truly read minds, you'd know I can't control the fire. It won't be of any use to you."

"What I know is that you're afraid that your ability will hurt people. It's one reason you isolate yourself in that bump in the road you call a town. To stay clear of fighting. And to avoid getting close to people, but that's just an added benefit."

"For good reason." She lowered her head. "What if I just lose it? Get angry, get crazy? I'm a bomb, ready to explode."

A frown crossed his face. At her age, he too had wished for control. Having an extraordinary gift that couldn't be tamed felt the same as being powerless. "I'm telling you otherwise. Everything can be controlled. We will train you to control it. You're a great fighter, Mirari. You can learn discipline, and turn from a wild street fighter to a battlefield warrior."

"The flames can't be controlled."

"That's your excuse to run away from life forever? Try it my way before you claim the impossible."

"And what happens if I fail?"

"Ability or not, I know you'll be good for the team."

She paused, then looked at him. "I believe what you're doing is right, and I fully support it, but you're aware that joining your cause poses a huge risk for me."

Fangbane leaned in closer. "I'm listening."

"First, you will do everything in your power to ensure that my real identity will not be exposed. I won't be trapped in that noble society again."

"Fair enough."

"Second, spare Gaven from the death sentence. Do anything. He doesn't need to be executed."

"You know that is beyond my control." He sighed, glancing

around. "I'm not a member of the Council. I'm without influence."

"But you have capital. Use it." Fangbane started to shake his head, but she insisted. "You just saved Althaea. You said it yourself. You earned their trust. It's time to cash in on it."

Fangbane thought for a long moment about her request. It seemed like an impossible demand. But it sparked another idea in his mind, a longshot, but it could be achieved if planned carefully.

THE NEXT MORNING, the courtroom was taut with all the tension of a fully drawn bow. Gaven looked defeated, scarcely listening to the back and forth. He knew a death sentence hung over him.

"His Honor, Region Leader Gaven, had no capacity in his mind when these acts took place," Starlight explained, offering her medical expertise to support Gaven. "He is abhorred by the violence that took place in his name. He has no memory of it. He did not act with free will or intention."

Starlight slid a long parchment, scribbled with notes, to a large black platform at the center of the table. It was a brand new device, another breathtaking invention of the Hale family. An image of the paper was projected onto six smaller black tablets, one in front of each of the five Councilors. The sixth seat was empty.

"It is clear that he was unconscious of his actions. As such, these acts were beyond his control, and this court should find it as so."

Starlight rubbed her fingers together as she waited for the Councilors to read her notes. She held her chin high, back as straight as a spear. Her composure was nothing short of the highly acclaimed medic she was. She was confident that her status, along with being a frontline witness to Gaven's attacks, would have an upper hand in making sure Gaven would be spared the death sentence.

But Fangbane witnessed the opposite. He could hear her inner turmoil and feel a gentle tug in his chest that echoed the butterflies in his wife's stomach.

The rigid Minettan scoffed at the notes. "Are you suggesting there is some mysterious, malevolent force, some invisible hand of evil at large? Is that what you claim impaired his judgment?" Dareh bellowed. "Because regardless of the motive, someone must take responsibility for the damage. And until we have proof of this invisible culprit, the one and the only person guilty for this tragic disaster is standing before us."

Starlight sighed. Nothing had changed. It wasn't about the evidence, not to Dareh. His objective was only to see Minetta take advantage of the situation to punish Althaea. Not for justice, but to weaken an opponent.

Fangbane agreed with Starlight. As a fellow Minettan, Dareh's behavior was as shameful as it was an embarrassment. At the same time, it made Starlight more certain that her husband's cause was worth fighting for. They had been chasing peace for decades. This was their chance to act on it.

The Councilor who had been silent for the last two days, relatively younger than the rest of the Council, cleared his throat. He sat next to Suzan on Althaea's side, half his face concealed behind his tall collar and his dark beady eyes hidden behind his wavy crimson hair, as always.

"What would we gain by losing a valuable fighter?" They heard Adder's muffled voice from behind his collar. "He has steady control over Althaea Main's economics and its people, a characteristic of leadership rarely found in most fighters. Right now, there is no qualified Althaean to replace Gaven. His region still relies on him, the empire relies on him. And if his region falls, so will the rest of Althaea's balance. Other empires will undoubtedly follow. Are Minetta and Valenia prepared to deal with such recoil caused by their selfishness?"

Gaven glanced at Adder. He always had the utmost respect for him. Adder was a brilliant man, drawn to logic over bias. But in this situation, Gaven couldn't understand why Adder would defend him, especially after witnessing him kill his brother.

Gaven's lack of understanding of what he did only fueled the pulsing pressure in his head. The death penalty sounded like a solution that would end his pain.

"How about a temporary suspension?" Suzan suggested. "The medical report warrants it."

"Nothing less than a permanent suspension," Novinha insisted. "What guarantee is there that he won't go berserk again?"

The room grew loud once again as arguments erupted among the Council.

"If I may," Fangbane interrupted. He stood from his seat and cleared his throat. All heads turned to him, not having expected him to speak. "I would gladly take custody of him, and guarantee his actions on my own life."

"Custody?" Tarek questioned. "For what reason?"

Dareh stood up and pointed his finger at Fangbane. "Stay out of this, Helmet."

"Hush." Suzan silenced him. "Let him speak."

Fangbane nodded and continued. "The bottom line is this. We must be certain His Honor won't commit such an atrocious crime again. Strip him of his command if it is your will. But allow me to accept responsibility for him at my home in Minetta, where I can put his skills to beneficial use. The man's still young. It would be a waste to let him rot in the dungeon during his prime years."

The Councilors looked at each other. Fangbane had proved his strategic abilities during the Althaean Siege, but the fact remained that no one knew anything else about him. Many still did not trust him, especially because they could not see his face.

Fangbane continued. "Considering that I ask for no reward for capturing him in the first place, I would say this request is within reason."

"I see…" Shiba muttered quietly to Neo. "If Gaven helps with his army of Knights, Fangbane would gain credibility and trust of the Althaeans."

With Gaven *and* Shiba? That was a dream team. Fangbane had a stake in the verdict now. How would the Council react?

"As long as he does not set foot in Valenia, I have no issue," Tarek agreed. "Valenia has had just about enough of your petty arguments. We want nothing to do with this."

Adder turned to Suzan, who returned a nod. He spoke, "Fangbane, if you are willing to accept full liability for Region Leader Gaven, we will leave him in your hands until we feel enough time has passed."

Novinha expected as much – Althaeans defending their own kind – and called them out on their bias. "What? This is an outrage. We are just letting him go free with a warning?"

"He'll be closely monitored."

"He killed your brother, Adder! Don't let him walk free—"

"That was beyond his control," snapped Suzan.

Bickering broke out again.

Neo leaned slightly toward his partner and nudged him. "Hey, you should say something too." But Shiba kept his arms crossed over his chest.

"Like I care about what happens to him," he grumbled.

Dareh jumped up and roared in support of Novinha. "Minetta objects to such leniency. I say execute him! I will pay the headsman myself!"

The main doors burst open, heels clamored against the marble floor, as a dark-skinned woman cloaked in scaled pauldrons and plated paragon armor made her majestic entrance.

Her battle regalia was made with the finest materials in Valenia, a quality worthy of her status. Her long hair, darker than a midnight sky, swayed as she strode in with uncompromising confidence.

"Enough!" she roared, as effective in seizing attention as her dramatic entrance. Councilor Julie's appearance was rare, but she was ready to fill the sixth seat. Her priority was her duty to the Tribe of Paragons, and she was upfront about most of the Council's trials being a waste of her time. Still, Valenia saw no one more suitable for the position. In her absence, she allowed Tarek, her Valenian confrère, to vote as her proxy.

Yet, this was one trial she couldn't afford to miss.

"I can hear you nitwits howling from the other side of the mountain," Julie said, taking her seat. "So? Who wants to be gutted first?"

Julie looked at the Councilors one at a time, meeting their eyes. They all fell silent. No one wanted to argue with Julie. Not only was her logic precise and her judgment impeccable, but her debating skills could humiliate the best of them – she cut her opponents to ribbons.

"That's better," she said, enjoying the silence while making herself comfortable in her grand chair. "Starlight, a pleasure to see you again. Do you have Gaven's medical reports?"

"Y-yes, I do," Starlight said, panicking a little, not expecting to be put on the spot. She hastily shuffled through her bag for the folder, then paced over to Julie and handed her the documents with both hands.

"Thank you." Julie quickly skimmed through the first few pages. "Shell shock. Everyone has been apprised of this, yes?"

"Yes, Your Grace," Starlight confirmed.

"And there's clear evidence of memory loss."

"Yes. When he was captured, His Honor was unable to recall anything that happened during the riots."

"And now?"

"Only mild hallucinations. My opinion is that these memories are manufactured, formed with the information he has picked up during our interrogations. They are not his own recollections."

"Is it your professional opinion that the Valiant Tiger voluntarily started a war?"

"No, Ma'am. It is frankly impossible from a medical perspective."

Julie turned toward the rest of her confrères.

"You all hear that?" she said. "We can argue all day about whether or not his actions were intentional. But what's done is done. We all know Gaven, who doesn't? I have never met an Althaean region leader that dictates over his people with kindness and fairness." She turned to Suzan with a glare. "You raised a puppy, Suzan. He's got guts, but he's not a killer."

Suzan returned a nod. She had been criticized for this countless times, but she never regretted her decision to make Gaven her successor, not even now.

Novinha held onto her sharp tongue. The majority was not in her favor. "What are you suggesting, Julie?" she said, crossing her arms, abashed but defiant.

"Whatever he does or does not remember, he will never forget that blood was shed with his own hands. We all lost beloved companions. They were also his companions."

"Blasphemy! He won't even say their names."

"Iphigenia wouldn't condone your tone," Julie warned. "Now lower your voice."

Novinha turned her head and spat on the floor.

"Novinha," Dareh warned, placing his hand in front of her and drawing Julie's attention toward him. "Are you saying we should take Lord Fangbane's offer?"

"His offer favors all of you. Gaven stays alive, but not in command. Althaea's greatest fighter is now the pet of a Minettan lord. What could be more humiliating than that?"

Dareh nodded in realization. "What would become of Gaven's territory?"

"Althaea?" Julie turned her attention to Suzan and Adder. "Why don't you decide?"

Suzan sighed. "Let the man keep some of his dignity. His Second is more than qualified to hold her own, but I shall oversee their operations."

"Unbelievable," Novinha scoffed, not wanting to shelter a criminal in her empire. But there was no point in dragging this out. Dareh seemed to have given in to Julie's rhetoric, and she had to acknowledge defeat.

From the sideline, Starlight shrieked with excitement.

"Well then, don't fail us, Helmet," Dareh warned Fangbane, his tone both serious and teasing. "You can bet that we too will keep a sharp eye on him."

"We'll take good care of him," Fangbane said, an imperceptible satisfaction in his voice that only Shiba and Neo could hear.

CHAPTER FOUR

Fangbane held a burning candle over the flap of an envelope, melting a blob of crimson sealing wax. Starlight handed him their stamp, a circular crest with a phoenix's wings spread wide, and he pressed it onto the wax. Laying the sealed letter on a tall stack of precisely written letters, he said to his wife, "There it is. That's the one I was looking for."

"Why's that one so special?"

He smiled. "Because it's the last one."

Starlight rolled her eyes, trying not to return her husband's smile – she didn't want to encourage his sad attempt at humor – but she couldn't help herself. To hide her amusement, she adjusted her features to one of intense gravity. She took a look at the name on the envelope and her expression turned into a real frown. "Your odds of getting a fighter from Oban to join the Knights are probably close to nothing, considering how Councilor Novinha reacted at Gaven's trial."

"Well, we still ought to try, don't we?" he said with much optimism. He knew, of course, that he'd never get all of them to volunteer. He wondered how many would even bother to respond.

Starlight didn't look convinced. "You're starting to sound like Neo. Come on." She rose from her seat and gestured for him to follow her out the door. "Suzan and Gaven will be here soon."

Stepping out the front door, they heard the neighing of horses crossing the wooden bridge to their estate.

The estate sat on a secluded island in a quiet bay just off the coast of Avon. A wall surrounded the palatial structure, and a wide golden gate served as the entrance. The island spread into the distance, a vast property of open land with an even bigger forest behind it.

Gaven and Suzan arrived at the gate and dismounted from their horses, a bit dazed at the sheer size of Fangbane's property. The gleaming white stone structure stretched across a wide swath of lawn. Though pristine and elegant, the property looked like it was in need of serious care. Gaven gaped at the sprawling building, and muttered, "I expected a mansion, but that's a damn castle."

The man in the mask threw his arms open and embraced his new guest. "Your Honor! Councilor! Welcome to our humble abode."

Suzan looked around, curious. "Only the two of you live here, right?"

"Well… the three of us, actually." Starlight smiled. It was no secret the two were expecting, but Starlight's 'baby bump' was more visible now.

Gaven passed on his turn, asking, "How far does your fief go?"

"Oh, the whole island is mine. Courtesy of Region Leader Shiba. He practically gave it to me for free."

"Sheesh." Gaven shook his head. "Why not ask him to build a kōnvoy line for you while you're at it?"

As they entered the imposing building, Starlight explained they had looked long and hard to find an isolated location this huge. "I wanted an herb garden, and he wanted a training ground. So, we saved up and took our time finding a patch of land big enough for both."

Big enough for an entire army, you mean, Gaven thought.

"Not quite," Fangbane said aloud. "But it's big enough to house a whole company of fighters."

Startled, Gaven recalled Fangbane's ability to read thoughts. Now he knew the rumors were true. He ignored it, returning his attention to the size of the mansion. He wondered how many servants it took to run a place like this.

"Actually," Fangbane spoke again, "we don't have servants. Don't believe in it. Everyone is going to do their share in this new program. It will help promote cooperation."

Gaven shot a snappy look at Fangbane.

"I wish you'd quit doing that," Gaven said. *Nosey bastard.*

"Sorry, I can't help it."

And to make Gaven do his own chores? That may have been the tipping point.

Starlight touched Gaven's arm to distract him from his discomfort. "We have a special suite for you, Gaven. It'll feel like a vacation."

"Call it what you want, but I'm still here against my will," Gaven said, turning to the staircase and making his way up to his new room.

THAT AFTERNOON, Fangbane talked in detail about the plans for his Knights. Before he started, Suzan offered her reassurance that Gaven's death sentence was permanently off the table as long as he behaved under Fangbane's supervision.

"It's alright," Gaven sighed, looking more than just tired. "What's done is done. You have every right to punish me as you see fit."

"Fangbane was smart to offer this deal." Suzan lectured him, as she always did when he was still a soldier-in-training. "It saved your life. You owe him one."

"I'd rather die than be a slave to Minetta."

"Show some respect." Suzan lightly smacked the back of his head. "We're keeping the details of your sentence confidential. The public will know you're on suspension, just not where. You haven't completely lost your honor yet."

"You're hardly a slave to us either," Fangbane said, opening his spiel. "You're free to travel as you'd like, so long as you help me with my project, and I know where to find your dead body."

"What *is* this project anyway?"

"We want to steer society in a new direction," Starlight put in.

Fangbane nodded. "We believe the three empires should assist each other, instead of constantly fighting for dominance. We're operating on a system developed hundreds of years ago.

"Fighting classes were created back when towns would murder each other over conflict and resources. When the towns began to form alliances to create regions, each region appointed their strongest fighter as region leader, who then formed armies to defend and govern the towns. But these militarized states only led to larger conflicts between neighboring regions. Rather than develop trade and prosper, this constant state of feudal warring brought only poverty and death. Some region leaders were desperate to find ways to help the impoverished, but others ruthlessly sought the power to rule and fought to claim more territory for themselves. While the creation of the Council may have minimized the violence between neighboring regions, it also created three hostile powerhouses. And here we are today, living in the same hostile empires."

"For a good reason," Gaven said. "Every empire is different. You worry about how to feed your chickens, while I, and the rest of the Althaean region leaders, worry about how to feed our people. Our resources and our priorities are different...

And Valenia? We call them swines for a reason. Those naturalists roll in wealth and see our empires as nothing but a market to profit off of. Other than that, they want nothing to do with Minetta or Althaea. They don't even have region leaders. The Council is the only thing we all have in common, otherwise the flatties, featherpits, and swines wouldn't be speaking to each other.

"Of course they are all different," said Fangbane. "All the more reason to create a single force for the common good. We were once a big nation hundreds of years ago. It's possible."

"That was *hundreds* of years ago. With all due respect, Fang, you seem to be wanting to fix a problem that doesn't exist," Gaven argued with a slight frown. "Region leaders already handle things in their respective regions, and Councilors speak on behalf of the empires. Why confuse people with a third system?"

Fangbane knew this would come up. "Oh, but young warrior, when was the last time you collaborated on good terms with the Shadow Soldier of Minetta or the Tribe of Aegises in Valenia?"

"Every empire operates in its own way. I cannot tell Shiba what to do any more than he can tell me what to do."

"True. And neither one of you considers the welfare of the other. When you disagree, where do you draw a line in an area so gray?"

"But that's what the Council is for," Gaven insisted.

"You just experienced how the Council operates, Gaven. They have raised bickering to an art form, but have no real incentive to act for the benefit of all. No offense, Suzan."

"None taken." Suzan shrugged. "Why do you think I waited until retirement to join the Council? Any earlier and it would've taken away the few youthful years I have left." She turned her attention to Gaven. "You are revered not only for your bravery, but also for your determination to pursue success in all that you attempt. I believe you're essential to make this a reality."

"You're supporting this, Suzan? I thought you hated going out of the norm."

"I do hate going out of the norm, but I am not against efforts for peace."

"If we are all truly the same," Starlight added, "there is no reason for us to operate separately. You lifted the restraints on foreigners settling in your region. That's all Fangbane is saying. We don't need invisible walls. You two have similar goals."

Gaven understood the point she was making, but he still thought his ideals were far different from Fangbane's.

"My decision to revoke the Separation Law," he began, "was for the benefit of the people in Althaea Main. If we open our doors to foreign settlers, our people wouldn't have to live in poverty. What I did was for the people of Althaea Main, not for Minettans or Valenians. Fangbane, you want to unify every region, and every empire. That's too ambitious. I would never tell another region leader how to do their job. Plus, I highly doubt the Council will ever support this. It would defy their authority."

"Correct," Suzan said. "The Council believes this Knights project won't succeed. It's the only reason we are willing to let you try."

"What's so special about me? Why do you want me to participate so badly?"

"I'm naming you as my training supervisor for the Knights project. Because, as I'm sure you're well aware, I can't keep my spear up to save my life," Fangbane said.

"I wouldn't put it that way, exactly," Starlight giggled, patting her belly.

Fangbane blushed but powered through. "I'm saying, you are Althaea's finest warrior. People will follow your lead. I can set up the gears, but it will take you to turn them. People aren't going to trust an old man who can't fight."

"Cut the crap, Fang," Suzan said, showing off her braided

gray hair. "I bet there's not a single strand of white in your hair… if you even have any."

Fangbane could tell that Gaven still had his doubts. Fangbane was a mediocre fighter. But no one denied he was a brilliant strategist. The battle of the Althaean Siege proved that. He had somehow convinced Althaean and Minettan fighters to unite under a common banner.

Gaven shouldn't have underestimated this man, but Fangbane planned to start this grand scheme with only five Knights? He thought it was a minuscule number for a job so enormous.

"Yes. But five is statistically the best number to have an effectively functional team," Fangbane explained.

"Stop that."

"I can't control it."

"Then tell me, oh great fortune teller. Will I be assisting you on your project?"

"I know you will accept my offer. You have personal reasons motivating your decision." Gaven raised a brow. What secret information did he discover this time?

He changed the subject. "These Knights, who represent all the empires, I assume you want only the best fighters, correct?"

"Yes and no," Fangbane said. "We'll be sure to have a Knight from each fighting class: umbra, paragon, aegis, and celta. Skill is essential, but the most important factor is cooperation. How do they make up for each other's weaknesses, that's how I will choose them."

"Enlighten me. Who's on the recruitment list so far?" Gaven asked as he knew every noteworthy name there was on the battlefield.

Fangbane handed him a long scroll of names, the same people he wrote letters to earlier that day. They were first sorted by the empires the fighters were loyal to, then their fighting class. Gaven's eyes zeroed in on the latter.

First were the paragons. They consisted of the brawlers and

the warriors, those who relied on physical strength, and close combat weaponry. It was traditional for them to bond with another fighter of any class to magnify their strength.

Second, the celtas, gifted with high kore capacity, were capable of harvesting elemental energies to create spells, heal others, and enchant objects.

Third, the aegises, allies of nature who often partnered with animals to fight by their side. Their primary weapon was the bow.

Lastly, the umbras. They rose from a group of mercenaries who practiced self-defense with various weapons. It was still the most preferred fighting class among commoners.

Addressing Gaven's question, Fangbane said, "I am pleased to have confirmation from Region Leader Shiba Zabato, the Shadow Soldier of Minetta, and his partner and second in command, Neo Xanth, the Silver Fist."

Gaven groaned. "Why does it have to be Shiba?"

"Shiba is your equivalent in Minetta, a significant influence for his people and a formidable fighter."

"You're well aware that we're acquainted. No need to rub it in."

"Just acquainted? I'd say the phrase 'mortal enemies' is more appropriate," Suzan teased. "Fang, you really think you're capable of making these two hard heads work as a team?"

"If the two of them can cooperate, it'll inspire people to put aside their differences. Worst case, I have no doubt Neo will be a sturdy barrier between them."

Gaven, crossing his arms, said in his most petulant tone, "Why would Shiba agree to join your cause?"

"Because when I turned down the offer to become a region leader, it allowed Shiba to keep his title. He owes me a favor."

"Ah. That explains it."

"He's a practical man who can recognize our mutual benefit."

"He's an avaricious narcissist. I say he's a bad fit."

"Put aside your childish rivalry. That is the point we're trying to get across, after all," said Fangbane, Gaven's petulance catching up to him.

Suitably chastised, Gaven looked down at the scroll in his hand again. He recognized most of the names but wondered how efficiently these people could work together. Most fighters worked alone, and the idea of uniting ones from different empires was undeniably a challenge.

"You didn't pick many paragons," he pointed out.

"You're the absolute master of that style. Plus, I already have one other in mind. She hasn't accepted my terms yet."

"She? It better not be one of those savages from Oban." Gaven gaped at him until he saw the look Suzan gave him. "Sure, I have no problem with a woman... but who would that be?"

"I'm going to keep that one a secret for now."

"If I help you, I have one condition."

"Speak."

"I need to approve every recruit before they officially become a Knight. I won't just train anyone."

"Fair. Starting with the next one, that is. Shiba and Neo are non-negotiable."

"Fine, I shall judge whether your female paragon will be a good fit."

CHAPTER FIVE

A lone soldier dragged himself through the streets of Solarin, the metal of his armor clanging loudly with every turn, drawing the attention of the shopkeepers nearby. He wore a sky blue cape and an army crest engraved in white and gold, colors that indicated that he was an Althaean, which made the locals keep their distance.

The man could only scratch his blond hair, wondering where in the world he was.

"Excuse me? Do you need help?" Mirari called out to the strange man standing in the middle of the street.

"Oh! By the Gods, yes ma'am." The soldier smiled with relief that someone had finally noticed his cluelessness. He was over a head taller than Mirari, but she could see the dragon-like insignia on his shoulder pad, the emblem of Althaea Main. He would not be familiar with Minettan territory.

"Thank you. Uhm, well, you see," the man stuttered while unfolding a small crumpled paper. "I'm looking for, well, this?"

There was a poorly drawn scribble on the paper. It looked like flower petals.

"Ah," Mirari examined it, trying to figure out what it was. "Could this be cryphedeon?"

"Yes!" the soldier said. "That's the word I was looking for."

"Those are sold at the lower market. I can show you the way."

His name was Haynes, and Mirari was right. It was his first time in this town. His first time in Minetta. She noticed the suspicious stares he drew. Why were people so wary of strangers? It made Mirari all the more willing to help him, and it had nothing to do with the fact that he was from Gaven's army. She directed him to a store selling flowering herbs and helped him negotiate the purchase of cryphedeon.

"I can't thank you enough for your help." Haynes bowed. "A-actually, if it's alright, I am looking for a few more things."

She felt mildly shamed that no one else in town would help the Althaean. She would feel guilty for leaving him unattended.

"Not a problem, I would be reassured knowing you won't end up lost again."

After a few more stops, Haynes had collected all the materials he was looking for. "I am meeting up with the rest of my team for supper. Allow me to repay you by joining us for a humble meal."

"It's alright," Mirari said. The sight of the Althaean was drawing attention, and that was something Mirari always tried to avoid. "I wouldn't want to interrupt your party."

"Nonsense! Let me introduce you to my mates." He was a rough looking man, with the eyes of a sad puppy. Mirari gave in and followed him into the tavern. She told herself it was on her way home anyway, so why not.

THE TAVERN WAS BUSTLING with Althaean soldiers bearing the same crest. It was loud in a way only a dozen drunken armored

Althaean soldiers could be. Solarin was always bustling with travelers. Most locals didn't care where the travelers came from as long as they were respectful and free spending. Haynes guided Mirari through the crowd to a table teeming with the not-so-sober men, all of them barely able to hold their liquor. The merriment droned out, and she could feel their gaze boring holes into her.

"Hey, look who finally made it," one of his soldier friends called out.

"Already picked up a featherpit too," another snickered, and Mirari raised her hand to the back of her head to the feathered pin, which was common in Minetta but not to these foreign men.

She began to feel apprehensive around them. Not scared – she could take care of herself if anything were to happen. But she remembered Neo's advice. She was more concerned about the unwelcome attention another brawl might invite.

Haynes interrupted her thoughts. "Don't mind them. I'm very grateful for your help, and your gracious company."

"You're okay hanging around with Minettans, I take it?"

Haynes chugged the rest of his beer, and got that philosophical look alcohol was so good at inspiring. "Aside from the land we were born on, there's no difference among us." Haynes already had another mug in his hand, thanks to his buddies. "We're all human. At least that's what our region leader tells us. He's a great man. I hope you can meet him someday."

"Spoken like a true commander, Haynes," a soldier praised.

"Oh, you're a *commander*?" Mirari raised an eyebrow.

"Did I leave that part out? Commander Haynes of Althaea Main, proudly serving His Honor, the Valiant Tiger!"

"You're talking to a woman whose empire sings the praises of Lord Fangbane, Haynes," muttered one of the drinkers.

"The very man who annihilated His Honor," someone else said.

"Ah, I'd like to see that guy in person," said a third drunk. "I hear he's just an old man with a toothpick for a spear."

"Why does he hide his face behind a mask?"

"Maybe he's as ugly as you, Rohan."

This remark garnered an enormous gale of drunken mirth. The laughter stopped just as suddenly, though, as a sturdy figure entered the tavern. His eyes swept the room, searching for someone. Not far behind were his escorts, Shiba and Neo. They slouched by the door as Gaven shoved his way through the crowd.

"Your Honor!" one of the soldiers greeted, and all other heads at the table turned to greet him with smiles gleaming with the energy of youth. By now, they should have received the message that their esteemed leader was on indefinite suspension. But the public had no idea where Gaven was serving his time. Gaven wanted to keep it that way. There was no merit in fighting under a man who had dishonored his name and region.

Althaea Main's leadership now rested in Gaven's second in command, Erel. She was a talented fighter in her own way, a former rogue, and could command soldiers with the fearful glare in her golden eyes. But she held no real influence, and people were reluctant to follow the leadership of a woman. But even if the new recruits did not respect Erel's position, anyone who followed Commander Haynes would.

Another soldier hollered at him. "What brings you here? Are you off the hook?"

"Just here to see you off. I'll need you all to return to Althaea tomorrow. Make sure you continue to behave and listen to Erel. Do as she says. Any mishaps, you can guarantee I'll hear of it."

"Your Honor, join us!" Someone tried to hand him a drink.

"Where's Haynes?" He asked, pushing the drink away. He peered beyond the other tables and found him and his men happily feasting. He made his way toward the back of the room. The least they needed was bad news.

Haynes looked up, and when he saw Gaven, his face bloomed into an astonished smile. "Look, it's the big boss himself!" Haynes yelled as he stood up. "C'mon, I'll introduce you to him." Haynes dragged Mirari by the arm until they both stood by the horde of Althaean soldiers. Mirari tried to keep herself out of Gaven's sight, hiding behind the substantial bulk of Haynes.

"Haynes, quit goofing around," Gaven said in his authoritative voice. "Did you get everything on the list?"

"I sure did." Haynes smiled as he nudged an unwilling Mirari forward. "This lady helped me out."

Gaven did a double take at the sight of Mirari. "You…" He paused.

"Ah…" Mirari was struck awkwardly speechless, recalling her last unpleasant conversation with Gaven. She felt his gaze bore into her.

"You're that girl…" he said, almost dumbstruck himself. "The warrior from the battlefield."

"Girl?" Mirari's voice reached the highest pitch. "We're practically the same age."

"Oh?" She watched a mischievous grin cross Gaven's face. "You followed me to Althaea… and for some reason, you know my age. Did you look up our constellations as well?"

She felt her face grow flustered, and she was left speechless.

"Eh?" Haynes turned back to Mirari. "You're a fighter? Why didn't you say so?" He hollered at his comrade at the bar. "Hey, Rohan. Get one for the lady, will ya?"

But Gaven nudged Mirari away, separating her from the rest of his loud men with the safety of his body. She felt trapped, sandwiched between him and the table behind her.

"This isn't the kind of place you should be in," he whispered in her ear. His voice wasn't friendly, and yet there was something protective in his tone.

But Mirari was not the kind of damsel who appreciated a male savior.

"Well excuse me, let me just move out of my own town for you."

"Your town? You live here, in Solarin?"

"You have a problem with that, oh Valiant Tiger?" Mirari asked. "These flat-faced soldiers of yours have no problem drinking in a Minettan tavern."

"That's not what I meant. I mean I don't trust these brutes around a decent girl. Besides, it's late. No woman should be wandering by herself at this hour."

That did not calm Mirari down in the slightest. She grew angry at the way he underestimated her. "I can take care of myself, *Your Honor*. But you wouldn't know that, would you? After all that time you spent away from home."

With that, she shouldered her way past him, storming for the tavern door before he could get another word in. She brushed past Shiba and Neo, who gave her a slight nod, but she ignored them both in her fury.

"I take it she's not going to buy us a round, then," Neo said.

As she calmed down on her walk home, she puzzled over what Gaven was doing in Minetta in the first place. Just like the rest of the town, Mirari had not known the result of Gaven's trial. He was alive, obviously, which meant Fangbane upheld his end of the deal. Seeing Neo reminded her of his earlier visit. Fangbane must be moving ahead with his plans to gather a force of warriors. She realized Neo's return meant she better start thinking about packing her belongings.

CHAPTER SIX

Two weeks after her encounter with Gaven in the tavern, Mirari arrived at Fangbane's estate. As Starlight welcomed her into the grand entryway, she told Mirari that Shiba and Neo had already moved in. Her baby bump had become much more prominent since the last time they met, but Starlight was still as cheerful as always, skipping over to reach for the bag in Mirari's hands.

"Don't be silly," Mirari said, refusing to hand over the luggage. "You look like you have enough to carry around already."

"Well, suit yourself," she said, scurrying toward a grand stairway. "Come, come, let me show you to your room. The men are living in the East Wing, ladies will be in the West Wing; the wings have a shared bath."

"Really? You must be aiming to spoil me." Mirari complimented the marble stairs, the soaring ceilings, the exquisite baseboards, and crown molding. Of course, this was not the first time Mirari had lived in such a luxurious manor, although she had never intended to live in one again.

"Directly upstairs is the library, and the big room next to it is our room," Starlight chirped. "We don't have servants, so you'll need to clean up after yourself and take turns with the chores. Everyone does. That's the cost of living here, in addition to your service as a Knight, of course."

Starlight unlocked the first door in the West Wing. Mirari peered into the spacious bedroom. It was fully furnished with a table, bed, and a bookshelf, and had far more space than she needed for her belongings. It reminded her of the house she grew up in before she met the family that saved her. Now, they were all gone, as were Gaven's memories of her.

"Feel free to make yourself at home. We'll all gather in the reception hall around sundown and have some refreshments."

<hr>

MIRARI EXPECTED she would be the first one to appear, but found that Neo was already in the reception hall.

Neo greeted her with a nod, waiting to speak as he was chewing a large piece of crusty bread with a hunk of cheese. He swallowed and said, "Well, you caught me. Quick, eat something so I don't look like the only pig at the trough."

It was a generous spread with cold cuts of roast boar, fresh norkfruit salad, deviled eggs, and many more mouth-watering dishes prepared by Starlight.

Mirari caught a whiff of a familiar smell – the overpowering aroma of rosemary dancing on the oily surface of smooth mountains of chicken.

She turned her attention to the dish, almost expecting to see a familiar face standing next to it. Instead, her heart sank; the chicken looked nothing like she expected. The color of the skin was light and garnished with spinach and tomatoes. It was beautifully assembled, but nothing like the homemade masterpiece Salathiel used to make.

"You want some?" Neo offered, seeing her eyes locked on the plump chicken.

"N-No..." Mirari resisted the urge to gravitate to the dish and covered it up with a lie. "I'm... not big on chicken. Actually, I wanted to come down early, and help set this up, but..."

"Yeah, you have to move fast if you want to keep up with Starlight."

Mirari extended her arm for a handshake, but Neo had his hand in a ball. Unsure of the protocol, she hesitantly clenched her hand, hoping that she was doing it correctly.

Still munching, Neo lightly tapped his fist on hers. "No need to be formal, M. We're teammates, after all."

"Actually, I'm not official yet. Lord Fangbane said I need to pass some sort of a test first, so he can properly assess my skills."

"Either way, you'll be staying with us for the next few months. Stunning place, isn't it? Nothing like this in Solarin."

"Most people in Solarin can't afford to build a manor on an island."

Fangbane entered, in rapid conversation with Shiba. The famed Shadow Soldier nodded to Neo and didn't even bother to look at Mirari.

"And hello to you, too, *Your Honor*," she muttered. He was a familiar face she wasn't thrilled to see, but Shiba and Neo were a package deal. Mirari expected to continue receiving the same hostile treatment she received back when they first met on the battlefield.

"Ah, don't mind him. You two will get along, I promise," Neo smiled as he pulled a drumstick off the rosemary chicken she tried so hard to avoid, and tucked out a chair for Mirari before taking the seat next to her.

Gaven strode in like a man used to being the center of every room he entered. When he saw Mirari, he stopped short. Mirari stared back, eyes wide.

Starlight noticed the sudden tension in the room and perked

her head up. She quickly shifted glances between the two. "Oh, sorry I forgot to mention. Gaven is staying with us too, at least for the duration of his suspension."

They said nothing, and now Shiba was scowling too, his cold stare fixed on Gaven. Their continued silence made Starlight scramble.

Mirari blushed, feeling a bit sorry she'd been so rude to him back at the tavern in Solarin. He made eye contact with her, but it was impossible to read his attitude.

"Ah, Gaven," Fangbane said, reading his wife's troubled mind, and breaking away from Shiba. "And Mirari, how wonderful. Welcome, welcome. Well, I think you've all met one another, no? Shall we get started?"

Starlight took this opportunity to leave the room.

Gaven turned his gaze from Mirari, and said to Fangbane, "So, this is your surprise candidate? Are you serious?"

From a door in the back, Starlight swept in with another platter. "Oh, yes," she said. "We all saw how great Mirari was on the battlefield. Fang couldn't resist asking her to join."

"Plus, Gaven wanted a fighter from the paragon class, and he got one," Fangbane said, unsuccessfully hiding a snicker.

"Very funny," Gaven rolled his eyes, clearly not amused as he shifted his attention to Mirari again. "But no one is official until I sign off on them. Right?"

"Well, I am," boomed Shiba. "And same for Neo."

"Yes, that's correct. But all the rest who join us will be evaluated for their abilities." Fangbane turned to Mirari. "But I expect that anyone I've selected will pass with flying colors."

"But that will be my call. Right?" Gaven asked again, his glare roasting at Mirari.

"Yes, yes. Mister Valiant Tiger here is going to be supervising the Knights," Fangbane said to ease the tension.

"So you're willing to commit suicide with this fool, My Lord?" Shiba said, cutting Gaven a taunting look.

"Shiba, I made it perfectly clear that he would be staying with us," Fangbane said.

"You didn't say he was going to be my chief."

"He's not your boss. He's your supervisor, manager, trainer, or whatever you want to call it." And then, in a more serious tone, he added, "I'm your chief, Shiba."

Shiba continued to scowl but kept quiet. Mirari had a bad feeling about all the existing rivalry in this group. Neo leaned in, and whispered, "Well, here we are. One big happy family, eh?"

Fangbane clapped his hands, rubbed them together, and put a cheery enthusiasm into his voice. "Well, then. First, let's go over the training schedule, shall we?"

AFTER THE MEETING BROKE UP, Mirari stayed to help Starlight clean up the buffet spread. Starlight tried to shoo her away, but Mirari insisted. After all, if they were to share in the chores, she wanted to do her part. When they were finished, she left the reception hall, heading for the stairs to return to her room.

"And where are you going?"

She turned to see Gaven, standing in the grand entry foyer with a spear in his hand. "Back to my quarters, your majesty," she said curtly.

"Do you need to get changed?" Gaven inquired calmly, looking her over. "Wouldn't want your nice clothes to get dirty."

"What do you mean?"

"I thought you wanted to become a Knight. Or did you forget about the little matter of passing my test for approval?"

"We're doing this now?" Mirari asked, genuinely surprised. She hadn't expected to have her evaluation tonight.

"Sooner the better." Gaven grinned. "Grab your weapon, and meet me in the courtyard."

She opened the doors to a patio behind the manor, dodging a minefield of luscious plants until she arrived at a wide, inviting courtyard. Her eyes were drawn to a source of light – a lantern with a glowing lumastōne inside – that sat on a table not far from where Gaven was stretching and warming up. He was unaware of her watching him as he twirled his spear in sharply executed drill moves. She was almost hypnotized by the sheer poetry of his fluid motion, in awe of his powerful body moving with the grace and perfection of a dancer.

For a moment, she drifted back to a childhood memory. Was this man truly that same determined young boy who taught her how to hunt down a wild boar? Showed her how to trail the dangerous animal, how to defend herself, how to make the kill safely and successfully? How could this grim and serious warrior have been that kind and loving friend who was so welcoming and warm to a lost young girl on the run, who welcomed her into the family?

"Ah. You showed up," Gaven said, stopping his drill as he noticed her with her sword sheathed and slung over her back.

"Well?" she said with a brash challenging tone. "Are we doing this, or are you just going to show off all night?"

Not waiting for an answer, she drew her sword, spinning it with a flourish. She took a couple of swings, feeling the balance of the blade in her hand, loving, as always, the sound of the weapon cutting through air.

"Nice blade," said Gaven. "Let's see if you know how to wield it."

It was astonishing how quickly he closed in, lunging at her with his spear. She swept it away and countered with her own attack.

Gaven took a step to the side to dodge Mirari's lunge, blocking her with his spear with ease. He held her gaze, anticipating and evaluating her every move. She was fast, faster than he expected, but wild and reckless.

Gaven escalated his attack, probing her defensive skills, forcing Mirari to adjust to his tempo, and was impressed as she successfully blocked every attack.

When given space, Mirari cast small barriers, using the tiny circles that hovered over her arm like a shield while she attacked with the sword in her other hand. He noticed that was the only time she used her kore.

Gaven shifted his tempo again in an effort to catch her off guard. And he did.

His spear lightly tapped her leg. A warning.

She blocked the next one, but Gaven moved too fast and nudged her roughly against her shoulder with the blunt end of his spear.

He expected that to throw her off balance, but she stood strong. He took mental notes, admiring her balance, flexibility, and ability to pick up his patterns. But her bizarre style made him furrow his brow. He had never seen such a strange combination of swings and footwork, and even if such a wildcard could catch him off guard she was not physically strong enough to throw him off.

He felt a strong breeze rush under him. He was on his toes, almost ready to be carried off. But Gaven commanded the earth to rise to firmly plant his feet back on the ground and block the flow of wind. He followed up with a flying pebble, just large enough to smack Mirari's sword out of her hand.

"That's enough," he suddenly said. He paused, planting his spear in the ground. "You went easy on me. How can I evaluate you like that?"

"You could tell?" She couldn't believe it. Mirari glanced at her fallen sword as she caught her breath.

"Of course. Explain yourself."

"I don't want to hurt you," she admitted, but he laughed at the very idea.

"Is that a joke? You're afraid of hurting the Valiant Tiger of Althaea?"

But she could hurt him. Gaven didn't remember their battle during the Althaean Siege. Neither did she, but she knew how deadly those flames could be. Suffocate, or char like a roasted goat – she had no control over the flames that overpowered him. He could've died. Much like a time when they were mere children. She recalled that day they had been hunting in the woods with Salathiel. Fire. Destruction. No memory. And she nearly killed Gaven. It was all repeating.

Now, she realized what she had never admitted to herself.

That incident changed him forever. She recalled the fearful look in his eyes, the way he avoided her touch ever since she had set that forest on fire. And not long after, he left home. He said he was determined to train himself as an invincible warrior. He'd left his family behind and never looked back.

But what if he left to get away from her? Was it Mirari who drove Gaven to prove himself? So devoted to his single-minded drive to be the best that he pushed his family out of his heart? Was that the real reason he couldn't allow himself to recognize who she was?

"Mirari! Are you even listening?"

She snapped out of her musings.

"I… No. I mean yes. I'm sorry, I was…"

"You fight like a commoner – reckless, spontaneous. If you want to be a paragon, you must learn to fight with tactics. Bonking things until they break will get you killed on the battlefield."

He was right, of course. Her only experience was fighting with drunks and louts.

He continued, "You only focus on your strikes. Are you paying attention to your breathing? What about your opponent?

Can you hear their breaths or how fast their heart is beating? Do you have any idea how hard you have to train?"

"I… know how much you have sacrificed to become who you are now."

Gaven's eyes narrowed at her. She stirred something strange in him, something he did not understand. "Never mind me. It's Lord Fangbane who wants you to be a Knight. I say you're not ready… but I'm willing to give you a chance. Every day, at the break of dawn, we'll train out here. Starting tomorrow. Prove to me that you can learn how to be a real fighter, and I'll reconsider your nomination."

"I'm glad to hear that," Fangbane interrupted. Gaven turned to see him standing in the doorway, watching them. "She'll be a fine warrior in your hands."

Gaven scowled at the flattery. "It would've been a lot easier for both of us if you just picked someone who already knows the battlefield."

"But you have agreed to train her. What changed your mind?"

"I want to understand what you see in her." That was half the truth. What Gaven didn't want to admit was that he didn't want to let her out of his sight. There was a sense of duty to protect her, for whatever reason. Perhaps, out of his own guilt for failing to protect his loved ones when he was younger. She resembled innocence, a time when life was simple and the most he had to worry about was catching a boar for supper. For this young girl to be forced into battle and bloodshed? He wasn't sure she could take it. "Besides, I owe her one, don't I?"

"Oh, there is a lot that you don't see," he said and looked at Mirari. "So much you can both discover."

"We'll see. I'm not here to babysit," Gaven grumbled. "She needs to be at her best or she's out." Gaven walked away without listening to another word.

"So, you still haven't told him. Why is that?"

"You're the mind reader. Figure it out."

"You wanted his life spared." Fangbane shifted the blame back to her. "I thought you would be happy to have a family reunion."

"He hates me," she mumbled. "I can see why he doesn't recognize me. But… I didn't expect him to be a prick."

"He was raised by egoistic Althaeans, what did you expect?" He stopped, staring into her eyes.

Beyond her fear that Gaven was possibly still upset with her over the time she nearly charred him alive as children, she realized that the rejection wasn't just about her. It was Gaven's denial of anything in his past, of his life in Minetta. He had been putting up the act of being an Althaean for so long that he probably believed it himself. If she were to let him learn the truth about her, he'd have to admit to being born a Minettan. He was no longer a Minettan child, but a respectable region leader of Althaea.

If he was truly pretending to not know who she was, she would be okay living with it. Mirari was ready to sacrifice whatever relationship she had with him in the past to let him continue living his legacy.

Her trail of thought surprised Fangbane. She wasn't worried about whether she would be able to keep up with Gaven's training regime, but rather…

"How do I know… I won't hurt him again?" She trailed off.

"You may have used the flames subconsciously, but you also managed to control it. You could easily have killed him, but you didn't. That's how I know we can learn to harness your… unusual ability."

"By the Gods, I pray you're right."

"I am. Fear is often the stepchild of ambition. The time you spend here may help drive that ambition. I sense that something very powerful motivates a man like Gaven to push himself to the limit. That might just be you."

CHAPTER SEVEN

There was little improvement in their relationship despite two weeks of training together. Every day, they were up long before anyone else. But as she yawned on her way to meet Gaven in the courtyard this morning, she noticed Fangbane awake and dressed, holding a cup of hot buzzbean with milk and sugar.

"Morning your lordship," she said. But as she passed, she was thinking: *If you think getting to know each other will help us bond again, you obviously haven't gotten to know what an asshole Gaven is.*

Fangbane burst out with a snort, splattering buzzbean all over the floor.

"Tsk, tsk, Lord. Some thoughts should stay private."

Gaven was waiting in the courtyard. Of course. He made a point of always getting here before Mirari no matter how early she arrived.

What a dick. Somewhere behind her, Fangbane did another spit take.

But at least they were making progress in the physical aspects of training, even if they weren't on a personal level.

"Pick up your sword, and practice your form," he ordered.

Though petty, it irked her to see Gaven sitting back with his gear on a table, enjoying a nice hot cup of buzz while she worked up a sweat. She wouldn't be surprised to learn Gaven didn't even like the drink, and just pretended to enjoy it in front of her while she went through her paces, practicing each sequence of moves that she had learned yesterday, repeating each pose, and movement in perfect form.

"I find it interesting that you fight like an umbra with a sword."

"My brother was a better teacher than you," Mirari grumbled under her breath. It was half a lie, but she was unwilling to get into the details of her real trainer.

The thought of her trainer and brother tingled a discomfort in her stomach, and she felt the hilt of her sword slip slightly from her hand. She tried to tighten her grip, but her hand was still trembling on its own. She drew her attention back to the sequence of moves, ignoring her unsteady hand until she regained control.

"Really? Was he a fighter?"

"He was an excellent retinue."

"Aah. You learned the sword from an umbra. It all makes sense now."

"And the bow, and the spear, and the throwing star, and… and many other techniques, from other people. It's called diversification."

"It doesn't work that way if you don't have the basics down." Gaven shook his head. "It will only weaken you. You're better off mastering one class. Only when you're as good as you can be at one thing, then you can expand to another. It's easier to learn skills that will complement your fighting style that way. No wonder your techniques are all messed up. You're a mongrel."

"Mixed breeds fight harder." She growled.

"On the positive side, it does make you unpredictable," he

admitted. "But that won't matter if it also makes you more vulnerable."

He took another sip of his buzzbean. "Speaking of your sword…"

"What about it?"

"It's nicely crafted. Where did you get it?" He tried to sound offhand, but she still heard a compliment hiding under there somewhere.

"I killed a region leader, and took it." She smirked.

"Liar."

"I stole it."

"Okay. Don't tell me."

She considered that very seriously, but she couldn't help wanting to reach out to him. "It belonged to my father."

His brow wrinkled, convinced she was still having him on.

"Uh-huh. And where would a common peasant obtain such a quality weapon?"

"What's wrong with common peasants? Or are you too good for an honest farmer?"

"I didn't say that."

She instantly regretted trying to open herself up to him, and she hated bringing up her past, both of her aristocratic family and her missing brother. She told herself that she had accepted Salathiel as deceased, but in truth, there was never a day when she didn't want to keep searching, no day when she thought about abandoning the Knights and returning to Solarin. Now that Gaven was here, however, she didn't want to let him down. Despite their time apart, he was the only family, blood or otherwise, that she had left.

"So?" Mirari said. "Tell me about your family. Grand aristocrats, I suppose. Wealthy, no doubt. Powerful. The kind of family anyone would want. The perfect life, no?"

"You still haven't learned your manners, have you?"

"Maybe I did my best to forget them. Just for you."

He almost threw another sharp barb back at her. "You have some talent with the bow," he said, reaching for something he could compliment. "Where did you pick that up?"

"Childhood hobby."

"Really? What were you, a highway bandit?"

"If you want to survive outside the city, you have to know how to hunt."

"Why the sword then?"

"For control." She paused as she recalled the first time she laid hands on her father's sword. "The bow is defensive. The sword is offensive."

"Well said." For a commoner with a poor upbringing, Gaven didn't expect her to be well-versed in weaponry.

"But the good thing about the sword is, it can be both. It all depends on how you want to use it. I'll show you," he said as he finished his buzzbean and snatched up a sword of his own. "Overhead blocks. You'll need perfect technique because this is usually a strength move. If you try to block and hold, the way most warriors will, your head will get split like a melon."

He took an overhead swing, Mirari blocked it, but he forced her sword down, stopping an inch from her scalp.

"So, what am I supposed to do?"

"Well, you could die…"

"Any other options?"

"I've come up with a move I call the roof slide. Instead of trying to block the standard way, the idea is to deflect your opponent with a parry riposte. Let me show you. Come at me. For real, I mean. Like you're chopping firewood."

Mirari brought her sword straight down like she was trying to pound a railroad spike. Gaven met the swing with his blade slanted at a forty-five-degree angle as he stepped sideways. Instead of stopping her blade, it slid off to the side. Having all her momentum deflected sideways threw her off balance, turning her body away, and Gaven made the point clearer by giving her a light kick in the rear.

"See? If you can't use power, then use your opponent's strength against him. Perfect for someone with twig arms like you. Go again."

They practiced the move a dozen times, then reversed roles, and he coached her through the move at half speed, again and again. Gaven was agile, and even when his sword was deflected, he kept his momentum under control and kept from being turned sideways. Until Mirari added her own twist, a flip of the wrist while his sword was sliding. The unexpected move made him turn to keep from falling over. She waved her hand and a pocket of wind followed her movement, smacking Gaven in the rear. He was so unprepared that he stumbled and fell on his belly.

Mirari was about to run, thinking he would explode in fury. She was pleasantly surprised when he sprang to his feet, his effort to control his smile evident.

He did give her a solemn nod, and said, "Brilliant! That was brilliant!"

Mirari was so delighted, she threw her arms around him. Gaven froze, eyes wide in shock as he let her embrace him. After an awkward moment, Mirari realized what she had done. She broke free and stepped back. "S-sorry, Your Honor."

It took effort, but Gaven managed to put a scowl back on his face, pretending it never happened. He cleared his throat. "Again."

Gaven snatched up his sword, and came at her, a swift attack, forcing her to move fast to fence his swings away. "Quick. No, quicker. You leave yourself too open for the opponent to strike." He kept up a string of criticism with every stroke.

He was attacking harder this time.

Finally, he stopped, leaving her panting.

"Left-handed now," he commanded and took the sword in

his left hand. Without pausing, he struck again. Mirari was caught off guard; she panicked and raised both hands to the handle to block his strong attack.

"What? That's… I can't do that."

"What if your right shoulder is cut wide open? Or your arm hacked off? All you have is your left. Are you so eager to die? Fight. Keep fighting."

He didn't go at her hard. But she thought it felt so awkward, she went red with embarrassment. She got angrier and angrier. She was sure he was just doing this to humiliate her.

"You're pathetic at this," he said, stopping.

"I've never even tried it before!"

"Like your kore? You're a mess. As a paragon, casting baby wind gusts won't fly. I'm assuming you were born with low kore capacity, which is why you chose a two-handed sword as your main weapon."

Mirari didn't argue. He was right, after all. She had an abysmal kore affinity.

"Didn't they say you know how to use fire? That's not as easy to master."

"I- No. I can't."

"You're right. I highly doubted it. I'll have to see it for myself."

Mirari was more than happy to drop that conversation. She still had no idea how the flames were triggered. She feared that simply talking about it could set it off.

"It's probably the bellberry juice you keep having for breakfast. It's not healthy."

She raised her brow at such superstition. "You're questioning my diet now?"

"And…" He continued.

Mirari groaned again. "What is it now?"

"I'm seeing a weak grip technique." He walked over to her side, then casually flicked his wrist on her sword, causing it to slip right out of her hands and fall on the ground. Mirari was shocked at how easily he disarmed her. She flushed red, embarrassed. "Wipe that pity off your face."

"You're a bully, all up on your high mount like Shiba."

"Don't you dare compare me to him. Look, I don't want to be here any more than you do. The faster you learn, the sooner we won't have to deal with each other."

"Fine with me!" She snapped and chucked her sheathed sword at him.

<hr>

GAVEN ENTERED Fangbane's private study, grumbling quietly. It was pitch dark, the way Fangbane liked to work. He was writing notes at his table when he heard something collide with his end table, followed by a series of hissed profanities.

"It's daytime. Why in Inferna are you working in the dark?"

Fangbane pulled back the curtains behind his desk, shining blinding light in Gaven's face.

"Sorry. Habit." Fangbane waited for him to give updates on the Knight's training progress, but Gaven's scowl was hard to ignore. "You seem a little grumpier today. If that's possible."

"Mirari is a handful." Gaven groaned. "She's beyond rebellious and always on the defensive. And impertinent? Not a shred of propriety."

"But she does as you ask? And she learns quickly?"

"Thank the Gods. Otherwise, I would've staked her to a gibbet by now. She's a mediocre fighter, but..." He almost didn't go on. "I can't believe I would say this, but she's very observant, quite intelligent for a peasant. She may be useful to the Knights one way or another."

"And how is it going with training Shiba?" Fangbane asked.

"How do you think?"

"I think he has an ego so insufferable you haven't made any progress."

"You read my mind," Gaven said. "The slackard refuses to bother with training at all."

Fangbane decided not to pursue it. Shiba was the best at what he did and had no interest in anything else. He shrugged. "We should work on creating a strategy that could be effective when all the Knights work together."

"Now that you mention it. How soon will we bring the group up to strength? We don't even have your magical number five yet."

Fangbane came clean. It had been nearly a month since he sent out invitation letters to fighters all over Althaea, Minetta, and Valenia. He received a few rejection letters, polite platitudes. They supported his idea. They wished him the best of luck. Prior commitments. Apologies they had to decline…

The majority never bothered to respond.

"On the positive side, your rebellion made the common people reconsider the current political system. People are in favor of what you are doing, and as a result, promising support for the Knights. Unfortunately, most of our supporters are not fighters, so our response rate has been… low."

"I didn't expect this to grow into a conversation outside of Althaea Main," Gaven said with a hint of regret in his voice.

Under the mask Gaven tried so hard to put on, there was a dash of guilt. He wasn't content with how the battle ended. His memories were still missing and he was being punished for something beyond his control. How his people would treat him when he resumed his position as region leader was a mystery, but to Gaven, it felt as if the world had already turned against him.

"I heard Althaea Main is recovering well." Fangbane tried to soothe him. "You are not hated. None of this is your fault. This conversation, this desire for change, it's something that has been in the minds of commoners for decades but no one dared to act on it. It's why I'm here and why I'm assembling the Knights."

Fangbane pivoted to a lighter note, reaching under his desk for one of many boxes that lay by his feet. He pulled out a box of finely tooled wood and leather.

"We got a new comstōne today," he chimed like a child opening gifts on his birthday. The large communication rock, as beautiful as any titanium-coated geode and erect and heavy as any grown man, was rare and expensive to come by. Large communities shared one in their town center. Region leaders and nobles owned one of their own, and now Fangbane was privileged to join this elite league who had a personal comstōne.

"I'm putting it in the library," he said. "It has contact with all the region leaders and the Council registered, including your region. Feel free to use it."

"Thanks, but I already have a clōve." Gaven waved his hand in the air, showing off his rare and costly black glove laced with pulsing blue threads of hāstals, a must-have for any leader on the battlefield. Though the clōve wasn't as beautiful as the comstōne's rainbow coat, it was invented to replace the stationary rock. However, it was full of limitations, and since Gaven was under house arrest, mountains and valleys away from his contacts in Althaea Main, his clōve was essentially useless.

Fangbane opened the package to reveal a dozen pairs of gloves that looked just like Gaven's. "One more for me." There was excitement in his voice. "Compliments from Lucan Hale of Valenia. He's been taking care of Hale's product distribution in Minetta and wanted to donate to the cause. This is exactly what we need."

"Oh, joy. How festive."

"So, in general, it sounds like you're happy here."

"Well, I suppose you make it quite a home."

"Minetta is your home, after all," Fangbane said, to gauge Gaven's reaction.

"What did you say?" the warrior snapped.

"I meant only that you are welcome here in Minetta any time." Fangbane noted the anger at the suggestion he was from Minetta.

"You should be more careful with your words," Gaven grumbled.

"Yes, no doubt. I suppose the problem is that no matter what people say, I can usually see the truth of what's really in their minds."

"That ability could make some people think of you as a dangerous man."

"Gaven, old chum. I am a dangerous man. I should think you'd have figured that out by now. Speaking of which…"

Fangbane got up to lock the door and reached into a cabinet to remove a file hidden under piles of other folders.

"The Council issued a report on the Althaean Siege. Frankly, I don't believe their conclusions."

"What do you mean?"

Fangbane grew serious. "There's not all that much information, and little we weren't already aware of. I'm pretty confident that the Council is hiding something. What I don't know is whether it's something they don't want us to know or something they're unsure about themselves."

He handed Gaven the folder in question. Inside were reports, statistics, interviews of people debriefed on their battle actions, along with copies of Gaven's medical report from Starlight.

"You really are a dangerous man." Gaven shook his head. "You're already defying the Council's system. Now you want to overrule their judgment?"

"There may be a greater danger out there we don't know about. Gaven, if you truly had no control over your actions during the Althaean Siege, surely it's not something we can sweep under the rug, wouldn't you agree?"

"Why would you want me to look into it? Aren't you afraid that my biased opinions will taint the research?"

"No. In fact, that's why I want your opinion. Only you can tell me how what happened to you made sense. Something polluted your mind. But what? What caused you to go berserk? Something attacked you, got inside you?"

Gaven wished he knew, not for his own closure, but to prevent the same thing from happening to someone else.

"Exactly." Fangbane read his mind. "We may not have a lead, but we can't close the investigation. There is an answer out there, somewhere. And we damn well better find it. Do your best to retrace your steps."

"What about all these other folders?" He waved at the mountains of paper behind Fangbane.

"Ah, that. More claims and troubles and complaints. They have been pouring in from all over the world. People are starting to hear about the Knights."

"What is there to hear?"

"Nothing, yet. Except, the idea of a force to help others seems to have appeal. Rather than ask their region leaders for help, people are coming to us in hopes that we'll do a better and faster job."

"I don't blame them. As a region leader, I receive hundreds of these. Sadly, most requests went unanswered simply because we lacked the resources."

"I think assigning some of these mundane tasks to the Knights is a good way to start building trust with the people."

"Not a bad idea. Should I have the Knights get started on these?"

"Absolutely. You be the judge of who gets assigned to these tasks."

"I'm on it like white on Valerian rice powder." Gaven gathered a stack of the folders, and started out of the office, shuffling through requests. "Anything to keep me from going crazy with that pain in the ass, Mirari."

In fact, Gaven thought it was the perfect way to keep her busy, and get her off his back.

Fangbane smiled at Gaven's parting thoughts.

CHAPTER EIGHT

Hooves drummed across the wooden bridge to the estate. In the distance, Mirari could see two silver horses, stalwart and energetic, with legs so muscular they could sprint for hours without stopping. She could barely make out the riders whose dark cloaks blended with the manes of their mounts, but she had seen the spirited mammals enough times to know that they belonged to Shiba and Neo. She walked over to the end of the bridge and greeted them upon arrival.

They were returning from their fortress located in Avon's capital city, Agna. Shiba was still the region leader of Avon, and he had this duty on top of being a part of the Knights. He and Neo frequently went back to Agna to check on the welfare and balance of their army while still living in Fangbane's estate. As a result, Mirari rarely saw them. It was also the excuse they used to dodge Gaven's training regime.

Neo greeted her with a fist bump. "How did training go today?"

"Decent, I suppose." Mirari shrugged.

Shiba was not as friendly. "In other words, a tragedy," he sniped, exchanging glares with Mirari. But starting an argument hardly seemed worth the waste of breath. As he sulked, Neo turned to Mirari with an apologetic shrug.

"Is he going to be like this all the time?" she asked Neo.

Shiba barked, "If you can't handle it, you shouldn't be here."

"The only thing I can't handle is your attitude. No wonder Minettans lost faith in you."

Shiba dismounted his horse and aggressively shoved her. "Listen here, kid. You're new to this, so I'll say it only once. Every day is a game of life or death. If you can't put a grip on that sword, you won't live to see another day."

"Asshole," Mirari growled under her breath. "You're a waste of skin."

"You impudent pup. I demand you duel with me," Shiba challenged, his pride stung. "I want you to show me why Lord Fangbane would ever choose you in the first place, and I promise my evaluation will be as easy as Gaven's."

"Please don't," Neo mumbled to himself.

"Will it make you happy?" she asked.

"It might make me consider upgrading you from bait to maid."

Mirari smiled and started to walk past him. Then she sucker punched him, leaving him with a bloody nose. Furious, he grabbed her wrist and twisted it at a painful angle. His knee rammed into her stomach. The force of his body weight slammed her into the ground. Mirari scissored her legs, locking them around his ankles, and down Shiba fell, face first into the loose dirt.

She struggled to stand back up before he could, but something was tugging at her arms. Mirari looked down to see a black, semi-transparent shape encircling her arms. Mirari couldn't break free from it. Shiba was standing, ready to attack again. He backhanded her across the face, following up with a boot to the kidneys.

"Shiba! That's enough!" Neo warned as he stepped between them and easily held Shiba back with one meat hook of a hand.

"She started it," Shiba said, sounding more like a playground bully than a revered leader.

"No, you did, you bilious skunk." Gaven stood with his arms crossed, clearly irritated with both of them. Gaven had watched the whole dispute and had been waiting for the result of this pissing contest before stepping in.

"Using your shadow on a novice is a dick move, you coward," Gaven said. "Next time, fight the little girl like a man."

Gaven held out his hand to Mirari. She stared at his hand in consideration, but decided to stand without his help.

"I'm not little…" Mirari said, loud enough for Gaven to hear, but his glare was fixated on Shiba.

Gaven pulled out a sheaf of papers and waved them at the Knights. "Read these. Since you're all so hot to trot, this will keep you busy."

"Passing out homework now, teacher?" said Shiba.

"Not homework. Orders."

Bristling, Shiba snatched the papers. "Since when do you—"

The sound of ringing steel cut Shiba's complaint short as he saw the gleaming edge of Gaven's spear sparkle in the sunshine. "Now here is your choice. You three can take this mission, or you can go polish every tile of the estate as training."

Shiba and Mirari glared at each other.

"You can always refuse. If you're tired of living."

Neo stepped up and took the papers, not even bothering to glance at them. "We'll do it."

"Hold on," Shiba said. "I'm not going without knowing what I'm getting into with her."

"Don't come with us, then," Mirari snarled, and tried to get a peek over Neo's shoulder, whispering to him, "What is it?"

"His Lord and I have agreed that we should spread a little

goodwill to get the Knights rolling. Pass out favors to some influential region leaders."

Shiba perked up. "Ah-hah! So we can call them in later. I like it."

"No. No strings. We just help out and gain their trust. That's all we're after."

Shiba grumbled under his breath, "Knights of the Order of Ass Kissers."

Gaven ignored him. "We'll spread awareness, get people on our side. We'll do this in all three empires, but we'll start with Evaleen in Althaea." He nodded at the papers in Neo's hand. "Landon runs that region."

"That halfwit can't run his own nose," said Shiba.

Gaven actually had to hold back a smile at that. "I'll grant he is sort of a weasel, but he's well-connected to the Tepis."

"Translation, he's a glorified pimp."

"The fact is he has problems that he's too lazy to attend to himself. So helping him makes it easy to sway him to our side." Gaven put the patented scowl in place and glared at Shiba one last time. "Now get moving."

* * *

SHIBA, Neo, and Mirari crossed the border to Althaea and rode to Elegen, the capital city of Evaleen where Region Leader Landon resided. Compared to the desert lands that plagued Ophallen and Axillaire, Evaleen was an oasis. It thrived off the benefits of being near the ocean. The capital bloomed with tropical nucifera trees as high as the white stone buildings, and pink orchid ivies wrapped around pillars.

They found the dissolute young wastrel lavished in gold jewelry and surrounded by several female servants whose garb – or lack thereof – left little doubt as to their gender, or their qualifications as personal assistants. The scrawny figure cut by Landon didn't look like he could win a duel with an asthmatic octogenarian. His clean shave and fair skin indicated that all his devotion to religion went into his beauty routine. Only the few who had seen him fight knew that the young blond was no joke of a spellcaster, a fighter who possessed a seemingly limitless amount of kore and could use it in place of a physical weapon.

"What a pleasure it is to be visited by… what is it you call yourself? Knights?" Landon asked with uncertainty, looking them over skeptically. "We are unaccustomed to visitors from Minetta." His tone implied that it was fine by him. His eyes looked askance at their peculiar clothing. "While you're here, I can refer you to an excellent tailor, by the way."

Their capes and armor were decorated with a few feathers – a fashion that was only common in Minetta, and over time became a signature insult favored by Althaeans. Landon found it strange and lacking in taste.

"Our stylist favors the functional." Mirari smiled.

"We work with Lord Fangbane," Shiba said. "We hear you're having a problem with some bandits in your region."

"Indeed, we are," he concurred, seeming to recognize Shiba. "I'm a bit scandalized to see you take an interest in it, though, Shadow Soldier."

"When your problems began to affect Minettan merchants traveling in your region, you made it my problem." While Shiba was not wrong, it was a harsh way to put it. They were supposed to help Landon as a favor, not confront him.

"We want you to know that we're here to assist you however we can, regardless of nationality," Neo said.

Landon was paying them scant attention; his eyes were taking a sight-seeing tour of Mirari that she didn't appreciate.

"This beautiful lady behind you is also a 'Knight'?"

Mirari was too diplomatic to say what she thought of this vain poser, so she kept her mouth shut.

"Yes," Neo confirmed. "She's with us."

"What's your name, darling?"

Mirari was gritting her teeth by now, clearly uncomfortable with this lecherous philanderer. "The name's Mirari," she said bluntly, then remembered to add, "Your Honor."

"Mirari… what an enthralling name." He could see she found his leer unwelcome, which only flamed his interest. "You are most certainly welcome to linger in my region anytime, Princess. How old are you, Mirari?"

"Nineteen… Your Honor." The hostility in her tone was hard to dismiss.

"Nineteen! With those melons—"

But before Landon could finish, Shiba interrupted. "Landon, do you have something for us or not?"

"Hmph. Impatient as usual," Landon muttered. "Very well. My advisors," he gestured at two of his ladies who appeared semi-clad at best, "Will update you on the matter. Handle it as you like."

"Follow me, Your Honor." One of the women addressed Shiba.

Neo and Mirari trailed behind them to another room. The women showed them to a table with a map spread out on it. It had markings indicating where bandit raids had occurred. They explained in detail what little information they had, including names of merchants waylaid, bills of lading, origins, destinations, and itineraries of the victims. The advisors withdrew to allow the Knights to converse in private and returned to other pressing duties.

"Disgusting. Utterly disgusting." Mirari trailed on once Landon's advisors had left the room. She nudged Neo. "What are they even wearing? How is this pervert a region leader?"

"Landon may have the brain of a weasel but trust me, you don't want to see what he can do with his kore. Unlike Minetta, in Althaea, the strongest fighters become region leaders. They know how to defend their territory, but they're useless diplomats. Why else would most of Althaea still live in poverty?"

"Does he even do anything about these bandit raids?" Mirari frowned as her fingers ran through dozens of letters from merchants pleading to have the bandits caught, and their goods returned.

"If it has nothing to do with women, he won't touch it," Shiba said.

Neo nodded, adding, "And the Council won't kick him off the throne because his family's filthy rich. That's just how they run things in Althaea. Money talks."

Shiba drew their attention to the map and pointed to an area with the most incidents. "The largest concentration of raids is right around here, between Kishnin and Ekvelt. That's where we should take a look."

Mirari analyzed the documentary evidence, matching letters and waybills to various points on the map. Her eyes flicked back and forth between the documents and the map.

Neo took notice of her intense concentration, and asked, "Did you find something, M?"

"A pattern, I think. Most of the robberies have targeted Minettans…"

"As one would expect," Shiba said dismissively. "Minettan merchants send most of the goods through here."

"I'm well aware of merchant trade," Mirari sniped back. "What I'm noticing isn't where the stolen goods are from, but where they are going."

"I don't take your meaning."

"There are quite a bit of trade goods heading for Altha Hills."

"A wealthy region. Nearly every object in Altha Hills is made of hāstals. No surprise they import a lot of goods."

"They do indeed. But for some reason, the cargo headed

there seems to get through without interference. The robberies only target caravans headed elsewhere."

"I'm sure you must have a point," Shiba said, pretending to be bored by faking a yawn. "I simply don't care what it is."

Mirari knew Shiba was goading her. She maintained a calm tone. "I'm saying these robberies can't just be random. These bandits target Minettan merchants. But they don't target Minettan goods headed to Altha Hills."

Neo caught her point. "You're suggesting someone in that region is tipping off the bandits?"

"That is not part of our mission," Shiba cut in. "The job is to catch some bandits and make a friend of Landon. Not to dig up dirt on 'anyone else', or piss off rich and powerful leaders in Altha Hills like the Bishop or the Priest."

"And what if they are behind these robberies?"

"That is outside the scope of our mission," he insisted. "We're after the bandits." He stabbed his finger at the map. "This area, here. That's where most of the attacks take place. That's where we'll catch them."

"Fine. Never mind who is directing them. But look at what's being stolen." Mirari slaps a report of stolen items. "Here – 'a sachet of tea, two barrels of wheat, ten stacks of wood'. Just ordinary commerce, being hit by random bandits, it appears."

Shiba rolled his eyes once again. "I don't see why—"

She interrupted him, slapping down another report. "Compare it to this; 'five pounds of iridium, a sack of topaz, ten bags of leather'. The Minettan merchants who carry more valuable goods are targeted more specifically."

"Ugh. Obviously, foreign merchants will have better goods."

"Minettan merchants always keep the most valuable items hidden, often under the cart or even sewn into their clothes. They put cheaper goods on top. Thieves don't want to linger or take time doing a thorough search on the off chance they might find more valuable goods. So? Tell me. How would the bandits know which ones to target?"

"You're overthinking," Shiba shook his head. "We're not here to speculate."

"I'm not speculating. I know all the tricks and trade secrets to move merchandise safely. It was my trade, after all."

"And fighting is mine. We just need to find some bandits quickly and deal with them. Landon will be happy with the results. Mission accomplished."

"What about these Minettans? Your own people. And mine."

"This is not a debate. Do your job. Get it over with." Shiba turned, starting to leave. "Neo, let's go kick some bandit ass."

Mirari seethed. Swallowing her fury, she followed Shiba and Neo out the door.

THE THREE KNIGHTS reached the rolling plains where a rash of bandit raids had been reported. Most of the terrain was wide open and grassy. But there were areas where the trail had to cross wooded ravines – areas with suitable cover to stage an ambush. And sure enough, they spotted busted carriage parts and scattered broken crates, their contents long gone.

They picked a quiet, isolated stretch of road that traversed a section of forested ravine. It looked promising for setting up a stake out. They watched several merchants passing by, some singly, some in convoy. Neo stopped several carriages to ask if they had encountered trouble. Not one of the frightened merchants had seen any bandits. But they were anxious to be on their way.

"They think *you're* a bandit," Mirari teased, amused at the friendly giant standing in the middle of the road like a bull ready to charge at the incoming carriages.

"Let's just get under cover and watch the road," said Shiba.

They settled themselves in a grouping of boulders, which concealed them but offered a good view of the road in both directions.

Several hours passed.

"You, girl," Shiba called, not even looking at Mirari, "gather some wood, make a fire, and brew up some buzzbean. I'm falling asleep with boredom."

"Great idea," Mirari replied with much sarcasm. "And I'll be sure to use green wood. It will make better smoke signals to tell the bandits we're hiding here."

"Shhh!" Neo hissed.

"No, you shut up, Neo," grumbled Shiba. "I'm sick and tired of you taking her side all the—"

Neo clapped an enormous paw on his lord's mouth. Shiba was ready to explode in fury, but Mirari pointed at four men across the ravine, dressed in full black on horses pulling up on the crest. After they gathered, appearing to confer with each other, they rode into the ravine, and scattered on either side of the road, concealing themselves in the woods.

They had timed their ambush very well. In the distance, a traveling carriage approached, unaware as they rolled along the main road. Mirari started to get up, but Shiba grabbed her elbow.

"Are we going to do something?" she whispered.

Shiba held her back, cautioning her. "Not yet."

As the carriage got closer, Mirari grew anxious. "What are we waiting for?"

"How many bandits are hiding down there?"

"Four," she snapped but kept her voice low.

"And how do you know that?"

"They were up on that ridge. We all saw them."

Shiba gave her a withering stare, and his point dawned on her. But he couldn't help rubbing it in. "You saw four. How many bandits are there?"

"I get it."

"At *least* four," he hissed with satisfaction. "Now sit still, and let's see how many others we didn't see."

"But the coach—" she started. It was getting close now.

"Yes. The coach is what they're after. But we're after them. Let's make sure we know what we're charging into before we jump into the lion's den.

Two of the bandits let the coach pass them, and the other two charged out to the road. The sight of the bandits closing in from both sides spooked the horses, forcing them to veer off-road.

The carriage flipped over into a grassy ditch. The other two bandits chased from the rear now, and as soon as the driver and his terrified merchant passenger staggered up from the wreck, they could see they were surrounded. The bandits circled the carriage, and two of them dismounted. They began to tear through the goods, some of which were scattered on the ground. They ignored the injured merchant, who huddled in with the driver in fear.

Shiba turned to Mirari. "Well, you were right. Just the four. Let's go!"

The Knights emerged from the trees and charged at the bandits. Neo jumped high and tackled one of the circling bandits off his horse. They tumbled and wrestled on the ground while the spooked horse shrieked and trotted in place.

The other mounted bandit charged at Mirari. He wielded a long spear, thinking he'd picked an easy target. Mirari unsheathed her sword and prepared to counter his attack.

Her sword clashed with his spear every time he lunged at her. Mirari was on the defensive, as the bandit had the advantage of being on a horse. She wished she had a long pike instead of a sword. She needed to get him off that horse, where she could get close enough to put up a decent attack.

Shiba approached the other two bandits, who were busy pawing through the spoils. One had just taken a small leather pouch from the merchant. He looked inside, and his eye caught the twinkle of jewels.

"Look!" he cried out to his partner.

"No, you look," the bandit answered, pointing at Shiba, who was striding toward them, grinning a cold-blooded smile. They each drew a sword now, thinking they had an advantage.

Shiba sneered with amusement. He pulled out a pair of throwing stars. "One for each of you," he said without holding back his sinister excitement.

The bandits stopped, realizing this was no merchant, but a real fighter. They caught a glimpse of the white insignia on the shoulder of his cloak – a spiral design that was modeled after the unique fighting style of the Zabato family. One look at his vibrant, blood-colored eyes and they instantly recognized him as the menacing legend Althaeans came to fear.

"The Shadow Soldier!" The bandit's knees grew weak.

"No need for bloodshed, friend," said the other, trying to convince Shiba to spare their lives.

"That's right," his partner nodded. "Plenty of loot to go around, right?" He held up the little sack of jewels and rattled it.

"Not for you," said Shiba. "Drop your weapons and run."

Something in the way he said it chilled them to the core. They glanced over at their two fellows, each of them in combat with Neo and Mirari. They exchanged a look and decided this was every man for himself.

They took off running, hoping to reach their hidden horses and live to rob another day.

"No, no, I said drop your weapons, *then* run," Shiba called. "Ah, they never listen."

He certainly didn't want to chase them. He whipped a star, and another, in less time it took them to travel a single step. He nailed each of them in the same place, just below the calf muscle of the right leg. The bandits fell to the ground, shrieking in agony.

"Now, don't go anywhere," he taunted. "I'll be back with some questions in a moment."

The bandit Neo had knocked off the horse wasn't in the same state. Shiba was shaking his head.

"Oh, Neo. Not again. I told you I wanted to get some information out of them."

"I didn't mean to hit him so hard," said the giant. He tried to pick up the limp, lifeless bandit. "Wake up. Hello? Wake up."

"Forget it," Shiba said. "He's robbing souls in the afterlife already."

Mirari saw that her lancer was the last bandit standing. Riding, actually. He decided it was the only advantage he still had. He hurled his spear at Mirari who batted it away as he spurred the horse. He charged past Mirari, galloping toward where Shiba and Neo stood over the lifeless sack of jelly, who had found himself on the business end of Neo's fist.

Mirari screamed. "Stop him! He's getting away!"

But Shiba put out his hand to stop Neo from interfering and said to Mirari, "Who, me? He's not my bandit. You're the one letting him get away."

"Bastard," she grumbled and ran to grab the last remaining horse whose rider had the misfortune to run across Neo today. She vaulted into the saddle and took off after her escaping bandit, cutting a look at the smirking Shiba as she galloped past.

As she chased, her spearman slowed for a moment as he passed the two fellow bandits whose running days were over. One of them tossed the small leather pouch up, and the rider caught it. He spurred his mount back into high gear, leaving his crippled accomplices behind.

"The topaz!" the merchant shrieked. "They took the topaz."

Mirari was starting to catch up to him. The bandit rode into the dense forest, slapped by branches as he whipped his horse into a panic. Mirari kept going, chasing as the bandit flashed in and out of sight, screened by the trees. She weaved her horse between the narrow trunks in desperate pursuit of the bandit. Low branches brushed against her skin as she pulled the reins left and right, masterfully dodging through the forest.

The thief rode on, reckless, desperate. He hoped he was pulling away, and turned back for a glance. Mirari was still chasing him, her horse slamming between the pines, but losing ground. Gleeful, he turned forward again, just in time to see the heavy bough that struck him under the chin, nearly decapitating him. The heavy branch knocked him from the saddle. He was barely conscious when he slammed to the forest floor. The horse, still in panic, kept running hard, and although the animal felt the loss of the weight of his rider, something was still slowing him down. The bandit's foot was caught in the stirrup, and he bounced and slammed viciously as the horse kept weaving between trees. Every sharp turn the horse made threw the bandit to the side, his unconscious body smacking against tree trunks and fallen logs.

Mirari felt her stomach clench in horror as she saw her bandit being hammered into trees, dragged until his ribs were smashed and his skull cracked open. He was dead by the time his foot tore free, and his body came to a stop. The horse probably didn't slow down until it reached its barn.

Mirari stopped when she reached the bandit's body. She didn't want to look at him too closely. But just as she wheeled the mount to return to the road, a sparkle caught her eye.

Then another. Then several more.

She saw the leather pouch and hopped down from her horse to pick up the bag of jewels the bandit almost got away with. She scooped up the loose stones, and secured the pouch to her belt, and rode the tired horse back to where Neo and Shiba waited for her.

They had the two remaining wounded bandits tied up and the merchant's carriage repositioned back on the main road.

"I'm sorry, I couldn't catch him, but…" Mirari took the pouch from her belt and gave it to the merchant.

"How did you get that if he got away?" Shiba demanded.

"He didn't get away. I just couldn't catch up to him before he…" She stopped as the gorge rose to her throat. "The fall from his horse killed him."

"Ah, well. Too bad," Shiba said. "You can't count him as a kill."

She ignored his callous remark but wondered if he was serious. Did he keep score of all the men he killed?

What chivalry.

She turned away and said to the merchant, "At least I got your jewels back."

The merchant took the small sack gratefully. "My sincerest gratitude. I've already lost too many of these."

"You've been robbed before?"

"We used to deliver a handful of them every month, but these bandits… it's getting worse every time. Now I only carry a small amount in my pocket. It's not worth risking my life over fake gems. The bandits can't tell the difference, you know."

Mirari and Neo shared a look.

"*What?*" Mirari asked.

"Did you say they're fake?" Neo said, confused by the revelation.

"My cousin's a tailor. His family uses them to decorate fabric. They look just like the real thing but at a fraction of the cost."

Mirari felt her heart drop again. Her chase had cost a man his life, and for nothing but a sack of phony rocks.

"EXCELLENT." Landon was pleased with the result. "Don't worry about these thieves. I'll make sure to have them interrogated. Thoroughly."

"Glad to be of service," said Shiba, signaling for them to leave. Mirari pulled Neo by the arm. "I think he's going to torture them."

"I think he'll enjoy it, too," said Neo, unconcerned. "But maybe, if you're right, he'll find out who's tipping off the bandits."

Mirari shook her head, unhappy with how this was turning out. "Well, at least those Minettans will get their goods back."

Neo turned to look at her and realized she was serious. He began to shake with laughter. "Mirari," he chortled, "you're too good for this world. But I like your spirit."

"What do you…?" She got the picture. "Are you saying Landon won't return their merchandise?"

"Don't take it too hard. We came here to make Landon happy. Well, he's happy."

"I'm not, damn it."

Neo gave her a sympathetic look. "Neither am I, M. It's not exactly justice. But look at it this way. There are four fewer bandits on the road."

***

"Congratulations," Gaven said as the Knights returned to the estate. "I spoke with Landon on the comstōne while you were on your way back. He's quite delighted with the results."

"Wonderful," Mirari grumbled. "How festive. Let's throw a party."

Gaven scowled at her sarcasm. "What's your problem now?"

She ignored this and said, "It's late. I'm going to get this mud out of my hair."

"What's she bitching about?"

"So is this your idea of the Knights?" Shiba said. "Doing chores for other region leaders?"

"It's a good start. We earned a strong ally with Evaleen."

"Isn't that grand? I'm so thrilled."

"We have to start small. Then again, I don't expect someone who had everything handed to him to understand."

"At least I haven't lost everything."

"Guys." Neo stopped the conversation from getting any worse.

Neo looked at Shiba with a warning glare, causing him to sulk and turn away, while Gaven shook his head. At least Shiba was following his instructions. For now, anyway.

MIRARI WAS UNDRESSED, standing at her washbasin, sponging off-road grime when Gaven knocked on the door. She grabbed a robe, barely having enough time to wrap it around her body before the door creaked open.

"What?" she said sharply with water still dripping down her hair and body.

"Nothing. Just…" He stopped. He followed the sound of water droplets tapping the ground, and moved his eyes up her body, realizing she was barely covered. He watched water fall from her hair onto her silky skin, disappearing into the arch of her cleavage.

"Oh… I'm sorry."

"You're blushing." She turned away, fixing the rest of her robe. She wasn't bothered by his gaze. In fact, it reminded her of when they used to fight as kids about who would use the bath first. "Well? Don't just stand in the door. You're letting a draft in."

"Look, I just wanted to say… I'm impressed," Gaven said.

"You pervert."

"No, I didn't mean—"

"Good. Don't get your hopes up."

"I'm serious. I heard you figured out there's more going on with this. Someone targeting Minettan trade?"

She was surprised. But it made her happy that he was taking an interest in it, unlike Shiba.

"Could be. I don't think it's a pattern to be ignored. It's likely these bandits are being tipped off, and I'm willing to put my money on someone in Altha Hills. But Shiba doesn't want to get involved. So, I guess it doesn't matter."

"I can understand where Shiba is coming from. As a region leader, you don't want to tell another one how to do their job, especially if you're from a different empire. But that doesn't mean we have to sweep the issue under the rug. I'll keep this in the back of my mind. Either way, I am very happy with your work."

Mirari noticed goosebumps on her arms, but upon hearing Gaven's words she felt anything but cold. She turned to him. "Do you really mean that?"

"Why wouldn't I? Do you think that ill of me?"

"I know you think I'm incompetent. I'm not the Knight you were hoping for."

"I won't deny that." Gaven shrugged. "But you exceed my expectations."

"A pretty low bar, though."

Gaven frowned and tried again. "You're more than just some merchant, Mirari. Merchants don't know how to ride a horse, nor do they know how to speak like a lady. You probably have a dozen other secrets you refuse to tell us."

"You got that right." She wrung out the water in her hair, gently reminding him that she was still in the middle of her wash and that he had been staring at her skin for much too long. He didn't seem to take the hint.

"That flame, for example." Mirari grew alert at the mention of her power. He went on. "Are you really not aware of your own abilities?"

"I already told you. I don't know anything about the flame."

"I don't care if you keep secrets," Gaven continued. "But the only person you will hurt is yourself."

"Said the fire to the kettle."

"Listen, you chose to fight the paragon way. If there's one thing that differentiates paragons from everyone else, it's honor. Your greatest strength comes from your will. But to get there, you have to have trust."

"Wow. You could crochet that on a throw pillow."

"Section Two of the Paragon's Conduct: trust in yourself and trust in each other. Whether or not you like your team, you have to trust them."

She rolled her eyes. "Tell that to Shiba."

"Shiba isn't a paragon. He could never be one with that level of arrogance. That's why you have to be different. Trust applies to Shiba just as well as it applies to me. You don't have to like any of us, Mirari. But if you want to be a good fighter, you have to trust and respect your teammates unconditionally."

Tensions lifted as Mirari let his words sink in. Despite how cold he was toward her, she appreciated the effort he put into their training.

"But your sass is unattractive," Gaven said, spoiling it again.

"You better have said 'sass'. Not—" She looked down at her hip. Gaven's eyes diverted to the end of her robe, so short it was barely covering her cheeks. He turned away, face flaring crimson.

He forced himself back to the point. "We clearly have our differences, and that is understandable. But trust me when I say that everything I tell you is in your best interest. I truly am trying to train you to be the best Knight you can be."

"Thank you, Gav," Mirari whispered under her breath. She smiled slightly with nostalgia, finally seeing that he still had the same kind heart behind all that sternness.

"Huh?" Gaven questioned, not sure if he heard her mutter the right words.

"Thank you for training me, *Your Honor*," Mirari repeated louder, with the same sarcastic tone she used when they first met in the boulder field. Her voice switched to pure sincerity as she clarified, "Thank you for believing in me."

"Ah." Gaven was speechless, not expecting gratitude, and it made him stutter. "Don't stay up too late. There's another rough day of training ahead."

CHAPTER NINE

Four Years Ago…

"Why are you here?" a young Shiba asked the recruit. Though he was a commander, Shiba still had little say about the people that were being recruited.

Mecate questioned what he meant, but paid little attention to the young lord as she continued polishing her breastplate in the armory of Avon's fortress.

The elegant, young lady was infamous across the empires. Her emerald eyes complimented her blueberry hair like healthy leaves that garnished the ripe fruit. Her straight hair created a curtain over her back, shielding the silk robes wrapped with pink floral décor. From those features alone, anyone could tell from a distance that she was a celta of Altha Hills.

She sat as tall as the dozens of axes and halberds that decorated the walls. Her aura captured the room like a fortified shield and Shiba knew her kore would be more powerful than all those weapons combined. But was this sheltered noble prepared to face the cruel world or would she split like the wooden poles behind her?

Imagine, a direct descendant of the High Priest turning against her own people, running away from her duties to fight on the enemy's side. Shiba had nothing against a celta princess joining their army. In fact, being a celta princess meant she had exceptional kore abilities, and Shiba was eager to witness such power.

But his mother's decision to shelter the Althaean princess meant that they were drawing Althaea's attention to them. They would have to make more preparations to ensure that the celtas of Altha Hills would not try to wage war.

Shiba wanted to know why Mecate was chosen to join his army.

"To serve the people, what else?" she answered bluntly.

"No, why are you on this side? You're a flatty."

"Oh." She paused and thought for a moment. "I forgot about that." She shrugged it off just as quickly and continued polishing.

"That's not something you forget."

Shiba already knew the story. Mecate had a passion for fighting, but her father, the Priest, wanted her to be a diplomatic beauty, not a war maiden.

"I've lived in Minetta for the last three years. I like it here, and Minettan is what I identify with." Shiba had always thought she was the silent type. Her words projected more confidence than he had expected, but he still looked at her with the same degrading glare he gave all Althaeans.

"You're not going to like what they say about you."

"I know what they say. So what? Are they going to deport me? It's disappointing for anyone to believe that they can decide what's best for someone else."

Shiba could only question where her logic was coming from. Normally he would've punished any soldier who sassed him as she did, but he found her quirky remarks entertaining. She seemed like a loyal fighter, and her record was beyond impressive. Either way, Shiba knew he was lucky to have her on his team.

Most importantly, he would not forget that day when someone taught him the importance of not letting anyone else judge you but yourself. She had moved him deeply, and he felt his heart opening to this strong, beautiful young woman. He didn't know then that when he lost her, his heart would slam closed again...

Word began spreading quickly that Fangbane was running a team that would assist people with anything. Packages of letters began pouring in. Their success with Region Leader Landon a month ago had been followed by several other missions, and even Mirari had to admit, this venture of the Knights had potential.

Gaven had been assigning them minor missions, mostly from small towns, without any wealth or power, seeking assistance. With the completion of each successful mission, more and more letters would arrive. With just three of them, the Knights couldn't respond to every request. Gaven and Fangbane were forced to prioritize them. Or to try, at least. But there was no denying the reception of the Knights had been overwhelmingly positive.

Mirari continued her training with Gaven and sparring sessions with Shiba. With each encounter, she learned and adapted to the way they fought.

"We'll stop here for today," Gaven said, throwing his spear to the ground and wiping the sweat off his forehead. "By the way, did you finish reading those mission requests?"

"Right." Mirari walked over to her bag and pulled out a small stack of papers. "The one about the border; the town should create a schedule to make sure everyone can use the river. With the aluminum ores; I'd suggest crossing through the lower plains, even if it takes more time. The savings in travel aren't worth the loss from accidents."

"How about the one at the Upper Forest? How would you deal with the herd of yetis?"

"I'm not sure, to be frank." Mirari always considered the round furballs with long hairy arms to be harmless. They spent their days swinging on branches and rolling in the snow. But she had heard enough stories to know that when yetis were provoked, their arms became strong enough to topple a carriage or snap a human body like a twig. She continued, "But even without the yetis, crossing the mountains will always yield plenty of problems. It's going to be extremely dangerous for merchants to cross either way. I would take my chances with the yetis. It's the least of their worries."

"Very analytical. Thanks." Gaven took the papers back.

Her suggestions were different from what he would do, but he valued her perspective and took it into consideration. He was pleased with this test of her reasoning.

Mirari's fingers glided lightly across one of the worn-out papers from a possible mission in Altha Hills. Her thoughts went back to the bandit mystery. Her finger traced the circle lining of the strange symbol that was stamped on the form.

"What does this mean?" she asked.

Gaven looked over at the unusual seal. "Probably just a signature from the person who ordered the case."

"No… no, signatures are made up of crests and letters, but this… this looks more like a figure, or a person…"

Gaven peered over again and took a closer look. The symbol did look more like a figure than a crest, two figures actually, though it still meant nothing to him.

"I'll keep that in mind. You seem to know a lot about seals." Gaven thanked her as he took the paper.

"As a merchant, I saw all sorts of seals on orders all the time."

"Even so, you have no trouble reading these orders. Most merchants I know can't even read. You continue to surprise me."

Even though she had long abandoned her noble family, Mirari had always kept up with her knowledge of the world, buying books whenever she could and studying in her spare time. She enjoyed it, especially when she didn't have to consider it a chore.

Gaven packed his training gear and made his way back to the manor first. Mirari stayed outside, resting under a shaded tree and enjoying the calm breeze on a sunny day. Neo was enjoying the sunshine in the courtyard and went over to greet her.

"Hey, M."

"What's new?" she said, looking up at him with a friendly smile.

"Thrills and chills. I just took care of wild rabbits destroying crops in Venne." He mimed a bored yawn. "Honestly, it was the most eventful thing that's happened all week. Not going to lie, but as an elite fighter, it feels weird doing so many of these petty chores."

Mirari chuckled to herself.

"We used to have a battle with bunnies back in Solarin. You'd be surprised, but most people simply can't catch wild rabbits."

"How are you holding up, by the way? Homesick yet?"

Salathiel's face flashed in her mind. She could imagine the friendly smirk he would give her before he left for work, and the aroma that would remain in the kitchen – carrots with roasted chicken, sautéed in butter and seasoned with rosemary. It was a dish that told her he was in a good mood, and no matter how scrumptious Starlight's version of it was, it didn't taste the same. Now the smell of rosemary only made her lose her appetite.

"I... a little." She shook off the image and changed the subject. "Training's been tough. I just want a nice break after all of it."

But after a break that seemed far too short, she caught sight of Shiba approaching them from across the courtyard. As soon as Gaven left her, the bastard would show up, ready to pick a fight. Whenever he was on the property, he would do it without fail.

"I'm not in the mood today. Go away." Mirari mumbled, clearly irritated. She could always sense his sinister presence before she even saw him.

"I guess that's too bad," he taunted before his shadow warped from the ground and grabbed Mirari's ankles to secure her to her position.

"Shiba!" Neo said. "Give her a break."

Mirari stared him down but kept her poise. She didn't want to give in, even though she was well aware that Shiba would never take no for an answer.

"Are you going to duck a challenge, and prove to me that you're not good enough for my team?"

"This is not your team," Mirari corrected. "You are serving the Valiant Tiger and Lord Fangbane. You have no power over me."

"I'm still your region leader. If you're not going to respect me, I'll make sure you'll never become a Knight." Shiba leaned in for a punch, but Mirari dodged it and quickly tackled him.

The shadow released its grip on her legs, and they both tumbled to the ground. Shiba and Mirari began struggling with each other, throwing punches whenever possible. Shiba's shadow emerged and catapulted Mirari off of him.

She stood back up and charged at him.

A translucent barrier formed between the two, and Mirari nearly ran into it, stopping just in time. She placed her hands on the barrier, admiring how tall and sturdy it was. She also knew neither she nor Shiba had made it.

"Whatever this fight is about, I'm sure we can settle this peacefully." A gentle and sincere voice called from the sideline. Shiba and Mirari looked to the side and noticed a young girl standing by the courtyard door. She had a peaceful smile on her face, and her hands were locked in front of her waist.

"Excuse me, miss." Neo approached her. "May I ask who you are?"

Shiba had a bit of a quizzical look.

The girl had short, light blue hair, and vibrant blue eyes that were the color of a translucent sea. The quality of her silk robes indicated that she was a celta from Althaea, and the floral patterns on her unstained white garment suggested that she was from a well-respected and holy family.

"My name is Hime." Her cheeks perked up like a baby quokka. "Pleased to meet you all. I'm looking for Lord Fangbane. Perhaps you know where he is?"

Shiba seemed to be lost in thought as she spoke, and continued to analyze the young girl who was definitely under the age of fifteen. Thirteen, maybe.

A chord struck in his heart. But despite the resemblance, he tried to put the thought out of his mind. Her memory only made his heart more bitter.

"Come, we'll take you to him." Mirari gestured to the door, glaring at Shiba, indicating that their battle was over. The four of them went inside and up to Fangbane's room.

The more he looked at the girl, the harder it was for him to hold back his thoughts. He couldn't help but ask her directly. "Hime. Are you related to Princess Mecate?"

"Yes, she was my older sister."

Shiba's face brightened for a second – but as soon as it had come, the lightness was gone, and he turned gloomy and pitiful. It was an expression that Mirari had not seen before.

"I thought you looked familiar," Shiba admitted quietly, but that was all he could make himself say on the matter.

She didn't seem bothered at all by Shiba's comment. "But my familiarity is nowhere close to one of Minetta's greatest fighters, Your Honor."

"That was a long time ago," Shiba replied humbly. "I'm not that person anymore."

Mirari knocked on the door to the Solar. Fangbane opened it and gestured for them all to come in, stepping out of their path.

Hime entered the Solar first, and noticed a fair-skinned healer resting near the fireplace. She had a thin book placed in front of her baby bump, one book out of the hundreds that were displayed in a row of shelves against the brick wall. Rows of wooden trinkets were proudly displayed on the other wall, a souvenir from each of the tribes and territories the couple had visited during their years together. The cozy room, decorated with fur carpets and feathered blankets hung over chairs, was a stark contrast to the white buildings in Altha City. Hime assumed only peasants lived in homes that weren't built with hāstals, but she found the decorated room favorable to the bland one she grew up in.

"You must be Lady Starlight." Hime curtsied.

Starlight flicked her wrist several times to brush off the formalities. "Simply Starlight will do, Princess Hime."

The couple were not shocked to see a visitor. Hime had Fangbane's letter in her hand, the one bearing a red seal with the crest of a phoenix. Starlight motioned for her to take a seat, but Hime refused, leaving the seats open to the superiors in the room.

"I've been following what you and the Knights have been doing," Hime explained. "At first, I wasn't sure how to respond to your invitation, but I think what you're doing here is truly remarkable, My Lord. Please allow me to be a part of your cause."

Behind the mask, Fangbane's face lit with delight. Hime was an exceptional healer, almost at par with Starlight. But for someone of her young age, Hime was anything but average. They were desperate for someone with her talents.

Mirari couldn't help but wonder if the young girl was ready to be a Knight. She was convinced there was nothing but pure goodness in Hime's soul. When she thought about the bandits near Hime's home – the sheer disappointment of being unable to help those in need, forced to become a slave to the politics surrounding their empires – Mirari wondered if she was prepared to deal with the cruel reality. Even if she was a celta of Altha Hills, Hime appeared to be very delicate and fragile, and it seemed that Neo had many of the same thoughts, but Shiba and Fangbane had different opinions.

"I have no doubt about your capabilities, Princess Hime," Fangbane said. "But I do have to perform a physical evaluation to ensure you will be able to handle what we deal with."

"Thank you, My Lord," Hime bowed, and after a few more pleasantries was shown to her room for the night.

HIME WANDERED into Mirari's room, immediately captivated by the wooden animal trinkets pinned over her bed and the ceiling decorated with dangling strings of fluorescent hāstals. The rest of Mirari's room was bland, but to Hime it was a refreshing sight. She had three thick books on her shelf and an amethyst-colored quill on top of her notebook, perfectly centered on her desk. They were items that weren't native to Hime's homeland, and she examined them with interest.

That night, Hime stayed in the West Wing next to Mirari's room, but she spent most of the evening bombarding Mirari with inquiries about her personal life as a trader and her transition to training as a Knight.

"I was so nervous coming here," Hime admitted, fiddling with the edge of her garment. "I thought all the Knights were going to be fighters much stronger than me. I-I mean, with all due respect, Lady Mirari, I simply have never heard of your name before."

"Mirari. Just, Mirari," she corrected with a nervous smile.

"And I'm not a Knight yet for the very reason you speak of. I'm not a real fighter like the rest of them. I came from a background of merchants."

"And yet, you have the courage to tackle the Shadow Soldier!" Hime's eyes sparkled with admiration. "You are undeniably worthy of becoming a Knight."

Mirari chuckled and brushed it off.

"Why do you fight with Region Leader Shiba?" Hime asked with a worrisome tilt to her voice.

"It's not serious," Mirari smiled reassuringly. "He wants me to prove that I'm worthy of being a Knight, so he picks a fight with me every day."

"It looked pretty serious to me. But I can understand why he does it. It's not that he hates the weak; he's just trying to make you stronger."

Hime recalled the letters her sister wrote to her during her time in Minetta, where she often spoke of the Shadow Soldier:

A chained spirit, bound by his duties and obligation to succeed, striving to impress those around him while neglecting the love his soul so desperately desires. I know that feeling all too well. And I know that when you meet him, my purest Hime, you can be the light that guides his lost soul.

Hime never imagined she would meet the Shadow Soldier, but now, here they were. She was doing exactly what her sister had done at her age. And Hime could only pray that she would be able to live up to her sister's purpose.

CHAPTER TEN

The next morning, everyone sat outside in the courtyard to watch Hime's test. Even Gaven had joined in to make the final judgment. Hime peered at the small crowd of familiar faces with a smile but froze in fear upon seeing Gaven.

Rumors had been flying over the last few months about his whereabouts. Where the famous fighter was serving his suspension was a complete mystery to anyone outside the Council. Yet, here he was, in Minetta. And Hime never thought she would come face to face with the famous warrior.

"I was not aware that the Valiant Tiger was a part of your mission, Lord Fangbane."

"He's helping me decide on the Knights we recruit," Fangbane explained. "You'll have to impress him as well."

"How nerve-wracking."

"The evaluation is simple," Fangbane began. "Use whatever you can to defeat your opponent. First one to the ground loses."

"My opponent?"

A voice called out. "That would be me."

A boy walked onto the field directly across from Hime. His

spiky white hair with brown roots was swept to the side and held neatly. Despite his mature appearance, he looked just as young as Hime. He held a golden bow in his hand, an indication that he was a skilled aegis. His glare remained unfazed, possibly even full of disdain, as he judged his opponent.

"This was a last-minute call," said Fangbane. "He just arrived this morning."

"Well, this is a surprise…" Neo couldn't help but stare.

"That bow is a dead giveaway." Shiba leaned forward to get a closer look. "Yep, that's Dareh's son."

"Looks like we got two young'ins," Neo stated. "Same age, I believe."

"A pleasure to meet you, Dorain Kampht of Klad Academy," Hime smiled. There wasn't a lady of Hime's age that didn't know of the handsome aegis who was at the top of his class.

Dorain was well aware of who his opponent was, but her status didn't matter to him. He had to defeat her to earn a place in the Knights. And he was more than happy to fight an Althaean.

"Well met, Princess Hime of Altha Hills." A wave of kore swirled in Dorain's hand, forming into the shape of an arrow. He pulled back the arrow and shot at her without hesitation.

Stunned, Hime vanished in the blink of an eye. She reappeared a few feet away.

"I didn't say you could start yet…" Fangbane said. But reading the thoughts trailing in Dorain's mind, he knew there was nothing he could say to make him yield. His mind was too focused on the prize at hand.

Hime didn't wait either. She took the lead, rapidly teleporting to different locations so that Dorain couldn't lock in an accurate hit. She could tell his eyes were following her closely. The confusion wasn't a reliable strategy, but she hoped it would create an opening.

Dorain readied his bow and took his time pinpointing her location. He gracefully raised a single arrow and shot it wherever he thought she would be. It was an accurate guess, and the arrowhead barely slid past her skin. Dorain continued shooting one bolt at a time. He showed no signs of panic. Instead, it seemed like he was taunting her to prove that he had the capability of shooting her down. His arrows continued to swish past her, missing her only by hair's length. Hime knew she had to change strategies soon.

"She's... very fast," Neo noted. "And Dorain's mark is absurdly on point. They're both great candidates."

"A real celta would learn to do more than just cast in one spot," Shiba agreed, and secretly, he was incredibly proud of what he was seeing. "She is well-trained. I expected nothing less of a direct descendant from Altha Hills."

"She's almost as good as—" Neo stopped himself short of speaking her name. But Shiba knew what he was going to say.

"She is," Shiba answered. "A little more reckless, but her kore is just as powerful as Mecate's. The main difference is that Mecate played in the offensive, while Hime seems to be trying to cover her skin. Dorain is landing his shots perfectly, but, if you look closely, there's not a single scratch on her. She's using a very minimal level of kore to act as armor. Hime is and acts like a healer. There's only so much offense she can do. This match is unfair to say the least."

Watching Hime fight must have brought back some bittersweet memories for Shiba. Maybe, he saw Hime as an opportunity for a second chance at redemption.

As he caught onto Hime's pattern, Dorain shot multiple arrows in the air around her next location. His arrows transformed into large spirits in the shape of an eagle. The eagle searched for a heat source and locked on, its eyes focusing on her as it dove.

Hime knew she would be unable to outrun the eagle. As it

flew toward her, Hime stood in place and pointed both her hands toward the ground. She waited for a split second until the eagle was right in front of her, then flapped her arms up. A large wave of ice rose from the ground and froze the eagle in place, its beak just a few feet from Hime's face, surprising everyone, including Dorain.

"She's an ice caster!" Neo stared in shock.

"So it seems she does know how to play offense," Shiba said. "Perfect. That's the kind of people we need."

Dorain launched more arrows into the air. This time he was more cautious, knowing that his opponent could cast ice spells.

Hime teleported to a farther location to gain more time for her next move.

She whispered a few words under her breath, and swung her hand in Dorain's direction. Ice quickly wrapped around his legs, limiting his mobility, and to his surprise, it was sturdy enough to keep him stuck for some time.

The arrows caught up to Hime. She waved her arm in front of her, and a dozen icicles encircled her like a barrier. She launched the icicles upward, and they neutralized Dorain's arrows. Seconds later, Hime teleported behind Dorain, ready to take her victory attack. She elbowed Dorain in the back, but her swing went right through his body. The illusion dispersed into a light mist. The mist reconstructed to reveal itself as Dorain's eagle, wrapping around Hime's body. Hime touched the bird, and ice began to spread from her fingers. She broke free of her constraint and quickly searched for Dorain's whereabouts.

By the time she found him, he had already shot an arrow at her. She neutralized it inches from her chest with a single shard of ice. Upon impact, the arrow detonated, and the smoke from the explosion engulfed her vision. As soon as she could see clearly, Dorain had closed the gap between them. Surprised, she raised her hand and began casting another attack, but nothing came out.

"Kore neutralizer," Dorain stated without losing his posture. "You won't be able to use kore in this mist." He nonchalantly twirled the bow in his hand as it disassembled back into a pocket-sized stick.

"I see." Hime looked back at her hand with interest. She had read about all the types of arrows that Dorain had used but never came face to face with them. She pondered over the fact that had this been a real battle, she wouldn't have known how to save herself.

She was slightly disappointed but more curious.

"You have to show me more of that." Hime beamed. Dorain's jaw dropped, expecting hostility from her. He tried to keep his face straight, ready to gloat over his win. Yet, his cheeks grew crimson upon seeing her broad smile.

"I… Of course, you Althaeans probably have never seen these advanced types of arrows."

"I haven't, and I've never seen an aegis move like that. You really are as skilled as they say, Master Dorain."

Dorain could not hold his resentment any longer. There was nothing more he enjoyed than high praise from beautiful ladies.

But something was holding him back from swooning over this lady – the fact she was Althaean. Dorain tried to remind himself of all the savage ways his father described these people.

"Good work both of you," Fangbane said as he strolled toward them. He gave a heavy pat on Dorain's back, as a warning to drop his act.

"The purpose of the Knights is to counter the hostility and hate against people from different empires," Fangbane said, almost fully directed at Dorain. "Unfortunately for you, Hime, it looks like Dorain has won this round."

Hime nodded and curtsied to the two, accepting her defeat. Her smile vanished, and it broke Dorain's heart.

"My Lord," Dorain said, finally giving up his tough act, "I don't think any other healer could perform the way she did. After all, it is unfair to compare our strengths when our area of expertise is tremendously different."

"You are much more skilled than me, Master Dorain," Hime said. "You deserve this position."

"I object!" Dorain was fully ready to forfeit for Hime. In fact, he had arrived at the estate simply to test his luck, not expecting to be recruited.

But before Dorain could bargain further, a tall warrior stepped in front of him. The hairs on his arm grew erect and his numb fingers let the bow slip from his hand. Dorain was skilled in reading the aura around him, and this warrior's aura trapped his soul in quicksand. Panicking would make it worse, he couldn't show fear, but it was a checkmate.

Dorain eased his head upward and took a quick glance at Gaven. His heart skipped a beat seeing the undaunted glow in the tiger's eyes, and he turned away.

Dorain trembled. He was well aware that the Althaean warrior was witnessing their match. Dorain was ready to challenge Gaven after his match with Hime. But he had underestimated just how powerful the Valiant Tiger was. Dorain's father had always described him as a kitten with tiger stripes. A typical Althaean full of arrogance, all bark, no bite. But now that he was finally face to face with the famous warrior, he realized just how wrong his father was.

If Dorain challenged him, he would lose without a doubt. Dorain was sure he wouldn't even be able to hold his bow steady. No sane person would challenge someone this strong. His father was clearly the one on his high horse.

"We currently don't have long-range fighters on the team," Gaven said. "We could use both of you. Congratulations."

"Oh…" Dorain paused, breaking from his mental panic. He was expecting to be challenged or at least scolded. Instead, Gaven was… rewarding him? Dorain's muscles relaxed once he realized that the Valiant Tiger wasn't going to eat him alive.

Hime, on the other hand, squealed with happiness.

"Two runts," Shiba mumbled. "That's just dandy."

Neo applauded the two newcomers with a smile. "Sulk all you want, but don't deny that you agree this is starting to become one interesting team."

CHAPTER ELEVEN

The Knights now had their army of five. Shiba, Neo, and Mirari did their best to become well acquainted with their new team members, and Starlight joined in on the fun for the evening while Fangbane and Gaven had their meeting.

They quickly realized that Dorain was certainly not the mature young man they all expected him to be. He loved to have fun, and he made the most unbearable jokes, often complemented with heavy sarcasm.

Every aegis had a companion, and Dorain's was a beautiful red-backed kite with a snow-white body named Kea. Though, Dorain hardly acted like the kind of person who could responsibly care for one.

Kea perched on Dorain's shoulder as Dorain spent hours telling stories in the Great Hall.

"So, I told him he couldn't use an arrow because it's *pointless*," Dorain blurted out, grinning at his own joke. "Get it?"

Neo snickered a little, but everyone else looked a little disturbed at the weak joke. Kea cooed softly and nipped at her feathers as if she had heard the story a thousand times. She gently pecked at Dorain's newly earned brooch pinned on his

123

jacket. The red and gold crest resembled a phoenix, similar to that of the Minettan flag.

"C'mon, that was pretty clever." Neo gently elbowed Shiba, but Shiba only rolled his eyes.

A faint laugh escaped Starlight's lips at Neo and Shiba's exchange rather than the joke itself.

"Where's Mirari?" Neo whispered, leaning toward Starlight as he stared at the empty seat across from him. Starlight quickly swallowed the food in her mouth.

"She said she wasn't feeling well." Neo stared at the empty seat for a few more seconds before returning his attention to the others.

After the meal, he made his way to Mirari's room.

"M...? Are you okay in there?" Neo knocked gently on her door. "I brought some food for you in case you're hungry."

"Uhm, I'm not hungry, thank you," Mirari called from the other side of the door. Neo tried a different approach.

"That's good because we're all heading into town for some beer to celebrate. Hope you're ready for that."

"Oh, I'm not really a drinker."

"That's okay too, but you have to watch Shiba duel with the regulars. It's quite a show."

"Sounds like a lot of energy for me. You go ahead, I'll pass."

"You sure?"

"Don't worry about me. Have fun."

With a sigh, Neo gave up trying to push her. He could tell something was troubling Mirari deeply. And clearly, she was not ready to share whatever it was.

***

"How are you feeling today?" Starlight asked kindly as she caressed Mirari's head between her hands. Starlight was reading her aura, feeling the energy interlace around her fingers, an advanced practice only the highest skilled healers could perform. Though the process was insensible, Mirari could swear it had a calming effect.

"Same as last week," Mirari replied, now half asleep. "Nothing different."

Starlight was their official medic. She regulated – or tried, at least – to make sure the Knights stayed healthy and got enough rest. She kept a record of their weekly examinations and panicked over the smallest scrapes and bruises. Nothing could get past her. She was basically everyone's mother.

"Your endurance seems to be improving, the same with your kore. Looks like all that training is paying off."

Fangbane, unbidden, stuck his head into the exam room. "I think it's safe to say that physically, you're in stable condition."

"Darling." Starlight smiled at him. "I don't suppose you ever considered that some people expect their relationship with a medical caregiver to be confidential?"

Mirari shrugged. "Thanks, Milady. But I don't suppose privacy means much to a man who can literally read your thoughts."

"Forgive me." Fangbane turned to Mirari. "I just don't want you to worry about your ability resurfacing. The stronger you get, the more you'll be able to maintain control if and when your power to generate fire returns."

"My Lord, while I trust your judgment, are you sure it's wise for me to try to invoke this ability?"

Starlight knew that Mirari's biggest fear continued to be that she would accidentally produce some uncontrolled conflagration and hurt everyone around her. She was convinced that her next incident would be inevitable, and it wouldn't be as merciful.

But Fangbane wanted to witness and research the anomaly behind Mirari's flames. The fact that he was unable to read her thoughts throughout her enraged state during the Althaean Siege told him that the flames weren't just cast from kore. There had to be another cause.

"You need not worry about us, we are all capable of defending ourselves against any 'accidents'."

"Thank you, My Lord."

"Actually, I was hoping you'd deliver this to Gaven on your way out." Fangbane waved a stack of papers in the air and Mirari took it with both hands. They were heavier than expected.

"More requests?" Mirari asked.

Fangbane perked with pride. "What can I say? We're practically celebrities now."

Mirari rolled her eyes and headed for the door with the documents cradled in her arms. "Enjoy your evening, my Lord, Milady."

As soon as Mirari was gone, Starlight began to review Mirari's evaluation with Fangbane. "Her mind is a mess. She is struggling with her grief."

"I've put my faith in the discipline of training to ground her, hoping that will take her mind off it."

"Perhaps because she put it off, relying on false hope. But if she can't handle loss, I'm not sure this is the field for her. Death is inevitable. We don't want her ending up like Shiba."

"She can do it. Somewhere in her mind, she's still hesitant to give up on her old life. I suppose it's to be expected. Before we took her in, she always leaned on one person."

"You're right. It's got to be damaging when that person vanishes without a trace, and she doesn't even know what sealed his fate."

Mirari approached Gaven's room with the file in her hand. His quarters were right next to Fangbane's, a room that was significantly larger than the others. Of course, the entitled egomaniacs felt they deserved the better end of the manor.

Mirari knocked on the door. There was no response. She tried again, calling out to him this time.

Silence.

She was about to turn and leave when she heard something massive tumble to the ground.

"Your Honor!" Mirari called out. "Are you alright?"

Still, he did not answer. She gave up on decorum and barged in. The door was unlocked and flew open with ease. She found Gaven sitting on the floor, head lowered, and leaning against his bed. He was panting, out of breath. Mirari realized he was hyperventilating, or having some kind of panic attack.

She dropped the papers and rushed over to him. "Your Honor?" She tried to look into his eyes, which were hidden under his hair. Nervous, she reached for his forehead. Her palm glided gently across his skin, but Gaven's hand snatched her wrist abruptly. Mirari was jolted by the intensity of his grip. She almost flared in anger but stopped herself. She could tell he was in pain, so she gave him time to relax, dismissing the fact that he was about to break her wrist.

Gaven realized how hard his grip was and released her. They both remained still for quite some time as he forced himself to gain control of his breathing. When he was calm enough, Gaven finally raised his head and met her kindly eyes.

"Sorry…" He mumbled softly as he rubbed his hand against his tired face.

"Are you alright?" Mirari asked again.

"I'm fine," he said, almost gruff, trying to hide what he considered a weakness. To switch focus, he gestured to the scattered papers. "Are those for me?"

"Oh, yes."

"You can leave them on the desk." Gaven nodded at his table, already overrun by an ocean of files. She stood, scanning the desk for the best possible spot in the chaos to place them without mixing it with the others.

When she turned back from the desk, she found his eyes were pointed to the ceiling, intentionally ignoring her gaze. She tried to ask him why – but the words caught in her throat. She could tell he didn't want to talk about it, and would only start to bluster as he always did if she tried to press him for any kind of emotion.

"Would you like me to bring you anything?" she offered, keeping it neutral.

"No, thank you."

Mirari hesitated a bit, but it was obvious he wasn't going to open up. So she quietly took her leave, and closed the door behind her.

"He experiences flashbacks nearly every other day," Starlight continued, discussing Gaven's medical chart with Fangbane. "The medication I gave him can only lessen the severity of the headaches. Frankly, I don't believe it's a side effect from whatever attacked him. It's his guilt. To fully address the problem, I'll need to run several therapy sessions with him."

"Good luck getting him to sit still for that."

"He can be resistant. But, unlike Mirari, at least he's trying." Starlight flipped through a couple more pages of medical records.

"Neither of them have recovered their memory from the Althaean Siege?"

"Unfortunately not, but perhaps they could help each other."

"You think?" Fangbane perked up.

"I know it's ironic, but out of everyone here, Mirari is only comfortable around Gaven. She's been retreating to her room whenever we have gatherings. The only time she consistently shows up is to attend Gaven's training sessions. It's clear that she still doesn't trust the rest of us yet."

Fangbane nearly revealed Mirari's real identity to explain her behavior. But he would not betray that confidence, even to his wife.

"Gaven was the one who taught her about the paragon's honor," he recalled. "Imagine if he taught her the rest of the Paragon's Conduct."

Starlight could sense the mischievous tone in his voice, and it made her smile affectionately.

"Whatever you have up your sleeve, I know you're not going to tell me anyway, so I needn't bother to ask you what plans you're hatching."

"You know you can trust me, darling."

Starlight rolled her eyes, trying to hold back the grin on her face. "I know I don't have any other choice, my dearest."

PART II

CHAPTER TWELVE

Gaven was tossing small clay targets in the air for Dorain's target practice. He analyzed how Dorain moved, noticing an inefficient hitch in his form.

"I want you to lean back a little before you fire each shot," Gaven said. "See if that makes a difference." He carefully readjusted Dorain's stiff body position, lightly touching his elbow.

Dorain jolted at his touch, his body as stiff as a deer in headlights. But Gaven kept his hand on his elbow. Dorain took a deep breath and forced himself to relax, knowing that Gaven wasn't going to let go until he did so. Gaven nodded, glad that he got the message, then stepped back to let him try again.

Gaven had high hopes for the teen. As Councilor Dareh's son, he was one of the best aegises they could ever hope to join the team. But his knees turned to jelly whenever he got near Gaven, and he was underperforming during his training. Gaven knew he could land every shot, but his presence gave Dorain an unsteady hand.

He didn't think too much about it. He figured Dareh would have spread all sorts of campfire horror stories about him. The best he could do was give Dorain space to adjust to his new trainer.

Gaven threw clay targets into the air again, making adjustments to Dorain's stance and motion after firing each arrow. At first, the change felt awkward to the boy, who managed to hit only six out of the ten targets before they reached the ground.

"How did that feel?" Gaven asked.

"I didn't hit all the targets." Dorain frowned. "It slowed me down."

"It didn't slow you down. It made you more hesitant to take a shot. Try it again, get comfortable with it, until you don't think too much about your position."

Dorain did as instructed. He leaned slightly back and rotated his body before taking every shot. This time he landed eight shots.

"How did that feel?"

"A lot smoother," Dorain agreed. "I can transition into my next position much easier."

"It will take the stress off your shoulders, too. You'll thank me for that when you get older."

Dorain was left speechless from his words of encouragement. The way Althaea's fearless fighter spoke to him was kinder than his own father. Dorain felt a bond forming between them, a bond he had always wished his family shared with him. Dareh had only ever told his son how much of a failure he was. Despite being the best performing aegis in his class, mastering every kore skill ever taught to him, Dorain was never enough for his father.

"Your Honor, I don't understand," Dorain began, swallowing his fear. "Why are you helping a group of Minettans?"

Gaven raised a brow. "You still don't get it, do you? The Knights are a team for all empires. We don't care who is from where. Why bother accepting the invitation to the Knights if you don't understand what we're doing?"

But Dorain didn't have time to respond before the answer clicked in Gaven's mind.

"Does your father know about this?"

Dorain pouted and turned his head away.

"Dorain! Don't tell me you ran away from home."

"And what if I did?" Dorain snapped, keeping the childish pout on his face. "It's none of your business."

"I can't believe it. Did you really join the Knights just to defy him?" Gaven flailed his arms and turned to face the mansion, tempted to head back inside. He considered ending the training session then and there. "By the Gods, you better hope he won't charge us for kidnapping. I'm telling—"

"Please don't tell Lord Fangbane!" Dorain stopped him. He leaned his body forward into a respectable bow as he pleaded. "You know how my father is. He would never let me join. Please, I want to make my own decisions for once. I want to be somebody, not just the son of Dareh. You said I would be good for this team, right? Let me stay, Your Honor. I promise I will prove myself useful."

Baffled at Dorain's sense of desperation, Gaven refrained from taking another step toward the mansion. It was then he remembered that Fangbane probably already knew of Dorain's circumstances from reading his mind and allowed him to join the team. Dorain was right. His father, Councilor Dareh, would be furious if he found out his son was dabbling in social justice with a group that threatened the very existence of his job.

Gaven released a heavy sigh, then turned back to Dorain. "Practice your technique until it becomes second nature. Keep at it, and you'll hit all ten quickly."

"Yes, sir!" Dorain saluted with full confidence.

Gaven couldn't help but feel that this would come back and bite him at some point.

In Fangbane's quiet library, Gaven kept the doors locked as he conversed with his substitute leader in Althaea Main. On a long wooden table lay confidential files Fangbane had given him, each significantly thinner than the walls of books that stretched beyond the crystal chandelier hanging from the mosaic skylight.

"There is benefit to what you have done." Erel's voice projected from the illuminating stone that hovered in the corner of the library. He could hear her fiddling with the items on his desk. "Businesses are thriving. People are finding jobs and roofs over their heads. Of course, you still get the occasional bar fight between foreigners, but you'd be surprised, Your Honor. Althaea Main seems to be on a good path to recovery. At this rate, we'll surpass the riches of Evaleen by next year…"

Her voice turned sharp, and he could envision her placing her hands on her hips, leaning over him, and her long hair dropping along with her excessive amount of sass.

"But not if you keep pursuing these mundane things! You are lucky to be alive. If the Council finds out that you've been investigating to overturn their report of the Althaean Siege, that's it. It's over."

Gaven couldn't stop brooding over what caused him to lose control of his will, and his mind, during the Althaean Siege. He felt no closer to getting the answer than he had the moment he snapped out of it.

Gaven had asked for simple updates from his second in command, a few questions that could help him with the files Fangbane had given him. Instead, Erel scorned him like the mother he never had. He ignored her warnings and picked up the next file, skimming through the pages.

Erel continued. "There's nothing to search for. The person responsible for tainting your mind may as well be dead. We have nothing to work with. Next."

Gaven sighed, shutting the file and waving it in the air. It was a relatively thin folder with less than a dozen reports of incidents across the empires. If he had received something so insignificant back in Althaea Main, he would've simply tossed it. He couldn't understand why Fangbane wanted to keep this one.

"Okay then. Tell me, what do you know of… the Blessed?"

Erel fell silent, then scolded. "What in Oris' feces are you doing in Minetta? You shouldn't be looking into these things!"

Gaven's eyes narrowed curiously. "So, you've heard of them?"

"I said no such thing."

"Tell me everything, Erel."

"You know what? I don't feel comfortable talking about this over the comstōne," she complained.

"That's an order."

Erel sighed and Gaven could hear her lean her head back on his squeaky chair. Her tension betrayed her knowledge of valuable information.

"They are a society that fantasizes about a world different from our current structure. There are many beliefs about the Blessed. Some are peacemakers, others are murderers. It all depends on which leader you follow, but they consider themselves one organization. The worst part is, you never know who's in it." She spoke as if she had personal experience with them. "You could have soldiers in your army who are part of this cult, and you would never know. I could be a part of it, and you wouldn't know. Even the Knights…"

"Are you accusing the Knights of being a part of the Blessed?"

"Well, from what I hear you're doing, it sure sounds like it."

Gaven opened his mouth to retaliate but stopped short when he realized Erel was right. The Knights were a threat to their current political system, and that was enough to consider themselves equal to the Blessed. But Fangbane wouldn't be giving him information on it if he was truly a part of it. Still, Erel had a valid point.

"All I'm saying is they hide themselves very well. I hope you plan on incinerating that file because I guarantee you're not going to get anything out of it. I'd rather have you stick your nose in the Althaean Siege investigation than this."

"Are the Blessed that bad?"

"Your Honor, I'm serious. Do not speak of that name to anyone. It could get you killed."

Gaven snorted at such superstition. "Whatever you say, Erel."

He could hear her groan on the other side moments before she severed the connection, and the stone stopped glowing.

Gaven flipped through all the files once more. He had made little to no progress on most of them. Erel's insight helped him get a head start, but he knew there was no chance she was going to help him any further.

He stacked the files nicely on top of each other and noticed a creased and worn letter that poked out – the letter from the Bishop in Altha Hills regarding bandits in Evaleen. He recalled Mirari had raised a question about the seal, and Gaven had thrown it in a random folder to remind himself to look at it later.

Carelessly, he threw the letter on top of the folder labeled 'The Blessed'. A mysterious organization for a mysterious seal. Why not? Gaven couldn't think of a better place to stick the letter.

He heard a knock and pushed open the locked double doors, leaving them wide open as Mirari entered with more files in hand. She offered him the cases she had finished working on. Gaven gestured for her to place it on top of the other folders.

Before she set down the files, she couldn't help but notice 'the Blessed' written on the top folder. Her heart skipped a beat when she read it.

"What is this file?" Mirari asked, unable to hide her curiosity. Gaven looked over and quickly snatched the case, hiding it behind his back.

"That one's top secret."

"Can I just take a look?"

"You can't. You're not authorized to look at it."

"I can handle it, Your Honor."

Mirari was unusually persistent, and Gaven found it suspicious.

"Do you know anything about that? The Blessed?"

Before she could justify her curiosity, Fangbane knocked on the open door, capturing their attention.

"Sorry to interrupt," Fangbane spoke up as he peeked into the library. "I have something quite urgent for Gaven."

Fangbane handed him a pure white long scroll. A request, written in flowing calligraphy on the elegant paper.

"Altha Hills?" Gaven frowned, before even reading a word.

"How can you tell?" asked Mirari.

"Who else?" Fangbane told her. "Only celtas would use such a majestic method of communication."

"You can put shoeshine on a turd, but it's still shit," Gaven grumbled.

He read it in silence, while Fangbane took notice of the rushing thoughts in Mirari's head. It greatly piqued his interest.

His uncomfortable stare told her he was absorbing her thoughts.

"What's in that case?" Mirari insisted in a low whisper, pointing at the folder in Gaven's hand.

"It has nothing to do with you, Mirari. Let it go."

"The Blessed took my brother," she snarled. "And I deserve to know what's going on."

"Excuse me." Gaven interrupted their intense whispering. "The Bishop is arriving in Oban in two days. Did you just receive this request, Fang?"

"Unfortunately so."

"Rather short notice. It's insulting."

"I think so too. But it's important for the Knights to take on this one. There are already protests brewing in the area. I spoke with Region Leader Hilda. She'll appreciate all the help she can get. If you would be so kind as to let the Knights know as soon as possible…"

Gaven nodded, understanding the urgency of this request. "Mirari, gather the Knights in the dining hall."

Despite the order, her eyes were still locked on the file Gaven had in his hand.

Fangbane guided her out of the room and whispered to her quietly. "Let it go."

"My Lord, please," Mirari begged, desperate for answers about Salathiel. That file might have information that meant nothing to anyone else but could provide vital clues for her.

"Knowing won't bring him back. Go call the other Knights, Mirari."

Fangbane retired to his room, leaving Mirari alone with unresolved tension, the name stuck in her mind. Neither one of them would let her access the file. But its very existence proved that the Blessed were more than just a myth.

IN THE GREAT HALL, Gaven unrolled the long scroll in front of the Knights, reading the relevant parts of the grandiose proclamation. His voice echoed across the high ceiling of the room.

"Oona has had a rowdy bunch of protesters over the last couple of days," he summarized. "A lot of folks are none too happy about the Bishop from Altha Hills coming to Minetta. Which is their right. We're not trying to bust that up. Tomorrow you'll be helping Oban stay on the defensive. These protesters can make all the noise they want, we just stop anyone who crosses the line. Your rank is above any other officer out there, so you get to call the shots."

"It's about time," Shiba said, a big grin forming on his face.

Gaven gave a seething look to Shiba. "Just keep your heads, and don't overreact. We can't afford a bad reputation this early."

"What kind of trouble should we expect?" asked Hime.

"There are rumors of a possible assassination attempt."

"Only rumors?" asked Shiba. "Pity. I was looking forward to some action."

"Neo, I expect you to restrain your liege, as usual. Unfortunately, I will have to leave Shiba in charge of this mission."

Mirari tilted her head. "You won't be coming?"

"I can't. Oban is the border region to Althaea. I'm sure there's no one in Minetta who hates Althaeans more than them. So, unfortunately, I'll have to sit out. It'll be good practice for the five of you to work together on your own without my guidance."

Shiba didn't say a word, but they could all sense his thrill of being in control.

"Your Honor," Dorain spoke up.

"Yes?"

"Do people even know who we are? I mean, will they listen to us?"

"We'll find out."

CHAPTER THIRTEEN

Upon their arrival at Oona City Hall, the Knights met Heisa, a newly appointed commander of Oban. There was a formation of Valkyries clad in heavy armor arrayed in front of the imposing building, a towering structure of marble and granite with massive fluted columns topped by elaborately carved lintels, and a frieze decorated with mythological figures and symbols.

Standing at the side of Commander Heisa was a tall, slender man in monkish robes, his long navy hair tied in a ponytail. As the Knights approached, the female guards clashed their spears against their swords, stamped once, and impressively presented arms in a more formal stance.

"Wow, Oban's army really is made up of all women," Hime whispered to herself with much admiration for the confident ladies before her.

"I'd hate to see how long the line to the latrine is," Dorain whispered back.

"Your Honor, sir," said Heisa, snapping into a crisp salute. "May I say it's an honor to meet you, Shadow Soldier."

"Thank you, Commander." Shiba basked in the praise, and he returned the salute. He introduced each of the Knights.

"Thank you all for coming," Heisa said, and gestured to the tall man beside her. "May I present the first acolyte of His Eminence the Bishop, who is here ahead of the visit to arrange security, protocol, and… uh… er… and did I mention security?"

"You did," Shiba said. "As for protocol, we are honored to be of service to Region Leader Hilda. And of course, especially to His Eminence, the Bishop."

Shiba turned to the tall man and his body grew tense, but Shiba's face showed no sign of discomfort. He extended a hand to the first acolyte. "Shiba Zabato. A pleasure to meet you…" he said, pausing for the man to introduce himself.

"I'm called Laikos." He spoke with a rich, commanding intonation, and offered Shiba a cool, dry hand.

Neo leaned into Dorain, whispering with sarcasm. "He must be in charge of security, ya think?"

"And protocol," added Dorain, as they both stifled their laughter.

"Shut it, you clowns," hissed Shiba, who had more appetite for formalities of honorifics – especially his own.

"Our greatest concern," Laikos informed them, "is the local unrest. Disgruntled citizens have become vocal and unruly. We would suggest you might disperse these undesirables today to avoid any unpleasantness tomorrow."

Shiba listened carefully to the rest of Laikos' plan, noting that Heisa didn't add much other than to nod enthusiastically at whatever the first acolyte was saying. "And you agree these demonstrators might constitute a threat, Commander?"

The commander glanced at Laikos as if for approval, and recited a response that appeared programmed. "A disgruntled element of citizens. They are undesirable. We must avoid any unpleasantness."

Shiba shifted his eyes from Heisa to Laikos, who seemed

more in charge than the Commander of the Guards herself. "Very well. We'll take a look at the situation and evaluate the nature of any threat."

Laikos made eye contact with the flustered commander, who rallied to her duties, saying with a little bow, "If you will all accompany me, I will present your company to Region Leader Hilda."

The commander ushered the five Knights up the gleaming marble steps of the imposing edifice of City Hall.

If the exterior of this palatial building was magnificent, then the Reception Hall where the Knights were ushered for a meet and greet with Region Leader Hilda was nothing short of spectacular. Richly veined marble columns rose from the polished stone floor to the vaulted ceiling, which was graced by a breathtaking painting that featured the image of the great Goddess of War, Cordelia, with a spear in hand, posing on a horse with poise and elegance. Nooks and naves were filled with statuary, paintings, tapestries, and stained-glass windows.

The overall impression was more of a cathedral than a municipal building. It was so awe-inspiring that neither Mirari nor Neo could manage to crack wise. Dorain, however, could not restrain himself from cracking up with laughter when a guard's boot skidded along the gleaming floor, making a farting sound.

"Shiba, Neo, my two favorite Avonians." A tall, muscular woman greeted them as she paced down the hall. Dorain abruptly stopped his laughter, the blood now drained from his face as he saw a giant who looked like she could crush his skull between her thighs. She was nearly as tall as Neo, yet it wasn't her size that made her stand out from a crowd, but rather the rare combination of her dark complexion and wavy, ginger hair. She was a familiar sight to the Minettan fighters.

"Hilda!" Neo met his elbow with hers, followed by a fist bump, and a sequence of hand gestures. "How are you enjoying the throne?"

"It's no joke, I'll tell you that. Never in a millennium did I expect to have this job. You know, we were going to give it to… Iffy." It took much effort to speak her name, and Shiba and Neo sympathized dearly. It seemed like only yesterday they were with her on the battlefield during the Althaean Siege. Dissipating the gloomy tone, Hilda roared, "Come, come. We have a feast waiting for you."

She guided them to a long table of refreshments just as a large four-legged creature with black fur and golden eyes stood up from the edge of the wall. Dorain shrieked, not having noticed the beast before. It looked at him briefly with a low growl and showed off its razor-sharp fangs before following Hilda closely like the shadow it was.

"Not a fan of cats, Master Dorain?" Hilda laughed, mocking Dorain's fright. "Councilor Dareh has his own saberlion, does he not?"

Dorain wasn't a fan of large beasts, creatures who were twice his weight, had teeth that could kill, and were prone to slobbering pints of drool that could stain his clothes with foul odor for days. He was thankful for Kea, a small and light fellow without any bad qualities.

"I can hear Pierce purr from the other end of a hallway," Dorain defended, recalling his father's striped companion. "But yours makes no noise, and its fur is darker than night."

The saberlion named Fig gave a snort, then crawled under the cloth of the long table. While everyone helped themselves to the curated delicacies, Dorain no longer had an appetite. To him, approaching the table would be asking for death.

LATER THAT DAY, the Knights were stationed at different intersections of City Hall, overlooking crowded streets paved by both nobles and commoners rallying and chanting their message.

They each commanded a squad of guards assigned by Commander Heisa. These troops were not armed with swords or spears, but they did carry shields, helmets, and hard wooden batons. The Knights equipped themselves with a pair of clōves that Fangbane had given them before they left. Shiba and Neo already had their own, as every region leader should, but the others tugged at and admired the new piece of technology around their wrists.

"Hellooo?" Dorain yelled loudly with his mouth just inches away from the glove.

Shiba flinched as Dorain's garish voice came out from his clōve. The unpleasant sound struck his nerve.

"Watch it, kid," Shiba said, but Dorain paid no attention to his leader and continued to rub his fingers over the gloves with immense interest.

Shiba and Neo had been stationed together in front of City Hall, where most protesters were crowded. They chanted their unwelcoming message, calling for the Bishop to return to Althaea. Neo ignored them, walked over to Shiba and leaned into his ear.

"My Lord," Neo whispered. "I couldn't help but notice your discomfort since we arrived..."

Shiba's eyes remained locked on the angered civilians in front of him. He waited until he was sure that the noisy group had no ill intentions before he held his hand in front of his mouth and leaned into Neo's ear.

"That acolyte's aura is too strong to be just an acolyte," Shiba said.

"You think?"

"A spellcaster like that wouldn't be under the Bishop, more like a commander, or the Priest's right hand."

Neo pondered over his words. "Mecate said there was a name for such people... what was it? An... Acker? Ass—?"

"Aster," Shiba answered. "The strongest type of spellcasters, but no. Kore is what makes spellcasters strong. His kore is average at best. There's something else powering his aura, but I can't figure out what."

Hours passed, and the demonstrations remained peaceful. The Knights watched from corners of the street as hundreds of locals chanted to ban Althaeans from entering their town. The Knights ignored this political expression. It didn't matter whether they agreed or disagreed with this display of bias of one empire's citizens to the other. They had a right to their opinion. As long as they remained non-violent, no action appeared to be necessary.

"This is going to be a long day…" Shiba sighed over the transmission.

"Good. Easy brownie points for us." Neo joked in response.

"Can we not talk about food? I'm starving," Dorain complained.

"I heard that there's a nice bakery down the street on your end, Dorain," Hime said. "Maybe we could all go there for our lunch break."

"I don't know about you guys, but I'm flat broke." Dorain scratched his head.

"Do we even get breaks?" Neo asked. "We don't have anyone to take over our shifts." He noted one voice had yet to speak. "M?"

"Huh?" Hearing Neo's voice boom from her glove, Mirari jolted out of her trance. "Did I miss something?"

"Uhm… no, but you're awfully quiet. Just making sure you're still alive."

"Mirari, you like norkfruit, don't you?" Hime asked.

"Ah, yeah, it's alright," Mirari said.

"I think something is happening here," Dorain spoke up. He heard some angry, disturbing yelling above the mostly peaceful chants in his area. The Knights went quiet and waited for Dorain to follow up.

"Well?" Shiba said.

"I'm going in." Dorain called moments later.

"Wait, Dorain, explain your situation—"

But Dorain had already sprinted down an alley, moving toward the angry noises he was hearing. He was eager to get a second of excitement on this long, uneventful day.

He saw several dozen protesters being detained by a handful of Commander Heisa's soldiers. As the protesters were herded against a wall, more demonstrators yelled at the soldiers from the sideline, some throwing trash at the ladies.

One of the soldiers couldn't contain herself and struck out at the protesters with her riot baton. Dorain grabbed onto one protester's hand to prevent him from throwing any more soup bones at the guards.

"Stop it," Dorain warned.

The peasant took a glance at the boy, ready to dismiss him simply for his age, until he noticed the unfamiliar badge on his chest.

"Whose side are you on?" The man yelled and shoved Dorain to the side. He was instantly tackled by a guard.

"How dare you assault the son of Dareh!" she scorned. The Valkyries grabbed hold of the man and cuffed him.

Hearing his father's name, Dorain groaned. For once, could people call him by his name? He was known as the Councilor's son. Nothing more than that.

Before Dorain could protest, an empty can struck him from the back.

"Get out of the way, traitor!" a protester yelled.

"Get your ass back to school, kid!"

"Come back when you can shave!"

Shiba grew concerned over the escalating unrest he was hearing. "Dorain. Answer me. What is your situation?" When Shiba didn't get any response, he turned to Commander Heisa. "Commander? Who ordered your men – I mean, Valkyries – to detain those people?"

Heisa turned to Shiba with a glassy look in her eyes. "There is a disgruntled class of citizens. We must avoid any unpleasantness."

Shiba shook his head. Dumb or delusional, she would be of no help. When Shiba turned to seek the acolyte's assistance, he found Laikos absent. Frustrated, he tried again to reach Dorain.

"Answer me, Dorain."

Back in the alley, Dorain clenched his teeth in disgust as insult followed insult. The shouting and cursing drowned out the sound from his com, and the escalation of violence made the youngster anxious. Guards were clubbing demonstrators. The crowd pelted the guards. He knew the situation was out of control and felt powerless.

Then, something struck him – a rotted chunk of chicken guts from a trash heap. Reaching for the only thing he was confident with, he whipped out an item from his pocket. It was a small brassy-looking stick, no longer than a pen. But at his touch, the stick expanded, transforming into a perfect golden bow.

A light arrow appeared in his hand, a demonstration of the control he had over his kore, and he twirled it with a flourish.

"Stand fast, all of you!" he shouted, as he notched the arrow to the bowstring. The crowd saw the young archer, who had suddenly turned from a slender youth to a deadly threat. The guards and would-be rioters stopped attacking each other, and all eyes were fixed on Dorain, waiting to see what he would do.

They were not alone in watching him. Hidden in an alley, a shadowy figure in a hooded robe watched the developing scene with interest.

"Keep it up, and all of you will be under arrest," Dorain warned.

"You see?" called a rabble-rouser. "Brothers, the mayor has sent this assassin to take care of us!"

"He means to murder all of us!" a protester shouted, igniting panic among the others.

"Everyone, please stop!"

A familiar voice yelled from a distance, and Dorain looked behind him. Hime strode up, cool, calm, and dignified as the royal princess she was. She stood close to Dorain and spoke in a quiet, steady tone.

"Are you planning to slay a couple of hundred peasants with that thing?"

"What? No, I—"

"Then lower that bow before you start a riot."

He did so just as Hime turned to address the crowd in a loud, clear voice that resonated with reason.

"We are the Knights of Lord Fangbane!" Maybe it was her noble beauty, or maybe her steady, soothing tone of voice. But the crowd hushed to hear her. "Under His Lord's command, we wish only to see your demonstrations carried out peacefully. We shall not harm you as long as you do not inflict harm on others."

This caused murmurs to ring out in the air as the crowd spoke to each other. They seemed to have calmed down.

"The Knights?" a woman repeated in a questioning tone.

"That's the first time I heard of them…" another responded unsurely.

"She said Lord Fangbane is their leader," a man noted. "They must have honorable intentions if they act under someone as dignified as him."

Dorain let out a heavy sigh of relief, glad he wouldn't have to fire an arrow after all. "Thanks…"

Hime looked over at him with a big smile.

"No! She's lying!" A woman yelled from the crowd, gaining attention. "She's a celta from Altha Hills. She's working for the Bishop."

Hime's smile faded as she realized her mistake. She had completely forgotten that she was cloaked in royal raiment from her hometown.

Dorain reacted quickly, hoping to stop the crowd from turning on them again.

"Didn't you hear us, woman? We're Knights. We're independent!" Dorain tapped on the badge on his chest to prove it. The crowd broke into factions, some believing him, and others still ruled by anger.

The two young Knights scrambled to come up with another plan. Hime took notice of a few civilians who had been tied and herded into a corner behind a handful of aggressive guards. She hurried over and addressed them politely.

"Honored guardians of the peace," she said gently. "Please release these citizens you arrested."

The Valkyries looked at Hime, bewildered by her request. A sergeant spoke up, but her voice had a flat affect to it.

"I'm afraid we can't do that. These are violent peasants."

Dorain noticed that as she spoke, her eyes did not focus on Hime, but seemed to wander to a dark corner down the street. Dorain swore he saw a movement in the alley, but it was too dark to see.

"Please," she said evenly. "Give them a chance to change. It's up to us to turn the tide."

The Valkyries went silent, uncertain how to respond to her reasoned tone.

"In case you weren't aware," Dorain interjected. "That is an order, not a request. Or would you rather I inform Councilor Dareh that you disobeyed my orders?"

Dorain hated uttering those words, but it always worked. He hoped this would be the last time he had to use his father's name to make something out of himself.

Hime took notice that the sergeant refused to meet her gaze. She reached out and lightly placed her hand on her shoulder. A faint blue glow radiated from her palm for a split second.

"Do you understand?" Hime asked again in a low, delicate tone such that only the sergeant could hear her.

"Yes, sir." The sergeant shook her head as if clearing the fog, and she turned to focus on Hime, then Dorain. "Uh… Yes, Milady. Sir, I mean."

The other guards took their cue from the sergeant and obeyed without further objection. They unlocked the handcuffs and released the civilians. Grateful, the prisoners dropped their hostility. Without further resistance, they disappeared into the now peaceful crowd. Clearly, the citizens were moved by the noble young lady's grace. Their suspicions evaporated, and their opposition to the Knights vanished. It was as if the air had gone out of them, and the crowd slowly dispersed, moving back into the main street.

"How in the name of the six wise wizards did you do that?" Dorain said, breathing a heavy sigh of relief.

"Negotiation is a skill we practice in Altha Hills on a daily basis." Hime responded with modesty. "People are not bad. You just need to find the right words."

"And that spell you used?"

Hime was impressed that he noticed.

"Not a spell. A muscle relaxer. It helps clear one's mind. Exceptionally useful under stressful conditions."

The rest of the day went by without further incident, and the Knights were installed in comfortable lodgings of the guard's quarters. To their surprise, Fangbane was present in the barracks.

"Neo pulled a few strings," he explained. "Who knew. Hilda was delighted to have me come over."

Shiba added his snarky remark. "Would've never flown if Councilor Novinha found out."

"Won't argue with that. I reckon she dislikes the very idea of the Knights."

Hime looked over his shoulder. "And the Lady?"

"Resting. I advised her against further traveling until after the baby is born."

Shiba snickered, understanding that now Gaven had to take care of Starlight. "You put the kitten on nurse duty."

Fangbane simply shrugged and diverted Shiba's attention back to the debriefing. "Hilda gave me the rundown. She had nothing but good things to say," Fangbane said. "You can all learn a little from Hime. There are times when reason and fairness are stronger than brute force. Good job today, everyone. Rest up. Tomorrow will be harder."

Hime beamed with delight, thanking her lord for the compliment. She was shortly pulled aside by Neo and dragged along to the refreshment table. Shiba and Mirari followed them, but before Dorain could take a step, Fangbane stopped him. He gestured Dorain over to the side. In a low voice, he began.

"I know Shiba is an ass, but you didn't respond when he asked you to report your status. You need to give your team full transparency."

"My Lord," the youth said. "I'm sorry I failed to respond. I am ready to accept whatever punishment is appropriate."

Fangbane shook his head. "You are not a child anymore, Dorain. You're fourteen. You don't need punishment to grow. More importantly, did you learn something from today?"

Encouraged that Lord Fangbane was turning the incident into a lesson, not a discipline issue, Dorain thought for a moment. "I need to maintain my focus?"

"Exactly. Battle is always chaos, son. That's when you really need to think clearly, and listen to your leader. That's what it means to be a man."

"Thank you, My Lord. I'll remember that."

He gave Dorain a strong pat on the back and nudged him toward the other Knights. Fangbane retreated to his own quarters, giving the Knights time to themselves.

"They said there may be an assassination attempt, right?" Dorain asked in a muffled voice, his mouth full of bread. "Do you really think so? The protesters today sounded like they just wanted their voices to be heard."

"The Bishop owes a mountain of coins to investors and merchants in Oban." Shiba agreed with the boy. "They have every right to protest his presence in Minetta. It's dangerous for us to even defend someone like him."

"But, that's our job," Hime said.

"Hime, I agree with you, but…" Neo looked concerned. "The Bishop is from your own capitol, after all. What's your opinion of the man?"

"He's… not pleasant, but…" She tried to put her own feelings aside. "He's not popular, I admit. But I trust that Lord Fangbane and Region Leader Gaven have a reason for agreeing to protect him."

"I don't take orders from anyone," Shiba said. "And whatever you think of this Bishop, my impression of his acolyte doesn't inspire me to risk my hide for him."

"That's no surprise," Mirari sniped. "You'd only risk your hide to benefit yourself."

"You're here on order from Lord Fangbane," Neo reminded him. "Not as Region Leader of Avon. Now's not the time to act on your own, Shiba." Neo steered things back to Hime, saying, "I'm just worried your own people back home might think ill of you if anything goes wrong tomorrow…"

"I can't worry about that," Hime answered. "My father is the region leader of Altha Hills. He knows the Bishop is a powerful force. It's a delicate balance. He needs the Bishop's support to remain in charge."

"It sounds to me like you'd be better off without this Bishop," Shiba said. "But still, you'd rather follow Fangbane's orders to keep him alive. Why?"

"When I face a difficult decision, I ask myself *what would my sister do?* And I try to be as brave as her." Hime looked Shiba in the eye as she drove her point home. "What do you think? What would she choose?"

Shiba grew pale. He opened his mouth, then stopped himself. He appeared to be in the throes of a terrible emotional conflict and seemed overwhelmed.

Neo felt his turmoil, and put his massive arm around his master's shoulders.

"Come, partner. We *do* have a big day tomorrow. Let's get some rest." The big brawler tenderly led Shiba away, down the hall to their bunk room.

CHAPTER FOURTEEN

The Knights arrived at the town center early in the morning for recon, checking the scene before their back-up guards arrived. The crowd of civilians was already teeming, and continued to grow by the hour. Shiba had determined that he would support the protection of the Bishop after all. He reviewed the plan with the others as they stood before the magnificent City Hall. The edifice of rose marble stood across from a lush city park. The Bishop was due to arrive soon.

"Here's the plan," Shiba began. "Neo, Mirari, you're both close-range combatants. Stay close to the Bishop at all times. Dorain will keep watch from a distance. From that roof, over there." Shiba pointed at a tall structure full of bureaucratic offices, on the edge of the park, and kitty-corner from City Hall.

"Gotcha," Dorain said, approving the favorable view from that angle. "Gives me a good field of fire."

Shiba nodded. "I will blend in with the crowd and stand by, looking out for anything unusual."

"And for me?" Hime asked eagerly.

"You're quick on your feet," Shiba noted. "Let's station you on the other side of the crowd. If the need arises, you can back up Mirari and Neo."

"Good," Fangbane nodded. "And I'll stay with Hilda."

Fangbane watched the Knights disperse, heading to their assigned posts. He walked inside the building to join Region Leader Hilda just by the doorway.

"Everything's in place."

"Good. Commander Heisa has a full company in reserve, in addition to the royal guards." She pointed at the three ranks of well-armed troops in formation at the bottom of the steps where the Bishop's carriage would deliver him.

Fangbane looked down at Commander Heisa in full command of her soldiers. As he did, the commander looked up at him. But her eyes didn't meet Fangbane's, nor was she looking at Hilda. Her gaze was somewhere off to the side. Fangbane turned to see what had Heisa so transfixed.

Behind him, with a purple cape around his shoulder, over his monk's robes, stood the tall, blue-haired acolyte. He turned his gaze on Fangbane, and a thin smile crossed his lips as he extended his hand. "Laikos."

Fangbane carefully reached out his hand as if he was ready to submerge it in boiling water.

"Fangbane." Laikos shook his hand firmly but didn't let go. "I've heard of your good work. We need more people like you, those who are willing to defy the system."

"I… am not defying the system," Fangbane said. "I am improving it."

"Well, any intervention into our current system is good, wouldn't you agree? Even thousand-year-old traditions need to adapt to modern times."

But Fangbane was too distracted to appreciate Laikos' words. Rather, he was mesmerized by the soothing feeling this man emanated. His body felt light, almost as if he were levitating. His aura exuded a warmth he hadn't felt in a long time. It even reminded him of… someone familiar… the love resurfacing from the dark…

"All is in order, I trust?" Hilda spoke, drawing Fangbane back to reality.

"Yes. We're ready for anything."

"Wonderful," Laikos said, and then nodded at the commotion down the street. "Right on time. Here comes His Eminence now."

The Bishop's fine carriage, pulled by two gallant white horses, rolled up to the City Hall steps and came to a stop. The soldiers stationed outside did their best to restrain the surging crowd, but the masses continued to encroach. As the Bishop stepped out of the carriage, he was greeted by Neo and Mirari on each side. He waved to the onlookers, now a fired-up crowd, smiling gently over all the boos and foul words as compliments. The holy man – short with baggy wrinkles across his face – was escorted across the plaza, passing the ranks of guards at attention, and toward the base of the steps.

"You're those Knights of Fangbane's, aren't you?" the Bishop asked.

"At your service, Bishop." Mirari said.

"Why is it then that you perform the peasant work that you do?"

"We are here to protect you, sir," Mirari replied with a hint of discomfort in her voice. "Surely you don't see that as peasant work?"

Mirari saw a light smile come across his face. She wasn't sure if it was an old man's kindness or laughter at her ignorance. But despite his kind nature – gentle and elegant like a fully-bloomed rose – Mirari started to see his true side; his thorns were hidden in his words.

"Do you actually believe that such a small organization as yours can bring peace? Of course, you do. You have to listen to your master."

"I believe he knows what's best," Neo said.

"Aye, the Silver Fist. How could Minetta's greatest brawler become a slave to someone else?"

"I don't see it that way, sir."

"Suit yourself."

Mirari's nostrils flared. The Bishop was undeniably one of the rudest people she had ever met, and Mirari wouldn't mind slipping a dagger into the seam of his velvet robe and slashing it open, revealing the insides of his soulless, hollow body. She admired Neo for maintaining his composure in the face of insults. He knew how to handle pressure well.

They arrived at the top of the staircase, where the town's mayor and other diplomats bowed and greeted the Bishop with obsequious solemnity.

From his rooftop perch, Dorain kept a watchful eye on the City Hall steps and the immediate area around the Bishop. He could see all the others. Mirari and Neo flanking the rotund bulk of the Bishop. Shiba and Hime were at the far end, monitoring the mood, and watching for any sign of the crowd turning into a mob.

He watched a hooded figure move through the crowd notably faster than the rest. He seemed to be in a hurry to get to the front. Dorain watched for a few more seconds, then looked up ahead. The person was going straight for the Bishop.

"Shadow Prick," Dorain alerted through his communication glove. "Man in a gray hood, two o'clock, maybe thirty feet from you. Suspicious movement."

"Got it." Shiba looked in the concerned direction. He caught a glimpse of the dark hood weaving toward the front, but he would have to course through a lot of people to catch up. Shiba cast his shadow to slither after the figure.

It traveled underneath the feet of the crowd and reached the suspicious man within seconds. The shadow reached up and grabbed his legs, holding him in place. The man began to panic, realizing that he had been caught. He struggled to break free from the shadow, but couldn't budge.

The man noticed Shiba moving through the crowd and getting closer. With no other choice, the man reached into his pocket and pulled out several deadly looking throwing stars, and quickly whipped them toward the Bishop.

"Neo, look out!" Dorain warned as the figure began throwing stars at the crowd and diplomats too. In an empty street, Dorain might have fired arrows, so accurately they would intercept the stars with ease and finesse. But in a crowd like this one, it wasn't possible. Dorain didn't want to risk taking a shot.

Neo heeded the warning and stood directly behind the Bishop. He lifted his fist, the armor gauntlet deflecting the weapons. Neo was unscathed.

While all eyes were on Neo, Mirari noticed Commander Heisa making nervous eye contact with her instead of focusing on Neo. The next instant, she pulled out a razor-sharp throwing dagger. Heisa was yet to raise her arm to make the throw when Mirari drew her sword. Heisa's blade caught the sun when Mirari swung her sword, and the flat side of the blade slapped the dagger out of the commander's hand.

In response, Commander Heisa drew her own sword, moving aggressively toward Mirari. She had a crazed, wild look in her eyes.

"Commander? What the—"

Heisa had barely cleared the scabbard when Mirari closed in on her. Their swords clashed. Mirari could tell Heisa's skills were no match. As an experienced street fighter, Mirari could easily kill her at close combat, but held off, hoping the seemingly mad woman could be taken alive.

Dorain's attention was focused on the sword duel rather than on the surroundings. He realized the error of his distraction when he heard the faint sound of a bow being drawn backward.

He quickly turned and noticed another assassin, aiming from a balcony below him.

Dorain reached for an arrow and aimed his bow. He fired a paralysis arrow at the archer below, but as he let fly, he heard the simultaneous twang of the assassin's bow as the man got his shot off. Dorain's shot hit him before the man ever saw his own arrow strike.

But strike it did, and Mirari felt a rush of pain centered below her knee. The arrow's shaft was buried in her calf. She stumbled forward, dropping her sword as she fell, crying out in pain. Commander Heisa saw her advantage, raised her sword, ready to strike the injured Mirari. She was too slow, however, as her own soldiers quickly piled on top of their traitorous commander. They wrestled and restrained her, causing her to drop her blade.

"Mirari!" Neo shouted.

"I'm fine!" she lied, but her strained voice gave her away. "Get them all inside."

There was no time to help Mirari. Neo gave her a once-over and hustled the diplomats into the building. The traitorous Commander Heisa was bound up tightly, giving Mirari a moment to look at her leg wound. Thanks to her leather leggings, the wound was shallow. She gritted her teeth, took hold of the shaft, and steeled herself to yank it out of her flesh.

Just at that moment, Hime teleported to her side.

"Gods on donkeys!" Mirari yelped. Hime's sudden appearance startled Mirari almost as much as the arrow had.

"Are you alright?" Hime said, examining the wound, voice shaky with worry.

Mirari took a deep breath and gripped the arrow shaft again. She pulled it out, and a trickle of blood seeped out.

"Oh!" cried Hime, shocked at Mirari's grit. "Gods, that must hurt!"

"I wish it did. I can't feel my leg…"

Hime's hands glowed vibrantly as they rested on Mirari's calf, and gradually Mirari felt the numbness fade. A soothing aura wrapped around her leg and sealed her wound. She felt a sting of pain, but it relieved her knowing she could feel her leg again.

"It's just a paralysis arrow," the healer reassured her. She looked at the arrow in Mirari's trembling hand, noting its thin point and flimsy material. "That arrow can't kill. It seems you were the target."

A moment later, Shiba hurried around the corner of the building, jerking the hooded man along, hands cuffed behind his back. He gave the man a driving kick, which shoved him toward Hilda's waiting soldiers, who hustled him off quickly but not gently. Another squad of soldiers was dragging the archer from the building where Dorain had shot him.

Mirari pushed herself back up. The diplomats were inside, safe and sound. But the day was long from over. Mirari let out a heavy sigh as she walked back to the side of the building, hoping she wouldn't have to take another arrow to the knee.

***

At the end of the day, Fangbane offered his condolences to Region Leader Hilda in her private study.

"I'm still shocked about Commander Heisa," Fangbane said. "Has she said anything about why she committed such treachery?"

"Not yet. In fact, she's putting on an act to try escaping responsibility."

"An act? How so?"

Hilda stopped herself, brushing the whole issue aside.

"Oh, who knows. It doesn't matter, she will be interrogated soon. It won't take long to clear up all the mystery."

There was no need. Fangbane heard the results of the interrogation. It felt like a puzzle piece tilted in the wrong direction. If only he had been there when the attack happened, he could help solve the mystery. Now he was left wondering if he had been careless in picking up the thoughts of the incoming assassins, or if they had somehow truly blocked his mental ability.

Fangbane's eyes shifted to the portraits behind Hilda. Generations of region leaders were recorded in flawless paintings secured in gold frames. It stopped at Nivenda, meaning Hilda's portrait wasn't finished yet. She had only been in service for a few months, taking Nivenda's place after the Althaean Siege devastated her.

The sight of Nivenda threw Fangbane back to the fierce debate in the courthouse. Though the twins had opposing personalities, Nivenda and Novinha looked exactly alike, radiating purple eyes and waves of flawless brown hair. Fangbane couldn't help but recall Novinha scorning at Gaven with disgust.

"How is she? Nivenda?" Fangbane asked out of genuine concern. Hilda followed his eyes, turning around to look at the portrait herself.

"She's doing fine," Hilda assured him. Then she contemplated whether or not she should speak out of turn. "Listen, Nivenda and I don't blame you for what happened to Iphigenia. After all, we sent her there to help you. She died for duty and honor."

Fangbane looked away, still ashamed to face the fact that one of Oban's best warriors died under his command. He was thankful to have received any help from fighters following him into the Althaean Siege. But Iphigenia's death, he believed, could've been prevented.

"I offer my deepest condolences. Whatever your region needs, Hilda, I will make it up to you and Nivenda."

"With all due respect, Helmet, you seem to be the one needing our help right now." Fangbane chuckled, and his reaction lifted a smile on Hilda's face. "This is between us, Fangbane.

I'm still new to the throne and I don't want people to know we're getting soft on Althaeans, especially not to sister Novinha."

"I understand."

"I support what you're doing with the Knights, but Althaea will always be Minetta's enemy, and as long as Valenia doesn't back us up, they might as well be the enemy too."

Before Fangbane could challenge her choice of words, a knock on the door interrupted him. Without waiting for a response, the door slowly crept open. Fangbane didn't sense anyone approaching. Was he losing his concentration?

"Pardon my intrusion," the old Bishop chimed as he invited himself into the room with a tiny spring in his step. "My carriage has arrived and I wanted to give a proper farewell. Any progress with the interrogation?"

"Not yet," Hilda responded in a dismissive tone, but the Bishop simply smiled with unctuous servility.

"I am most anxious to know what motivated the cowardly and despicable attempt on my life today. Do let me know once you find out."

"Let me assure both of you, we intend to pursue that information with the most extreme interest."

"Thank you, Your Honor," he said. He turned to Fangbane, pushing an air of humble gratitude. "I wish you well, Lord Fangbane."

The Bishop crept out of the room as gracefully as he had entered. As soon as the door clicked, Fangbane realized he had been holding his breath the entire time.

"That man is strange." Hilda laughed as if she had read his mind. "But he's loyal to his duty, and I won't challenge that."

Fangbane slowly nodded. The series of events today were too peculiar for his liking. He couldn't wait to go home.

Upon their return to the mansion, Starlight and Gaven greeted them with refreshments in the dining hall. Fangbane complimented the Knights on their first successful mission as a team of five. He relieved them quickly, giving them the rest of the evening to relax.

Mirari turned to the stairway, ready to disappear into her room without celebrating. The room erupted in a loud bantering, a perfect opportunity for her to slip away. She placed her hand on the railing, but before she could take her first step, Shiba brushed by and roughly shoved her against her shoulder.

"What's your problem?" Mirari growled. Shiba turned back and gave her an equally harsh glare in return. Mirari regretted her words as she saw that he wasn't messing around this time. He was genuinely furious about something, which made her wary of his next words.

"Did you see the arrow?" he demanded.

"The arrow?"

"Don't pull that crap. The arrow that hit you this afternoon."

"No, I didn't," she said softly.

He looked ready to spit on her. "What if that wasn't just a paralysis arrow? Even worse, what if it hit the Bishop?"

"I'm sorry." She had never imagined apologizing to Shiba, but she had been awash with guilt over her failure to avoid the shot that hit her. It was no excuse, she knew, but she'd been so shocked at Commander Heisa's treacherous attack that it distracted her. She had failed to keep herself aware of her surroundings. It was an inexcusable mistake, and one that put them all at risk.

"Sorry doesn't make up for mistakes. Quit slipping up, before you get someone killed with your incompetence."

Shiba turned and strode away in utter repugnance, leaving Mirari feeling even more guilty than she did before. She was ashamed to admit it, but Shiba was right. She was lucky her careless failure hadn't led to something much worse. She might have gotten the Bishop killed, and destroyed the Knight's reputation. Or worse, get one of her comrades killed.

As Mirari climbed the stairway and shuffled to her bedroom, she couldn't stop the bitter tears from erupting like a fountain of grief. She knew no amount of training could make up for the lack of instinctual fighting.

Gaven had observed the entire conversation from the sideline. He ground his teeth and forced himself to hold back his anger. It was supposed to be a moment of celebration, and Shiba was making team collaboration more difficult than it needed to be.

His thoughts were disrupted by a tap on his shoulder.

"Come." Fangbane signaled to his room, and Gaven tread with curiosity. Fangbane locked the door behind them.

"We caught the assassins," Fangbane began, "but they're dead."

"What?" Gaven was stunned. "Hilda executed them?"

"No, they committed suicide."

"What?" This time the question was laced with anger, fumes rising from his ears. "How could that happen?"

"Hilda wouldn't tell me, but I heard her thoughts. The assassins swore to have no memory of what they did. As soon as the guards turned around, the Bishop carelessly left one of their daggers within their reach, and they took it to their necks, one by one."

"The old prune? And why would he have any business in the interrogation room?"

Fangbane shrugged. "He may have bribed the guards. Hilda didn't let him in, that's for sure. Once she heard what happened, she dismissed it as a clumsy old man's accident."

Gaven continued, "It sounds very suspicious. If they were truly innocent, why did they kill themselves?"

"That's the important question. Because if they weren't lying, and they were acting beyond their own will, without any memory of it…"

Gaven furrowed his brow, realizing how familiar it all sounded.

Fangbane voiced Gaven's apprehension. "It appears an awful lot like your case, doesn't it?"

CHAPTER FIFTEEN

"You never want to step forward if the center of your sword is this far out," Gaven explained to Mirari. "It's a high-risk situation. You wouldn't have enough momentum to change directions should the pursuit fail. It's adapted from the Zlan Tribe, so not a lot of paragons know about it. You're very nimble. This will work to your advantage."

Gaven was working her extra hard, knowing it might help her get over the self-doubts and shame she felt. She was following his demonstration, seemingly focused… But Gaven knew her so well by now, he could tell that her mind was elsewhere.

"Focus," he said as Mirari readjusted her position slightly, nodding at his warning. "Or I'll make you take notes."

"Sorry," Mirari muttered. Her body was being crushed with disoriented grief, and it was making their training time less efficient. Gaven released a loud sigh.

"You're thinking about what Shiba said to you last night."

Mirari's eyes lit up, astonished that he had heard their conversation, but more ashamed that he was able to read her so well. Her spine continued to slouch from the weight of her shoulders as she raised her sword again.

"I have to prove that I'm strong enough to be here…"

She practiced the swing that Gaven had just taught her. He looked like he was about to say something, perhaps in regard to Shiba's message, but he stayed quiet about the incident and resumed the lesson.

Memories of the last few months at the estate flashed in her mind. It wasn't just Shiba's constant harassment that was driving her to the edge. Her relationship with Gaven was still an icy brick wall.

While she had always known of the bad blood between Althaea and Minetta, the past few months had driven it in like a tent peg. Since she started fighting on behalf of the Knights, the extent of just how much the citizens of each empire hated one another became clear to her. Even though full-blown wars were rare nowadays, the hostility remained. All regions and empires were at risk of exploding into the next great war if there were no Knights to suppress it.

Gaven himself barely escaped the death penalty for the rebellion he allegedly led. He was only granted mercy because he was Althaea's great fighter. But if Althaea learned that their warrior hero – let alone the bloody traitor of the rebellion – was, in reality, a Minettan, his fate would be sealed. He could not be both Althaean and Minettan – the current system forced him to pick a side. And so, as much as she missed their childhood relationship, she had to let him be the Althaean he believed he was. But the secrecy was destroying her.

Suddenly, she felt a tug as her sword slackened from her grip, and clattered to the ground while Gaven held the point of his sword at her throat. She tried to snap her attention back to the present, only to have an outburst of rage aimed at her.

"By the bloody stumps of the Martyr Aggrecio! Are you trying to have your limbs hacked off? Where is your mind!"

"It's not that easy, alright?" Mirari shrieked. Her voice

cracked, trying to hold back rising tears. She picked up her sword in frustration. "This isn't how things should've ended. I never asked you to train me. Leave, for all I care."

"Gods, calm down," Gaven yelled as his brows furrowed. "If you need a break for the day, say so."

She didn't want a break. She wanted to go home, go back to Solarin, and open her front door to Salathiel in the kitchen, hear his lecture against street fights with the drunks, and banter and wrestle with him late into the night.

But that was a reality she knew she could never return to, for he was gone, and the Knights were all she had left. If she failed here, she would fail Gaven, the one who had put so much effort into her training. All the chances she had of finding the people responsible for Salathiel's death would fade as well. What purpose would she have left in this world if that happened?

Mirari took her sword in both hands, walked to a wooden chair sitting in the shade of an oak, and chopped the blade down on it, hacking and smashing it to bits as she let out a bloodcurdling howl of sheer misery.

"This is why women can't be warriors..." He cursed to himself. Gaven kept his silence and gave her a moment to let go of her frustrations.

"Mirari, what do the Blessed mean to you?" Gaven asked her almost cautiously.

"What?" She turned around to face him.

"This is about the Blessed case, isn't it? You've been acting up ever since you saw the file, and Fangbane told me that you have personal ties to them. I want to hear about their relevance to you, from you, if you would indulge me. What do they mean to you?"

Mirari took a deep breath, processing her thoughts and carefully choosing her words, not knowing how much she would be able to reveal.

"I need to know what happened to my brother," she said. "All I know is the Blessed did it."

"Did what?"

"They…" Mirari paused, not wanting those words to slip out of her mouth. Even though it had been six months since Salathiel's disappearance, she still hadn't entirely accepted it.

"My brother was a retinue. He guarded merchants and their valuable cargo. Sometimes the clients… well, they weren't exactly saints. But the more dangerous they were, the better they paid. I told him not to do it… I told him. That night, his clients must've been members of the Blessed. He never came home from the job, and those 'clients' just disappeared with no way to track them. No one knows what happened. Nothing." Mirari looked into Gaven's eyes with utmost certainty. "They killed him. I'm sure of it. And I will find them."

Gaven bit his lip. Her story was much like all the other cases in that file. It would be insensitive to tell Mirari that her brother's death was just another number in the Blessed's roster.

"The Blessed isn't some mysterious boogeyman you can blame just because your brother went missing. There are only a few people in this world who know they exist."

"Well, I'm one of them. And I have every right to know more." There was such pain, such urgency in her plea. Gaven looked at her with uncertainty. She wasn't ready. The fact that she was so persistent made him that much more hesitant to reveal the details.

"Your Honor, please… I need answers."

"But, would *he* have wanted that?"

"Who?"

"Your brother. Would he want you to spend your life agonizing over his fate? Or would he want you to move on?"

Mirari's eyes widened. Gaven's words made her recall a time when Joachim, her retainer, had said the same to her. He was the one who helped her discover the Blessed in the first place, but he also refused to let her pursue the mystery further. He too insisted that Salathiel wouldn't want her to put herself in danger of suffering the same fate. Could they have known what was best for her?

"I… I can't just forget about him."

"Don't forget him. But stop torturing yourself."

Doubt flickered across her expression, but the depth of sorrow in her eyes showed that no advice would ever stop her. She would keep at it until it killed her.

He let out a loud sigh and decided to indulge her, only enough to feed her curiosity and get it out of her mind.

"The Blessed appear to be some kind of vigilante group, people who think they're saints, on an equal level with the Gods. And like Gods, they think they're above the system. They commit petty crimes of theft and assault, but some will go as far as to slaughter entire villages. But I have no leads and no evidence. The file you want so badly is small, Mirari. Any person who looks at it would think it's nothing more than a bunch of miscellaneous complaints. They're as good as a myth."

"But, they're not! If I've heard of them, and Lord Fangbane gave you a file on it, that certainly means that they're not a myth."

"The Blessed might as well just be a term that people use to blame someone who they can't describe. It happens. I hate to admit it, but people go missing all the time. We can't solve every mystery in this world. I know this means a lot to you, but I can't have you looking into this file when your only real interest is revenge. That doesn't mean you can't ever see it. I'd like you to recover first. Don't make it personal. We've all lost someone. Shiba, Neo, and I have seen more losses than we can count. And I…"

He paused. She could tell he was fighting not to allow his

memory to affect him emotionally. He went on. "I took the life of my friends with my own hands, and with my lost memory, I may never know why. I really hope you never go through that, Mirari. Just take it easy."

Mirari turned away, sulking in silence. She missed Salathiel beyond words could describe. What if he was alive and needed her help? No matter what anyone said, she couldn't just put that thought out of her head.

Yet, perhaps they were right. It might be best after all to accept his death and move on. No vengeance would ever bring him back…

AN HOUR LATER, Gaven walked past a window and noticed Mirari outside, dueling with Shiba again. And getting beat.

As she dragged herself off the ground, Mirari scowled at Shiba's twisted smile. He was enjoying her humiliation too much.

"You'll never get by with endurance like that!" Shiba scoffed.

Mirari cursed under her faint breath. She seemed to not want to go on, but Shiba wasn't giving her much of a choice. She tried to stay composed and not show her fatigue when a door slammed open, hitting the wall like the boom of a cannon.

"Shiba!" Gaven growled as he stomped into the courtyard.

"Kitten," Shiba taunted in return.

"Quit playing around," Gaven said. "You're supposed to train your team, not bully them."

"How can anyone train someone like her? She's even worse than you were when I—"

"Enough, you scheming featherpit!" Gaven said.

Shiba bristled at the insult to his nationality, but Neo grabbed his shoulder to prevent him from attacking Gaven.

"Language, Your Honor," Shiba said.

"I swear," Gaven said in disgust, ready to throw a punch at

Shiba. "You act like you're trying to make the world your enemy." Gaven pulled Mirari up from the ground and guided her into the manor by the arm. She was exhausted, too tired to resist. Her mind wasn't in the right place either way.

"Typical flatty…" Shiba muttered to himself as they left his sight.

"Mirari," Gaven growled as they entered the manor, "stop fighting him."

"But, I can't just let him—"

He cut her off harshly. "You don't have to prove anything to him. He's a bitter scamp. What he thinks doesn't mean shit." He saw his words cut her, and softened his tone. "I'll make sure he stops goading you. But focus on what's important. You need to take care of yourself first. All that built-up anger about your brother? It's destroying your concentration. Fighting with Shiba just makes things worse."

"You would know."

"Listen, I know you're having a hard time." He sighed, scratching his head. "That's it. You need to take a break. Take some time off to process everything. Once you're ready, let me know and we'll resume training."

"I don't need time off."

"Don't argue," he sneered. "I'm excusing you from all missions for the next two weeks. No exceptions. You'll work no files, stay out of all investigations. Period."

"I don't need rest, Your Honor."

"Enjoy the time off, Mirari. That's an order."

She raised her eyes. "What would you have me do? Bake? Garden? Iron your sheets?"

"Actually, here," he said, stopping by a bookcase in the upper hall. He searched through the titles, finding a thick book titled *The Paragon's Conduct.*

Mirari noticed the book was in mint condition.

"When you're not meditating, study this."

"I have already read this…"

"Memorize it. You'll be tested. Enjoy."

MEANWHILE, Shiba was making his way back to his room. Neo trailed behind, his displeasure obvious. But there was little Neo could do to tame Shiba's aggression. Shiba was his liege, and was free to run things the way he wanted.

He followed him into the room. Shiba was still seething by the way he pulled out a set of throwing stars and began hurling them at a wooden target board on his wall.

Thunk. Thunk.

"Shiba, please," Neo said. "You're being too tough on her."

"I'm only trying to strengthen this team," Shiba spat back in response.

"But in your world, Lord," Neo argued, "the team currently consists of just me and you. Everyone else, you simply deem unworthy."

Shiba chose to ignore Neo, and continued hurling shuriken stars at the wooden target, throwing harder and harder each time, trying to wear out his fury, and hitting the center target every time.

"Is it your job to question me?"

Neo ignored his partner's bid to remember his boundaries. "It's my job to make sure you're the best region leader you can be."

"I told you a thousand times, Neo. You can resign at any time." Shiba recalled the last head count of his army, a significantly smaller amount compared to when his mother had left the throne to him. Ever since he had been neglecting his duties, his people also started to lose faith in him. But Shiba had nothing motivating him to do better. "Maybe I should've let Fangbane take over."

"Not in a millennium, partner. This is your birthright. I'm not letting you give it up so easily."

"And yet, you're the one who urged us to join the Knights. We already had enough on our plate."

"It's the least you can do for Lord Fangbane. He's helping you restore your fallen reputation." Neo chose his next words carefully. "Besides, if Mecate was here, she would've joined in a heartbeat. You don't need to play tough around me, Lord. I know you wanted to do this… for her."

This stung Shiba, and his next throw missed the target completely, knocking a chip out of the wall and clattering to the floor.

"You'll never let go about that, will you?" Memories of Mecate brought him misery, and he could picture what she would've said to him. Neo was not wrong.

"You're the one who's refusing to let go."

He spun, and barked at Neo, "And what if I don't want to?"

"Well, that's why I'm still here, isn't it?"

Shiba couldn't deny Neo's words. This man spoke too freely sometimes, but Shiba had too much appreciation for his partner to lash out at him. Neo was the man who had always been his better conscience.

"She's a lot like her, isn't she?"

"How could you compare Mecate to that talentless piece of—"

"Oh, cut the shit, My Lord. Be honest with yourself. She youthfully radiates with courage. I know you see it because you haven't given up on her yet."

"How would you know?"

"I can count all the people you've ever given attention to in your life. It's fewer than the number of fingers on my hands."

Shiba thought about it for quite a long moment. "Mirari radiates nothing but soul-ripping grief."

"And doesn't that sound familiar?"

"You can't deny the loss of her brother is deeply engraved in her mind. She's stuck in the past, dwelling on revenge. Until she lets go, she won't reach her potential."

"Perhaps what she needs is someone who can truly understand her loss."

Shiba walked to the target and pulled out the stars.

"There are some things you never get over."

CHAPTER SIXTEEN

Dorain was prowling the empty kitchen. With Kea on his shoulder, he snagged slices of ham and cheese, and a tomato secretly plucked from Starlight's garden. As he made his fourth meal of the day, Kea helped herself to a few galuchi seeds scattered on the floor.

He noticed how quiet it was today. Dorain had to be extra careful with handling the glass jars and squeaky cabinets. He stuffed his mouth quickly before anyone could find out that he broke Gaven's diet regimen.

As soon as Dorain got rid of the evidence, he peeked into the next room, hoping to find Hime. She typically read in the dining hall during lunchtime, and he always looked forward to seeing her. Her very presence always brightened his day. But today, he found Neo sitting where she normally would be.

"Where's Hime?"

"No idea. I didn't see her yesterday, either."

Starlight, who had heard Dorain's inquiry as she approached from the other direction, said, "I believe her father asked her to return to Altha Hills."

"Oris, be merciful," Dorain muttered. "She just got here."

"Well, Hime is a princess after all…" Neo said.

"That's true enough," Starlight said and continued about her work, setting freshly laundered towels on a side cabinet, and tucking them away in drawers.

"But… why would she just leave?" asked Dorain.

"Her father, I assume. As you might expect, the Priest has strong, conservative opinions," Starlight said. Then she added, "And like most Althaeans, he no doubt frowns upon Minettans."

Dorain knew exactly how that felt. "So, it's not some emergency? The old blister just called her home to bust her chops about hanging around with us?"

"Most likely."

He couldn't help but feel sorry for the girl. She was sweet, submissive, and undoubtedly responsible. But Dorain understood how toxic family ties could be, and if he could, he would help her break free from her family's shackles, much like how he broke his own.

"Well, that's a steaming pile of pig shit," Dorain grumbled. "She ought to stand up to the old demon."

"It's not so easy to take a stand against one's father."

"Why not? I sure did."

Kea cooed in a low tone as if she disagreed.

Neo took the hint. "You did?"

"Damn right I did," said Dorain. "He wanted to stop me from joining the Knights, and I just told him to…" Dorain trailed off, lowering his eyes. "Well, I told him I'd think about it…"

"…And?"

"And I just bugged out when he went on a hunting party," Dorain admitted, but quickly put back on his brave face. "I would have told him off if he was home."

Kea cooed again and pecked the feathers under her wing.

"Ahh." Neo turned to Starlight. "I take it you don't expect Hime will do a runner on her old man, right?"

Starlight frowned. "Actually, maybe Gaven should take all of the Knights on a field trip."

"To Althaea?" Neo questioned. "You think he'd do that?"

"He would indeed," Gaven answered as he entered the dining hall. "It's about time all of you get more familiar with the Althaean territory." He turned to Starlight, and with a light smile, he added, "Unless you think Lord Fangbane might give me a spanking, that is?"

"Somehow, I doubt it," Starlight grinned.

<hr>

AT ONE TIME, hundreds of gods were celebrated across all the lands. But as time passed, the tradition was lost. Devotion to gods gradually diminished, fading from memory until their existence only remained in ancient scriptures and children's folklore. The celtas of Altha Hills, however, never wavered from their undying devotion to Oris, the God of Judgment. As the worship of Oris grew, so did the healing powers of the celtas of Altha Hills.

Located in the northernmost part of Althaea, Altha Hills was known to be a holy place. Here was where the most prestigious celtas in the world thrived. Nearly every civilian in Altha Hills who was capable of harnessing kore was a celta healer or spell-caster. They grew in renown such that every region leader in Althaea had celtas from Altha Hills in their army.

Most of the population lived in Altha City, among the vast, white temples caressed in the arc of high mountains. Streams of translucent water hugged the edges of every path, reflecting the color of the flawless sky. The waves of neon light coursed between every crack and tile as if the buildings and stone-covered walkways were alive. In Altha City, kore was considered alive. There was no other settlement better at fusing hāstals with kore than the celtas of Altha Hills.

The man in charge, the region leader, was known as the High

Priest. The celtas of Altha Hills followed the old tradition of appointing the eldest child to become the next priest. Hime, as it happened, was next in line.

"Abandoning your duty is truly an embarrassment to all celtas," the High Priest lectured her.

Hime was used to enduring her father's endless scolding. His voice echoed loudly across their grand hallway. She didn't mean to upset him, but Hime believed that she truly had done nothing wrong. She had to gather every shred of her courage to face her father.

"I'm doing what is right, Father," Hime said, trying to keep a respectful tone.

"No. You're doing the same incredibly foolish things your sister did!" The High Priest's face grew red as his fury escalated. "How dare you run off on this insane quest of Fangbane's? Have you not learned your lesson?"

It was the High Priest's greatest shame that Hime's older sister, the late Princess Mecate, had stubbornly rejected her pampered life as a royal of Althaea, and became an honored fighter in Minetta. What was worse, she got betrothed to the Minettan region leader, Shiba Zabato.

"My sister was not foolish! Mecate cared only about helping others. She knew she couldn't do that being trapped in this place."

"Trapped? She turned her back on her own kind. Mecate threw away her life for the Minettans, and in the process, she left Altha Hills to rot."

"She followed her heart and her conscience."

"And paid the price, as the judgment of Oris fell upon her," thundered the Priest. "Is this the fate you seek for yourself?"

"Of course not."

"Then why is it so hard for you to understand your duty?"

Hime seethed quietly when she heard that. She respected her

father's concern, but why did he always refuse to even try seeing her point of view?

A scrawny boy about Hime's age, called Liber, urgently shuffled toward her, oblivious to his untimely interruption. Liber was Hime's retainer, and looked perpetually confused, overworked, and gave the basic impression he'd have trouble figuring out how to lace a boot. The High Priest constantly nagged Hime to appoint a better retainer, someone reliable and confident. His dissatisfaction with Liber was Hime's foremost reason not to fire the boy. Besides, they had been childhood friends, and she loved him in spite of his undeniable deficits.

"Forgive me, Your Holiness," Liber mumbled, with a groveling bow to the High Priest, before turning to Hime.

"We are having a private discussion, you blithering twit!" the Priest roared.

"Yes, sorry, your Glorious Holiness," Liber said, bowing so low he started to pitch forward on his head. Hime caught him and set him back on his feet.

"Bless your kindness, Venerated Princess."

"You're welcome, Liber. Can this wait?" asked Hime, kindly.

"A thousand pardons, your most Gracious Ladyship. Please forgive my untimely intrusion, I humbly apologize for—"

The High Priest exploded with impatience. "Stop groveling and say your piece, you duck-footed simpleton!"

"Forgive me, your Honorable Reverence."

"By the sacred blood of Oris, boy, spit it out!"

"Yes, my Righteous Lord Most Exalted." Before the Priest burst an artery, Liber turned to Hime. "Princess Hime, your Gracious Eminence, your honored guests are waiting for you by the gate."

"Guests?" Hime said with an air of confusion.

"Oh, yes. By all means, Hime," said her father. "Don't let the crucial affairs of state distract you. Let's have a party. Or perhaps a Grand Ball. We can roast a goat."

"Excuse me, Father. I shall be right back." With a quick curtsy, Hime followed Liber out of the chamber.

The High Priest blustered after her. "Of course, my darling. Bring your visitors. Why not throw open the City Gates while you're at it? Let the peasants in, I could use a good case of fleas."

Just inside the courtyard by the gate, Hime saw her fellow Knights gathered. Gaven and Shiba, region leaders themselves, stood almost rigid with solemnity. Neo waved his hand up high from across the courtyard with a hearty smile.

But Hime's attention drew to Dorain, who hollered, "Gods be hammered, what a classy joint!" He gawked one way, then another, as excited as a dog with two peckers. His eyes locked on the flow of kore in nearly every building and object, as if it was the first time he had ever seen hāstals used in such a way. "Hey, can we get the grand tour?"

"Oh, Gracious," Hime said. "What are you all doing here?"

"Looking for you," Neo said. "You just disappeared on us."

"Sorry, it was a… family emergency."

"And it's settled, right?" Dorain said, knowing that there was no emergency at all. "So, when are you coming back to the manor?"

"Uhm, I don't know, honestly…" She frowned. Hime was not her cheerful self. She noticed there was one person missing. "Where's Mirari?"

"On probation," Gaven said.

"Oh…" She was afraid to probe any further.

Shiba stepped forward. "I know the Priest isn't happy about you joining the Knights, and I clearly haven't made things easier. If it would help, I can speak to him."

Hime crinkled her nose, imagining all of the things that could possibly go wrong if Shiba were to speak to her father. They might as well all be deceased.

"I don't want to burden you with this," Hime said. "Besides, I don't think he'll listen to a Minettan, in all honesty."

"What about me?" Gaven spoke up. "A fellow Althaean region leader?"

Hime didn't decline, though she clearly didn't really want him to either. "You needn't bother. Really. This is my issue, not yours."

"Correct me if I'm wrong, but since you're a Knight now, doesn't that make it our problem, too?" Dorain piped up, not catching the mood.

In fact, Hime realized that he was the only one in this caravan who had no idea of what was going on. The issue was far more personal than he could ever imagine, an animosity that had been avoided for years, and now it seemed like it was ready to burst.

But Dorain had a point. She wasn't the only one being affected by this, and her decision couldn't be a selfish one.

Liber leaned in and whispered a question to her. "So, are we really having a feast, then?"

With a smile frozen in place, Hime answered. "Looks that way."

"Okay. Umm… Should I round up the peasants after all?"

As Hime led her fellows in through a grand entry foyer, Dorain spoke in a voice that bounced off the marble and tile. "Fact is, we came to help you put the squeeze on your old man."

"Shhh!" Gaven gave Dorain a light rap on the skull. But it did not stop his unfiltered thoughts.

"What? You're definitely going to stand up to your father, right? You have to."

"I'm… well, the truth is… I mean, it's difficult to give up all this…"

"Hime, I know exactly how you feel. But you're not your father and at thirteen you're old enough to make your own decisions. You don't have to put up with this. Forget about what he wants. What do *you* want?"

"I… can't just do that, Dorain," Hime said, her eyes now

wandering across the white floor. They were now in front of the throne room, and on the other side of the door, they would have to face the High Priest.

"Shut it, kid," Shiba warned Dorain, as he took the lead and pushed the door open. "If you want to help, *do not* say anything."

Hime reentered the throne room with a retinue of Knights and introduced the High Priest to her teammates. He looked at them all curiously, even though he had met most of them already.

"Your Honor, you look well," said the High Priest, turning his attention to Gaven. "So the rumors are true. You did take up that Knights project with Lord Fangbane."

It was no secret to the Priest. He was there during Gaven's trial, and by now, leaders across Althaea and Minetta swore to have seen the Valiant Tiger working with members of the Knights. Gaven knew he couldn't keep his interaction with the Minettans a secret for long. But he felt no shame standing up for their cause.

"Indeed I have, Your Holiness." Gaven gave a slight nod. "I understand you have some issues regarding Hime joining the Knights. Rest assured she will be safe in my hands."

"It is not your hands I'm worried about, Valiant Tiger." The High Priest glared at Shiba. "My concern is with the people you have formed an alliance with. I expected better from you."

Gaven's face went cold. "Nobody joins this order unless I say so. Do you question my judgment about their character?"

"No, certainly not. If you vouch for them, that is. But still… Princess Hime." His face creased with genuine worry. "Surely you understand my dilemma."

Hime kept her silence, afraid that anything she would say will surely start a war between the two region leaders.

Now putting steel in his voice, the High Priest announced, "Princess Hime is next in line for the throne, as you are certainly aware. Her duty is clear. I will not have her meddling in Minetta's business."

Gaven challenged him. "Your Holiness, the Knights serve Althaea as well. And Valenia, too. Equally. There are no borders where our mission is concerned."

"I fail to understand what exactly the mission is. And that is the problem. The way we've governed our regions has been working successfully. For us in Altha Hills, we have a tradition to uphold. As long as we keep it that way, I see no need to fix something that isn't broken."

"So, you don't think things can be improved?"

"Ah, I nearly forgot…" The High Priest let a smile crack, as he taunted Gaven. "You started a whole war over this childish idea, didn't you?"

Gaven's nostrils flared as he tried to hold back the building rage. The Priest was making it personal.

"Father, please," Hime interrupted before things got worse. "If you think it is childish, then it must be harmless. Surely you can have no objection."

"Princess Hime, your clever tongue doesn't work too easily. Don't meddle in matters that don't concern you."

"I want to help people as my sister did!"

"And it is her sorry fate I am trying to spare you from." At this, the Priest burned another bitter look at Shiba, who glared back, ready to draw steel and put it to use.

But Shiba knew better than to fall for such a trap. He kept his mouth shut, for he knew it was the best thing he could do for Hime.

Hime hated to have anyone, even her father, insult Mecate. She knew many other celtas would agree with her. Mecate had been a tremendous inspiration to everyone, even if she did abandon her duties as a princess.

"Princess Hime," her father pontificated. "It is your destiny to be next in line for my throne. I expect you to acknowledge your obligation to continue upholding the ideas and customs of our people. This is not about right or wrong. It is more than a simple tradition. The succession to the throne is determined by Oris in his wisdom. If you do not wish to follow his design, I fear for your soul. But I will pray to find a new successor. You cannot be a Knight and a Princess."

Hime held her silence when she heard that. The High Priest mistook her unresponsiveness, assuming she accepted defeat. He took his leave without another word to anyone.

Taking the throne wasn't something Hime dreamed of. But she felt a sense of responsibility to honor her obligation as the last direct princess. On the bright side, if she did inherit the throne, she would have a chance to change her people's beliefs from the inside.

But it was not what Mecate would've done. Hime was beyond conflicted, knowing she would have to sacrifice one path for the other.

CHAPTER SEVENTEEN

"Hime's nothing like you…" Shiba seemed to be talking to himself as he peered at the water. There was no answer. The only sound was the musical burble of running water as it trickled down from a small waterfall into a shallow pond – the sacred Fountain of Hope. Shiba sat on a flat rock at the center of the pond, surrounded by the gentle ripples in the holy water.

He spoke again, not to the water, but his lost Mecate. "What do you think? Your father seems dead set against Hime leaving Altha Hills."

Shiba paused as if waiting for her response. He desperately wished to believe he could hear Mecate responding to his questions…

But he couldn't. He knew that. He could only guess what Mecate would say. And yet, in a way that hardly mattered. He felt as if her spirit was present, if only within his own heart. The fountain allowed him to listen to that voice inside him.

"I tried to move on, Mecate. I know that's what you would've wanted. But my soul is captive to your memory… I can't. I'm not like you. I don't have half your courage."

Shiba admired the shallow ripples appearing in the clear

water. He wished for Mecate to offer a solution. He knew she would have a way and would stir up enough trouble to force the old man to let Hime go. Shiba had no idea how he could do that. But coming to the fountain, he hoped she could lend him her wisdom – a way for him to help her sister. He felt like a sitting duck, more powerless than the rest of the Knights. How much longer could he hold his silence?

He watched his reflection in the water become obscure. Another ripple formed, colliding with the small waves formed by the previous ripple. He could only make out the dark silhouette of his hair and clothes reflected upon the water.

As he continued to watch the ebb and flow, an idea began to form and take shape in his mind – it seemed someone had planted it there.

"You're a genius!" Shiba said, grinning at the waters. "As always."

Having heard his beloved, he was now radiating with confidence. He picked himself up and skipped over smaller stones out of the Fountain of Hope.

FOLLOWING A FINE DINNER, Hime eased open multiple doors in a long hallway, one for each guest. The inside was furnished in all white, just like the building. Dorain's eyes were drawn to the only speck of color in the room – raw, purple hāstals, used as decoration only. He began to feel like a prisoner after visiting several rooms all filled with the same bland décor. He was glad they were being forced to leave in the morning, but if it was the last night he was going to see Hime, he didn't want tomorrow to come.

Hime stayed silent on the matter. Her smile never left her face, thinking little of the decision she had to make by dawn.

"Where's the grumpy prick?" Dorain asked, looking over at the room designated for Shiba. But he couldn't find the dark-

fashioned grump in the plain room. Shiba had been missing since long before supper. "Who does that? Bail on free food?"

"I think he went to see some fountain or something," Neo said.

"Ah," Hime said. "The Fountain of Hope."

"Yeah, that. What is the Fountain of Hope, anyway?"

"It's a place where people go to speak to those who have passed."

Dorain was skeptical. "Seriously?"

"It's a very sacred place. Many pilgrims visit, filled with… hope, to reach out to their departed loved ones."

"Oh. And… do they… The departed ones ever… I mean, they don't really come back, do they?"

Hime smiled and shook her head softly. "That's why they call it Hope."

While they were busy mingling, Gaven slipped out of his chamber and found his way to the kitchen. A scullery maid was dozing in the corner, but he knew no one would have stopped him from taking anything he wanted either way and what he wanted was a drink. He entered the wine cellar, browsing shelves full of locally-grown wine. He looked at the labels and made his choice.

"You might not want to drink that."

Startled, Gaven turned to find Shiba, smirking as usual.

"It's no business of yours."

"Up to you. But I happened to notice Starlight prescribed you nemaphora. For your headaches, am I right?"

"You could lose that nose. Be careful where you stick it."

"Just saying. Nemaphora won't do anything if you rinse it down with alcohol. In fact, it will make your headaches worse."

"As if you would give a damn."

"About you? I don't. But you have no partner so who else is going to send you to bed?"

He held his hand out, wanting Gaven to surrender the bottle.

"If you want to recover, you have to take care of yourself."

Gaven let out a light chuckle. "You know the last time both of us were here, you wanted me dead… but now…" Gaven ignored Shiba's hand, but he placed the bottle back high up on a shelf. "Happy now, Mother?"

"No. I'm still worried about what you'll do if the High Priest keeps Hime from leaving freely. It wouldn't surprise me to see you try dueling the old bastard."

"Funny, isn't it?" Gaven let out a snicker. "Dueling is more of your style. I'm surprised you haven't challenged him yet."

"Because unlike you, I won't rock a boat that's already drowning."

"I'd be happy to, after the way he challenged me. And I still haven't gotten over how they talked about Mecate at her funeral."

"Mecate… I agree with. But that time has passed, and now, this is about Hime. Deal with your problems in your savage Althaean ways in your own time. If you duel the High Priest, people are going to hate us for telling Altha Hills how to do their business."

"And? People already hate me."

"I'm talking about the Knights, you self-conceited mongrel. Even so, you're a region leader on suspension. Duel another Althaean, and people will think you can't uphold your punishment. They'll think you really are a traitor."

"People already think that, too. So why does it matter?" Gaven argued, despite the fact he knew Shiba was right.

Shiba shook his head. "You're just like Inigo."

"Don't you dare compare me to him!" Gaven lashed out. But Shiba had expected this response and was unfazed by his uproar.

"If you don't like him, don't act like him. You're better than that… Kitten."

Shiba's words hit him like stone. That was the last thing Gaven wanted to do, to be the cruel image of his former self.

Gaven was nothing like the prick of his former partner, but still, he believed Shiba had every right to blame him for Mecate's death.

Gaven's anger quickly dispersed into pity as he heeded Shiba's words.

"Sorry. And… Mecate, I'm sorry about that too, the whole raid. I never formally—"

"We can both agree that was stupid." Shiba quickly brushed off the mention of her name. Now was not the time to relive that tragic day. "Forget it. It's in the past. Look, I have an idea."

Shiba diverted the conversation to the item in his hand. He tossed a velvet sack full of gems at Gaven, who caught it and peeked inside with a curious gaze. They shone a bright yellow, but Gaven noticed that they were a bit heavier than they should be.

"They're fake."

Gaven's eyes widened, realizing where he was getting at. "Are these the fakes you recovered in Evaleen? They were returned to the merchant, weren't they?"

Shiba continued to smirk. "Go on, ask me where I found them."

"If you're going to drag this out all night, we better open a bottle after all."

"When we arrived, I noticed that all the guards had gold bracelets, the high-end kind. While you guys were stuffing your faces in the dining hall, I snuck a quick look into their kitchen and saw more norkfruits than they had the space to store them."

"And your point is?"

"Those are Minettan imports, and by some luck, they have a surplus of them. Then I remembered the scrooge of a man we had to save, that Bishop. He lives here too… So I visited his room. And what did I find?" He gestured to the gems in Gaven's hand. "These. In his drawer."

"Why, that old swindler…"

Gaven realized that Mirari was right all along. The person who was tipping off the bandits did come from Altha Hills.

"And I'm willing to bet you my best horse against a bucket of puke that we can find a lot more stolen items if we search that 'old swindler's' residence."

Gaven shook his head, impressed. "I knew you were a sneaky bastard. But I didn't give you enough credit as a *scheming*, sneaky bastard."

Shiba shrugged. "I can't take all the credit."

"You went to that fountain, didn't you?"

Shiba nodded and filled Gaven in on his plan.

IN THE VAST COURTYARD, Gaven admired the golden glow rising behind snow-capped peaks. It kissed his frozen cheeks and comforted him with a speck of warmth. Below him was the grand stairway leading down to the deepest parts of the sierra, where the light never touches. That was the way home, but first, he had to find the Priest.

As soon as he heard the sound of their heels clacking against the stone floors, Gaven turned around. There was the High Priest, in the company of a handful of obsequious retainers escorting him across the palace.

"Your Holiness," Gaven greeted as he paced toward him.

"Ah, the Valiant Tiger himself. How kind of you to seek me out before you go."

Among the disciples behind the Priest stood the Bishop and his acolyte. Gaven grinned, pleased with the Bishop's timely presence. But his attention shifted to the monkish man next to him, who held a similar grin on his face. He stared at him with much curiosity, as if he had just heard the mischievous plan play in Gaven's mind. Gaven glared back at him with caution, but the man stretched out his hand from under his long sleeve.

"We have yet to meet, Valiant Tiger. Laikos."

Gaven hesitantly took his hand and shook it. There was something about his aura that gave him an unsettling feeling, perhaps it was the uncanny smile, but he wanted to give him the benefit of the doubt.

Gaven noted that the monk was trying to cover his aura, but such tactics couldn't hide from a sense as strong as his. It was the question behind why this man would feel the need to refrain from showing his true power that made Gaven act with caution.

"If that will be all…" The Priest's husky voice jolted Gaven back to the moment. Gaven gently squeezed his hand and recalled the velvet sack that rested in his other palm.

"Actually, I wanted to ask you about this." Gaven held up the sack of gems. He slowly poured them from the bag, a shimmering waterfall of jewels cascading into his hand. "We found these in your Bishop's possession. Any idea where they came from?"

"Why would I care?" the High Priest asked with a frown. "It's not uncommon for anyone in Altha Hills to carry gems."

"But you would care about how they are acquired, Your Holiness. A group of merchants in Evaleen had a bag of topaz just like this one stolen by bandits."

"Those are some nice bracelets on your guards," observed Shiba dryly. "Yates gold. These minerals are only found in the region of Avon. I don't recall any of them being imported to Altha Hills."

The Priest turned around, not having sensed Shiba's presence, and his calm demeanor quickly turned to disgust. He knew they were scheming something, and this confrontation began to anger him.

The Priest bristled at Gaven. "Are you insinuating that these goods were stolen?"

"Oh, no. I'm not insinuating," Gaven said. "I'm accusing."

"How dare you!" The High Priest's hand started toward the

hilt of his sword, but he checked that foolish idea. "My condolences go to any victim who has suffered at the hands of the wicked. But how can you suggest I have any connection to this?"

"We call it 'evidence'," Shiba said with snide delight. For the first time, Gaven liked the man's nastiness.

"I will concede I've heard of a bandit issue in Evaleen," the High Priest admitted. "Our regions share a border, after all. We even heightened our security to ensure that no such piracy exists within our region."

"Then you might want to speak to your Bishop about it."

"Are you challenging my word, Shadow Soldier?"

"Absolutely not, sir," Shiba smiled. "We are challenging his." Shiba turned, pointing a finger at the Bishop.

"Your Grace!" fumed the Bishop. "You cannot permit these barbarians to abuse me in this villainous manner!"

"Go ahead, your Most August Eminence," Shiba said to the High Priest in an ironic stage whisper. "Ask the old fraud yourself."

"Ask me what? This is blasphemy!" The Bishop pouted like a child with his toys confiscated. "They're just gems, gifts from a family in Evaleen. A simple thanks for our blessings."

Gaven poured the gems back and forth from his left hand to his right and back again.

"Really?" Shiba said. He decided it was time to slip another dagger into the Bishop's back. "And tell us, my dear Bishop, how such a devout family would dare try to show their pious devotion by gifting fake gems?"

"What… I do not understand… Fake?"

"It's a simple matter to verify," Gaven said. "The merchants were transporting fake gems to Elegen. If inspecting them shows they are counterfeit, then you are lying. If so, I suggest we investigate how you obtained the other 'gifts' of Minettan origin."

"Bishop?" the High Priest said, his trust evaporating.

"I… I was, uh, that is, they told me the stones were real, Your

Holiness…" He now turned to his acolyte. "Laikos, did you not say they were real?"

Laikos cast his eyes down, humming with regret. "Alas, I have no personal knowledge of the nature of your… acquisition of…" He hesitated. "These items." He turned to the Priest. "I'm sure the Bishop would be happy to have his quarters searched to clear his good name."

"We've taken the liberty to review some documents." Shiba smiled, as he held up a file of paperwork. He slid out a crumpled paper with a seal on it. "This order is from you, Bishop. This is your seal, is it not?"

The Bishop kept silent, but the Priest needed only a glance. "Yes, this is certainly the seal used by the Bishop for confidential communications."

"This letter provides very specific instructions on which caravans to raid. It even lists what goods they are carrying. If I compare this to the shipment records that pass through Evaleen, I'll bet the mines of Venne that they were all Minettan imports headed for Elegen, not Altha City."

"Preposterous! That… that… forgery you're waving around proves nothing!"

"I suppose you figured as long as you were fingering Minettan imports, nobody in Althaea would investigate?"

Gaven spoke now. "But the Knights don't pick sides. They seek only justice."

The Bishop turned on Laikos, his voice bitter. "You… you sneaky little—"

"I have never sought any path but that of righteousness, good Bishop." Laikos lowered his head with a sincere apology.

Mortified, the High Priest turned and signaled to a pair of guards. "Please return the Bishop to his quarters, and keep him confined there until we give him a trial."

The Bishop put up a good struggle, kicking the guards and

attempting to snatch Laikos by his long hair. He was hurriedly escorted out of their sight, the courtyard quiet once again.

"Good riddance," Laikos sighed, relieved to give up his act. He lowered his head to the Priest, then to Gaven and Shiba. "I am truly sorry for the mess he has caused. Yes, it was I who planted those gems. As he is my superior, it was not within my right to accuse him, but I could not put up with his mischievous ways any longer. My greatest blessings to you, Valiant Tiger, and to you as well, Shadow Soldier."

Watching his close ally being dragged away, the Priest began to understand the purpose behind the Knights. He added, "No thief shall reside in my kingdom. Oris shall not permit such a sin."

Gaven was about to respond, but again, Shiba beat him to the punch. "This is the reason we exist, Your Holiness. You may think that this is not your problem, but everything has a chain reaction. I once thought the same of Althaea's troubles. But when we turn a blind eye, we become a part of the problem."

"Those aren't words I expected out of you, Shadow Soldier," the Priest said. "I see Princess Mecate had an influence on you after all."

"She was the strongest person I've ever known. You should be proud of her," Shiba said. "It may not have been the path you expected, but she found her calling. We do not pick our destiny; that is in the hands of Oris."

"Rightly said." The Priest nodded. His opportunity to apologize to Mecate was long gone. He would take that regret with him to the grave.

"You shouldn't deny my destiny either." He heard a sweet voice, delicate and shy, but Hime's spirit beamed with as much confidence as her sister. They turned and saw her coming up the stairs, with the rising sun casting a golden halo around her royal presence. She took the old Priest by his arm. "Mecate brought nothing but honor to this house. And I hope to do the same."

The High Priest let out a sigh. "Mecate…" But instead of pain, her memory brought him a smile. He turned to Shiba. "You heard her speak at the Fountain of Hope, didn't you?"

Shiba smiled. He didn't hear her. But it was as if Mecate had planted her thoughts in his mind, and through those thoughts, he heard her message. His visit to the fountain gave him insight into his motives for joining the Knights. He hadn't stayed out of coercion. No, he truly believed in Fangbane's cause, because Mecate would have too. The responsibility he bore as a region leader wasn't limited to Minetta. The justice he sought, the freedom Mecate dreamed of, had no borders.

Laikos spoke up now. "This world is filled with mysteries, Lord. We cannot question what the Gods intended. But in his wisdom, perhaps Oris can even permit evil to inspire good men to help each other. We must all try to do that."

The High Priest nodded. "Though Mecate's calling cost her life, I am learning to respect the decisions she made." He turned his watering eyes to his younger daughter and opened his arms. "Come to me, child."

Hime threw her arms around her father, and they hugged each other tightly. "You are a wonderful soul, dear girl. You will take care of yourself, won't you?"

"Of course I will, father," Hime said. "Does this mean…?"

He nodded and released his hold on her. Turning to the two region leaders, he said, "Valiant Tiger, Shadow Soldier, I entrust her to you."

CHAPTER EIGHTEEN

Not long after the Knights returned with Hime, a letter arrived at Fangbane's estate from the Council.

"By the Gods…"

"Is something wrong?" Starlight turned away from the scarf she was knitting.

"The Council. It looks like they are not pleased. Not at all."

Fangbane called Gaven to his study and showed him the letter.

"I don't understand," Gaven muttered, looking up at Fangbane in shock. "We've had nothing but positive results. Besides, the Knights were a part of your compensation for the war. They can't just take it back."

"We still have permission, just no support."

"They're asking you to disband. That doesn't sound like permission to me."

"But there are no consequences listed if I don't. So there is no way to enforce it."

"They'll find one if we defy them."

"Disbanding the Knights is not an option. Period."

"I feel like this was not a unanimous decision." Starlight pitched in, her eyes still concentrated on knitting the scarf in her hands.

Fangbane took a look at the seal on the letter again. Sure enough, the shining gold seal was the emblem of the Council.

"I wonder who had the biggest mouth in this ruling…" Fangbane pondered, recalling how disoriented their decision-making process could be. He could only imagine that this decision too involved endless days of bickering.

"If you ask me, it's the work of Novinha." Gaven was disappointed in the Councilwoman from Minetta, suspecting she had organized the vote against them. "After we helped the Minettan merchants in Althaea, and even Region Leader Hilda, you'd think Novinha would be more on our side."

"Actually, I think Dareh is behind this," Fangbane grumbled.

"What makes you say that?"

"Novinha gains nothing from doing this." He rubbed his jaw, lost in thought.

"I don't see how it would help him, either," Gaven said.

Starlight was quick with her opinion. "Aah, but it would hurt his son. We all hear the way Dorain bitches about his father, and how he's trying to be better than him. Since Dorain loves being a Knight, it would please Dareh to no end to bring his son to heel. He wants to control everything in his son's life."

Fangbane nodded excessively. "Brilliant observation, my darling. The Council is a political circus, after all. They no doubt make things a personal matter."

"Why don't I have a little heart-to-heart with Dorain," mused Starlight. "Maybe we can find something to, ah, persuade his father to overcome his reservations."

"Like what?" Gaven asked.

"I don't know yet…" Starlight gave a little shrug. "But a little blackmail is always effective. I'll see what I can come up with."

With that, she made a cheery exit from the study, leaving Fangbane and Gaven in a daze.

"Remind me to stay on her good side," Gaven muttered, watching her close the door behind her.

Gaven could tell how much this project meant to Fangbane. He was willing to protect it at all costs as if it was the only thing he had ever wanted in his life. It made him suspicious.

"Fangbane, I must ask for your honesty," Gaven began.

"I will be as frank with you as possible."

"What relation do you have with 'the Blessed'?"

"I'm not sure what you're implying." His voice grew cold, daring Gaven to continue.

"You gave me a file on them. Did you know that the Blessed is an organization seeking to overthrow our political system?"

"I did."

"Is that what the Knights are? A division of the Blessed?"

Fangbane turned his body to face him and leaned in closely. If it weren't for the mask, Gaven would've felt his flaring breath brush against his skin. His long pause made the quiet of his study feel as still as the graveyard.

"We… are *not*… the Blessed. We fight to protect the Council, region leaders, politicians, and mayors, not scheme against them."

Gaven stood as firm as ever, unwavering in the wake of Fangbane's rare loss of calm and control. "So you created the Knights because you knew they existed?"

He began to pull away from Gaven, returning to his relaxed state, and paced along the edge of the room.

"I didn't know if they were real or not. I've only heard rumors, as you have. But if we can make our current world a better place, show them that putting together our strengths can eliminate our hardships, groups like the Blessed wouldn't need to exist."

While he respected Fangbane's goals, Gaven couldn't make

himself feel as dedicated to the cause. Yes, he was proud of what they had accomplished. But he still believed there were issues far beyond their control. Gaven felt a sense of duty to help the Knights, if only to repay the debt he owed to Fangbane for sparing his life. But once his job training them was complete, that debt was repaid. He wasn't sure if he wanted to stick with the Knights after that.

He was in no position to. One day, he assumed, he would have more personal duties to worry about. Once he returned to his role as region leader, that would be his only focus.

"I gave you that file," Fangbane spoke up again, "because I think the Blessed were the ones who possessed you. That's why the Council swept it under the rug. They pretend the Blessed doesn't exist to avoid public chaos. I just don't have any evidence to prove such wild theories."

Gaven's jaw dropped in disbelief. How had he failed to see the connection before? Still, without any evidence of their existence, no specific name to work off of, there was no one to go after. The Blessed were just someone to blame for all things evil.

"You believed in my innocence. Is that why you convinced the Council to spare me?"

Gaven fixed his look on Fangbane's mask, waiting for the news.

Seeing the desperate need to know in Gaven's eyes, Fangbane confessed.

"To be honest, your execution was none of my business. Whatever the Council was going to decide, I was resolved to respect it."

"What? But I..." Gaven was shocked by his answer. "You stood up for me."

"I defended you, yes," he said. It was hard to say the rest. "But I stood up for Mirari."

Gaven tilted his head, unsure of how these dots connected. "Mirari...? I don't..."

"She came to me. Begged for your life to be spared," Fangbane said. "So, I made a deal with her."

"A deal… but what, I mean… why?"

"She agreed she would join the Knights, but only if I would fight to convince the Council to spare your life."

Fangbane vividly recalled the day Mirari approached him at the Hearth. It was a bold and selfless move that he never would've expected from anyone, and he admired it.

"But that… it makes no sense. I was just a stranger to her."

"Are you so certain of that?" Gaven's eyes darted away from the question, as he changed his focus. "And you? What did it matter to you if she joined the Knights?"

"She didn't want to, believe me. To this day, honestly, she still doesn't."

"Then why did you force her? She isn't even a skilled fighter. What's so special about her that you needed her to join the Knights?"

Fangbane turned away to run his finger along a shelf of books, and Gaven was getting antsy with puzzlement.

"Are you looking for an answer there in the Classics? Answer me."

Fangbane turned back to Gaven.

"When Mirari was fighting you during the Althaean Siege, she did something no one else could."

"You mean that fire ability you all claim she has? I'm telling you, she doesn't have enough kore to—"

"It's not kore. It's more than that. I still don't understand it, and neither does she. Her memory is as hazy as yours, but I'm confident that both of you lost your memory from separate causes."

"What has that to do with the Knights?"

"Everything. Gaven, I always believed you were truly possessed. And that girl… whatever she did, it was the only way to knock you out of that trance. She has something special, a power, something unique. And I mean to find out what it is."

"So, you're saying if anyone else ends up like I did, she would be the only one who could stop it?"

"Her fire might be the only thing to hold back the Blessed."

PART III

CHAPTER NINETEEN

"**P**oint up your spears, or you'll never survive your first charge. That's it. Brace yourself. I want to see those spear-shafts bending when you strike… Sokal!"

Sokal flinched beneath the weight of the spear he held pressed against the training dummy with the blunted end of the spearhead. Sweat ran down his face, and his hands began to slip on the rough wood. The damp earth was slick beneath his feet, and the air had a musty, wet smell from the rainstorm that had slowed down to a drizzle. He was soaked and chilly despite the warmth in the air.

He glanced nervously at Teng, who was now stomping past the row of boys, all bigger than Sokal. Sokal tried his best to emulate the others, but his arms were easily half the thickness of most of them.

The spear was particularly heavy that evening. After ten hours of training in the rain, his right elbow finally buckled and gave out on him. To his horror, the spear point slipped from the dummy and planted itself into the mud at Teng's feet.

"Clean it up and get back into position," he growled as his jaw took on a scowl. *Useless, waste of my time.*

Sokal flinched as anxiety and frustration came over him. He could hear the instructor's thoughts clearly in his mind. It was an ability he had from birth, a curse from his mother. Teng was standing too close for Sokal to be able to ignore the man's oppressive presence.

Gritting his teeth, Sokal cleaned the spear tip with his palm and reset his position. The spear shaft continued to slip between his sticky, dirt covered palms, the blunt point wavering before the dummy.

Pathetic. Teng stepped behind him. "Now strike."

Sokal glanced at the other boys, all standing with spears up, watching him.

"Focus, Sokal. Head up. Eyes ahead. You are one with the spear. Let it become an extension of yourself. Now strike!"

Sokal grit his teeth and pulled back, all of his strength went behind it, and the spear struck. The shaft didn't flex but sent a small puff of dust rising from the sackcloth dummy.

He expected laughter, but the silence he received was much worse. Teng stepped in closer, his breath brushing against Sokal's ear.

"When your father sent you to me, I thought I was getting a true son of Sarkan. Your father is arriving tomorrow. I'd hoped to show him a warrior worthy of his name."

Teng put down his own spear in a gesture of giving up and turned away in disgust. He called out for the rest of the trainees to resume their drills. Sokal bit back tears of embarrassment. His father, a commander of Saon, had duties which seldom allowed him within a hundred miles of home. Sokal's mother raised him to study literature and science. He'd been restricted to quiet libraries and religious studies. Never had his father taught him a thing about holding a spear, or any weapon for that matter. He hated it.

He should just stay in a library.

He's so weak.

What were they thinking, letting him come here?

All around him, he was bombarded by his comrade's thoughts of disapproval. It was the worst thing about being here. His ability to hear their thoughts was a double-edged sword. He knew what people were thinking, but he also took on their emotions and experiences. He felt not only his grief and torture but also that of those around him. If he could, Sokal preferred to not be able to hear at all.

Teng's voice brought him back to the muddy courtyard. "Strike!"

Thud. The spear struck the dummy as Sokal tried to force away from the barrage of thoughts and emotions.

Thud.

Is he even trying?

Thud.

I can't believe the son of Lord Sarkan is that pitiful.

Thud.

Some people just aren't cut out to be a fighter.

THUD.

Sokal stopped, panting and shaking from the exertion, his eyes downcast.

Freak.

Sokal looked up at the boy next to him, a tall boy that moved like a panther. His name was Aulus.

"What did you say?"

The boy simply smiled, reaching out his hand. "We all start somewhere. Don't be so hard on yourself."

His smile eased Sokal's tensions as he reached for his hand, thankful that someone was bothering to interact with him.

Sokal was distracted by the sound of Teng's whistle, directing his attention to the rest of the trainees. "Time to clean up. We have a big day tomorrow."

Sokal turned back to Aulus, but found that he had left already. His heart sank, as his hope that he had finally made a friend in this crew broke into pieces. He should have known that it was too good to be true.

Although he was saddened by Aulus' quick disappearance, he wanted the evening to himself. As his comrades dragged themselves back to their tents, Sokal crept down a path on the side of the hill, one that he knew would lead to the herb gardens.

THE HERB GARDEN was open for anyone to walk through, though picking anything without permission was strictly forbidden. He had no interest in plucking the herbs. Instead he was there to admire the fragrant plants. It was a way to calm his mind.

His favorite display was a large water fountain with an ancient statue of a warrior in the middle. The statue's torso was worn with age, blunted and chipped away. Only the right shoulder and arm remained undamaged. The fountain was festooned with lichen, creeper vines, and many exotic herbs and fungi that clung to the stone. Sokal imagined the warrior wearing a uniform of green.

Sokal took a deep breath and closed his eyes. He tried to release his mind, letting it expand across the garden. It was a technique his mother had taught him to grasp the sense of every life force around him. Birds, plants, water, even the air surrounding him. These pure thoughts brought tranquility and peace to his mind. The plants never spoke, but the life inside them gave off a feeling as if they were singing. He tried to absorb their song, to make himself forget about the rough time he was having at the camp.

Engrossed in this moment, he felt a strange tingle interrupt his rapture. It was like a mental tug from his left, pulling him toward the cliff side beyond the railing. He tried to ignore it as a passing distraction, but the feeling only grew more insistent. He allowed his awareness to shift toward the cliff. He could no longer hear the vegetation's life song, only the sense of distress coming from the other side of the rail.

It was a person in danger on the cliff.

Snapping out of his trance, Sokal raced to the railing and looked over the edge. A network of terraces, steps, and ladders were arranged on the cliff face, with a rocky patch of ground some hundred feet below. His eyes swept the cliff urgently, searching for a sign of the person whose thoughts he had felt. He spotted something on the third terrace from the top. He could see nothing more than a pair of hands grasping at the ledge. He leaned farther, and saw a girl his age clawing desperately for a handhold.

Adrenaline overtook him, and he leaped over the railing, barely touching the rungs of the ladder as he descended. He skipped over the second terrace, then the third, and sprinted toward the dangling figure as fast as possible. Her fingers were at the last knuckle as he dove and snatched her hand as it released its hold.

He heard her scream and his shoulder felt as though it was being pulled out of its socket. Gritting his teeth, he worked his way to his knees, pulling with all his might. Though he struggled, he succeeded in getting his other hand around hers. She used her feet to push off against the edge as Sokal pulled her up. She made it up and over, and the sudden release sent them both tumbling in a heap.

They lay there panting for a brief moment before he sat up. "Are you all right?"

The girl got up and began brushing herself off. "I am now, thanks."

"Just fortunate enough to have heard you."

She squinted at him. "I didn't call for help." She grew suspicious. "Were you watching me?"

"What? No, I swear. I didn't even know there were more terraces on this side of the garden, let alone you being here."

She didn't believe him.

"I am grateful, but how did you know?"

Sokal stopped himself for a moment. The more he stared at the girl, the more he felt like he was reaching into her mind. It was pure, much like the herbs around him. Their auras were nearly identical.

Sokal decided he could trust her. "I-I can read minds."

"Oh?" She cocked her head to the side inquisitively before frowning at him. "What am I thinking now?"

Sokal waited for her to think of something. It came rushing in like a vivid memory. Through her eyes, he saw her hand reaching for a fully-bloomed yellow flower over the ledge. She managed to pluck the flower but lost her footing in the process. The flower wisped away far beyond her reach. She grabbed onto the closest ledge with one hand, unable to pull herself up.

"You were stealing herbs?" Sokal's mouth dropped open, almost wanting to confront her for it. But her oppressive glare made him hesitant to speak.

With her arms crossed on her chest, she tested him further. "What color was it?"

"Yellow. But… why would you steal it?"

Sokal quieted down as he realized the girl was responding to him with her thoughts.

This plant hasn't bloomed in the wild for forty years. It has a healing power that can cure nearly any human-transmitted disease. The nobles have been keeping it to themselves. Do you understand? They want the commoners to stay sick so that they exert power over them.

Hearing her voice in his mind felt like a melody of tumbling leaves. He could sense that her intention was pure, and her words were heartfelt. Having lived around backstabbing authorities all his life, he knew what evil felt like. She was not one of them.

"I'm… sorry."

You're a noble, aren't you?

"I am."

"Wow, you really can read my mind." She reached out her hand to him. "Fareeha."

He took her hand and shook it. "My name's Sokal."

Sokal, you have a powerful gift. Imagine if you could use that gift to change the minds of others.

His forehead wrinkled at the thought. He had never been confident enough to persuade others. Besides…

"I can't control other people's minds. I wouldn't want to either. It wouldn't be honorable."

"Not control, persuade."

"My father would never allow me to get into politics. My duty is to him and the region leader."

"I don't have to be psychic to know that's a stupid excuse." She squinted and held her fist to her mouth. "You should come with me."

"Come where?"

He caught an image of a boat on the ocean. Fareeha was there along with two other hard-looking men armed to the teeth. Though it was frightening, he couldn't help but entertain the idea.

"I… can't." He was stammering.

"Fine, but if you change your mind, I am leaving at sunrise." She turned away from him, and proceeded to climb down the ladder leading to the lower terrace. She paused at the top rung. "It was nice meeting you, Sokal, and… thanks." She winked and smiled at him and disappeared down the ladder.

He stood there for a while and stared at the sun as it sank low into the horizon.

SOKAL AWOKE SUDDENLY. It was hours later, and the rest of the troop had filtered into the tent. Peeking from his covers, he could barely make out the shapes of the others upon their cots. But a strange aura made him feel uneasy. Where was it coming from?

His heart froze for a moment as a pair of legs strode past his bed, stopping before him for a moment before moving on and out of the tent. Sokal shook with fright. The shadow left an eerie mark in his mind. There was something dark and sinister hanging about it.

Sokal pulled the sheet off his head, his eyes still fixated on the entrance of the tent. Something told him to follow the stranger. Regardless of whether it was his duty as a soldier or out of sheer curiosity, he knew he wouldn't be able to go back to sleep without finding out who it was.

Thankfully he'd fallen asleep with his training clothes and cloak on. He left his boots behind for the advantage of silence as he moved through the sea of cots and out into the night.

The air was chilly, but the dewy grass hadn't yet gone to frost. Closing his eyes, Sokal scanned the direction the figure had gone and found that it was heading away from camp toward the edge of the steppes, leading into the deep woods. Instinctively his hand went to his belt to ensure he was armed; it wasn't much, but it was better than nothing.

As soon as he entered the woods, he caught an unprecedented change in the smell and feel of the air. The moonlight filtered through the deep shadows beneath the trees and deadfall. Heavy underbrush became wells of darkness. It concealed the person he pursued.

Cursing silently, he closed his eyes and listened for movement. He was overwhelmed as all of the surrounding forest's life energy, insects, rodents, and worms, overpowered him. For a moment, he felt nothing but awe for what he was experiencing.

Sokal opened his eyes again, realizing he was giving into the distraction. He couldn't sense the presence of the person he was pursuing or any human being for that matter. Hesitantly, he continued forward, farther away from the camp and into darkness.

"Ha! I knew it."

As soon as Sokal heard the voice, he turned to the sky, his eyes searching for the source. Something leaped from a branch overhead, and he sensed it move away from him silently in the air, a bird, most likely an owl.

Before he could look back down, he felt a cold blade touch the back of his neck. Sokal flinched, unaware that the person he was pursuing had trapped him. He raised both hands over his head.

"Got ourselves a little spy here now, do we?"

Sokal immediately recognized the voice. It was Aulus, the boy whose presence gave him an uneasy feeling.

"Why are you following me?"

"I wasn't."

"You would never come here willingly, even to piss."

"I…"

"Quiet." He gently shoved him with the handle of the blade against his back. "I saw the way you looked at me. Do you think I don't know? My father trained me in the old ways. He trained me to kill freaks like you. What's the matter, empath? Can't read my mind now?"

It was true. Aulus was good at hiding his thoughts. Sokal couldn't hear a thing.

The blade came away from Sokal's neck, and the boy turned him around. The moon enhanced Aulus' menacing features as he glowered down at him, easily a head taller.

Aulus moved away and circled to Sokal's left. "What would happen if the region leader found out about your power? Would he award you with a high position by his side, or would he think you're too dangerous to live?"

Sokal kept his hands raised as Aulus continued to orbit him

with the blade pointed at him. "I'm not doing it on purpose, I swear! I can't control it."

Sokal turned his head, following Aulus' footsteps in the darkness, when a vision flashed in his mind.

It was his father lying dead on the ground with his throat cut. A crowd of people gathered about the corpse. A knife lay beside the body, bloody and familiar to him. It was the knife Sokal had in his belt, engraved with the crest of his family house.

Sokal blinked himself back to reality. How those thoughts came to his mind was a mystery… unless… Aulus was planting them in his mind.

"If you can't control it, then how are we supposed to trust you?" Aulus' voice had faded further behind him, and Sokal turned but couldn't see him. The hair on the back of his neck rose, and he tried to sense him, but Aulus kept his thoughts locked up.

"You have no place in this world, freak."

Sokal heard the sound of an object gliding in the air and promptly spun, dodging Aulus' attack from behind. Aulus lost his footing, having missed Sokal and stabbed at nothing. He turned and charged at Sokal with the knife again.

Sokal grabbed hold of Aulus' wrist with both hands. The blade swung back and forth wildly, Sokal trying to push it away and Aulus trying to push forward.

"The Blessed has determined your fate. Now die with honor!"

"No, I can't…" Sokal thought back on Fareeha's words. She gave him light, a hope that he had a greater purpose, and he wanted to believe her. He couldn't let her down. "I won't die here tonight!"

Sokal let out a scream as he pushed forward with all of his body weight, charging Aulus into the nearest tree. Aulus' body bounced off the stump. The blade, now pointed at his chest, followed a split second later. With the force of both Aulus' and

Sokal's hands pressed against the hilt, the blade lodged into Aulus' chest.

He coughed up blood as he fumbled to try to pull the blade out of his body. Sokal stepped back, terrified of what he had done. He didn't want Aulus to die, but he didn't want to help him either.

Aulus lost his balance and fell forward. As his body hit the ground, the knife shoved in deeper. He laid there lifeless, his face on the ground.

Sokal stared at the dead boy. The enormity of what he'd just done struck him hard, and he became sick; gagging on an empty stomach, he held himself up taking support of a tree. His eyes were wide with shock. He had doomed himself, dishonored his family.

"You there, Sokal? What's going on?"

Sokal reeled around to see Teng. Not far behind trotted the region leader's second in command, Maddock Grint, and his father, Commander Sarkan of Saon.

Teng only then noticed Aulus' body on the dark earth. "Don't move." The man drew his sword and stepped toward Aulus' body. He had one eye on Aulus, checking his vitals while keeping the blade pointed at Sokal.

"I didn't mean to," Sokal defended himself. "It was an accident."

"He's dead." Teng stood back from Aulus' fallen corpse. He turned to his two superiors, waiting for their judgment.

"What's the meaning of this, Sokal?" his father roared, almost in disbelief that his spineless son was capable of committing murder. His father was lithe and dressed in dark black and crimson clothes, carrying an air of cold authority. Sokal's heart sank. He couldn't read his father – he never could. Sokal had always figured that his father had learned to protect himself early on after meeting his mother.

"It was self-defense!" Sokal pleaded. "He attacked me first. And… and he fell. I didn't do it."

The men peered at the blade lodged in Aulus' chest and thought otherwise.

Sokal's eyes widened. It was likely Aulus brought him out there knowing they would cross paths.

"I would like to speak to my son alone," his father said. But Sokal knew the chances of his father believing his story were close to none.

"There is nothing to speak of." Maddock Grint denied his request, pointing once again at the dead body. "Your son has clearly committed murder."

"But—"

"Teng, inform His Honor of the tragedy that has taken place. Schedule this boy's execution for tomorrow in the courtyard."

Before Teng could respond, Sarkan objected, "You can't."

"I can, and I will. Such crime will not go unpunished in this region."

Despite the fear and panic swarming in Sokal's mind, he noticed a faint breath of emotion from his father. For the first time since his mother's death, Sokal felt a hint of sadness in his father's heart. It was followed by confusion, anger, and distrust.

Then a flash of violence. His father debated drawing his sword to kill both of them, eliminating all witnesses, just to save his son.

Sokal couldn't tell if he was serious; it was a move he never expected his father to make just for him. Sokal could feel his mysterious thoughts amplified. It was soothing and warm, like…

Love?

Sarkan's eyes shot up to his son. He was not mad, nor did Sokal feel that he was going to shout at him. The warm feeling was an unsettling one as if his father was ready to say goodbye.

Maddock spoke up once again.

"Since he is your son, Sarkan, I'm willing to offer you a second choice. May the boy learn his lesson when he realizes what a privilege it is to be able to hear and follow the orders of those he serves."

Maddock moved up next to Sarkan, pulling the knife from his belt and handing it to him with grace. Sarkan looked down at the blade, now in his hand.

"An ear for an honorable discharge and his life will be spared."

Sarkan stared at the knife as though it were a snake. "You cannot…"

"This is the price for your son's life."

The knife wavered in his father's shaking hand, and Sokal relented.

Sokal's thoughts returned to Fareeha and her boat, wondering if he had made the wrong decision in choosing to stay. If he had gone, the boy's life would've been spared and he wouldn't have dishonored his family. Now he would surely be expelled from the army, his family name tarnished. It would benefit everyone if he just disappeared.

Maybe it wasn't too late to change his fate…

Sokal leaned forward, eyes wet with emotion, yet not a tear fell. Sokal felt his father's anger directed at Maddock and watched his hand tighten on the grip of his knife. Sokal reached out and grabbed his hand gently.

"I will dishonor you no further, Father."

In a flash, Sokal took his father's knife. With one hand tugging at the end of his ear and the other holding the cold blade to his skin, he sliced it from the bottom up. He could feel blood running down the side of his neck, the smell of metal filling his nose. The world around him began to wobble. He felt no pain. His mind was clear, but he couldn't think.

Sokal saw the anguish in his father's face, his spirit filled with intense guilt and shame.

It was then that Sokal realized that something was different.

He wasn't feeling his own emotions at all. The shock from the pain had numbed him to his body. Dizzy, he dropped to a knee as his ear began to ring. A high-pitched stabbing sound dug into his brain.

Hearing had always been a curse to him. He was going to break this curse.

With resolve, Sokal held the wet blade up to his other ear.

This time there was pain, and a sudden flood of emotion came over him. Sokal felt its energy. He felt shock exude from the others as he stood stolidly holding his ears for them to see. The pain turned away from him.

"I, Sokal, son of Sarkan, am no more. I have no name and no life among the army of Saon. I reject you as you have rejected me."

He tossed the ears to the floor and became almost giddy at what he'd done. Standing there, he relished this decision as his and no one else's. It gave him strength, and he handed the knife, handle first, back to Maddock, who stared at him wide-eyed, impressed with Sokal's resolve.

To his surprise, he sensed respect and awe from Maddock as he accepted the knife. Maddock gestured toward the doors. "Go with grace, young one. You have served your sentence. I advise you never to return."

Sokal turned, his head buzzing with energy, as he began to feel lightheaded. He walked past his father and heard his words.

You will always be my son.

His father's words were spoken like a plea, begging him not to leave. They both were well aware that this may be the last time they would see each other.

His father wanted to say goodbye, but he didn't have the strength to speak. He focused on Sokal's bloody ears on the ground and listened to his footsteps tap against the soggy earth until he was gone.

Drifting on strange winds, he knew he was dreaming. Before him, he saw a single point of light that spoke to him. It was calling his name, and he felt love behind it. The light grew, and he reached out to it. The light enveloped his fingers, traveling up his arm and embracing him in white light.

It was an entity, he was sure of it, the entity wrapped him in a cocoon – it was like the blanket in his cot – comforting and warm. He felt safe and drifted over the cradling waves.

After some time, a crystalline voice called out his name, and he stirred in the cocoon. It didn't resist him, and he felt it remain as he began to smell the sea.

Sokal woke as his head thudded against something hard.

"Easy with his head, you idiots. I swear you dolts have no sense." It was her voice.

He couldn't make out any forms but registered the morning orange glow of the beach as it slowly moved away from him. Trying to remember what had happened, he dared to reach up to his ears and found them covered with bandages. A scent of pungent herbs hung about him.

"You're awake," said the young female voice. He finally dared to look around. Fareeha sat beside him, dressed in a heavy wool cloak to ward against the frigid night air. She smiled, her eyes glinting in the orange glow of the sunrise. Sokal blinked a few times. Her voice sounded like it was drowning in water.

Sokal glanced around at the two people – both men, burly and mean looking. One was pulling on oars as the other handled the rudder of the craft. Sokal watched them as they operated in unison, but could only hear muffled sounds.

You can't hear me? Well, that's expected. It'll take some time for your wounds to heal. But at least you can listen to me like this. I'm glad you were able to make it to the beach before we left.

Sokal had no memory of how he got there, but that didn't matter to him.

"Where… are we going?" Sokal said, but he couldn't hear his voice.

Far away from this place, where people need our help. Fareeha examined the patch of herbs wrapped around his ears, checking to make sure it was intact. *These men are from a resistance group. I'm bringing the flower back to their tribe.*

"Isn't that dangerous? The Council would kill you once they find you."

I'd rather die trying than to let those who do terrible things get away. She looked up at the stars, toward the far end where the light of the rising sun had not yet touched. *Most of all, I would like to help people – really help them, in my way, with the freedom to live as I wish to live. I want to show people the error of their ways – living in war and oppression that has caused chaos and grief… I'm tired of it. All I want is to have my own herb garden someday and to settle in peace.*

Sokal watched her, and he could imagine it. What if there was no division between the people any longer? What if the empires were unified?

He felt a pull – something bigger than himself and found that he deeply cared for this girl. He wanted her to have that garden someday.

"I wish I could help, but I'm no longer noble. There's no power to my name."

So let's pick new names. She looked up at the sky thoughtfully. *In the past, ancient heroes would take the names of constellations, or nature, but usually the constellations to remember them. What should my name be?*

Sokal looked up at the handful of stars in the sky that had yet to disappear. "You came to me in the darkest hour of my life as though fate itself was pushing us together. In darkness, you have been my saving light." He looked at her. "You are my Starlight."

He could feel her heart flutter as she let out a small gasp. *I like it. It's also the first letter of your name.* He felt a warmth bloom from her as she looked up at the stars, marveling at them. *You know, there is a legend among my people – the tale of the boy who stole the serpent's fang.*

When a terrible scourge came upon the land, many died. The only known cure laid in the venom of a great serpent's fang. A young boy, desperate to heal his dying mother, entered the caverns of the great serpent and took its fang as it slept. But he did not kill the serpent, and the serpent did not rouse in anger. The people were spared its wrath, and their lives were saved from the plague. He became known as the serpent bearer, bane of evil, and wielder of peace. His constellation is there, close to the horizon.

Sokal turned to where Fareeha pointed and saw a curving arc of five stars coiling over the shadowed peaks of mountains on the coast. It held him spellbound as he listened. He felt her move next to him, and she whispered close to his ear. Muffled and soft, it sent tingles down his spine.

"You are Fangbane."

CHAPTER TWENTY

I n Fangbane's room, Gaven pondered over their next course of action. Starlight's plan of using some form of blackmail on Dareh had been unsuccessful. Dorain's relationship with his father was more broken than she could ever imagine. Fangbane had written a heartfelt letter back, swearing to train Dorain into a fine fighter, but the letter returned with cold words. The man practically denied ever having a son.

Fangbane concluded, "Unfortunately, if we plan on keeping Dorain on the team, this is what we will have to put up with."

Gaven agreed. "Perhaps we were too hopeful after Hime resolved her issues with her father. Dareh is a different kind of windstorm. We have no leverage over him."

"Yes, family ties can be hard to break." Fangbane thought back on the day when he had to choose. Though it was decades ago, he could still feel the warm blood seeping down his neck as his hearing faded away. It was the price he had to pay for freedom, a choice he often looked back on with regret for leaving his father. But he never doubted his decision.

His heart sank, not knowing what became of his family after he left. Was his father still alive? Did he resent him? Does anyone still remember the son of Sarkan? Questions Fangbane would take to his grave.

"It also says 'stop sticking your buzzbean in religion'," Gaven read. Its inelegant writing and crooked position on the paper told him that it was added just before being sent off. "Sounds like something Dareh would write. What does that mean?"

"I assume it's referring to the Blessed. That means he knows we're trying to dig up evidence of their existence. Perhaps that's why he's so against his son getting involved."

"Ah, so if it isn't Dorain's daddy issues that shut down the Knights, it will be your nosiness."

"But in a way, he just admitted that the Blessed exist," Fangbane said as if he had won the battle, but Gaven knew it only put them in a more dangerous situation.

"So now what?" Gaven probed.

Fangbane leaned back in his chair. "We ignore them."

"That could be… dangerous."

"We're not shutting down. Period." Fangbane was calm. "I don't need their support or their gold. I have the resources to keep operations going."

Fangbane's stubbornness caused fumes to come out of Gaven's ears. "Defying the Council isn't something you can solve with money. Besides, how rich can you be? You don't make anything. You're not even a noble. You just have dozens of sponsors from who knows where."

"I'd say with our current expenditure, we can last… a little over a hundred years."

"You're kidding."

He heard a light snicker behind that solid mask. "No servants, fewer expenses. Besides, who said I wasn't a noble?"

Gaven rolled his eyes. "You're right. I wouldn't know. No one would know. But I bet most of those funds come from that Sorren guy, whoever he is. You probably have a whole drawer of letters from him alone."

It was no surprise to Fangbane that Gaven had caught a glimpse of his daily mail, so he played along.

"Most of our funds come from a new investor in the Hale family," Fangbane explained.

Hearing the name sent butterflies through Gaven's stomach. Memories that he had long buried struck him like lightning, and he could feel his heart pounding harder. He wondered… was it the person he was thinking of?

"A Valenian," Fangbane said. "He has shown interest in becoming a Knight. He is on his way as we speak."

"He?" Gaven was mildly disappointed, but still just as curious. "I thought you were capping the Knights at five."

"He's from Valenia. If we are going to appeal to the three empires, we should include people from all three empires on our team."

"That's what I've been trying to tell you. And… there's no doubt that someone from the Hale family will be beneficial to the team." Gaven was still curious as to who this person was. Would he be like the Hale he once knew or the materialistic mammon that she claimed they all were?

Fangbane nodded. "Perhaps with the support of the Hale family, the Council will reconsider its decision. But until then, we ignore them. And if they send the royal guards to our doorstep, we will defend the estate with all we have."

Gaven shrugged with defeat. He knew Fangbane was ready to defend the Knights project with his life. On the other hand, Gaven wasn't willing to commit career suicide.

"Before they do kick us out, let's speed things up, shall we? What of Mirari? She should be off probation now, no? And she is becoming quite a fine warrior, don't you think? Practically fights like you. How much longer are you going to hold back from granting her badge?"

Gaven shook his head in response. It wasn't the first time he asked, and his query was more of a nudge, but Gaven did not deny that Mirari now had the capabilities of a noteworthy fighter. She had, for a while. But the fact that she was only here because of Fangbane — serving the Knights in exchange for mercy on his life at the trial — was stopping him from declaring her as an official Knight. If she didn't want to become a Knight, then granting her a badge would feel like branding a slave.

She has to want it, Gaven thought, as if he was telling Fangbane directly. And Fangbane nodded, acquiescing to Gaven's justification.

"Here is a task that will hopefully change your mind." Fangbane handed him a piece of paper with a poorly drawn map scribbled on it. It looked like he spent no more than a few seconds on it.

"Take Mirari with you to get some Luxaniform Alponia."

"The wha-?" Gaven stammered, trying to comprehend the drawing given to him.

"You'd call it lumapetal. They're very useful for medicine. Starlight is nearly out of it."

"Why Mirari and I?"

"Those are the mountains by Solarin. No one will be more familiar with that area than her. You can use that travel time to catch her up to speed."

Gaven mumbled something to himself, too low for Fangbane to hear, but he didn't need to. Fangbane knew he didn't like running errands.

But Gaven knew it was time to put Mirari back on the field, and the long journey would give them enough time to reflect and deal with their problems.

GAVEN CHECKED in on her later that day, and found her curled in one of the small velvet nooks in the library. She chose the one with a view of the back forest, the sun bright and refreshing, but unless one admired seeing the same type of tree over and over again, it was a bland sight. She paid no attention to the scenery, just the book in her lap on the history of Valenian fighters.

"Good morning," Gaven said. "How are you feeling now?"

Mirari didn't bother meeting his eyes. She kept her gaze on the book. "I'm fine. Always have been." But when she felt he was still staring at her, she clapped the book shut impatiently. "What? Is there something you want to say, or are you just going to keep staring?"

"I do have things to say. But first, let's get a little sunshine and fresh air."

He guided her out of the library, and to the courtyard. He was still mysteriously quiet, puzzling her even more when he led her onto a path that meandered into the forest.

"I don't have my bow… if we're going hunting," she said, rolling her eyes and pretending to turn around to go get it.

"I guess you could say we're hunting. Or searching for something, anyway."

"What is it? A leprechaun with a pot of gold?"

Gaven just smiled. "You'll see."

They climbed a steep trail, picking their way up a rocky hill until they reached the peak. The view from the summit took in almost the entire island. Scattered pockets of floating cotton hovered over iridescent meadows of shrubbery and wildwood. Mirari noted glittering streams that she never knew existed. It was breathtaking.

"Worth the climb, isn't it?" Gaven said, sweeping his arm across the vista.

"I'm so… this is amazing. I had no idea the island was so big!" She was as excited as a child. "Look at the pond, there. And that river. I can practically see the trout jumping."

"I can hear you stretching the truth." Gaven gestured for her to take a seat on a flat stone pavement, and then sat down directly in front of her, and crossed his arms. "Now… close your eyes."

"Why?" she asked, suspicious.

"Test time. Can you recite the three virtues of the Paragon's Conduct?"

She rattled them off without hesitation. "Courage, Justice, and Loyalty."

"Good."

"Of course, I am good. You made me memorize the whole damn book." She turned to look at him. "Is that what we came up here for? Are you going to quiz me?"

"Not exactly," he said, his voice calm and cool. "But we are going to search for some answers."

"Answers to?"

"In an honest self-evaluation, which of those virtues do you currently possess?" He asked her this in a gentle, non-confrontational tone.

But Mirari remained silent. She didn't know how to answer. She should've seen a question like that coming, but frankly, it had never crossed her mind.

"Your silence is appropriate, Mirari. At this point, I don't see you display any of these qualities."

She opened her eyes, stung, glaring at him. "Excuse me? I've done everything you asked, and—"

Gaven cut her off. "And yet, you dread being here at all. You work when I ask. But your heart is always somewhere else."

"You know nothing about my heart," she said, looking grim.

"I know that it's still chained to your past." She didn't deny it.

"Says the paragon who refuses to have a partner. You're one to talk."

He rolled his eyes. He didn't like it when people brought that up. There was more to that story compared to the public version everyone knew, but he brushed it aside. "Yes, you have trained very hard. You've made tremendous physical progress, far more than I expected."

"Then what's the problem? What more do you expect from me?"

"More. So much more. And I think you have it, locked inside you." He turned, seeing a tear swimming in the corner of her eye. She was determined not to let it spill, though. "Courage, Justice, and Loyalty. They are more than words. To attain the three virtues, you need to go forward and never look back. Now close your eyes again."

When she closed them, a single tear escaped her eyelids.

"I'm telling you this because I believe you do have all three virtues inside you. That's extraordinary, believe me. Very few paragons have all three. But you? It takes tremendous courage to fight in a war. Through the missions, I've seen you stand your ground on what you believe is right, even if it defies tradition. And you are dedicated in everything you do, loyal to the people by your side. The three virtues are within your grasp, if only you surrender your doubts. I was hoping that during your time off, you would reflect on your commitment to these virtues."

"Why didn't you say that?"

"I hoped you would come to it on your own. But I can see you need more guidance." She turned to him, opening her eyes. "Ah ah. No. Keep them closed. Quiet yourself. Just let go…"

He watched her face as it relaxed.

"Better. I'd like you to meditate now. Until I tell you to stop, let your mind focus on the three virtues. It may help you to envision something. A triangle, or a three-leaf clover. See them: Courage, Justice, Loyalty. You are so capable, Mirari. If only you can let yourself push forward. Your past has brought you many fears. Leave them behind, and face only the future."

Mirari did as he instructed without a word in response. She sat up straight and closed her eyes, focusing on the wind, visualizing it passing through her body. Gaven observed for a few minutes. She was as steady as the rocky cliffs of Nanaka. When she didn't move in the slightest, he found himself impressed at how much her concentration had improved.

Mirari felt a peace she had not known before. She realized she could trust Gaven, and do what he asked of her without hesitation. She remained still, her eyes closed, her focus held on the wind that gently danced around her, letting herself feel it slide tirelessly on her skin.

Gaven locked his eyes on her. He paid attention to the rhythm of her breathing, and found himself pacing his breaths with hers. Without any conscious decision, he found himself joining her in the meditation.

CHAPTER TWENTY-ONE

"This area is infested with griffins," Mirari said, as they trudged up a steep goat trail. "I can't believe Lord Fangbane wants us to get lumapetals."

"Couldn't we just buy it in Solarin?" Gaven said.

"It's a lot more potent when they're freshly plucked. I admit, despite these mountains being close to Solarin, lumapetals can be hard to come by. They're almost always guarded by griffins, and most herbalists aren't fighters."

They plodded deeper into the snow-covered mountains until they found a medium-sized cave and went to explore. They each held a luminous crystal to guide their way into the dark cave.

Mirari scanned the corners of the wall for a faint light. The flowers they were looking for gave a soft pink glow when in full bloom. Most only bloomed in the darkest and most wet parts of the cave.

She caught sight of a few bulbs and plucked them. There weren't many, but the presence of a few was a sign that they should venture deeper into the cave.

Gaven's attention drew to the splattering sounds his feet made over the shallow puddles of the damp cave. A medium-sized feather blew into the radius of his light, dancing between their feet, then vanished into the darkness. Then another. And another. He grew suspicious.

"The aura around us is tense," Mirari spoke up, but her eyes were still searching the cave for lumapetals.

Gaven blinked twice, not expecting her to be thinking the same thing. It took immense concentration to read the aura in the atmosphere. He opened his mouth, ready to compliment her, but decided to let it go.

"My bet is those overgrown chickens aren't hibernating," Gaven agreed.

Several minutes later, they reached a part of the cave so vast that their light could not touch the walls. But on the ground, they saw faint patches of swaying pink light that could've been easily mistaken for dancing fireflies. They rushed to the glowing flowers and plucked them until their pouches were filled to the top with lucent bulbs.

"That should be enough. Let's hurry and get out of here," Gaven said.

They could hear low growls accompanied by the tap of slow-paced footsteps splashing through the wet caves. Gaven and Mirari looked at each other and kept quiet as a griffin walked into their line of sight, sniffing around the den for their scent.

Gaven nudged his head toward the direction they came from, and Mirari nodded. They stored their lumastōnes back into their pouches, and the cave became pitch black. One careful step after the other, they crept toward the side of the cave, their hands wavering in the air until they felt the chilled edges of the wall.

Their hands glided against slippery moss as they staggered to the exit in darkness. But one misstep and Gaven kicked a small rock that bounced and echoed through the cave.

The winged beast perked up, attentive to the sound of the fumbling stone. It turned its head toward the direction of the sound and took another whiff of the air.

Amplified through the narrow passage, a high-pitched screech pierced their ears. Gaven wanted to cover them, but then he felt the ground rumble, followed by a strong funnel of whisking wind.

His instincts told him to reach for his spear. He pulled the compact stick from his back pocket, and it expanded in his hand. His other hand irradiated a soothing teal aura. As he slid it across his weapon, it immersed into the kore, transforming the basic pole into a gleaming, fortified spear. Its rough edges shone as if it were made of ice, illuminating the walls in pulsing blue light, just far enough for him to see the incoming opponent.

Mirari joined in, hoping to lend a hand. Her eyes darted left and right, trying to follow the chaotic gust in the tunnel. Once she was confident, she stretched her arms wide to absorb the element. The wind became confined in a ball around her body, whipping her hair in all directions. With the wind not pushing him off balance, Gaven could take a clean strike.

He took two prideful strides toward the inner cave, each step cracking the ground like eggshells. On the third step, a curtain of rocks rose moments before the first beast could reach him.

But the headstrong feline did not stop and plowed into the rough wall, shattering it to boulders of all sizes. It fumbled to the ground like tumbleweed, but the ground continued to vibrate. Its allies were close behind, Gaven and Mirari had no idea how many.

Mirari swept her hands forward, redirecting the wind to lift the mixture of gravel, dirt, and boulders. They were carried away in the gust and rained on whatever was in the shadows. The stones struck the beasts' wings and limbs forcing them to cover their heads under a veil of feathers, but pebbles were not enough to scare them away.

Gaven charged ahead with a valiant cry, leaping high in the air and taking a strike at the closest griffin with its head tucked under its wings. Blood splattered against the walls and slid down his tainted glowing spear. He had decapitated the beast with a clean cut. His eyes were drawn to its large brown feathers, which were bathed in crimson. Now that he could see the creature up close, he noticed that its wingspan was almost as wide as the cave itself. Its razor-like talons were longer than its beak, and Gaven knew he was lucky to have gotten the first strike.

He was engrossed in his assessment of the corpse for too long and didn't notice the dilated pair of beady eyes that flew toward him. It plowed its feathery head into his abdomen, with a force strong enough to lift his body and catapult him back toward Mirari. Before he could lift his head, he heard a loud thud.

The bird flew head first into a shimmering shield, and Mirari's feet slid slightly from the impact. Her barrier of kore was just enough to shield both of them. With talons as sharp as her sword, it began to swipe at the shield in an endless frenzy.

"I got this!" Mirari called out, and Gaven sought the chance to strike back.

"Lose the shield. Follow me," he ordered as he ducked under her barrier and pointed his spear at the rabid creature. His blade slipped through its chest like butter as it shrieked and withered in pain.

At his command, Mirari dropped the barrier and unsheathed her own weapon. She kept her blade pointed up toward the last winged beast inching closer. It was too far to see, but she could hear its stout huffs and grunts with every stride. She focused and recited its rhythm.

It came within distance of Gaven's light, pouncing with the sturdy legs of a saberlion. Its eyes were locked on Gaven, ready to avenge its friend.

Mirari leaped over him and delivered a mighty blow with her sword. It knocked the griffin back with a large gash running down its furry chest. It gave Gaven enough time to free his weapon from the injured beast, which was now drawing its last breaths.

He followed with a swipe. The griffin clawed to defend itself; Gaven was only able to get away with a flesh wound. Mirari followed his lead and struck immediately after him, drawing another shallow cut into its skin. They continued to push the feline back, one blow after the other.

Without taking their eyes off of the furry opponent, Gaven noticed that Mirari had learned his movements and copied them exactly. He was beyond impressed, as he had yet to meet someone who was able to follow his pattern.

With another battle cry, Gaven slammed his gleaming spear on the ground, and the crust began to crack faster than a parched desert. Confused and spooked, the griffin stepped back and its hind paw fell through the unstable earth. A chunk of rubble fell through the hole, depth unknown; there was no sound as the rock hit bottom. Its wings spread and fluttered through the narrow cave, creating another cyclone of wind that forced Gaven and Mirari to cover their eyes with their arms. The griffin was desperate to save itself from the collapsing ground and lucky for them, the beast turned around and flew into the deep parts of the cave.

They only celebrated for a second before realizing that the ground beneath them was shaking again. Gaven and Mirari stepped back cautiously, trying to keep their balance, but it wasn't long before the ground gave in and they fell into a dark abyss.

GAVEN STOOD UP, trying to find a way out, before he felt needles in his ankle and cursed softly. It had twisted but was not broken. He waved his luminous crystal as high as he could, but he knew it would be useless. He only saw towers of rocks in all directions. The light couldn't reach the ceiling, and he didn't expect it to. Their freefall felt like an endless heartstopper. He knew there was no way they would be leaving from the same direction.

He moved his lumastōne around the edges of the cave, locating Mirari next to him. It was their only source of light, and they could barely see each other. She sat on the ground, surrounded by rubble, rubbing her shoulder.

"Are you hurt?" Gaven asked. Mirari had wrapped them in a ball of wind to soften their landing, but they undoubtedly still suffered injuries from the long fall.

"I just fell at a bad angle," Mirari said with a frown. "You?"

"It's nothing serious, but I can't imagine walking all the way back to the estate like this."

Gaven took out a renastōne from his satchel and gestured for Mirari to take a seat. He rubbed the green crystal between his hands until a faint light appeared, then he pressed the stone on her shoulder.

"Would be easier if you could do this yourself," he teased. Mirari gave him a playful glare.

"You're one to talk. Your healing is no better than mine. I believe they call it nonexistent."

Gaven moved the crystal over his own ankle. It was only enough to temporarily soothe the pain for both of them.

"I didn't expect those things to be so big," Gaven confessed as he checked his bag to make sure the goods were still secured. "They're twice as big as the ones in Althaea. What do your people feed them? Cattle?"

"We leave them alone." Mirari smirked while rolling her eyes. "We don't kill anything that doesn't need to be killed, especially if they're just defending themselves."

"All that mercy will be the death of you one day."

"Perhaps. But it's the way Minettans live, and it's the honorable way, wouldn't you agree?"

Gaven thought back to his younger self when he would've still considered himself a Minettan. He would've never been able to become the impregnable warrior he was if he had stayed. Still, he knew he would be lying to himself if he said he didn't miss those simpler days. She was right – Minettans knew how to live with honor.

"You Minettans aren't so bad after all."

"Same to you. I meant your personality. It's not so bad."

Gaven grinned a little. They were both used to each other's petty retorts by now.

Once he moved his light in the other direction, he noticed an opening that led into the depths of the cave.

"These caves usually have multiple exits," Mirari said as she looked around with intrigue. "But, there's no telling how far they go."

"If we follow the griffins, they should lead us to another exit." Gaven waved his crystal over the ground to look for feathers. He found a few scattered on the side.

Gaven stood up, holding onto the side of the wall for support to avoid putting pressure on his injured ankle. He peered into the dark cave, finding nothing but deep shadows.

"Let's get going."

Mirari pulled out her luminous crystal and followed Gaven deeper into the cave. There were more feathers accumulating to quite an alarming amount. They both feared that the beasts would appear in larger numbers.

"May I ask you something?" he asked, a little unsure, hoping that the conversation would ease their fears.

"What is it?"

"You made a deal to save my life. Why?"

"What do you mean?"

"My sentence. Fangbane told me."

"Oh. Did he now?" Mirari mumbled, rather disgruntled. She knew a day would come when he'd learn of her role in his release from his death sentence, and ask her to explain her deci-sion. But she had always pushed the thought away. Now, here it was, and Mirari wasn't sure how to give a safe answer to his question.

She was stuck in the fantasy of their childhood selves, hoping that when they reunited, everything would be exactly as it was a decade ago. But they had taken separate paths and so much had happened in between. For starters, she didn't use her birth name anymore. She had a new identity, one that she hoped would forever deviate from the Hale family. Gaven also had a new identity. He couldn't risk anyone knowing that he was born a Minettan, for it would mean all sorts of trouble with his status as an Althaean warrior and leader. She had come to terms that it was selfish of her to want to bring back both their former selves, which they had tried so hard to leave behind.

She must move forward.

Gaven grew impatient with her silence and reworded his question. "Why did you fight in the Althaean Siege?"

Mirari was still silent. Over time she had come to realize that there was another danger if Gaven found out they had been raised together.

Salathiel.

He had been Gaven's sibling, just as he'd been hers. She was starting to put aside the mystery of Salathiel's murder, but if Gaven discovered that a family member who shared his blood was taken by the Blessed, the same people who brainwashed him into career suicide, would he be able to hold back his rage? She wouldn't want him to go through the same pain she did. If the Blessed was truly a powerful, shadowy enemy, the best thing she could do for him was to prevent him from being absorbed with vengeance.

"You don't have to answer if it bothers you that much…" Gaven was disappointed, but he could see his prying was disturbing Mirari.

"No, you're right, I do owe you some explanation," she said. "I know I've been avoiding the question." With a slight waver in her tone, she began to reveal a partial truth. "When my brother disappeared, I swore to find the people who took him. But I didn't have any luck. When I tried to ask around, everyone just… went silent. No one wanted to give up information on the Blessed. Nobody would even admit they existed."

"How long ago was this?"

"Around the time the Althaean Siege began."

"And is that why you fought me? You thought there was some connection to his disappearance?"

Mirari almost said yes – that would be such a simple excuse to explain her behavior. It would avoid all the problems that were sure to follow if she told Gaven the truth.

But there was fear in how he would react. She'd tried to explain when she first met Gaven at the battlefield, but he had been so aloof and arrogant as he scoffed at her and rejected her. She had kept her secret from him all this time.

Now, the words just came out. "I went to Althaea… for you."

His reaction was immediate. He became flustered at her words, his confusion palpable. "Me? I don't… What possible reason could you…" He trailed off, truly baffled.

Again, she found herself trying to fill the gaps with half-truths.

"It was because… well, my brother, you see. He looked up to you. He admired you. The Valiant Tiger, the greatest fighter alive. And the truth is, he was always jealous of you. He knew that he could never be a fighter like you, but still you meant so very much to him."

"Even so… what did that mean to you?"

"I felt in some way that if anything happened to you…" She looked at him, the tears in her eyes stinging him as well. "I just… it was like the last flicker of him, the little spark that was still alive within me… it would fade away to nothing if you died as well…"

"So you joined in the fight to kill my rebellion and me with it? How does that make any kind of sense?"

"Not to kill you. To save you. I knew in my heart you weren't a killer. I couldn't just stay out of it, and let you die."

Gaven could sense that Mirari was sincere in what she was telling him. Yet somehow, this only increased his painful anxiety. His terrible ignorance, his unending guilt over the bloody rebellion spearheaded by him.

"I still can't… I don't know how you could see anything good inside me. To this day, I don't even remember what I was doing. All I know is that my actions resulted in a terrible slaughter. Whatever the reason, my heart was filled with black and evil violence. Perhaps I truly deserved to die."

"No, Your Honor. I have never questioned your innocence. I'm certain some dark power took over your mind. I believe it not just because of my faith in you, but because the same thing happened to me. I can't remember any more of our duel than you can. Nor can I explain it. Something took over me, I'm sure of that. Whatever I was doing, it wasn't me."

Gaven bit his lip, recalling a conversation he had with Fangbane months ago. If only the mystery behind both their memory loss was that simple. He had to admit he was starting to believe in Fangbane's fairytale theory.

"I'm not quite sure if what fogged my mind was the same as yours. I caused destruction. You stopped it. Why would the same force want us to fight with each other? No, Fangbane believes you have some vast and mysterious power inside you, Gods only know what. But he's sure that whatever overcame me, you were the only cure."

"And… is that what you think?"

"Me?" He could only shake his head. "Mirari, all I've ever seen of you is an impossible knot of contradictions. Who are you really? I have no idea."

"So? Why do you put up with me?"

He let out a snort. "I don't know. Maybe because we aren't so different after all. People expect things from me, and I turn and do the opposite. Your rebellious nature is a pain in my ass, but I wouldn't trade it for anything. The world needs more people like you."

Mirari smiled.

"Tell me, Mirari. Do you want to be a Knight? Do you truly want to be a part of Lord Fangbane's team? Or are you only here by force of your bargain?"

"At first, I was only here by the bargain, but…"

"But?"

"I've been asking myself that question for months. I never thought I was even remotely qualified to become any kind of warrior. Certainly not the kind of elite fighter to be eligible to join Fangbane's ambitious mission."

"I certainly would have agreed with you then." Before Mirari could respond, he added, "But you showed me I was wrong. You do have greatness in you, and you do belong here."

"What about you? Would you still stay with us if your probation ended?"

He shrugged. "From the start, my role here has been only to help Fang build the Knights. Sooner or later, the Knights won't need my help."

She couldn't hide her disappointment at this. "You mean you would leave us if you could?"

"I admit I've grown fond of the team, but…" Gaven's gaze fell to the floor. After a moment, he cleared his throat. "If I could go back to Althaea Main, I would do it in a heartbeat."

"That's what you want, then?"

"It's my duty. I'm a region leader before anything else."

She didn't like this but understood his loyalty.

He looked up again, meeting her eyes. "You still haven't answered. Are you here only because of your promise to Fangbane?"

"I'm not good enough to be a Knight. I was not born to fight. You've seen me, you know. I can't even heal a papercut."

"Then tell me this. Deep in your heart, do you truly believe that the Knights can make the three empires a more peaceful place? Perhaps even one unified nation?"

"Without a doubt, Your Honor. I just don't know if I'm the right person to help make it so. Shiba and Neo rule a region. Hime and Dorain are from powerful families. Me... I'm just a merchant."

"Fate works in strange ways, Mirari. Despite my doubts, I'm delighted you came here and joined us."

She looked up, surprised. It was unusual for Gaven to project such kindness, but his words were genuine and comforting.

"You may not be the best fighter, but you have enough willpower to command an army. The other Knights lack that burning drive you can bring, and that's what makes you essential to the team."

"What's that supposed to mean?"

"It means I'm granting you your badge," Gaven declared proudly. He took out a gold brooch engraved with the phoenix insignia of the Knights from his pocket, and carefully pinned it onto her outer jacket.

Mirari seemed stunned to hear that she had earned Gaven's approval, but something didn't sit right with her. There was little excitement in her expression.

"Thank you, Your Honor. But I'm not entirely sure if I want it." She thought back to Fangbane's promise to keep her identity hidden, but as long as she was a part of this controversial group known as the Knights, she risked being found out that she was a Hale. As much as she believed in the Knight's cause, her personal need came first.

"I figured as much." Gaven didn't seem surprised at all. "Fangbane made you join the team against your will. I'm freeing you from that obligation. If you're going to be a Knight, you have to want it, and if you leave us to return to Solarin, I won't stop you."

But there was a reason that stopped her from returning to

Solarin, and that was Gaven himself. Even if their past relationship had faded, she cherished the time she spent with him now. She didn't want it to end.

"I need some time to think about it." Mirari's fingers glided across the new pin on her chest. The way she stared at it told him she liked how it felt, but her fingers refused to fully caress the foreign object.

"I understand."

Eventually, they reached an open area that stretched on for acres, light bouncing off from the walls and illuminating the room. The light was coming from the other end. Below, they could see countless griffins curled up. They have to cross over them to reach the other side.

"Something tells me that this is a bad idea…" Mirari whispered.

"It's the worst idea, but it's the only one we've got." Gaven realized something even direr – they were both useless in this situation. "Your wind abilities won't have any effect against them, and if I use my earth kore again, the cave will collapse. We must be careful."

Mirari nodded, storing her lumastōne back in her pouch on top of the precious lumapetals. "Let's go."

Gaven and Mirari carefully slid down the wall of the cave and crossed the vast area full of slumbering beasts. They did their best to not make any noise, but each step they took, getting closer to the beasts, brought them more and more anxiety.

Mirari felt a change in the wind's direction once they stepped past the midway mark. It made sense for the wind to be coming from the cave's entrance, but now she felt the breeze behind her.

It was insignificant enough that Gaven didn't notice it, but Mirari was observant and curious, so she took a peek behind her.

Her eyes wandered upward and widened, seeing a mouth full of piercing blades just inches from her body. She found herself frozen in fear, forgetting how to scream. The headstrong creature, master of the skies, raised its talons high in the air and prepared to step on her, but just at the right second Mirari waved her arm and blew a gust of wind at the griffin. It went through its body like nothing but spooked it enough to shriek in response.

Upon hearing the screeching noise of the beast, Gaven jolted and quickly turned around. It stood on its tree-trunk legs and flapped its wide wings aggressively.

Mirari stumbled backward by the force of the attack and yelped as she tumbled several feet out and landed on the soft fur of a slumbering beast, which slowly woke up as it noticed Mirari on its back. Blades fell upon Mirari, but she managed to roll out of the way in time.

Gaven raised his arms as a shield to cover his eyes from the dust. He kept himself grounded, but he was careless and allowed the blood-thirsted killer to seize him. It clawed at him and pinned him on the ground, the force of its body pressing into him like iron on fabric.

His spear had fallen out of his reach. He turned to Mirari, hoping to find assistance, but instead found that she was also fighting for her life. The commotion they were making had woken half a dozen griffins, and they were all focused on her. More were starting to slowly awaken. They were running out of time.

With her hands glued to the hilt of her sword, Mirari cut through every beast that dared to charge at her, and while it was not hard to land the hit, the numbers were overwhelming her.

On the other hand, Gaven was struggling under large talons, but it didn't budge. Overhead, more beasts began to take flight, circling them until they were ready to take a dive.

"Mirari, my spear!" Gaven called out, pointing to his abandoned weapon several feet from her. She glanced at the spear, then back at the hissing felines. At the first opportunity, she dashed for the spear as several griffins followed her.

She struggled to fight them off before she succeeded in grabbing the far end of the spear in her hand. She made a sweeping turn, dodging the rain of thorns swiping at her as she ran toward Gaven.

"Recite the partner bind!" Gaven shouted.

"The what?" She blew another puff of wind at diving birds, strong enough to make them yield and try again.

"From The Paragon's Conduct! Recite the oath of the partner bind!" He began:

"Mirari Zanette, by my blade, I hereby request your alliance to become my eyes and ears in the time of uncertainty!"

Almost instantly, Mirari could feel a surge in the energy radiating from the spear in her hand, and as if by instinct, or entranced by the spell, she reacted to his calling. She leaped with her renewed energy to hand Gaven the spear, responding to his call.

"Gaven Zanette, by my blood, I swear to be your sword and shield in the battles to come!"

As soon as Gaven's hand touched the spear, a pulse of energy could be felt levitating from the spear into both their bodies. They flinched. The sedative aura around them felt lightweight as their souls were pinched together. The adrenaline coursing through their veins was now amplified, but with patience and power.

Gaven felt his concentration improving, his breathing returning to a steady pace.

Mirari sensed a burning rage in her heart, but it wasn't hers. Yet, it gave her a much-needed focus.

That split second felt like minutes, and when Mirari finally released her grip on the spear, Gaven waved it upward and stabbed the creature that had pinned him down.

In return, the griffin gave an anguished shriek and backed away. The shriek was more pained than they had heard, and the other beasts around them also seemed to take the warning, growing suspicious, and started to play the defensive.

Gaven stood up tall and valiant, his ankle now fully recovered. He gripped his spear, targeted a herd and sprinted forward.

"Mirari, follow me!" he said in a commanding and urgent tone of voice.

Hesitantly, Mirari obeyed. As soon as Gaven's spear scratched the surface of their brown fur, Mirari leaped from behind and sliced through its organs. They moved to the next closest creature and did the same.

Gaven raised his spear and took a stab, and Mirari did the same with her sword. Their bodies weaved and dodged swipes and bites. She could feel her rhythm in sync with his, their footwork flowed identically like a dance.

After seeing a dozen of their kind injured, the other griffins stopped attacking. They hissed and surrounded the two, their ear-piercing howls reminding them that they were not welcome.

Gaven and Mirari took a few steps back, ensuring they would not be followed, before making a run to the cave exit.

The light blinded their eyes as they climbed out of the cave and breathed the chilly mountain breeze, their hearts pounding when the adrenaline started to wear off.

Together, they fell to catch their breath, relieved that they made it back out in one piece. Silently, they decided that they should wait until their eyes adjusted to the sunlight before they headed back to the estate.

Mirari looked at her hand as if a new power had just entered her body. She found that she felt more robust and much more confident. Her shoulder was fully healed, and she felt ready to fight off another army of griffins.

The partner bind was an ancient fighter tradition exclusive to paragons. Every paragon was expected to choose a partner, a fighter that could complement their style and enhance their performance. Gaven was an exception. He abandoned his partner long ago, and never sought a replacement.

Until now.

"I don't understand…" Mirari said, glancing over at him.

Gaven couldn't help but smile as he watched her. "Which part?"

"Why did you choose me? I thought you didn't work with partners?"

"Things can change, can't they?" Gaven said with minor embarrassment as he tried to come up with an excuse. "But you felt that, didn't you? That surge was strong."

With a nod, Mirari agreed, as the wave of energy that had sealed their partnership felt divine, and it meant that they had both greatly benefited from it. They were both so much stronger.

"You have reminded me that sheer willpower is all it takes to defy any level of physical strength. That's your unique value. Lend me your willpower, and I'll lend you my strength. I think we'll do just fine."

Once they had recovered, Gaven checked his pouch one last time for the valuable goods that had nearly cost them their lives. They took the abundant harvest of lumapetal they had gathered and headed back to the estate.

Mirari followed Gaven to his room and waited by the doorway. He came back out with a thin file in hand and gave it to Mirari. She skimmed the first page. Her eyes widened. The Blessed.

"I thought this was off-limits?" Mirari said in confusion as she turned to him, wearing an almost vulnerable expression.

"It was," Gaven replied. "But only until you proved to me that you were ready. You're cleared to read it now. I'm eager to hear what you think. I've seen enough battles to know if there was a strategy behind this. Yet, I see no pattern here…"

Running his finger across the map of the alliance, Gaven began briefing her on the major points of the case. All of it was new information for Mirari, but none of it came as a shock. The facts only confirmed her suspicions.

There were circles and crossed marks in every empire, identifying places where members of the Blessed were spotted and sites where they allegedly committed crimes. Mirari instantly understood why he struggled to find a pattern. The marks were as random as splatters of paint, and one of Gaven's fearful theories started to take light – *if they are real, there must be more than one leader.*

"You can start by lending me a fresh set of eyes. I know it's not much to work with, so we have to try to find the smallest of patterns and predict their next move, that is, if they really exist."

Mirari thanked him, leaving her pouch of lumapetals with him, and retreated to her room. Gaven proceeded down the hall to Fangbane's room and knocked. The door was ajar so he didn't wait for a reply.

The room was pitch dark again, but by now Gaven had grown used to Fangbane's strange habits; he even memorized how many steps to take in each direction without running into furniture. Even though he couldn't see anything, he had no doubt that the master of the house was in the room.

"Here's your lumapetal. Nearly cost Mirari and me an arm and a leg… each."

Gaven threw the sacks of flowers at the side wall, where he knew a table was standing. It landed perfectly on the stand and the bag opened slightly, revealing the glowing buds. Gaven heard a drawer open as a shadow reached over the radiating flowers and closed the bag again.

"But you came back with something much more. I can sense the difference in your aura. It's stronger, Gaven." His thoughts tingled in Fangbane's mind. "Oh, you have a new partner."

"Cut the crap, Fang. I know you did it on purpose. You had more than enough lumapetal in your pantry. You didn't need us to get these."

"The decision of choosing Mirari as your partner was purely yours to make." Fangbane chuckled.

"I know, I know," Gaven groaned thinking how his new partnership with Mirari would hurt his reputation even more.

There was no doubt that more would now question his loyalty to his empire. But the surge he felt was powerful, more powerful than with his former partner, and he knew there were greater things they could accomplish together.

"I see why Starlight calls you a fortune teller. You should consider changing it to manipulator."

Fangbane thought of his new nickname, nodding with satisfaction.

CHAPTER TWENTY-TWO

As the winter solstice drew near, snow was steadily canvassing the plains. As official partners, Gaven and Mirari began learning how to work together, but adjusting to their new strengths and synchronizing their fighting styles would take time.

A yeti stood on its long arms and tackled Gaven in the chest. He tumbled onto the ground, his body covered in snow. Satisfied with itself and the job it had done, the yeti turned around and walked away, ending its pursuit of Gaven. These furry creatures, passive and no larger than a bear, made perfect practice targets, but Gaven was tired of being knocked around.

Mirari watched the yeti leave, then looked back at Gaven. It had been her turn to block, and she had forgotten, letting Gaven take the hit. She felt a speck of his frustration sparking through her nerves.

It was the consequence of a partnership – the emotional link that came with it. Mirari not only shared Gaven's strength, but his emotions as well, and vice versa. The bond only picked up overbearing emotions, and the fact that Mirari could feel his rage meant that he was very upset.

In some ways, the bond could be strategically beneficial, but in most cases, it was a curse. They had to practice for this very reason – to maximize the full benefit of a paragon's partnership and to prevent their bond from becoming their weakness.

Standing up, Gaven brushed the snow off his body. He wanted to say something, but he knew that she could take the hint.

Gaven's emotions, she felt, were aggressive and fierce whenever he fought. It came as a surprise to her, realizing how well he was able to shield his emotions.

"Sorry…" Mirari apologized as she lowered her head, and while Gaven tried to brush it off, he was still quite disappointed at their lack of progress.

"Never mind that. Try playing defensive on that one."

Gaven nudged a yeti, who was minding its own business and had ignored them all this time. Gaven threw a medium-sized stone at it. That got its attention and it began approaching them slowly. Mirari got in a defensive stance, but the yeti read her movement as an attack.

It charged at them with rage, and Mirari, too, dashed toward it, stopping a couple of feet away to allow the yeti to close the distance between them. The furball tried to knock her down, but with each swing, Mirari moved between the attacks, circling and dodging to disorient it. Moments later, Gaven charged, taking a direct hit at the yeti with his wooden pole. Mirari stepped to the side, out of his way, but close enough to provide support. Gaven aimed for a follow up attack, but unexpectedly the yeti seized the pole with a hand twice the size of its head, and flung him to the side.

Mirari stepped into his position and fought on the defensive until Gaven got back on his feet. He dashed back toward the beast. Mirari stepped to the side, but as soon as Gaven got next to her, she pivoted to the front and extended her pole at the yeti.

Their movements aligned, perfectly synchronized as they

both knocked back the yeti at the same time. It suffered twice the blow, fumbling across the snow and tumbling down the hill, too far to chase as it kept rolling in the distance. Mirari felt a bit sorry for the beast, not expecting to hit it so roughly.

"How did you know?" Gaven turned to Mirari as he recovered his breath. "How did you know which move I was going to make?"

"Instinct, I suppose."

"But I told you to defend."

"Sorry."

"No," Gaven said, shaking his head. "That was… good. That was a good move."

When they returned to the estate after their training exercise, the other Knights were long gone. They had set out for missions that Gaven had assigned to them the night before. The estate was quiet as they headed for their rooms. Mirari wondered what she was supposed to do for the rest of the day.

"No mission for me?"

"Not today."

"So what, I get special treatment now that I'm your partner?" Mirari said, with a cheeky smile.

"You wish. I want you to focus on unfolding the Blessed's next move. If anyone asks, just say you're handling my paperwork." Mirari certainly had no objection to that – it might help her learn more about her missing brother.

Hours passed as she reexamined the file without any real insight. To maintain confidentiality, Mirari worked in her room, her door locked, rather than in the library. She absently scratched her head, vexed at the frustrating lack of meaningful details. She stared at the map of Althaea, marking incidents that might be related, hoping to discover some clue or pattern as she had when they were on the mission to stop the bandits.

Nothing.

She realized that Gaven wasn't exaggerating when he said there was so little solid information on the Blessed. She wasn't even sure if any of her markings were related to the Blessed or just another act of crime in their corrupted world. It was better writing them off as a myth, a random string of coincidences. Only she was certain that they existed – Joachim was never wrong – and she was determined to find at least one name to the mysterious organization.

Her thoughts were interrupted by a knock on her door. When she opened it, Starlight asked, "Are you busy?"

"Busy work, but no result. Frankly, I feel like I'm chasing my tail. Do you need something, Milady?"

"I got a message from Neo. He's worried that Shiba may need help with their mission in Narvi. It seemed rather urgent."

Mirari tilted her head. "It's unlike Shiba to need any help. And his ego wouldn't let him ask even if he did."

"I expect that's why the message came from Neo. He's tied up with another incident, so he and Shiba could use more back up. You can take Lightning. There's no faster mount in all of Minetta."

"Thank you, Milady. But are you sure?"

"Oh, pish posh, child." Starlight laughed. "Look at me," she said, patting her pregnant belly. "Do I look like I'm going on a fox hunt any time soon?"

Mirari noticed a large crowd huddled by the tall iron gates of Narvi. It was a well-developed community, slightly larger than Solarin, that rested in an open prairie. A wide river ran through the city, one that typically reflected the sky on a clear day, but today its surface was blanketed with mats of green foam. Mirari slowed down to investigate the commotion.

"Ah, Mirari!" Neo called out, waving so that he was visible in the large sea of hungry peasants. It wasn't hard to spot the giant among these scarecrows.

He was certainly occupied, fighting to control a swarming multitude of grasping desperate hands, pressing in all around him. He was surrounded by chaos, as he struggled to distribute bags of grain from the back of a wagon.

"What's going on?"

"What's it look like? I'm running a bakery."

"A do-it-yourself bakery, if all you're handing out is flour."

"There's been a blight, killing most of the crops this year. The mayor asked for our aid, so Fangbane has us delivering supplies," Neo yelled back, dodging the desperate hands that were clawing at him. "Shiba's in the Public Hall on the left side of town."

"What's Shiba passing out?"

Neo sighed. "Attitude. As usual."

Mirari hustled off to the building with a green awning on the quiet end of town, hitching Lightning outside as she entered. Inside, she found the wooden counter at the front deserted. She was about to call for somebody when she heard angry yells and curses from the basement.

That would be Shiba, the soul of kindness.

It didn't surprise her to find him having a noisy feud with two other men. She noticed their wrists were tied to an iron bench by an old-fashioned chain and lock.

"Oh great." Shiba groaned on seeing Mirari. "They sent you?"

Mirari ignored the slight, nodding at Shiba's prisoners. "What heinous crime did they commit? Aggravated hunger?"

"I ordered them to produce identification, and they refused."

"We reserve the right to not show you," the younger detainee spat. The youth had a sturdy build, sun-browned skin, and light blue curly hair. He was awkward in his movements, revealing he had only recently come to his height.

By the look of him, he had no relation to the older captive who was an extremely pale gentleman, likely in his early twenties, several years older than his companion. The man wore a gray vest over a loose white shirt, common garments for peasants, but there was not a single grass stain or wrinkle in his clothes. She could see his outfit was not only new, it was masterfully tailored. The clothes might have been cut to ape the style of an ordinary citizen, but the fine quality of the material and crafted bespoke tailoring belied this on closer inspection.

Her experience as a merchant taught Mirari that when the wealthy traveled, it was unwise to advertise their status. To confirm her theory, her eyes wandered to their chained hands. They were wearing identical gloves, crafted with the finest soft leather and decorated in brilliant gold, a flourish only the wealthiest could obtain. She could see decorative hāstals laced around the knuckles. It was a clōve she had never seen before. It was truly unique but she was confident it was made by the Hale family.

"Shiba, clearly these two are merely travelers," Mirari told him with a frown. "Valenian, if I had to guess. They don't use identification over there."

She looked at the man's face, but the glaring reflection from the man's unusual white-tinted glasses made it impossible to read his eyes. It gave his chalk white face a mysterious appearance.

"I don't care if they're swines. I caught them stealing from a fruit stand." Shiba whined like a child begging for an award, hoping Mirari would stroke his ego.

"Oh, I see," she said. "So you determined these arch criminals were worthy of intervention by the Knights, is that it?"

Shiba bristled. "If that were all, I could just leave them

locked up here. But their refusal to be candid about who they are, and what they're about, makes them worthy of suspicion."

"And what evidence do you have to back that up?"

Shiba gestured to the heap of expensive luggage stacked against the wall. "I want to know what's in the seven bags they're carrying. They won't say."

In truth, Mirari also found that suspicious, but she didn't want Shiba to be right. "Why not just open it?"

"I did open the first one. And look." With a satisfied smirk, he unzipped one of the bags, delighted to reveal that it was chock full of daggers, throwing stars, and other hand weapons. They weren't the cheap kinds used in war. The blades of the throwing stars were lined with a yellow coat of hāstal and so were the hilts of the daggers, each shining with a reflective polish only a newly forged weapon would have.

She also saw a number of bottles, which appeared to be filled with various herbs. The combination of these goods didn't add up.

"They won't explain what this crap is for." Shiba glared at the two prisoners.

Despite the obvious evidence, something about the travelers overcame Mirari's suspicions.

She turned to the pale man, and cocked her head, inviting his explanation without demanding an answer. Just offering her ear, if he cared to give his side.

The pale man leaned forward as if getting a better look at Mirari. He relaxed and finally spoke.

"The theft of fruit was an honest mistake." His deep voice was calm and even. "In our land, the townspeople share their resources freely. Please forgive the boy. He has never been outside of the empire. He doesn't know any better."

The man was sincere and respectful, and Mirari thought him credible.

Not Shiba. He was a congenital skeptic. "And how do I know

that the contraband you're smuggling isn't stolen? You don't even have a merchant permit."

"What is wrong with you featherpits?" the boy burst out. "Why can't you take our word and release us!"

"Pipe down, kid," barked Shiba, stepping toward him, his girth menacing.

"Shire. Enough," said the pale man, quietly.

"Apologies, my liege," the boy said, his eyes studying the floor.

Shiba frowned at his lost chance to enforce discipline.

But his vitriol was rekindled as the pale man said, "He's in the right."

"Shut your hole unless I speak to you."

"You have no cause to detain us further." The pale man never raised his voice and spoke plainly. "We have places to be."

Shiba got right in the man's face, and as he screamed Mirari could see spittle fly from his angry mouth at the man's face. "Quiet. Didn't you hear me? I said to speak only if I ask you to."

With the slow deliberation of a coiled snake, the man pulled an elegant embroidered handkerchief from his tunic. Slowly, he removed his glasses, and wiped the spit from them. He placed them carefully back on his face.

"You don't scare me, Shadow Soldier."

"Nor me," said Shire. "You're a pathetic swamp weasel compared to my liege."

"Is that why you're cowering behind him, you unbearded whelp?"

"Shire…" said the pale man, admonishing him at the same time as Mirari warned Shiba.

They looked at each other, and both started laughing at their identical instinct to settle down their hot-headed companions.

"Don't let down your guard with him, Mirari," Shiba said. "I'm an experienced hand when it comes to rooting out spies and traitors."

The man mumbled just loud enough for Shiba to hear. "Such a pity you don't have any instincts about who is innocent."

"They're hiding their identities for a reason."

"Really?" Mirari turned to the younger traveler. "Is that right… *Shire?*"

Mirari glanced at the two travelers. Clearly, the only reason for their irritation was being locked up for hours without cause. Mirari snatched the key from Shiba's hand, and began to unlock their chains, starting with the pale man.

"What are you doing?" Shiba fumed even louder than before, flailing his hands in the air. He gritted his teeth in disbelief and tried to reach for the key in Mirari's hand. Mirari nudged his hand away with her elbow.

"Well, I'm not being an asshole. You've got that covered."

"You are going to regret this laxity."

"This whole mission was for you and Neo to come here and help people. Not to round up suspects without a crime."

Suddenly, Mirari felt a cold breeze surround her hands. A dark form was wrapping itself around both her wrists. Then, the shadow abruptly yanked her back and pinned her to the wall, like a magnet against a steel door. The key dropped before she could free the man.

"I've had enough of your insolent sass!"

Mirari struggled, but couldn't break free. "Let go of me, you dickless toad!"

"Why can't you just do as I say for once."

"Kiss my ass, you strutting little eunuch."

Shiba lost it, raising his fist and taking a swing at Mirari with a roar of pure rage.

But his fist stopped, suspended in the air. Caught inches from her face, and held fast by the pale man's surprisingly powerful hand. He tried to pull loose, but could not budge under the slender man's hold on him. Instead, the vice grip tightened as a sharp pain hit him and his knuckles popped. It was then Shiba also noticed the man must have snapped his chain like a thread, and realized he had somehow crossed the room to seize him in a fraction of a second.

"You are just as ill-mannered as they say, Shadow Soldier."

"Let go of me you freak, or I'll… aaaAAAH! Stop! STOP!"

Shiba whimpered in agony as the hand squeezed down on his fist. The man yanked Shiba like a weightless scarecrow, roughly throwing him across the room. He hit the far wall so hard it scrambled his brain and crossed his eyes.

"Gods and monkeys," Mirari muttered in breathy astonishment.

Another dark shadow rose in front of Mirari and took on a human form. It yanked Shiba's shadow away as if it were but a cobweb, and tossed it across the room, where it wrapped around Shiba's face like a wet towel, and vanished inside its master. The man's shadow did the same.

Shaking his head, he tried to clear it. He picked himself up, looking around for his lost dignity. "If you can do all that, why didn't you evade me the first time?"

"Because I acknowledged my wrong, and accepted the punishment. You should learn to do the same."

At close proximity, Mirari could see his smooth, pale face more clearly. Behind those foggy glasses were cold white eyes. It was odd, yet mesmerizing, and it tickled at a faded memory.

"Miss, are you alright?"

Mirari was too distracted, struggling to place him and letting his deep voice drown in the din of background noise. The man blushed a nudge, although against his snow-white flesh, his cheeks emitted a flashing red light. She had been staring at him for a long time, and he couldn't help staring back at her shining, deep purple eyes.

"You…" Shiba muttered, still rocky on his feet. "You're a high-class umbra." He now understood why the man carried the weapons. "I know all the high-class umbras in Minetta, and you're not one of them. So you either tell me who you are right now, or I'll have you sent back to the border for theft."

"Shiba, quit while you're in one piece," Mirari said. "They're just travelers. Let them be on their way."

"Suppose we come to a compromise." The man's eyes were drawn to the shimmering badge on her chest. "Are you one of Fangbane's Knights?"

"I am. As is Region Leader Shiba."

"Will you escort me to Lord Fangbane, Miss? I would feel much safer with you guiding me over your aggressive teammate."

Mirari was again distracted by his elegant demeanor. But even more by his colorless pupils. She knew someone with that rare condition once.

And now that she was up close to him, close enough to pick up the scent of his lavender cologne, she noticed a jewel peeking out from under his belt. The purple gem was locked in a silver chain and hung like a fashion statement next to his daggers.

A kirinvā stone.

Her heart was racing as she realized…

"Lucan?" she murmured to herself, hardly willing to breathe the name out loud.

The man's mouth hung open a moment before he could answer. "I… that is, yes. Do I know you?"

Mirari cursed at herself quietly. She prayed she was wrong, that she hadn't blown her identity, that Lucan wouldn't see through her and recognize the little Hale girl, his cousin, gone so long ago.

"Me?" she squeaked. "I don't… that is, I'm sure you couldn't—"

And luck, it seemed, was with her, as the pale man said, "No? Pity. But you must be right. I'm sure I'd remember a woman with your… pleasing appearance, if I may be so bold."

Mirari felt her cheeks grow hot. Flushed with panic and embarrassment, all she could do was scream in her mind.

Shiba was starting to piece the information together from the daggers to the pale skin, and to the high-tailored clothing he wore. He, too, took notice of the kirinvā stone on Lucan's chain.

"Lucan… Hale?" Shiba perked.

A large grin appeared on Lucan's face. "Yes, Shadow Soldier?"

Shiba felt his knees grow weak. He had insulted and assaulted one of the youngest business titans in Valenia, an heir to the prestigious Hale family. Perhaps the richest, most powerful house in Valenia. Or even, in all the empires.

"And what brings you to honor Minetta with a visit?" Shiba said, in complete servitude to his new master as if he was dying to take Shire's job. He realized he was prying again, and tried to backtrack. "Not that it's any of my business, of course. A private matter. None of my concern. Ignore my curiosity. I can be a terrible pest."

Mirari was appalled at how fast his manner had changed.

"Don't worry yourself. I've come at the invitation of Lord Fangbane," Lucan said, turning to Mirari, reserving his smile only for her. "I hope to be worthy of becoming one of his Knights."

Shiba swallowed, his throat suddenly very dry. He felt bile rising and wished he could vanish as efficiently as his shadow.

CHAPTER TWENTY-THREE

Lucan and his retainer rode quickly along with the three Knights back to Fangbane's estate. As they rode, Mirari's mind was consumed with anxiety over the new guest. She could not help fretting over whether Lucan knew who she was. If he didn't yet, she had no doubt he soon would. Lucan was smart enough to figure out she was his long lost cousin, Roselyn Hale. Mirari considered him the smartest person she knew, even though her last memory of him was when she was merely six years old. She wondered if she should approach him first, and ask him to keep her secret before he exposed her accidentally.

As a Hale, Lucan descended from one of the most prominent aristocratic bloodlines. He was a child prodigy, mastering everything he touched. Mirari hated being compared to him when they were children. Their parents pushed them to satisfy their unhealthy competition, but Lucan never saw her that way. He was quiet, always keeping his face glued to whatever book he was holding, and Mirari too considered him a friend. Her only friend.

There was no doubt that he continued to overachieve into adulthood. She heard that the young lord saw boredom in everything he did. He hated… predictable.

Perhaps the invitation from Fangbane had intrigued him. He was ambitious, full of impetuous curiosity, and he was excited at the idea of leaving home behind and tripping off to Minetta. No matter what, it promised to be a stimulating new experience. Whether he ended up joining Fangbane's Knights, or he didn't, this would be an adventure.

When the party eventually made it back to the estate, Mirari didn't get a chance to speak to Lucan. He dismounted in a twinkle, leaving his horse and luggage for Shire to worry about. Before she could say a word, he rushed off to find Lord Fangbane, anxious to consult about his invitation.

"What exactly were you doing in Narvi?" Fangbane asked Lucan outright.

"To put it bluntly, I was dropped off at the wrong city," Lucan answered, chagrined. "I didn't know how to find a ride in your empire, so naturally, I walked." Despite the embarrassing mistake, Lucan was too enthusiastic to be here with the Knights to let it bother him. Fangbane warmed to him immediately.

"You declined my letter at first." He was grateful for the clōves Lucan had donated, but he didn't expect the noble to offer more. "What changed your mind?"

"I…" Lucan hesitated, seeming to avoid as much detail as possible. "There was some disagreement within the Hale family of course, but I managed to convince them to let me observe your movement."

"But you do intend to do more than simply observe, do you not? Your luggage speaks for itself."

"Of course, Lord Fangbane. It's not just a battle between empires, right? Nobles, peasants, we are all at fault for widening the gap in cooperation. So let's work together, and prove them wrong."

"What an honor it is to have such a wise man join our team," Fangbane said. "However, protocol compels me to evaluate your fighting skills before I officially appoint you to become a Knight."

"If it's a duel with the Shadow Soldier, I will accept with pleasure." Lucan practically licked his chops at the prospect, looking forward to a fight with Shiba, win, lose, or draw.

Mirari was sure he would win. He probably studied the Shadow Soldier's moves, the way he excessively used his shadow ability to confuse his opponents. Yes, by strength Shiba would win, but Lucan had the brains to put him in check.

"Mirari?" Fangbane called out. She'd been lurking just outside his study, waiting to buttonhole Lucan as soon as she could. Sheepish at being caught, she slunk into the doorway instantly, making the two men laugh. She leaned against the doorframe, not sure if she had been summoned, or merely caught eavesdropping.

"Yes, My Lord?" she responded, her face the picture of manufactured innocence.

"Do you mind dueling with Lucan? After all the good things I've heard from Gaven, I want to see your progress for myself."

Mirari was unsure of the prospect of a fight with Lucan. She knew she wouldn't be able to defeat him.

"Wait a second," Lucan interrupted them before Mirari could respond. "My Lord, I'm afraid I will not fight a woman."

Since when? Mirari smiled at such a lie, thinking back to all the times they wrestled as children. The way he flickered his eyes at her now spoke doubt. She felt his gaze judging every breath she took. That was it. It wasn't women he was afraid of hurting; it was Mirari specifically.

And though Lucan didn't say it, Fangbane heard his explanation loud and clear.

"Mirari is the only one available at the moment." Fangbane was unfazed as usual. "Plus, I don't think it would be wise to taunt Shiba any more today."

With a heavy sigh, Lucan gave in and accepted the duel.

ONCE THEY REACHED the open field behind the estate, Mirari and Lucan assumed their stances, roughly three carriages apart from each other. Only Fangbane and Starlight were present to observe the match. Lucan stood silent and confident, twirling a throwing star in each hand. Just watching him juggle these razor-sharp weapons like they were rubber balls was intimidating. But for Lucan, it focused his mind and allowed him to consider the ways an opponent might attack him, and how he might defend.

His patience alone started to drive her crazy.

It was a stalemate. They stood there for five minutes. Ten. Lucan appeared content to spend the whole week juggling shurikens, waiting for Mirari's first move. He didn't have to fight her to know that she wasn't a skilled fighter. He could sense her hesitation in the way she spoke and walked. Her body language told him she lacked the bold and militant behavior of a high-class fighter. Instead of claiming his easy victory, Lucan was thinking of ways he could put on a show without embarrassing the little lady.

She could stand it no longer. "What are you waiting for, Hale?"

"Ladies first is how I was raised."

"I doubt that's it."

"I don't want to hurt you."

"You'll need to do something if you want the position."

"There are other ways," he said, adjusting his glasses with a single finger.

A shadow slithered across the field of tall grass, much too quickly for anyone to see, before it rose directly behind Mirari. Without turning back or even looking at it, she unsheathed her sword. Her hand promptly gripped the handle as she did a full spin, slicing the shadow in a clean cut and then replacing her sword into her scabbard.

Her quick reaction awed Lucan.

"Impressive. You could sense that?"

"No. Predicted it. Shiba used that on me one too many times."

Lucan's shadow ability wasn't as strong as Shiba's. In combat, he'd merely do it for show, but it was an excellent way to analyze Mirari's reflexes. Lucan still didn't want to cause unnecessary harm to her. But he figured that if he took away her sword, she would be defenseless, and victory would come fast to him by default.

He took a deep breath and hurled his shurikens at her in succession. They were still in the air as he made a break toward her. Lucan was remarkably fast, although not fast enough to outrun a throwing star. But as he closed the distance, he watched Mirari's superior sword work, as she swatted the stars out of the air like annoying mosquitos.

His objective was to make her swing fast twice, to get her out of position while he dashed to catch the advantage.

She slapped the second star aside easily, but before she could unwind herself to face forward, Lucan sped past her, slapping the sword from her hand.

Her sword tumbled to the trimmed grass, but Mirari didn't reach for it. She turned around in search of Lucan. He stood still again, smiling, almost daring Mirari to make a lunge to pick up her sword. That would be the perfect opening.

She leaned down for the sword, and Lucan readied for a sprint. His back heel lifted from the ground ready to take off, but he stopped himself short when he realized she was running straight for him, not the sword. He wasn't quite ready to block the wild swing of her fist, as she knocked him back with a solid punch.

They began fighting fist-to-fist, and while Mirari had always dominated in close combat, she was now up against someone better than her. Lucan was incomparable to the dozens of drunks she scuffled in the streets of Solarin. As they grappled, each trying to gain advantage, Lucan leaned in close to her ear and whispered, "You're tougher than you look, buttercup."

The infuriating insult knocked her hollow, and she cut loose with a string of vitriolic curses. Wasting her breath, and breaking her concentration – exactly what Lucan wanted. He pounced to flip her and landed on top of her with the advantage of all his strength and weight. The only problem with this move was that she landed in reach of her sword. In an instant, Mirari had the sword within an inch of his neck. He managed to catch her wrist at the last instant, and they both strained for control.

"If you ever call me that again, I'll kill you."

"No, you won't," he said, and with his grip on her wrist, he pushed her arm away, then gave her arm a little twist until she dropped the sword again. But she took advantage of the shift in weight to break his position and escape his effort to pin her.

Now they were both on their feet again, circling like a pair of prizefighters, looking for the chance to land a blow. Without her sword, Lucan knew she would have to resort to physical attacks or kore spells to defeat him.

Mirari focused on charging her kore into a shield around her body. It was faint, just enough to repel a few impacts. But even Lucan wasn't going to waste his energy breaking that shield. He played the waiting game once again.

She defiantly raised her hands in the air, letting the kore shield collapse but drawing all of that energy and directing it to the sky.

Seeing her shield vanish, Lucan was about to make a dash at her. Suddenly, he stopped hard, and barely missed an arrow hurtling straight down at him. Wary, he glanced up. The sky became illuminated with strange purple crackles of light as a score of glowing arrows appeared above Mirari, circling her with a different kind of shield – an offensive one. With a delicate motion of her upraised finger, she moved the brace of arrows, until they were pointing directly at Lucan.

"Will you yield?" she called out. "Or will you treat us to a demonstration of the Valenian porcupine dance?"

Seeing her perform an aegis skill with such control piqued his curiosity. His opponent was full of surprises, and he loved it. "You'd be surprised, but for a tall man I'm very light on my feet."

Mirari roared as she whipped her hand down, releasing the full volley of arrows to rain down on the field like a hailstorm from the Gods in Nagama.

Lucan proved to be the faster fighter. It was a dance, the way he dodged every arrow. But it took every fiber of his concentration to focus directly above him. With his head pointed skyward, Mirari charged. She threw that same effective power punch she had started with. But Lucan was ready for it this time. He caught her fist in his hand just in time to block her blow and held on tight to her fist.

He smiled. Now she was in the same pickle Shiba had been. He began to squeeze very slowly. She tried to pull her trapped fist away, but of course, that was impossible.

Or so he thought. The corner of her lip perked up as she countered with her other hand. Not to hit him, though. She had enchanted her left hand and brushed it against the side of his hip, and the spell's energy sent crippling, deadening sparks through Lucan's body, effectively executing her misdirection.

Lucan twitched and struggled to shake it off, but he wasn't sure what had hit him, and his body reacted instinctively.

This involuntary instinct took over as Lucan's other arm counterattacked, shooting out toward her, charged with a massive blast of electricity. The instant his hand pressed against Mirari's chest, a pile driver of voltage crackled through her body.

A painful scream rang out in the courtyard as the massive discharge shot Mirari several yards across the lawn. Fangbane and Starlight cringed as she hit the ground. There was a sting of ozone drifting through the air.

Lucan's leg buckled from Mirari's attack, and he dropped to

the ground like a sack of wet sand. He was paralyzed from the waist down by Mirari's spell. He couldn't care less. His eyes drifted to Mirari, who didn't get up. Her body devoid of the slightest movement.

It was clear something wasn't right.

Seeing the damage he'd done, Lucan cursed under his breath and began crawling toward Mirari as fast as he could. He could only use his upper body to drag himself closer, but the paralysis was wearing off already.

Fangbane and Starlight raced across the lawn to Mirari's lifeless form. Starlight immediately began to check Mirari's core life functions. Her fingers glowed light blue as she firmly pressed onto the side of Mirari's head. She was trying to pinpoint a source of pain, a change in Mirari's aura, something she could identify and treat, but there was too much going on. Brainwaves and neural fibers discharging signals in chaos. No organization – just a buzzing field of static inside that skull of hers. Starlight thought it felt like a hopeless tangle of string, locked up in a thousand knots. Mirari was badly damaged – but Starlight didn't have a clue how to find an effective cure or even a treatment to ease the symptoms.

Fangbane moved over to Lucan, helping him stand up. The paralysis had worn off now, and Lucan could feel his legs again, while his opponent still lay unconscious.

"Is she alright?" Lucan asked.

Starlight removed her fingers from Mirari's skull and slumped back. "I can't… whatever is going on inside, I can read nothing." She turned to Fangbane. "Darling? Surely if she lives, you can read her thoughts?"

He shook his head sadly. "She lives still, but… there is nothing there."

Lucan recalculated what had just happened, how he could've made such a terrible mistake. Mirari's paralysis was weak, but it had caught him off guard. On the other hand, lightning kore was his specialty. A simple touch would've been more potent than the spark Mirari unleashed, but not enough to knock her unconscious. That meant his charge interacted with hers, creating an exponential effect. A deadly one.

A wash of icy water seemed to fill Lucan's guts as he feared the worst.

"It was an accident, I swear," Lucan pleaded, guilt coursing through his veins. "It was a reflex."

But it didn't change the fact that Mirari was still not responding.

"She was hit near the heart," Starlight said as she pointed to the light burn on the chest of the unconscious Knight. "It's highly likely that her nervous system won't be able to respond for a while even if we continuously healed her."

Lucan began to panic. He cursed at himself for accepting this duel. The thought kept running through his mind like a stinging wasp, jabbing his mind again and again. Accident or not, he hated himself for losing control.

"She'll be alright, Lucan, don't worry," Fangbane assured him, hearing his agony.

"But… can't we do… something?"

"Time," Fangbane said, laying a gentle hand on the grieving umbra. "It's all we have for now. We need to let her rest, while we figure out what to do."

And together, they lifted the inert bag of flesh, blood, and bone that might be Mirari again… or might not ever wake up.

THERE WAS an aggressive knock on Fangbane's door before Gaven shoved it open with his body. He was slouched over, breathing heavily while gripping tightly to his chest.

"Where's Mirari?" He asked, his tone harsh.

"She's… resting," Starlight replied vaguely as she could sense the frustration in his voice and didn't want to anger him any further.

"Your bond," Fangbane said as he observed Gaven grip the same place on his chest where Mirari was hit.

"Explain, now!"

Fangbane could hear a dozen questions running through Gaven's head, as the intensity of the pain made him uneasy. He had to know what had hurt his partner.

"Your Honor," Lucan said as he rose from his seat and bowed apologetically. "I take full responsibility." His cheeks grew hot as he nervously addressed the man he had long looked up to. Lucan did not expect the Althaean fighter to be in Minetta.

There was an evident rage in Gaven's eyes, and his presence gave an intimidating vibe. But the creases on his forehead and the way his chin perked into a snarl painted a handsome portrait that terrified Lucan as much as it tormented his hormones. He took note of his toned body, muscular in shape – proof that he was a hardworking man and living up to his title as the Valiant Tiger. He would hate to anger someone as strong as him.

More so than wanting to know why he was here, Gaven needed to know the cause of the pain in his chest. If he was hurting this bad, then his partner was hurting even more.

"Explain yourself."

"It was a dueling accident, nothing more, Your Honor. I apologize. I was unaware that she was your partner." Lucan stared at Gaven's hand, clenching his chest.

Attacking one's partner and triggering the recoil was usually equivalent to declaring war on the other partner. Lucan didn't want to enter that territory, especially on his first day.

Gaven scanned the chalky figure, intrigued but not surprised at his unusual features. He must've heard the rumors of the umbra with such a condition, even though they had never met face to face. His eyes drew to the decorative daggers and glimmering violet stone chained to his belt. The gem was identical to the one he possessed, and he knew what it meant.

"Lucan Hale, correct? From the Hale family of Valenia?"

"Yes, Your Honor."

"Did he pass?" Gaven asked, turning to Fangbane and ignoring Lucan.

"I would say so, yes."

"Good for him."

Fangbane wasn't sure whether Gaven meant that sarcastically or not. But the room was still tense, glaring daggers darting between Gaven and Lucan. Starlight placed a hand on Gaven's shoulder, inviting him to relax.

"We need to find a healer for Mirari. Maybe you can help Hime contact the celtas in Althaea."

Starlight gestured for Gaven to follow her, guiding him to the room where Mirari was sleeping. As soon as they left, Fangbane released the breath he had been holding.

"Gaven is helping us establish the foundations of the Knights," Fangbane said. "He'll have to approve you before we make you official."

Lucan's face grew paler than it possibly could. "And I just knocked his partner into a coma."

CHAPTER TWENTY-FOUR

Two days had passed without any sign of life from Mirari. Both Starlight and Hime checked on her regularly, but there was not much they could do. Her vitals were stable – that was a good sign. The pain in Gaven's chest had subsided, but he could not rest knowing that his partner's condition was ambiguous. He stayed by her side from dawn to dusk.

On an empty night, a lone candle in the dining hall was burning, sending shadows dancing in the deep gloom. Everyone should have been asleep by then, yet someone could be heard shifting through bottles in the cellar. Lucan peered into the room as Gaven appeared with a bottle of wine to end the evening.

Gaven glared hard at Lucan as if daring him to disapprove. He was tired and restless, sick with worry about Mirari. His droopy eyes and sluggish movement showed the toll his partner's illness had taken on him.

"I know it's late, but may I have a word with you?" Lucan asked, hoping the Valiant Tiger could see past the instinct to resent him for hurting Mirari.

"What is it?" Even his response seemed drained.

"Lord Fangbane informed me that you approved of my nomination as a Knight. I am grateful."

"You're a valuable fighter," Gaven said, but his voice held bitter irony. "That much is very clear."

Lucan swallowed. He went on, voice quavering. "I look forward to working with you, and… I hope we're not off to a bad start."

"Oh, it's a bad start. But not your fault."

"I can't accept that. This whole accident was undeniably my fault. But please believe I would never intentionally hurt you or your partner."

"Is that what you're worried about?" Gaven's unexpected smile made Lucan's cheeks tingle.

"I accept full responsibility for—"

Gaven cut him short. "Enough. I know it was an accident. Do you think I would want to recruit an enemy?"

"Of course not. I apologize for—"

"Stop apologizing. If you're going to be a Knight, then be stern. Have pride in yourself."

Lucan could feel the near-legendary awe people felt in Gaven's presence – his unnerving aura and blunt manner. Cold, perhaps, but not inconsiderate. They were both leaders in their own ways, but their styles were undeniably different.

"Knight or not, you are my superior in this company, correct?" Lucan asked. "How I handle my business is one thing. But I have no intention to elevate myself above anyone else here. Equality is our goal, after all, isn't it?"

"You know how to talk. I'll give you that. An umbra that's quite the opposite of the Shadow Soldier, that's for sure."

"I've heard Shiba can be… a strong personality."

"Shiba is a royal pain in the ass." Gaven tried to maintain a straight face, but a little smile forced its way onto his lips. "But you'll be fine teammates. Get some rest."

Clutching the bottle by the neck, Gaven took his leave with a nod and carried the wine back to Mirari's room.

But before he could walk past him, Lucan asked, "I do have a question for you, Your Honor."

Gaven stopped and turned to him. "Go ahead."

"Your skills are undeniably top tier, yet it seems you have chosen a partner who… well, she has the ability, certainly, but barely a fraction of your talents. Your own experience, sharing her injuries, proves it. Do you not fear she will weigh you down? I don't question your choice, but well, I'm curious about your decision."

"You may be known for your good judgment. But you've barely scratched the surface when it comes to Mirari. I've trained her for months. To say none of that has crossed my mind would be careless. But I do have faith in this one. She's stronger than she looks."

Lucan lightly rubbed the area on his hip where he could still feel the light tingle Mirari had inflicted on him.

"You are correct about that."

***

GAVEN WOKE to a light brush against his arm. He opened his eyes, blinking twice as he lifted his head. He realized he had once again fallen asleep by Mirari's bedside. The empty bottle of wine was still in his hand, and an early morning draft was seeping in from a small crack in the window. It was still dark outside, but from the faint chirps of rollobirds, he knew sunrise would not be long from now.

He felt the sheet underneath him shifting once again, ever so slightly. Gaven let out a soft gasp as his eyes landed on Mirari. Her movement was stiff as she tried to move her head. Begrudgingly, her eyes opened. His face bloomed with joyous relief to see her awake.

"Are you alright, Mirari?" Gaven said, his euphony as soothing as the pillow under her head.

"I… suppose so…"

She took a heavy breath with every croaked word escaping her mouth. As the numbness of her body faded, a warm radiance glazed in her hand. Her weighted eyelids worked hard to focus on the silhouette in front of her.

"You had a bit of an accident during your duel with Lucan. We're glad that you finally woke up."

"Sal…" She mouthed, but Gaven heard no more than a slither. He handed her a glass of water and gave her time to come to her senses.

Her eyes adjusted, and she saw an unfamiliar man. Similar in features, but he was not who she first thought it was. Then, she came to a realization.

"Gav… Is that really you?" She had never called him by his first name before.

He gave her a reassuring smile and lightly squeezed her hand in support. "I'm here."

"Where's here?" She began to scan the room, taking note of the lack of furniture. Bottles of herbs decorated the shelves and she was tucked in satin white sheets that she could not recall owning. A cold draft picked up from the edges of the sheets and tingled her naked skin. She realized that she wasn't properly dressed, if at all. But that didn't bother her. She forced her sore muscles to behave, adjusting her position to sit upright as she dragged the thin cover up with her. "Where's my brother?"

Gaven's worry shot up as the blood from his face fell with gravity. He knew very well that her brother was gone, and it was not something she should've forgotten.

At that moment, Lucan stepped into the room. He was relieved at the sight of Mirari being conscious, but she barely glanced at him.

"Please, go get Starlight," Gaven told him, trying to keep his panic in check. "Now. Hurry, she needs help."

"Of course, Your Honor." Lucan left to retrieve the healer while Gaven stayed by Mirari's bedside.

"Does anything hurt? What's the last thing you remember?" Gaven tried to probe her.

Before she could counter with her own questions, Lucan rushed back faster than lightning, his face showing alarm.

"Where's Starlight? I told you—"

"Forgive me, Your Honor, but we have a bit of a problem. Starlight's in labor."

"Right now?" Gaven was flustered at the timing.

"I'm afraid so."

"Then bring Hime. Quick!"

Lucan gulped. "But... I'm sorry, but... Hime? She's the midwife."

"Damn all the Gods!" Both women needed immediate medical attention, and Starlight's baby made that need two to one. He heard footsteps running down the hallway. The other Knights were coming, but everyone was heading for the room where Starlight was delivering.

Attracted to the commotion, Mirari removed the sheet covering her body and slowly got out of the bed, heedless of her nakedness.

"No, Mirari, don't get up yet—" Gaven tried to make her stay put, but Mirari ignored him, following the sounds of distress. He jumped from his stool, ready to drag her back to her bed, but his hand stopped inches from her shoulder when his eyes wandered down her body and realized she was fully naked. Gaven panicked, searching for her misplaced garment.

Mirari stood tall with the help of the bed frame, her feet pressed against the cold wooden floor. She seemed to have no problem walking despite the soreness in her body, and her strength was returning with every confident step.

Lucan stood in the doorway, unsure if he should restrain her, and even more unsure if it was appropriate for him to touch a nude lady without consent. His cheeks grew redder with every step drawing her closer to him, and he could only stare.

Gaven threw a nightgown to him and barked, "Get that over her!"

Without the shame that the men in the room felt, Mirari raised her arms and allowed Lucan to drop the nightgown over her. She ignored them and strode off toward Starlight's room.

Gaven and Lucan exchanged looks… then both burst out of the room to follow her.

In the birthing room, Fangbane was holding Starlight's hand, as the air was torn by the agonized screams Starlight could not contain. Frankly, no one knew how to deliver the baby, let alone what was causing such agony. They had planned to have an experienced midwife on hand when the time came, only the baby wasn't expected for at least another week. Dorain had darted with Lightning in search of a midwife from the closest town, but it could be hours before the woman arrived.

"Lay her on the side," Mirari instructed from the doorway. All heads perked up and turned to face the familiar voice.

"Mirari! Are you feeling better?" Fangbane asked, trying to unravel her thoughts, but she was focused on the screaming woman in labor.

Mirari looked at the crowd of anxious onlookers and firmly gave an order. "If you are not assisting, please leave the room. Bring towels and boiled water."

The men scurried out into the hallway, leaving Hime and Fangbane by Starlight's side. Mirari knew the young girl in celta robes would be of assistance, but she couldn't understand what the strange man with a mask could contribute.

"Leave." Mirari glared at him and pointed to the door.

"But I'm the husband," Fangbane reminded her.

"Unless you've done this before, leave."

Fangbane threw his hands up defensively as he side-stepped his way into the hall and shut the door behind him.

Mirari walked to Starlight's bedside and helped Hime turn Starlight on her side to prepare for delivery. Starlight groaned with each movement, now firmly grasping Mirari's hand.

"Don't worry. It's fine. We can handle this," Hime soothed her, placing a hand on Starlight's stomach. The soft blue glow radiating from her hand helped her relax, giving Starlight more control over her breathing.

The rest waited in the hall. All they could do was listen to Starlight's cries of pain, and pray…

A BABY's loud and healthy cry echoed through the estate. Dorain returned with a midwife moments later, who examined the infant's health and ran tests.

Starlight gently caressed the baby boy's cheek with her husband by her side, both of them beaming with pride. Hime sighed in relief as she cleaned the last bit of the room.

"I'm so glad you woke up, Mirari." Hime thanked her with a smile. "I've never delivered a baby by myself before."

Mirari nodded without a word, dull and expressionless. With Starlight's permission, Hime opened the door and allowed the worried men to enter the room and greet the baby.

"His name is Sarkan." Starlight beamed, showing off the tiny newborn in her arms.

"The God of Authority. What a powerful name," Hime said. Little did she know, there was much more meaning behind it.

Fangbane's eyes were glued to his new son sleeping soundly in his wife's arms.

We should tell Sorren he has a brother. He heard her communicate to him in a discreet manner behind her warm smile.

Fangbane nodded. He was ready to share the news with the world.

While everyone else was busy congratulating the couple on their adorable new baby, Gaven pulled Mirari to the back of the crowd to speak with her quietly.

"What were you thinking?" Gaven whispered in her ear. "You should worry about yourself first. You're uneasy. I can feel it. What's wrong?"

Mirari's face was blank for a long moment.

"Who are these people?" She finally asked in a low whisper with her back to them so they wouldn't notice. She looked up at him with heart-rending confusion in her eyes.

Gaven had hoped that when Mirari showed such skill and presence of mind while assisting with the delivery, she had come back to herself. Hearing her doubts, his throat dried up.

Overwhelming concern rolled over Fangbane as he registered the conversation happening between Mirari and Gaven, both verbal and non-verbal. Their distress was so strong it pushed right past the joy he felt for his wife and new child. Mirari's scrambled, confused, and frightened thoughts – her feeling of desperation and isolation – hit him like rollers flattening rocks.

"Hime, could you please run a diagnosis on Mirari?"

"Yes, of course." Hime scurried past the crowd and directed Mirari back to her room for an examination.

Mirari sat on the edge of her bed, her expression remained blank as Hime pressed her fingers lightly against her head to perform some assessments. The Knights observed Hime's work closely.

"Any pain or dizziness?" Hime asked, but Mirari remained silent in response and stared off into blank space. Her eyes focused on an empty wall in front of her.

"Do you see anything wrong?" Gaven asked.

"On the surface… no, I don't." Hime shook her head.

"Mirari, are you okay?" Dorain asked with uneasy concern.

"Are you hungry, M?" Neo asked. "I can go get you something."

Mirari gave no response to any of their questions. It was as if she wasn't even there with them at that moment.

"Can she hear us?" Shiba asked. They were all overwhelming Hime with questions that she couldn't, and didn't want to answer. Shiba moved closer, standing right in front of Mirari. "Hey kid, how many fingers am I holding up?"

"One," Mirari replied blandly, but a hint of annoyance was kindled at the idiotic question.

"Which one?"

Mirari's answer was flat. "Your middle finger."

The lack of anger worried even Shiba. "Something's definitely wrong with her."

Fangbane watched her look around, blinking, while they all talked about her. She searched for a face among them, hoping… but Salathiel was not there. He absorbed her emotions, feelings of confusion and uneasiness. With the concentrated attention of so many strangers on her, she began to fret.

How much do they know about her? How long had she been here? Those were only a few of the questions he heard in her mind. She remembered nothing more than waking up and delivering a baby. Whose baby? She didn't know.

"Do you mind?" Hime was startled when Starlight appeared by her side, beaming with her usual bright smile. She shooed away all the Knights, leaving only Fangbane, and Gaven in the room with Mirari. The baby was in the other room with the midwife, and she was still shaky from the delivery. But there was no denying Starlight was much better at diagnosing than Hime, if only because of her years of experience.

Fangbane and Gaven skulked at the edge of the door, watching with mounting concern as Starlight worked.

"She has amnesia. I sense abnormal activity in the cerebral cortex and her hippocampus. That electrical shock affected her neurotransmitters. If we don't act fast, her catecholamines may be depleted before she can recover enough to make more."

"What does that mean?" Gaven asked, shuffling his feet.

"Permanent memory loss."

"What would we need to help her recover?" Fangbane asked, determined to be the voice of reason and practicality.

"Frankly, we would need a genius," Starlight frowned. "She needs someone who can treat her frontal lobe, but all healers learn from the books and there has never been a successful study to prove how the brain does its work. Any trauma to the brain is deemed untreatable. Our only hope is to find a spellcaster who has experimented with the human brain."

"Mirari," Fangbane asked her politely, "can you remember the last thing that happened before you woke up?"

But Mirari still didn't respond. She didn't have to, though; Fangbane read the answer in her mind.

She wondered if she had been captured after being discovered as a Hale. Without Salathiel, she became uncertain of her position. Mirari wasn't even sure how much time had passed. Gaven's age gave her a good idea. She felt genuine kindness from those she met so far. Still, she questioned if any of them could be trusted, even Gaven.

Fangbane knelt closer to her bed and whispered so quietly only she could hear. "Mirari, I know how frightening this must be. But all of us are your friends. Once we help recover your memory, everything will make sense. Salathiel is safe, and we're your allies. We're here to help you."

But she already felt her trust for Gaven diminish along with her understanding of her situation. Fangbane was the only person who spoke any sense since she woke up, and he saw that his soothing voice gave her a speck of reassurance. Without much of an option, Mirari nodded in surrender.

LATER THAT NIGHT, Gaven brought some tea up to Mirari's room.

He pushed the door just enough to take a look inside, but it was much too dark to make out anything. He entered the room, treading with light steps, both to avoid waking Mirari up and to prevent himself from tumbling into anything, and placed the tray by the bed. He glanced over and immediately noticed that only a pillow was tucked underneath the blanket.

Before he could react, Gaven felt his wrist being jerked behind his back. A sharp elbow shoved him down and crushed him against the bed, pressing the cold blade of a knife against his neck, and preventing him from turning around.

It was only a butter knife, but sharp enough to cut through the skin.

"I need you to answer honestly." Mirari exuded a calmness Gaven had never seen in her before. She relaxed her stance but kept the grip on her knife taut. "Are you my friend or are you my enemy?"

"I'm your partner."

"What does that mean?"

"It means we're bound by blood. I share your strength. I feel your pain. My honor and loyalty are with you."

"What's my name?"

"Mirari."

"My full name."

"Mirari Zanette. You're a merchant from Solarin. You lived there with your brother, and…" He thought for a moment. "And you have an uncanny habit of having bellberry juice for breakfast."

Mirari paused to analyze the situation. All his claims were true. But he didn't know her name…

Roselyn Hale. It came to her in a flash, but…

If he doesn't know then why was she here?

She tried to focus, but she could not fathom her presence

here. Yet somehow, her gut told her Gaven was speaking the truth he knew.

She slowly released her grip on him and backed away.

"How do I know you're speaking the truth?"

Gaven gave himself a hard pinch on his own arm.

"OW! Quit that," she howled.

"Do you believe me now?" A realization bloomed on her face. Even if she didn't understand it, she knew he was demonstrating the truth. "I know things may not make sense now, but we'll find a way to get your memory to return."

With her trembling hand, she placed the knife on the table in defeat.

"I don't know what's going on..." Mirari whimpered to herself, tears ready to fall from her clouded eyes. Gaven stood back up and placed both hands on her shoulder. He looked into her eyes that still refused to meet, and pulled her in for a tight hug.

"You're going to be okay. I promise you that."

CHAPTER TWENTY-FIVE

"Lucan, how's your search for the specialist?" Starlight asked the next morning in the dining hall. It was a busy day and everyone jumped on their duties earlier than usual, most in search of a healer for Mirari.

"Shire contacted me an hour ago. He's close to the area where he's sure he'll find her. If she's willing to listen to him, we should hear an update soon enough."

Lucan's connections were their last hope. As a businessman, he knew a lot of powerful people across the empires.

He was standing in the shaded part of the room, back turned against the window where the sun was shining. Starlight had noticed this behavior of his for quite some time.

"Lucan, may I ask you something?" Starlight kept her voice low to be discreet.

"Yes, of course, Milady."

"I don't mean to pry, but I notice you carry an intriguing set of medications."

Lucan was surprised. He was very inconspicuous about his medications. It wasn't that he was ashamed, but… he had found it best kept private. People tended to get uncomfortable with his condition. So he simply avoided the topic.

"I was born with a rare form of albinism. Unlike most, my body still functions normally, except…"

"Extreme sensitivity to sunlight?"

"I'm practically helpless without my medicine."

"Does it hurt?"

"More like 'does it burn'. Sunlight seems to drain me of energy the instant it touches my skin."

"That must be very difficult for you."

"The medicine allows my skin to function normally, so I can step into the sun without incinerating," he said, trying to make light of his condition. "But I still try to avoid exposure, just in case."

"And your eyes?"

He takes a moment before going on. "So far, I haven't had any deterioration. But… I know I can expect problems as I age. It's inevitable, they say."

"I know you have excellent medical and research resources in Valenia. The best there is, in a conventional sense."

"Conventional? Meaning what?"

"There are many roads to health and well-being. Here in Minetta, I admit we are behind your empire in many ways, medicine included. However, if I'm not mistaken, those herbs and extracts you carry, didn't come from Valenia, did they?"

Lucan smiled. "For someone who doesn't pry, you manage to notice an awful lot, Milady."

"Sorry. But when you live with a mind reader like my husband, the boundaries of privacy do seem to blur at times."

"It's not a secret. I have a lot of respect for the folk knowledge of your culture, as well as the healers of Althaea, like Princess Hime. And you're right. The medicines I rely on do not come from Valenia but a spellcaster in Minetta, as you no doubt have guessed."

"And this person… that's who you sent your retainer to find?"

Lucan nodded, smiling. "Are you sure it's only Lord Fangbane who reads minds?"

ANOTHER HOUR PASSED before Lucan's clōve glowed as it received a call from Shire. He quickly activated it, its threads illuminating to blue.

"Found her," Shire said from the other end with frantic excitement. "She's willing to meet near Narona Peak, south side of the harbor in Akoun."

"Where, exactly?"

"She… won't say. She'll give further directions only when you get here."

Lucan shook his head. "I'd expect as much. Okay, we're on the way."

He delivered the news, and Fangbane assigned Hime to remain with Starlight to look after her and the new baby. Along with Gaven and Lucan, he rushed Mirari out into a carriage, and they were off to the neighboring town of Akoun.

"This woman," Gaven asked, "you say she's not a healer?"

"Not exactly," Lucan said, reluctant to provide details.

"Then what in Inferna does she do?"

Lucan shrugged. "She writes spells… among other things."

Gaven shot a worried look at Mirari. But she was just staring out at the passing scenery, her eyes serene but vacant.

"I mean," Gaven said, "how do we know she can help? What if she makes things worse?"

Fangbane turned his eye on Mirari, and said, "I'm not sure she could get much worse. As it is, she's lost to everyone, especially herself."

"She doesn't study medicine, but she is known to perform miracles," Lucan said.

Gaven frowned. "So, a spellcaster?"

"Yes, but more than that. She's… well, unique. She's an innovator in her own way."

"Ha!" Gaven huffed. "Sounds like some kind of witch."

Fangbane caught a glimpse of the person in Lucan's mind, and turned to him. "Ah, yes. I thought as much. She has quite a reputation, all right."

Lucan added, "She doesn't like to be called a witch. But people do call her the Witch of Aten."

"Ah, quit screwing around. I'm not some kid to frighten with ghost stories." Gaven recalled all the political studies that Suzan made him do before he was promoted to region leader. He was well aware of this witch from Valenia, but without concrete evidence, she was nothing more than a myth. He doubted there was even a spellcaster capable of what the rumors claimed she could do.

"Kylah Kein has a bad reputation, I'll grant you," said Fangbane. "But she's not a myth. I can attest to that."

"She's the only one who's ever been able to help with my medical situation. I'm privileged to be her longtime friend, but even I don't know her whereabouts most of the time."

"If she's real, then she's an outlaw. We shouldn't be trusting people like that."

Lucan didn't answer right away. "She is doing us a great favor revealing herself to us," he said, choosing his words carefully.

"You'd better be right," Gaven said and turned to look at Mirari who still stared blankly, a lost soul, wandering in the fog of her mind.

***

BETWEEN THICK SHRUBS AND TREES, Lucan caught sight of his blue-haired leprechaun waving from the side of the inclined dirt path. The carriage came to a halt in the middle of the forest. With his uncontained youth, Shire bounced toward the carriage and hastily opened the door for his liege.

"Is she here?" Lucan called, stepping out of the carriage.

"Follow me," Shire said, waving all of them forward in a hurry. As Gaven helped Mirari down, Shire pushed apart a gap in the bushes, invisible until he parted the branches to reveal a faint path into the forest. "This way," the boy said.

Fangbane pulled the carriage off the road, leaving it in a quiet, shady glen, and followed the others down the secret path.

After half a mile, Gaven grumbled aside to Fangbane. "Nobody said we should wear our hiking boots."

Lucan, hearing him, answered back. "Disappointed, Valiant Tiger? I suppose you prefer your witches to live in a spooky old castle."

"Right now, I'd settle for a tumble-down hut made of sticks and…"

"And mud?" Lucan mocked, pointing at Kylah Kein's home – a tumble-down hut made of sticks and mud.

A hooded figure sat in front of the hut poking at a fire, which had a steaming blackened pot hanging over it. Her back was to her visitors, and she did not turn to see who they were or offer any greeting.

"Hello, Kylah," Lucan said, doffing the wide brimmed hat he always wore to keep the sun off his face. "Thank you for allowing us to visit you."

"Is that her?" she croaked. She still had her back to them. "Bring her closer."

Gaven started to walk with Mirari, but Lucan blocked his path and took Mirari's arm.

"Fine," Gaven grumbled and turned to stand with Fangbane, his strides heavy as he displayed his annoyance. Lucan and Mirari took small wary steps toward the hooded woman who still wouldn't turn around. She continued watching the fire, tending to whatever was brewing in her steaming pot.

"What time is lunch?" Gaven called to her.

The woman froze and very slowly began to turn. A sense of impending menace radiated from her, or so it felt to Gaven. Fangbane could read his mounting terror.

"Steady, old man," he said.

"Why is she hiding under that hood?" Gaven said. "Have some manners and show your face."

"Don't worry. Not all of us aspire to show off our handsome countenance."

Gaven glanced at him, but as always, he met only the frozen expression of Fangbane's ever present mask.

When he turned back, he gasped in horror. The Witch of Aten was standing face to face with him, only a foot apart. He felt his knees turn to water, and he quaked with a fear he had never known on the battlefield. When she started to raise her hands, he took a staggering step backward.

But all she was doing was reaching to pull back her hood. Gaven panicked, terrified to see what lay underneath. He shut his eyes tight, almost like a child hoping to make her disappear.

"What troubles you, 'Valiant Tiger'? Is my face so hideous to behold?"

He pushed back hard on his fear and forced himself to open his eyes.

It was… staggering. His eyes were drawn to hers, wide and red as an apple. Small dimples hid behind her long, golden hair that looked like it had been brushed a thousand times.

"Your face is…" he murmured, captivated. "You… You're…"

But Fangbane was there to hear his thoughts and said them aloud. "Beautiful as a rising sun, Kylah. He is struck dumb."

Kylah laughed, and raised her hands in a playful gesture, freeing a tumble of lustrous hair. "Thanks. You're not too hard on the eyes yourself, Tiger." She gave him a wink. But during the time it took to blink, she was gone, back to her fire, where Lucan and Mirari stood in wait.

Lucan briefly described what had happened as he handed Kylah a hand-written medical report Starlight had taken down during her analysis. Kylah skimmed through, barely bothering to glance at the notes.

She turned to Mirari. She had grasped the gravity of her condition even before she lay her fingers on the girl's head. She closed her eyes, watching something only she could see.

She turned sharply to Lucan, wagging a finger at him. "You've outdone yourself this time."

"It was an accident."

"So is falling off a cliff. Doesn't make the landing any softer."

She inspected the patient more closely now, studying her face, reading her features, trying to work something out. Kylah raised an eyebrow and did a double take looking from Mirari to Lucan.

"Why, of course… you must be overjoyed to see her again."

"You know Mirari?" Lucan asked, quirking his brow in puzzlement.

He didn't use her real name, and she frowned at him. "You… don't?"

"What do you mean?"

Kylah stared at Lucan as if she was waiting for an explanation. But his silence was enough. He didn't know.

"Oh Mirari," she murmured, "what have you gotten yourself into?" Kylah shook her head and took Mirari's hand in hers as she examined her eyes.

"Your healers did a good job preventing the spread of damage," Kylah said, humming before she continued. "Luckily, it's not permanent. Her brain just needs a simple wake up call. I don't blame your healers for not knowing what to do. This is uncharted territory, which is why celtas are so stupid, always relying on books."

"Can you fix it?" Lucan asked, worry and guilt evident in his hope.

"You know, you really shouldn't rely on me for situations like this. I'm no medic," she reminded him, which told Lucan that Kylah knew exactly what to do. "It's a theory. Worked on frogs… but I've never done this on a living person before."

Kylah waved her wrist in front of Mirari, forcing her to focus on the colorful charms on her golden bracelet. They jingled hypnotically, and the blue and green gems began to light up. Kylah recited incantations in some unknown language.

As Mirari's eyes remained focused on the gems, they glowed brighter. She found herself in a trance, hearing only Kylah's foreign words and seeing dancing colors twinkle in front of her, increasingly bright, until she could see nothing else.

The gems stopped glowing. Mirari blinked a few times, slowly readjusting to her environment. She looked up at Kylah and Lucan.

"Next time, I would prefer that you finish your kills. You'd spare me a lot of bother," Kylah said, in a deadpan tone.

"Kylah, that's morbid." Her dark humor still made him smile, but this time it was no laughing matter. "This is the Valiant Tiger's partner. He would have my head if I killed her."

Kylah noticed Gaven trying to look inconspicuous. He kept his eyes on the fire. "If you're still thinking about lunch, Tiger," she warned him, "you'd best stay clear of that brew."

She didn't quite get how things were adding up, and she had more questions than answers looking at Mirari, Lucan, and Gaven. She turned to Lucan.

"His partner will be as good as new. You can pay me in two shipments of helmia and five boar tusks. Same location as usual. Let Mirari rest for a few weeks. A slow and gradual process is a healthy one."

Mirari looked at Lucan and then back at the person who had just healed her.

"Ky… lah?" Mirari mumbled in confusion and bewilderment. She had just the tickle of a vague memory of this woman.

"Yeah, she'll be alright," Kylah confirmed.

"How do you know her?" Lucan asked.

Kylah glanced at Mirari, then back at him, before she shook her head. "She needs to tell you that herself. It is none of my business."

Instead of pushing the matter, Lucan simply thanked her again and escorted Mirari back to the carriage. Once there, Mirari began recognizing faces, finding them to be familiar, but her memories were still fuzzy and vague.

CHAPTER TWENTY-SIX

A week passed. The occupants of Fangbane and Starlight's estate gave Mirari the time and space to recover. For days she stayed in her room and took walks through the empty halls. She daydreamed of moments spent with the Knights, the satisfying journey so far. Then she passed Lucan in the main hall and remembered that they still had things to discuss.

"You're looking well," he said, encouraged by the spring in her step.

"I feel great." Mirari smiled to reassure him. She spread her arms wide, even doing a little pirouette to show off her perfect condition.

"Once again, I apologize for what happened. It was—"

"An accident, I know." Mirari swept her hand through the air, gesturing to brush the thought aside. "Kylah is great, isn't she?"

"She is." Lucan paused. "How do you know her?"

"I…" Mirari thought carefully of her words. She had remembered a lot in the past week. About the time lost between Gaven and her. About Salathiel going missing. How she'd run away from her birth family, and kept her real name a secret. If she decided to keep her identity hidden from Lucan, her lie could not be sloppy.

"I met Kylah in Solarin. It was back when she was hiding from the Tribe of Paragons."

"Right. She still thinks they're after her."

"And are they?"

Lucan measured his answer. "Not… openly. But I've learned to trust her instincts." He switched gears. "Solarin, huh? Seems like an ideal place to go unnoticed. Lots of small towns in Minetta. Small, yet sustainable. They make for an ideal safe house."

"Solarin is a busy trading town. Anyone trying to hide there would be a fool."

"I suppose so…"

They were quiet for a beat. Uncomfortable with the direction the conversation was heading, she asked, "Do you miss Valenia?"

"Yes and no. Shire sends me messages daily. Gods, hourly it seems. So no. Sometimes it feels impossible to believe I've left home at all."

"I'm surprised they let you join the Knights. The Hales, that is."

"Well, no. They weren't happy about it," Lucan said with a speck of sorrow. "I believe in what Fangbane is trying to accomplish, and I know I can help, but as far as an endorsement from my family is concerned? Let's just say I came here out of my own will and I hope to prove a point. In the meantime, I must assume all my regular responsibilities, just from afar."

"They'd hate to let you go. You're a smart man."

"As are you. A smart lady, that is." Mirari tilted her head, waiting for his explanation. "I mean, I noticed you don't carry the mannerisms of a simple country merchant."

"What do you mean?"

"For one, there's a spark of grace in the way you speak."

"Gosh, mister," she teased in a country accent. "Them's mighty purty words of yours."

"Ah, no. You're more complicated than you let on. Why, if you told me you were a noble, I'd believe you."

Mirari snorted and faked a laugh, slapping her hand on her knee. "I appreciate the compliment… if that is one."

"If you don't mind me asking something personal," Lucan began with an air of curiosity, "are you and Region Leader Gaven related?"

"What? No, of course not." Mirari kept the smile plastered on her face, but alarms were going off inside her. "Our names are just a coincidence."

"To my knowledge, the Zanette clan has almost all male heirs in this generation."

"And how would you know a thing like that?"

"Oh, by the love of Candela, don't ask." But he could see Mirari cock her head in a look that he knew was both curious and stubborn. "My mother. Obsessed with breeding, lines of succession, genealogy. When I was a boy, she'd make me help her catalog practically every family line there is. Not just Valenia. The whole Alliance. She was relentless."

"I bet mommy was worried her little Lucan might breed with some young tart with peasant in her veins."

"Well, that worry is gone. Dear mother is communing with her ancestors now."

"And you've forgotten all about it."

"I wish. I'm afraid I have one of those memories that won't let me forget anything."

"Braggart, I wish I could say that."

"Well, anyway. As I was saying, the shape of your nose, the angle of your jaw, and the color of your eyes – you resemble more of the Hale family than the Zanette family."

"Me? A Hale? Don't get me wrong, I could use the money. But I'm just not cut out for a life of satin pillows and caviar."

"No. I understand. The truth is, neither am I." He smiled. "But that doesn't mean I'm any less of a Hale."

"Well… maybe somebody left you at the door in a basket."

"Mirari, is your blood truly of the Zanette family?" Lucan asked again.

Mirari felt cornered, and she didn't like it. "Frankly, your interrogation is making me uncomfortable. I am who I am."

"Oh, I do apologize." Lucan bowed. Getting Mirari upset was the last thing he wanted. "I'm sorry to be such a… well, I'm sort of a bore sometimes." He buried his hands in his pockets and shifted his gaze across the room, toward a plant and then the window. "I'm aware I tend to say… Well, not things of the ordinary, and…"

"Lucan. It's alright." Mirari smiled. "It's who you are, and I would never ask you to change that."

He turned so… not pale, it was almost like he blushed. It's true, she did find him rather adorable, but she would never have said that except it seemed like a good way to change the subject, and get his mind somewhere else.

"Anyway, I enjoyed chatting with you. But I am meeting with His Honor, so… See you soon."

She sighed with relief as she started walking away.

Genealogy. She rolled her eyes. Why was that not a surprise to her? Lucan always had to know everything.

"I'd like to treat you to supper sometime," she heard him call from behind. "If not to apologize… then to perhaps discuss your unique birthmark."

Mirari felt as if a big sharp icicle had dropped from high above, and pierced through her skull, and down her spinal cord. Her hand shot up her bare neck – her hair had been pinned up this whole time.

How careless she was. A birthmark on the back of her neck, no larger than the curve of her nails. Oddly shaped, almost like a plump songbird, and standing out against her creamy skin like a dark tan stain. He had the same mark. How could she have forgotten about that?

It wasn't something she could escape. There was no lie to cover this one. She had to admit defeat.

Mirari looked back at Lucan with guilt boiling up inside, wondering what would come next. But Lucan had a warm smile spreading over his face.

"Am I wrong, Roselyn?"

At the sound of that name, Mirari gulped hard. She had made it through weeks without being suspected, only to screw the pooch now. She was furious at herself for being so careless.

And yet... here was Lucan, with his arms wide open. A new feeling washed over her. He knew. And it wasn't the end of the world.

"Lucan..." she said, as tears choked her. "I'm... sorry. I didn't mean to—"

He threw himself to her. The arms were family, and she couldn't resist his embrace. The hug was the best thing she had felt in many years. For the first time since Salathiel's disappearance, she felt the warmth of familiarity.

"You were always a genius." She gave in eventually, letting a little smile cross her lips. "I knew I wouldn't be able to keep it from you for long."

To her surprise, Lucan didn't just hug her. Mirari couldn't help letting out a squeak of surprise as he picked her up and swung her body in a full circle like a child.

It felt like a door to their childhood had been kicked open. It was wonderful, and also strange. Lucan had grown into such a mature and serious man. She didn't expect he would still have his playful side. But Mirari could feel that connection they shared so long ago. It was the feeling, she realized, she had always longed for from Gaven, but never received.

"I can't believe it," Lucan said. "I'm so happy you're alive."

"I've missed you too, Lucan..." Mirari quickly wiped the

tears falling from her eyes before they landed on his expensive vest.

"If you don't mind me asking…"

Mirari hesitated for a second, but in reality, she had nothing to hide from Lucan anymore. She wanted to tell him her story. To finally open up to someone she could trust.

Her euphoria was interrupted by the echoing of footsteps. "What's with all the excitement?" Gaven called from down the hall. Mirari peered over Lucan's shoulder and let go, returning to her professional stance.

"He, uh…" Mirari struggled to make an excuse. Lucan took the hint. Their reunion would have to wait.

"I got her a gift to apologize," Lucan lied with the slick charm of a horse trader. "When you're free, you can stop by my chambers to pick it up," he said to Mirari.

Lucan bowed and left to give them privacy.

"Your memory," Gaven began, able to feel that she was flushed. "You seem to be recovering very well."

Mirari made a conscious effort to recall everything that happened over the past week. She remembered almost every event, with only a few fuzzy sections.

"I think so."

"That's wonderful. But I'm still not sure how you were only able to remember me and not—"

She didn't want to let him finish his sentence, nudging him with her own conclusion. "I must have said some crazy things, right? Off my rocker, and all that… Who knows? Maybe our bond kept my memory of you in place."

"I… suppose that's possible. Weird, huh?"

"Sure is." She shrugged, trying to look like it was no big deal. She wanted nothing more than this subject to end. "By the way, I'm sorry about that thing with the knife."

"You weren't yourself, don't worry, I understand. Remember, we're in this together." He held out a fist in front of her as a symbol of their collaboration, a Knight's code to stay firm and stay together. Mirari smiled and lightly tapped his fist with hers.

"So, can you fill me in on what happened during the Althaean Siege?" Gaven joked. Mirari tried to dig into the deeper parts of her memory, but it was still blank.

"Sorry," she shrugged. She too was hoping that the shock would reboot her lost memory. But maybe the memory was truly lost.

"We may never regain that memory, and perhaps none of it is really important. What we have now, in the present, that's what truly matters."

"You know, Your Honor," Mirari began, giving him a comforting smile. "When I had amnesia, it made me realize how lucky I am to be here, and to know you and the rest of the team. You are all very caring, like a true family. I know I'm not exactly perfect—"

"Who told you that?" he said, teasing her.

"I just mean… you never gave up on me, none of you. And now I have the honor of being your partner. I don't expect you to be perfect either, and I'll never give up on you."

"Does that mean you're staying?"

Mirari squeezed the badge on her chest. She was genuinely thankful to have met such kind people over the past couple of months. For the first time in her life, she felt that she belonged in a place where people truly wanted her to stay. Mirari could never walk away from this, never bring herself to go back to Solarin. Not only because she would miss the team, but also because she knew they would miss her.

They were doing something meaningful together, and it was a cause she didn't want to let go of. The thought made Mirari smile broadly.

"Yes, it means I'm staying."

CHAPTER TWENTY-SEVEN

K ylah waited at the entrance of a vast forest located miles away from the nearest town. She remained hidden in the undergrowth as she watched a stranger approach. He was a big man, sturdy as the surrounding trees, and in his arms were three wooden crates wider than the giant himself. She was expecting him but she left nothing to chance and remained cautious.

"Stop there," she said, and the big man did as she asked. "Who sent you?"

"Lucan said to tell you 'toads are better than frogs'. I think that was it, anyway."

Satisfied with the password, Kylah stepped out into the open. She went to the large containers and began to inspect them.

"Two crates of helmia and five boar tusks," Neo said.

She looked up and ran a critical eye over him in response. She was not comfortable with the new delivery man.

She raised an eyebrow to show her displeasure, whether at his words or himself, Neo couldn't tell. While she had trusted Lucan's choice in people he sent for the deliveries, she wasn't pleased with a change in routine. She could not afford to let her guard down.

"Normally, I get my deliveries in a wagon," she muttered. "You expect me to carry this?"

"I'll bring it all the way to your front door, Ma'am."

"That's not how it works," Kylah snapped. She scowled as she looked down at the crates. They were too much for her to carry, even one at a time. She had no choice. She inspected the big man again, noting the beautifully crafted iron gauntlets he wore.

"A brawler, then. In service to whom?"

"Region Leader Shiba Zabato of Avon. And Lord Fangbane at the moment."

"Oh, you're one of them? These 'Knights' of his?"

"I am. And at your service."

"Fine, then. Come along. This way." Kylah led Neo over narrow paths, and through dense trees. He humped along with the bulky crates until they arrived at her hideaway home. The fire pit outside was still steaming. Neo assumed she had put it out just before she went to meet him at the road. The fire pit was larger than the hut she lived in and was carefully constructed, with better care than her dwelling.

Kylah gestured dismissively for Neo to place the supplies next to her hut. He did exactly as instructed, but received not a word of thanks. She made a point of ignoring him and went into her squalid hut.

Neo shrugged. He was a friendly man unless someone crossed him. He could see this woman lived her life in constant fear. He examined the fragile hut and realized its rough quality was due to her frequent residential disposition. There was little sign of comfort in her camp.

She came back out and scowled at the sight of him. "Why are you still here? On your way, stranger."

Neo nodded at her decrepit lean-to. "This doesn't look safe," he said with genuine concern in his voice. "I could fix it up. Wouldn't take much of a storm to knock it to—"

"Leave, brawler," Kylah barked, cutting him off cold. She turned her back on him, picking through the bottles in one of the cases he brought. Whether she was about to prepare some noxious recipe in the blackened cauldron over her fire pit or was just making a show of ignoring him, he got the message.

"Well then, Milady," he said, "it has been a pleasure, to be sure." Neo turned, and walked away, hoping to remember the path back to the road.

***

KYLAH SAT HUNCHED near her firepit, squinting back and forth between some ancient tome and a leaf of parchment, scribbling notes for a new spell. The twitter of a songbird caught her attention, and when she looked up, she saw the sun starting to rise. She realized she had stayed up all night again. It was not unusual for her, and her habits were nobody's business since she lived all by herself.

She got up to brew herself a mug of buzzbean, and was about to set her kettle over the fire when an unfamiliar sound froze her in place. Something was shuffling in the shrubs nearby. She patted her hooded robe, reassuring herself that the dagger was where it should be. Last week she had concocted a new batch of the poison she used to coat the blade. She was confident it was at full potency and could drop a bear with the slightest prick. She carefully hid behind a tree, listening as the intruder drew closer. She was ready to kill at the least sign of threat. Whoever it was, they certainly did not bother to move quietly.

When she saw the lumbering giant haul into view, she relaxed. But that didn't mean she was happy to see him again.

"Why are you back? Do you not understand the concept of privacy?"

Neo only smiled at her, friendly and polite as ever. He was dragging a handcart behind him, carrying a large pile of freshly cut planks of wood. He stopped by the hut, and began to unload the lumber.

"What are you doing? This isn't a public trash heap."

"I imagine you have to point that out to most people."

"There is no 'most people'. Nobody is welcome here, and that includes you."

"I'm not here for a visit. I'm just here to fix your house," Neo said, pointing to her disheveled hut.

"I didn't ask you to, moron." An alarming thought occurred to her. "How did you get past my traps?"

Neo smiled. "I have to compliment your skills, Milady. You cast enough security spells around your camp to kill a small army."

"But not you, I'm sorry to say."

"Kore neutralizer." Neo grinned as he drew a chain from under his tunic. A glowing crystal was centered on the necklace.

"That isn't enough. What else did you use."

"Ah, I had help from a comrade. He's a master aegis, and he lent me a few of his enchanted arrows. I stuck some into the trees, to make a safe path for myself."

"That doesn't explain how you knew where to put them."

"Don't take this the wrong way, but I know exactly how aster spells work."

Kylah froze, now riddled with guilt. He must have noticed the cursed symbol tattooed on her right hand. The sign meant she could employ a type of spellcasting only an elite few could perform. But how could he have seen it? She had cast an illusion spell over it, making the mark invisible unless she chose to reveal it.

"So..." she said, wary. "You're not just some brutish brawler after all." She felt a foreboding chill, and had to fight the urge to run. Although the oaf didn't look like he intended any harm, in fact, his expression was more like a mooning school boy nursing a crush. She realized her hood was drawn back, leaving her face and scarlet tresses in full view. Quickly, she flipped the hood up, hiding in the privacy of her shadow of gloom.

"Well? What are you staring at, ox boy?"

Neo blushed, although he was unfamiliar with this strange heat flashing over him. "Ap-apologies, Milady."

His stumbling shyness put her at ease. Her eyes darted back to the pile of wood. "Well then? What are you waiting for? Are you going to fix my house or not?"

"Y-yes, Milady!" Without hesitation, Neo scrambled to the pile of wood and lifted a few planks to the side of her hut, making mental measurements. "These will support your foundation. At least when it rains, it won't collapse."

"I don't know why I should let you bother," Kylah muttered. "Now that you know where I live, and how to break through my traps, I would have to move again anyway."

Neo stopped and looked back at her. "Who are you hiding from, if I may ask, Milady?"

"Do you have to ask?" Her voice rising as she held her hand in front of her. "If you can see my aster crest, then you know who I am."

"Kylah, right? My name's Neo."

She wasn't buying. "Cut the crap, Na Ore. What is it you want from me?"

Neo was stunned. His birth name was a secret known only to him, and very few others.

He tried to brush it off. "Nothing. Or, what I mean is… well, I don't feel comfortable with someone like you living all the way out here on your own."

"Someone like me?" she seethed. "Would you feel more comfortable if this 'dangerous' spellcaster was locked in the dungeons of the Naito Mountains? Sorry, brawler. You're not taking me back to Valenia."

"No, no I'm not here to take you back. I meant it's heart-breaking seeing a pretty lady out here by herself." Neo grew flustered, then added, "Even if you are a capable spellcaster."

He left her speechless. Kylah turned back to her kettle to avoid his gaze. "I killed your people. You should hate me like the rest of your comrades in the Tribe of Paragons."

"I'm not an enemy, nor am I a member of the Tribe of Paragons."

Though, he couldn't deny he had friends in Valenia – Neo was born in Minetta, his parents were indeed from the Tribe of Paragons in Valenia, and he kept close contact with the tribespeople.

"What happened was truly a tragedy," Neo said, knowing why she was hated among the Tribe of Paragons. "But I don't see how any of it is your fault. You didn't know the Tribe of Celtas would use your poison to start a war."

"It happened regardless. And the paragons will never let it go until they have my head on a pike."

"You're protected under Minettan law. They can't detain you or send you back to Valenia."

"Yes. But nothing is stopping the swines from killing me right here on your 'protected' Minettan soil."

"That will not happen," Neo said, dead serious.

"And what would make you say that?"

"Because I would rip the arms off of any man who tried to harm you."

It was Kylah's turn to blush. She was glad her face was hidden. "That's very noble of you. I know you are a powerful paragon. Your partnership with the Shadow Soldier makes you twice as deadly as well. But however good your intentions, nobody can guarantee my safety."

"True…" He smiled. "But if I don't fix this hovel you live in, it will fall and kill you anyway."

"Just like a brawler. Stubborn as a mule."

"Which is it, Milady? Am I an ox, or a mule?"

"I suppose only time will tell." She laughed now and drew back her hood. "Well? Don't waste the whole morning. Let's see if you're a carpenter, instead."

"As you wish, Milady," he said, with a wide grin. He was reluctant to tear his eyes off her, but he made himself turn to the task at hand.

"How do you take your buzzbean?"

"Black is fine with me." Neo felt almost as high as the Tower of Axillaire. He didn't need any buzzbean. But he'd be very happy to have it if Kylah was drinking it with him.

PART IV

CHAPTER TWENTY-EIGHT

Tensions rose in Fangbane's study as powerful leaders quarreled among each other. Anyone who walked by the room would be able to pick up on their conversation, and the issue was not unknown to the residents of the estate. For months, they had wondered how long the Knights would last. They lived every day to the fullest, together, mingling and bantering, ignoring the cruel reality that the Council could shut them down as soon as the next dawn.

"Suzan, we went over this." It was Fangbane's turn to raise his voice. He stood as sturdy as the mask over his face that was made with cepha metals. They were hard to break, much like his pride. If the Council was going to burn his estate to the ground, he was ready to go down with it.

"You need to disband," Suzan warned one last time in a hushed tone that elicited more fear than her raised voice.

"You dare say that it's a wasted effort?"

"Of course not. But I couldn't persuade the Council to think otherwise."

"It's Dareh who's making this personal, right?" Gaven spoke

up, thinking back on Dorain's plea to stay with the Knights. "Let me speak with him directly. I'll—"

Suzan raised her hand. "You will not make things better." She saw Gaven snarl at her and continued, "No, it's not just Dareh. Even the Valenian representatives don't want this to continue."

"That doesn't make any sense. Why would they care? We even got Lucan deep-pocket Hale on the team."

"You're stirring too much attention. Everyone knows who you are now, even empires outside of the alliance. People are starting to talk about change, a new society. They want to be like you, and as much as I believe you have pure intentions, not everyone following your idea will. We have to suppress this before it becomes another revolution."

"Alright," Fangbane gave in, not seeming to care all that much about what the Council thought about him or his Knights. "That's fine. We don't need their approval."

Suzan turned to her protégé. "Gaven, please. Can't you talk some sense into him?"

"Fangbane? Arguing with him is useless."

She looked at the stubborn mind reader again. "I won't bother wasting my breath then. Just know that when the royal guards show up, I can't help you."

Fangbane gave a tiny nod of acknowledgment. "In that case, why don't you tell Gaven the good news and be on your way."

Gaven tilted his head, wondering what good could come after an hour of pointing knives at each other's throat.

Suzan cut another look at Fangbane. "You can't help stealing my thunder, can you?

"The Council has declared that you're free to return to Althaea. Your sentence is over."

"What?" Gaven was visibly interested now. "Is there a catch? It hasn't even been a full year since I was banished."

"Starlight's reports for the past two months deem you fully recovered."

Gaven was glad that he was 'medically cleared'. He still had headaches – though much milder and less frequent since he became partners with Mirari – and his memory was still lost in the universe, replaced by haunting guilt he wasn't sure he could ever recover from. Starlight's reports had been much too kind.

Fangbane didn't let him celebrate. "Honestly? Call me paranoid, but this has the feel of a set up."

"Because you don't want me to leave," Gaven said.

"Exactly. Without you, the foundation of the Knights will be weakened. The Council did this on purpose."

"What's the difference? To me, I mean. I don't have an ax hanging over my head, and I don't care why."

"I'm sorry you see it that way."

"Sooner or later, we all knew this day would come."

Fangbane made no reply. He already knew what Gaven was about to say, and it was true.

"Fang, you knew when we started, my duty as a region leader will always come before your project."

Fangbane knew very well that Gaven had an honorable commitment to take his position as region leader. By law, by custom, and by practice, he couldn't refuse his obligation to go home and resume his duties. The uncertainty lay in whether or not Gaven would want anything to do with the Knights once he left.

ON HER WAY OUT, Suzan noticed Shiba waiting at the end of the hallway. She was happy to see an old friend, and approached him with a smile. As usual, he skipped the chit-chat, and cut to the point.

"So, the Council still doesn't like us?"

"You can't tell me you're surprised."

Shiba fell into step with her. "Oh, I'm surprised. I expected they'd show up at the gate with a hundred armed men to enforce their will."

"Really? You think a hundred would be enough?"

"Not even close," he said and appeared to relish in the thought.

"It's not you," Suzan said while Shiba escorted her through the estate and back out toward the main gate. "Althaean–Minettan relationships have always been quite hostile."

"What a surprise."

"Funny. Look, it's not just the prejudice between the people. The rivalry in the Council is even worse. Each side wants to take power from the other. Along come the Knights with their high-minded ideals of equality and what have you. This little experiment of yours doesn't just pose a threat to the Council. Even within each empire, there are region leaders who look at their neighbors and desire whatever they see. All of this is threatened by the existence of the Knights. You've caused quite a stir over the past couple of months."

"All for the good. You can't deny that. People like us."

"And other people don't. People with power do not like change."

"They are all idiots. Too selfish to see that everyone wins if the three empires simply try to work together."

Suzan chuckled. "That doesn't sound like the fierce Shadow Soldier I know."

"But… just look at us here. We all get along fine."

Suzan smirked, almost playfully. "Since when have you been so passionate about Althaean–Minettan peace?"

Shiba grew flustered. "I… you know the reason."

Suzan realized that this wasn't something to tease Shiba about. He was still an aggressive braggart. But ever since an

Althaean princess gave up her royal privilege to join his army, and to capture his heart, he had lost the lust for war.

"You only joined the Knights out of debt to Fangbane, but I can see it has done you good. You're recovering. Your mother would've been proud."

"Too bad I'll never know what she thinks."

"You seek to follow what Princess Mecate can no longer do, and that would be enough for her. Unfortunately, most leaders don't see the need or urgency for the Knights."

"Ask the people we've helped."

"A wonderful thing, and a drop in the bucket." They had reached her carriage. Suzan became more urgent, wanting to convey the reasoning and the reality. "Every empire already has a dedicated class of fighters. That's who the Council expects to defend the respective empires."

"And we both know justice falls through the cracks of bureaucracy."

"The bottom line is, people don't see the point of a unified force. For that, you'd have to prove to the empires that they need the Knights…"

"How can we if the Council won't let us?"

"You're clever," Suzan said. "Surprise us."

———

GAVEN WAS ALREADY PACKING when Fangbane appeared at his door. "Not wasting any time, I see."

"No point in dragging it out."

Fangbane watched Gaven load the last of his belongings into his bag, but he didn't take everything. Stacks of paperwork were sorted on his desk next to his impressive collection of empty wine bottles. There was still room left in his pouch, but he didn't bother taking his chest of daggers or the notebook he used to log the Knight's training regimen. Some of his clothes were abandoned on his shelf, the rest tossed to the ground. It was unclear to Fangbane whether or not Gaven intended to return.

"I understand you want to return home very badly," Fangbane said.

"Do you?" Gaven turned to him.

"Of course. You are the Valiant Tiger of Althaea after all."

"It's not about being adored. There's much more to it."

"I just want to let you know… We've all grown pretty fond of you here. It won't be the same without you."

"Look. You know I respect all that you're doing. All the Knights do."

"I respect them just as much."

"Exactly. They're family. They depend on you. Now, imagine what it's like to have that feeling, that responsibility, only times a hundred thousand people. All of them depending on you. It's an obligation larger than the skies of Nagama."

"I admire you for it. I honestly do. Good luck."

Gaven offered his hand, but Fangbane pulled him into an embrace. Gaven waited, feeling Fangbane pat him on his back several times before pulling out of his arms.

Fangbane added. "What of your partner?"

"She's your Knight. I can't take her with me."

"This is not advised, Gaven."

"I'm not going to drag Mirari out of here. I wouldn't do that to you."

"But… you two are still partners."

"I wish I could…" Gaven stopped. "Look, I'm not saying this is forever. I mean, if Shiba can remain leader of his region…"

"You don't have to make any promises. I know your heart."

"Then you understand that at the very least, I need to check on my region before I consider… whatever is next."

"I know. I just want you to be careful. I sense that something isn't right."

THE FORTIFIED LAND of Althaea Main was the largest city in its empire, bustling with trade and produce on every stone-paved road. Merchant stalls decorated the streets and the packed crowds weaved fearlessly between carriages. It reeked of month-old piss and drunk man's spew. Despite the poor conditions of the city, vagabonds carried warm bread and blankets and fortress soldiers frequented the streets, arresting anyone committing the pettiest of crimes. It was crowded and chaotic, but ever since Region Leader Gaven took the throne, fear had vanished from the city.

Althaea Main was as he left it, running like clockwork. Gaven had no doubt that his second in command would be able to defend the region on her own. To his surprise, there had been fewer revolts since the Althaean Siege. His people were either worn out from the battle or had accepted his decision to open their doors to foreign settlers.

His carriage rolled through the upper levels that housed the servants and soldiers of the fortress and their families. It appeared to be a completely different city, one that was uniform – chalk-white walls and sky-blue rooftops, decorated with an abundant harvest of flowers and plants.

There was enough space to see stretches of the road beyond gated homes. Children played freely, running across green lawns with new toys in their hands and fresh clothes on their backs.

The center of Althaea Main was the fortress that housed the region leader and his army. It was surrounded by thick stone walls that towered over the courtyard, forever creating a cold shadow over the first line of defense. Once the carriage passed the shadow gates and dozens of guards, the land opened to an arcadia. Towers of pure white edifice were surrounded by yards of trimmed lawns and greenhouses. Statues of a merciless winged dragon decorated the edges of blue rooftops, and the hāstal resting in their mouths harvested the blaring sun.

Gaven took a deep breath and tidied his shirt one last time, stepping out of the carriage into his familiar home.

He kept his head as high as his wavering cape. His guards saluted him and paved the way to the golden doors where a distinguished lady, skin just a shade off from her cedarwood hair, stood impatiently waiting for his arrival. Though she was more than two heads shorter than Gaven, they had striking similarities. For starters, they both wore a blue cape wielding the dragon-like emblem of Althaea Main, a garment reserved for only the highest ranks. Her eyes complimented Gaven's in a commanding manner that matched the scowl they always carried. But while Gaven's eyes glistened like the coral sea, some soldiers went as far as to say she had the same eyes as the legendary beast tailored on their capes.

The soldiers in Gaven's army, and all the staff in his fortress, referred to this lady as Erel. The expressionless woman with a brown bob was known as Gaven's second in command. Only Gaven knew her by a different form.

He had barely greeted the woman he left in charge when she rushed him to his chambers, pressing him about an urgent message that was delivered by a homing kestrel. The short woman was moving at such a hurried clip, he had to widen his strides. Whatever was in this mysterious letter, she certainly didn't want to waste any time getting to it.

"I know you say this letter is urgent, but you're going to wear out your sandals." He said, teasing her as she led him to his study.

"This is no laughing matter, Your Honor," she responded in her usual dull tone.

"Why so serious? Aren't you glad to see me?"

"Why should I be?" she said, yawning and putting on a bored

expression as they turned down a wide corridor. "I suppose I'll have to work now?"

"All you did was pick up my mail for a year. And you're still complaining?"

"No one puts a bounty on mail."

But he trusted her judgment. That was why he left her to run things in his absence. If she thought it was urgent, he knew it couldn't wait.

"Your Honor, welcome back!" A loud voice echoed behind him. Gaven glanced over his shoulder and noticed the big blond man flaring his arm like mad, trying to get his attention.

"Not now, Haynes," Erel said. Gaven ignored him too as usual, and turned the corner, leaving his sight.

"Has Haynes been giving you a hard time?" Gaven asked, knowing how needy his commander could be.

"Let's just say it's a good thing you're back." Then she added, "You are back, right? Or is there a catch?"

"Seems like it's final. They're dropping my probation."

"Not out of kindness," she said, sounding grave. "If you want my honest opinion, Your Honor, they are acting out of their own interest. They need you back on their side... Something's wrong."

Gaven wasn't surprised. "You aren't the first to say that to me."

"In the last few days, some men have been demanding to see you. I hope you don't mind, I put on your suit and gave it a go down the street."

"Did they say what they wanted?"

They had reached the study now, and Erel checked behind them, making sure the corridor was empty. She closed the doors and locked them. As soon as they were alone, the gnomish woman transformed herself into her true form – a slender woman, now as tall as Gaven, who appeared to have little flesh to her bones. Her brown bob had cascaded into a curtain of honeydew hair that reached down to her knees. Her golden eyes were the one thing that always remained the same, except now there were faint wrinkles under them.

In his mind, this is how Gaven always thought of her – Erel Estel. She was very possibly the last surviving shapeshifter of the Belligmn Tribe. She had to live. Gaven did all he could to keep her identity safe, knowing that there might still be bounty hunters after her.

She hurried to Gaven's desk and picked up an envelope she had left waiting for him.

"They gave me a letter," she said, handing it over. "A trap, I would rather call it."

"They?"

"A handsome man. Long hair, slim face, probably from Altha Hills. He was escorted by a few guards. They appeared to be commoners, but the wealthy kind."

Gaven quietly read the offer to himself. "Your caution tells me that you don't trust them. Give me your reasons. I value your judgment, Erel."

"The man had a bad aura," Erel said, crinkling her nose as if she had snuffed a glass of month-old milk. "But for some reason, I felt safe around him. Safe, but… these feelings didn't seem to be my own if that makes sense. He might be an empath. Those people can't be trusted."

"An empath?"

"They're incredibly powerful people with the ability to read your emotions as well as the ability to project their emotions upon others."

"Psychics."

"Not exactly. They don't read the future. They read the heart. And the mind. They don't like to show themselves, so their kind is well-hidden."

Gaven instantly thought of the empath he knew, a person who didn't keep that ability hidden at all.

While Gaven was still reading the letter, Erel looked at him closely, squinting as she sniffed his body.

"Your aura is different..." Erel mumbled. "It's like—" She took a bigger whiff. "By the holy vision of the Blind Monk of Evaleen! You took a partner?" Gaven held back from answering her. Erel pranced to him and looked deep into his eyes, then took another whiff. "So it's true. You did, didn't you!"

"What's the big deal?"

"The Valiant Tiger, the warrior famous for fighting alone, now has a partner? That's headline news. Who is he? Is he a Minettan?"

"She."

"Wait, what? A Minettan woman? What in a bucket of blood from the Gods did they do to you? You're not the Valiant Tiger at all."

"A lot has happened, alright? But who knows? Maybe my time in Minetta will prove to be for the better."

Gaven broke away from her gaze and continued to read the letter. The writer wanted Gaven to grant him exclusive trading rights to ship and distribute a long list of goods in the Althaea Main region. The worst part was that a fraction of the items were considered illegal in Althaea Main. It was an extraordinary request – the boldness of it felt vaguely insulting.

"'If you are not satisfied with this offer, then I humbly ask you to pass along this letter to the next person in charge,'" Gaven read with an agitated grunt. "The next person in charge? Is this a threat?"

He put down the letter, then glanced at the envelope on his desk.

He felt a coldness wash through his guts, freezing away all his anger. The envelope bore a seal, a symbol that stirred alarm all through him. He had stared and analyzed this symbol for far too long. He could recognize it anywhere now.

"Erel, are you familiar with this seal?" he asked, and she glanced over at the envelope.

"Looks like… twin figures, some divine constellation, maybe a flame, or an aura." Something about that struck a nerve in her.

But Gaven could read the grim expression on her face, the way it tied a knot in her throat. She had to speak truthfully.

"It appears to be representing Moranity."

"Moranity…" Gaven thought hard, thinking back on his studies and trying to recall where he had heard that name before.

Erel gave him a hand. "It's a Plethorist religion. The Goddess of Fate and the Goddess of Devotion are deities of Plethorism, and Moras specifically worship the two goddesses."

"There are still Plethorists out there?" Gaven scratched his head, having been living under the impression that most people had committed themselves to only the main Gods.

Erel rolled her eyes, slightly offended at such an obvious question. "Everyone knows Oris isn't the only God. You Althaeans may only know a dozen off the top of your heads, but many tribes in Valenia still worship the hundreds of others." She took a pause, then added, "The Belligmn Tribe were Moras."

Gaven perked up with interest. What were the chances of all this being a coincidence?

"Does that mean this is the symbol of your tribe? Or someone from your tribe is using it?"

"To your first question, no. The symbol of the Belligmn Tribe is different. The latter, highly unlikely. I'm pretty confident that I am the only survivor of the massacre."

Erel gave a grim pause, glancing at the seal one last time before turning away. She looked queasy.

"I don't understand why anyone would use this symbol. You could say that being Moras was what led to the extinction of our tribe. Some people take religion to extremes. As the worship of Oris swept away the old Gods, anyone standing in the way of the broom had to go too. My tribe was no exception."

"And such fanatics still exist?"

"You know they do, Your Honor."

The first people to pop up in his mind were the celtas of Altha Hills. There was no group more devoted to the God of Judgment than the people of that region. But he found it hard to believe that this peace-loving region would destroy any other group who did not follow their beliefs.

Gaven recalled the last time he saw the seal – on the Bishop's letter. He had slipped it into a miscellaneous folder, the one labeled 'the Blessed'. There had been no progress with that case, nor with finding the culprit behind his memory loss, but now he wondered… What if these two mysteries were related?

He asked Erel, "Would the Blessed use this symbol?"

"Your Honor!" she gasped, hearing the forbidden words. "I told you to incinerate that file."

"Too bad, I didn't. Now you have to work with me on it."

Erel groaned as Gaven thought harder. "This is the same seal the Bishop used to hire bandits. Could this mean he's one of the Blessed?"

"The guy the High Priest threw in the dungeon? Now, why would someone that stupid be a member of the Blessed?" Erel raised her fist to her mouth and a lightbulb went off. "Ah, but if he seeks to rob the poor and hoard the riches, he very well may have been trying to mold society into a game of survival of the fittest. That sounds like something the Blessed would do, and with his position, it's possible he was a leader."

"But he's devoted to Oris. Why would he use a Plethorist seal?"

"He could be faking it. The Blessed are clever at hiding their identity, but this Bishop? Doesn't seem that smart. Besides, if he's in the dungeon, then who was the man who sent this letter with his seal?"

"You said he had long hair? Was he tall? Mole on his neck?"

"Do you know him, Lord?"

"That's Laikos. The Bishop's first acolyte."

Erel's heart stopped. No other words mattered to her. She took a deep breath to calm herself. "L-Laikos? Are you sure?"

"He *was* the one who put the Bishop in the dungeon…" Gaven thought carefully and asked again. "*And* you said he's an empath?"

"Might be. It's… I don't know." But up until that moment, Erel had been so sure that the man she had met was an empath. Her sense of smell was never wrong. She just didn't want to believe she was right, for that would answer the grim mysteries surrounding the annihilation of her tribe. Gaven saw a tremor run through her as she was gripped with a terrible fear. "It makes sense… Laikos is a Mora. This seal must be his."

Everything that happened in Altha Hills with the Bishop, Gaven realized, was a set up. And those assassins who had no memory of their treachery, along with Commander Heisa, were all under some hex.

Laikos may be the man Gaven had been looking for this whole time, the man who had cast him under a dark spell and started the bloody Althaean Siege.

And if he was truly a member of the Blessed, then there was a high likelihood that he had something to do with Mirari's brother's death.

Gaven was ready to hunt the man down like a hungry predator preying on deer, but his second in command wasn't going to let him slip out of sane judgment.

"Listen to me, Gaven." She'd never taken the liberty of addressing him in such a personal manner. "Whatever is in that letter, do it."

"Why? Just because he's a part of a cult?"

"He is no acolyte. I know for a fact, he's one of the *leaders* of the Blessed. A powerful one."

"What? And you never told me?"

"I told you not to get involved in this!" Erel snapped, slamming down her fist on the table. "That lunatic slaughtered my people. You can't run, and you're not strong enough to fight him. No one is. If you don't want Althaea Main to fall like my tribe, then you must stay on his good side."

"Stay out of…" Gaven's face darkened, and he grabbed the letter and tore it in half. "Erel, I intend to send this bastard to Inferna."

CHAPTER TWENTY-NINE

A few days later, Suzan made another surprise visit to Fangbane's manor. It had been a little over a week since her last visit, and once again, she wasn't interested in chit-chat. She came bearing confidential news.

"I know you're still mad at me for sending Gaven away, but I'm afraid the Council is in need of the Knights' assistance."

Fangbane crossed his arms like a sassy child. "Oh, *now* you want our help. Can I get that request written on a golden scroll, Suzan?"

"I'll serve it to you with a thousand soldiers if you want, but this is urgent." She lowered her voice and whispered into his ear. "At least three region leaders have fallen ill, dozens of their soldiers too."

Fangbane was about to reply when Starlight swept into his office, as always, inserting herself without the least bit of hesitation.

"I hear there's a terrible flu going around. I haven't taken the baby anywhere, just to be safe." But when she saw the grave expression on Suzan's face. "Oh dear," Starlight said. "This isn't about the flu, is it?"

"We think it's some kind of poison. Something we've never seen before. And we have no idea who's behind it."

"Whatever it is, our problem is to find a way to stop this poison from spreading."

"That sounds like quite a dilemma…" Fangbane put on a hang-dog expression, dripping with sarcasm. "If only there were some special group who could get to the bottom of this. An elite force dedicated to seeking justice, and keeping the peace in all the empires."

"I get the point," Suzan muttered.

But it didn't stop him from rubbing it in. "It's too bad, really. If only the Council had thought of creating a group like that in time to help with this."

Suzan gave him a withering stare, then turned to Starlight. "And you have to live with this guy?"

Just then, they heard a commotion from outside as a rider galloped into the courtyard. They peaked out the window and were left speechless.

"What is this fool doing back here?" Suzan snapped, but Fangbane had already sprinted out the room to greet their guest.

Gaven's exhausted horse was dripping with lather and heaving for breath as he trotted onto the estate grounds. Just as he got off the horse, the front doors swung open and the masked man hurried over.

"Is everything alright?" Fangbane asked, taking the reins from Gaven's hands. "Have you been poisoned?"

"Have I been what?" Gaven asked while wiping the sweat from his forehead. "No, I have something I need to tell you. It's about the Blessed."

"I'm afraid that may have to wait. Suzan is here with some dire news."

"Suzan?" But before Gaven could probe any further, Fangbane hustled him inside.

The entire company of Knights waited as Gaven tramped in,

covered in sweat and road dust. Mirari didn't hesitate to throw her arms around her partner, not caring about the dirt that had now stained her clothes as well.

"I'm so glad you're alright," she whispered, and he reciprocated a much needed embrace. He took a deep breath as if he was about to tell her the same, but with so many eyes on them he redirected his attention to the rest of the Knights.

"Ah, Suzan," Gaven greeted blandly.

"Gaven." She responded with the same tone.

"What news did you bring?"

"While you were traveling, region leaders across the empires were poisoned. Avon, Oban, Evaleen, and Ophallen have been hit. I have no doubt there will be more casualties."

"Dorain and I were in Evaleen when it happened," Hime said. "Landon collapsed, his temperature was spiking, and his face had streaks of purple. It was horrible."

"He must have gotten this poison or bug or whatever." Dorain piped in, unaware he was stating the obvious.

"Landon was so sick, I asked my father to help me, and he brought a whole caravan to investigate."

"Hmm," Shiba muttered. "Knowing your father, I'll bet he came to make sure you didn't get sick. He despises Landon, that lecherous satyr."

Gaven silenced Shiba with a glare, then nodded for Hime to continue.

"Father took one look at Landon and said it's the same sickness that was being reported in Ophallen, and had heard rumors of people with similar symptoms in Oban's capital."

"Although knowing Landon," Shiba said, "it wouldn't surprise me if he caught something from one of his—"

"That's enough, Shiba," said Starlight, cutting him off, but with the same cheery smile she always had. If one of the Knights had spoken to him like that, Shiba would not have caved. But no one in Fangbane's manor was dumb enough to challenge Starlight's authority. "Please continue, dear," she told Hime.

"Father concluded this must be a toxic prion that latches onto food and water." She noticed several puzzled looks, and added, "Meaning transmission occurs through ingestion."

"But is it curable?" Lucan asked, clearly worried.

"Our healers say it can be lethal, death as early as two days. But if it's treated immediately, they have medications that can reverse the damage. The patients can recover with the right treatment, and a week of bed rest."

"That's a blessing," Lucan said. But then his face darkened. "You said 'toxin'. So your father agrees with Councilor Suzan? This isn't a natural disease at all, but some kind of poison?"

"That's what the High Priest says," Dorain put in. "He told us it's a very unique poison, one that isn't easy to manufacture."

Fangbane shook his head and turned to his wife. "Who would make something like that?"

"I… have a hunch," Gaven said, sounding grim. "On my way here, I stopped in Olina, and Region Leader Cole told me about a suspicious letter he got, the same as I did," Gaven explained that he was convinced it was from Laikos based on the seal.

Shiba jumped in. "Laikos? I should've known that letter was from him."

"Wait. Did you get the letter too? How did you respond?"

"I told that bastard to pound sand. If I'd known, I would've chosen harsher words."

"The day after we sent our refusal, half of our recruits called in sick," Neo added. "Blamed it on lint beans."

"Neo and I skipped lunch that day. We got lucky."

Gaven turned to Hime. "What about Landon? Did he mention a letter like this?"

"I… don't recall." Hime frowned.

"He didn't," Dorain said, "but I overheard his servants

talking about it. They were cursing Landon and how he should be more kind to the way he responds to foreign affairs. They were sure that his illness was a reflection of his karma."

"Are you seeing a pattern?" Mirari asked Gaven. "There's the proof that Laikos is behind the poison. He's attacking every region that rejected his request."

"And what about you, Kitten?" Shiba asked. "How did you respond?"

"I…" Gaven slightly scratched the back of his head. "I just tore it up…"

"Well, your aggression saved you this time." Suzan rolled her eyes. She wasn't surprised in the slightest.

Fangbane now understood the urgency of this matter. "We need to stop him before he poisons all the region leaders. But how do we even go about finding him?"

"I can assure you he's no longer in Altha Hills," Hime said. "He disappeared not long after we arrested the Bishop."

"For now we need to warn everyone to be careful about what they consume," Starlight reminded them. "We'll need them to take precautions. There won't be enough healers if every region falls ill."

Suzan stood up. "I'll get the Council to notify every region leader right away."

As the meeting broke up, Gaven kept Mirari by his side and leaned closer to Fangbane. "I'm afraid the Blessed may be making their move."

"What do you mean? Laikos works for the Blessed?"

"He does, and it makes sense. Laikos wouldn't be able to travel to all those regions over a couple of days if he was doing it on his own. My theory is that the poison has spread so quickly because there are members of the Blessed scattered in every army. They can slip the poison without causing any suspicion."

"If Laikos works for the Blessed then does that mean he may be the one who possessed you?" Mirari realized. Her face went pale recalling the seemingly innocent monk. "He… killed my brother?"

Gaven unfolded a piece of paper from his pocket and tapped on the seal of the Bishop's letter. "Same seal on Laikos' letter. This seal represents the Goddesses of Moranity."

"Did you say Moranity?" Hime teleported next to them. Startled, Gaven jumped back with his hand over his heart, and Mirari felt the same jolt.

"Gods on donkeys!" They cursed at the same time.

"Sorry," Hime said. "But I thought it may help to know that my father said this poison was likely transcribed from the Mora scripture. Only aster spellcasters would be able to decipher or create something like that. There aren't that many of them around."

Gaven let that sit for a moment. "Well, that's a start. We'll track down whoever is making the poison and he'll lead us to Laikos. How many aster spellcasters do you know of?"

Hime shook her head. "None. At least none from Altha Hills."

Fangbane thought hard, then a light went off in his head. "One."

CHAPTER THIRTY

Neo looked inside the now empty hut. All that was left were loose papers scattered across the floor, stained in mud. There was one letter that caught his eye. Neo picked up the paper and saw the red seal – the insignia of the Knights – and on the other side, it was signed by Fangbane.

"You knew who she was," Neo said, holding the paper in front of Fangbane. Yes, it was his recruitment letter to the Witch of Aten. But Fangbane simply shrugged.

"She never responded."

Lucan returned, having searched the parameter, confident that Kylah had moved on to her next secret location.

Gaven grumbled under his breath. "That treacherous witch. I knew we couldn't trust her."

"Organize a search," Fangbane ordered, dashing Gaven's anger. "We have to find her, and quickly before she poisons another region."

"You don't know for sure she did it," Neo said, pointing to the abandoned hut. "She's just an alchemist living by herself."

"A runaway assassin, you mean." Gaven snapped. "She's the

one who poisoned the mistress of the Tribe of Paragons four years ago."

"She didn't! And I believe her."

"She's lying. She got close to Mirari, to Lucan, to you. Is that a coincidence? She was watching us. In the end, she was a spy for Laikos. She made lethal poison once, and she can do it again."

Neo turned his head to the engravings on trees and dirt around her home. It didn't sit right with him. Even if she left the area, he would think she would keep the traps in place.

"I want to hear her side of the story," Neo said with determination, before moving on to examine the other traps.

Fangbane nodded as well, confident that he saw no malicious intention. "Innocent until proven guilty."

Gaven spat on the ground, refusing to yield, but he knew there was no point in arguing. They had to find her regardless.

The Knights spread out across the forests and valleys of Avon, scouring the ground for clues – footprints, tracks, trampled grass or broken twigs, any kind of sign. The team raked through a wide area around Akoun, Three Rivers, all the way out to the Karkel Plains, without finding a single clue.

Gaven was an experienced hunter and skilled tracker, and so was Fangbane. But the 'game' they were seeking today was far craftier than any crow or fox. Kylah wanted to stay hidden, and she could employ all sorts of wards and charms and magical misdirection to conceal her true path.

The afternoon sun began to dip, and as the shadows grew tall, and the forest started to cool, Fangbane brought the party to a halt. "We only have a few hours of light remaining," he said. "We should split the company to cover more ground. Gaven? What do you think?"

Gaven nodded, gesturing Mirari over. "Shiba, take the Knights with you. We'll keep working toward the hills, and you guys work down, toward the shore."

They agreed to return to this spot at sunset, with or without success.

———

After an hour, Dorain sounded a shrill whistle, retracting Kea from her latest patrol. Hime shivered from the increasingly cold air, exhausted by the long distance they had covered. "The sun will be gone in half an hour. Should we head back to the rendezvous?"

"Frankly, it's likely she's not even in this region anymore," said Lucan. He was used to Kylah's disappearing act.

But Neo refused to give up. "Damn it," he grumbled, kicking a nearby stump. "She's not behind this. I know it!" He tried to calm himself with a slow, deep breath.

"Normally I trust your judgment," Shiba began, "but you've fallen for the wrong woman."

"Don't worry, we'll find her," Hime said. She wanted to believe that the woman was not behind the poisonings, but there was no other aster spellcaster they could blame.

Kea glided back from the mountains, soaring in low, and settled on her falconer's glove. She rested on Dorain's arm as she cooed her message that only Dorain could understand. His face lit up with a smile.

"Show us, Kea. Go!" Dorain said, and the kestrel flapped away, soaring through the forest. Dorian spurred his brown horse, chasing after the bird. "This way!" he called to the others. Neo took off at a gallop and Hime and Lucan followed after them.

After just a couple of minutes, Kea wheeled, and began to circle above a grassy clearing in the forest. Neo looked around, full of hope and then disappointment. There was nothing to see there. "What is it? Why'd she stop here?"

Dorain scanned the grass and surrounding brush, searching for something specific, as the bird kept circling.

"Where?" he called. "I don't see anything." The winged raptor dropped down in the center of the grassy glade. She began to peck at the soil.

Shiba chortled. "She's lookin' for worms…"

"By the sweaty balls of Engelburt the Untutored, what is your bird doing, Dorain?" Neo was angrier than anyone had ever seen him.

Dorain ignored his rebuke, partly because he was a little afraid of Neo and partly because he was worried about Kea. He watched his bird continue to peck the ground like a chicken, which is not something hawks do. A few more minutes of gawking and then he got it. He gave a whistle and the bird took his instruction and flapped over to perch on a nearby branch. Dorain dismounted and put his ear to the ground. He rapped on it and smiled.

"What? What is it?" Neo said, about to lose it.

Dorain produced his bow and aimed an explosive arrow at the spot. It flew, detonating in a small, controlled explosion. The surface ground collapsed, revealing a large, hollow cavern below. They could hear water in the distance, drip-drip-dripping on limestone. Neo dashed to the edge. He could see a path inside the cavern that led into the dark. He jumped in without hesitation. As soon as his feet hit the cave bottom, he pulled a lumastōne from his tunic, which began to glow, casting a soft light in the cave. He took off without a word, and everyone followed.

The cave tunnel extended several hundred feet until it ended at the entrance of an expanded chamber. Water dripped from stalactites, splashing against the stubs of stalagmites growing up toward them at an infinitely slow pace. In the corner of the chamber, a nook dipped into the cave wall, forming a space like a small room. Iron bars formed the fourth wall, making a tiny cell.

And there sat the spellcaster, locked inside, her hands bound. Neo rushed to the bars, crying out her name like a prayer.

She rose, squinting at him, her eyes unaccustomed to the pale light of his glow rock. "Neo? How did you…?"

"Kylah, are you alright?"

She kept blinking, her vision slowly returning until she was able to see the other Knights. "I'm fine. But you shouldn't be here."

Neo looked up and down the wall of bars, puzzled. "Who did…? Where's the door?"

"I'm afraid there is no door. It's an enchantment, of course."

Instead of giving up, Neo grabbed two bars and began to strain at them, his muscles bulging, thick as tree limbs, trying to bend the bars apart.

Kylah scolded him for his idiocy. "Neo. Stop straining, you'll get a hernia. Those bars are made of inconel alloys." He ignored her, grunting with even greater effort. "Fine. You want to wind up wearing a truss, be my guest."

Neo cut loose a roar that was an explosion of its own. As the echoes of his mighty cry bounced off the cave, there was another sound. A faint creaking noise, like the squeak of a rusty gate. Kylah blinked and rubbed at her dazzled eyes again. She must not be seeing right. But it looked like he was making a dent in the bars. As his face grew red with the super-human effort, the bars slowly started to bend. In a few more moments, he'd bent an opening wide enough for Kylah to squeeze through, although barely.

"Insanely impressive," she said, giving his bicep a short feel.

"You have a very stimulating effect on me," he said when he had gathered his breath. On a more serious note, as he untied Kylah, he added, "Who did this to you?"

"Not someone we want to deal with," she said. "We can worry about that later. We need to get—" She choked on her words, a voice booming through the cavern.

"Leaving already, Kylah?" The voice bounced around the cave walls, and seemed to come from nowhere, or everywhere, as it echoed through the darkness.

The Knights all turned, peering back down the cave's tunnel. The light from the opening where they had entered began to grow misty. A thick fog seemed to materialize in the tunnel. Slowly, backlit by the stream of light from the opening above, a vague outline began to take shape. The figure became the silhouette of a tall man, calmly approaching them from the opening.

As he finally drew close enough, the pale light of the lumastōne filled in the silhouette with details. He had long, beautiful navy blue hair tied back in a ponytail. The slender man wore a long purple cloak, trimmed in ermine. On his wrist, Neo noticed a gold bracelet, crusted with large gems. They flashed and sparkled, even though the lumastōne's glow was far too dim to cause this. But it was plenty enough for Neo to recognize the jewelry. It was Kylah's, and a glance confirmed that her wrist was bare. His blood started to boil.

"Who are you?" Neo said, searching for a clear view of the man's face. The rest of the Knights stayed on alert, cautious of whatever skills this man might have. Neo held the lumastōne closer to the stranger.

"The acolyte," Shiba said.

Hime said, "You betrayed our people!"

"My position was simply an alibi." Laikos spoke humbly with a dismissive wave of his hand.

"You kidnapped and imprisoned her," Neo said with a flat but deadly cadence. He flexed his hands, knuckles cracking. "You're about to become a new face in Inferna."

"Do with me as you wish if you think you're able." He leaned slightly toward Neo. "I'll allow you to do your worst, but only on one condition…" He glowed with a chilling smile. "Kylah? I'm still waiting for that spell you owe me. The recipe for the poison. The airborne version."

"Over my dead body, you blue-topped stringbean!"

Laikos let his gaze bore into her.

"Here," he said, pointing to a small wooden desk near the cave wall.

Kylah took a deep breath, then spat on his polished shoes.

Neo scowled at Laikos, danger in his voice. "You better shut your face while you still have teeth to chew wi—"

His words froze. So did his ability to move.

"Do stand still, all of you," said Laikos.

Kylah noticed what he was doing. She had no doubt that Laikos was ready to silence all of them.

"Leave them out of this," she said.

"Your threats mean nothing to me. You dare challenge me without the stones of Aten?" Laikos showed off the golden bracelet now in his possession. Then he reminded her. "The spell, Kylah."

Under her soft breath, Hime chanted a few verses in an unknown language while holding her palms together. A light began to glow from her hands, but it faded just as quickly. She tugged on her hands, but her palms would not separate. She could feel a spell bounding them together.

"Don't even, Princess."

Shiba and Lucan whipped out a pair of shurikens, their blades whirling in the air toward Laikos in perfect synchrony.

The small wet puddles in the cave began to flow, then suddenly shot up in ice form. They blocked the shurikens and knocked the Knights into the air, but they landed back on their feet without a scratch.

Kylah knew that he wouldn't miss. This was her last warning.

She looked back over at the wooden desk with hesitation. But he was right – the stones of Aten were the divine energy that allowed her to craft advanced spells like the poison. Without it, she was just a spellcaster with above average wit, and wits alone wouldn't be enough to stop him.

Kylah picked up the quill on the desk and began scribing complex symbols as fast as she could. Laikos waited patiently, but she didn't take long.

She put down the quill, rolled the parchment into a scroll, and slapped it in Laikos' hand. "There. You have your spell. Now let them go."

"Thank you, one and all," he said with a mock bow. "I hate to rush off, but needs must if you will. I would appreciate it, though, if you didn't attempt to follow me. Brawler?"

The frozen giant trembled with effort, trying to move a muscle. His every limb and digit was locked down tight. Then, he felt himself moving. But certainly, there was no will of his own involved. He took Kylah's arm, and led her over to the others, and herded them all into a tight corner. Neo's massive arms reached out like a pair of gates and pressed the others against the wall so that nobody could get past him.

"Neo, stop!" Dorain tried to break free from under his arm, even though he was well aware that there was nothing he could do to break him from his trance. They watched Laikos put on a grim smile and leave through the deep tunnel from which he came.

Neo's face blinked to life, with only a couple of flickers. "What the... sorry, friends." He let them free from his hold.

Kylah was about to step away, but she stopped – still pressed against Neo. The meat logs of his arms now encircled her in a gentle embrace. She raised her face to him, and their lips seemed to fit together so perfectly. She decided she wasn't in that big of a hurry...

CHAPTER THIRTY-ONE

"Why are you working with Laikos?" Gaven shouted at the spellcaster. "I knew we shouldn't have trusted her, Fangbane. Didn't I say that?"

The Knights had gotten back to the manor after hours of riding in the dark. They were weary, bone tired, and desperate to find a plan to thwart Laikos. Gaven kept insisting that Kylah was to be restrained, but Fangbane allowed her to sit freely.

Neo stepped between Gaven and Kylah. "She had no choice."

"That's her story. She's a witch who makes illegal poisons and we should be sending her back to Valenia. Let the Tribe of Paragons tear her apart."

"With all due respect, Valiant Tiger, I won't let that happen." Lucan stood close, ready to challenge the man he was sure to lose to, but to protect his friend he would do it in a heartbeat. "She did cure your partner. Is that not enough to prove she has no ill intentions?"

"How do we know she wasn't doing it to get close to the Knights? To tear inside our operations and leave us vulnerable to Laikos?"

"I don't work with him," Kylah finally spoke up. She kept her head lowered, gliding her palm over her bare wrist. "Yes, I made the poison, but I had nothing to do with his plans to administer them." She knew she had an obligation to stop Laikos, but without the divine power from her stones, her confidence was stripped away.

"Laikos can take over your mind," Neo said. "He can dance you around like a puppet. I swear to Celerimon the Swift, you've never seen anything like—"

Neo stopped, the words trapped on his tongue as he realized how wrong he was. Because Gaven had seen something like it. Exactly like it. "Holy wallowing mud skunks. The Althaean Siege. It was Laikos all along."

"Is that true?" Shiba turned to Gaven. "You really didn't know what you were doing?"

"Of course I didn't!" Gaven snapped.

"Sure, sure, I know that..." Shiba backtracked, then muttered, "...now."

Gaven shot a quick look at Fangbane for approval. After he nodded, Gaven began debriefing them on the confidential details of the Blessed, right down to Laikos' involvement with the Bishop and Commander Heisa. The Knights absorbed the information in disbelief, grasping just how powerful the man truly was.

"An empath... of course." Feeling dumber than a rittlefish on land, Fangbane slapped his hand over his mask. He forgot that there were people out there with abilities similar to his. "I should've seen this coming."

"Wow, we actually have our own super villain!" Dorain cheered, a thrill coursing through his body, but everyone ignored him.

"But if Laikos already had the poison, why did he need the spell from you, Kylah?" Lucan asked.

"The crap I gave him the first time was weak sauce. It wasn't the poison he asked for. He's too stupid to transcribe the spell himself, so he wouldn't have been able to tell the difference. Plus, only aster spellcasters can make the poison, and he isn't one of us." Kylah raised her bare wrist. "But with the stones of Aten he'll be able to make the poison on his own."

"It could kill you if left untreated," Mirari said, furrowing her brows. "You call that weak?"

To their surprise, Hime spoke up. "I call it smart." She gave Kylah a nod of admiration. "You passed off a puppy to Laikos, and told him it was a wolf hound."

Kylah was relieved to have a few of the Knights on her side. "Believe me, I would've never given him the more potent version of the spell. But that merciless monk would've killed all of you if I didn't give him something. I know he would."

Shiba broke in. With his arms crossed against his chest, he fumed at the witch. "Are you calling us weak? You think the greatest alliance of fighters can't handle a scrawny spellcaster?"

"He's an empath," she reminded him. "You saw what he can do. You let your emotions better you for one second, and that's all he needs to make you go against your will. You'd be dead in a heartbeat, Shadow Soldier."

"You shouldn't have given him the formula."

"I didn't have a choice."

"I'll remember that when we're all dead."

"If you're done whining, Princess Shiba," Kylah raised her voice like a scorned mother. She was starting to feel overwhelmed by the burning accusations roasting her, but still tried to maintain a professionality as she spoke. "Let's stop pointing fingers and focus on the present."

"Shiba, settle down. Please continue, Kylah," Starlight said, effectively ending the spat. Shiba yielded immediately. He turned his head to the side and pouted like a stubborn child.

Kylah continued. "It is more deadly and unfortunately contagious. But like Poison Lite, this version is curable too… if treated early."

"Oh, thank the Gods," Hime said.

She dug out a hand-written scroll with symbols and diagrams only celtas like Hime or Starlight could decipher. "This is how you brew the antidote."

"How early?" Mirari pressed her, challenging the legitimacy of the scroll she couldn't read. She would have to trust Hime or Starlight to decode the language and pray that it was not another poison in hiding.

"Right away is best," she said. "No later than six hours after infection."

That shut everyone up.

Kylah tried to find a bright side. She dipped back into her bag and pulled out five small vials. "But if you do give it right away, the victim recovers in about an hour. Three, at most, I think."

"That's not…" Dorain's eyes widened, afraid to ask. "Is that all you have?"

Kylah handed all the vials to Starlight and turned to Fang-bane. "You have to stop him. He's running a rebellion to end an era of region leaders and the Council. He wants to kill them all and unite all the empires into one, with himself as the head."

"And you? You're not trying to run away from this, are you?" Gaven was still towering over her, unwilling to step aside or let her leave his sight.

"No… but…" Kylah glanced down at her bare wrist again. How could she admit to such weakness? "I don't know how I can help you. Without the gems, the power of Aten, I'm just a basic spellcaster."

Starlight tried to cheer her on. "You're an aster spellcaster with or without the gems, darling. That itself tells us your potential." She wiggled one of the vials. "You can make more antidotes, right?"

"That… Yes, I can and I will." Kylah nodded confidently. The antidotes would be a piece of cake for her, but surely it wouldn't be enough to compensate for the damage she had caused and was about to cause.

"How hard can it be to take down one man?" Dorain sprung from his seat, with the ignorant confidence of the young. His chest out and head raised higher than the mountains of Nanaka as he said, "We're the Knights after all!"

"Think before you race off Dorain," Gaven said. "We don't know how many members of the Blessed are out there."

Fangbane raised his hands, about to bury his face in them, but that one small comfort was blocked by the presence of his mask. He took a deep breath and released his frustrations, clearing his mind of the uncertainties and volatilities he now faced, before it got the best of him.

He looked at his team – and saw it so clearly now. This was why he needed to make his vision work. This was the purpose of the Knights.

With his mind back in focus, he turned to Kylah, insisting, "I need you to make as many antidotes as you can. We'll stop him before he makes his next move."

"We have some time. It'll take him at least three days to make the new poison," she said. Unable to resist showing some professional pride, she continued, "if he does it without screwing up, that is. It's a delicate spell to pull off right. It's not like making instant buzzbean."

"Yes, yes, I'm sure you're as good as they come. So, how long does it take to make the antidote?"

"I'll try to finish before him, but in the meantime, you better find out where he's going next. Stay one step ahead."

CHAPTER THIRTY-TWO

As dusk covered the sky, Fangbane returned from his evening stroll. He stopped in the entrance hall, listening to the resonant chamber. He had always been comfortable in the dark, especially in his home. He was so used to the lack of a well-lit house, he could find his way around just as well in the darkness of the night. As long as some jerk didn't move the furniture around without asking, just to suit his fancy.

Not that he held anything against Shiba, but Fangbane still had a dark bruise under the nail of his big toe. Sooner or later he was going to lose it. But right now that was the least of his problems.

He tried to let the peace that darkness brought him settle his mind. This large, welcoming entrance hall that Starlight called the foyer was his favorite room in the house. He wasn't sure why, but the sizable vaulted ceilings seemed to give him clarity. Two half-moon curving staircases led to the upper balcony on either side. The broad, deep treads had a gentle rise, making it easy to climb even when you ached. Together with the chandelier between them, the twin ornate staircases made a grand impression. For most people, anyway. To him, the sweeping curves made it feel like the house was smiling.

Tomorrow would be another nerve-wracking day – the third day after Laikos had obtained the spell to generate his deadly poison. They still had no idea where he would attack next.

Before the Knights had staggered off to bed two nights ago, Kylah assembled a lengthy list of ingredients for making her antidote. These ranged from the arcane to the bizarre, with plenty of disturbingly weird animal parts. Obviously, not the kind of things one kept handy in the spice rack. But Mirari wrote up a list of her own, naming a dozen shops in Solarin that would carry everything Kylah needed. She offered to guide Kylah herself, but Fangbane insisted it was important for her to remain at the estate, where she could help Gaven and Lucan track and plan out Laikos' next move. The rest of the Knights followed Kylah to Solarin. Their assistance in finding the ingredients and making multiple batches would speed up Kylah's antidote-making progress and give her an extra layer of security.

Mirari offered her vacant home as their workstation to brew the antidote, handing over her set of spare keys to Kylah. She wouldn't need directions.

"Shire will bring in reinforced armor by dawn," Lucan said. "And the swiftest horses for all of us. I'll send them to Solarin as well."

"Can't you order a kōnvoy for us, Mr. Hale? At least some of those new weapons," Gaven said, assuming that the noble would provide better resources to help fight the enemy.

"Horses are twice as fast as kōnvoys. Trust me, you'll save time by taking transportation that isn't confined to the tracks." In a lower voice, Lucan came clean with his regrets. "I do not control the riches of the Hales, Valiant Tiger. I too have my limitations. In fact, my connection to the Knights weakens my credibility, but I'm here, hoping to do what's right."

"And you are," Mirari laid her hand on his shoulder with a gentle smile. In her guts she truly pitied Lucan. She ran away from her responsibilities, and Lucan had to fill her shoes. He was challenging the Hale family by joining the Knights. It was bold, something she could never do. "You are sacrificing so much for us. Thank you."

Lucan returned a kind smile. "You sure you don't want to take command, Lady Mirari? You clearly have the skills of a leader."

Mirari took the hint, but shook her head. She had already explained to Lucan her disinterest in returning to the Hale family, and he accepted it wholeheartedly. "No one can do a better job than you."

Gaven narrowed his eyes at Lucan. He seemed bothered by their banter. He hovered next to Mirari and looked at the map in her hand, focused on the few places that had no markings yet.

"I think he's going for Valenia next." Gaven's finger traced the lower land mass. "If not the main tribes, then the Hearth."

"The Hearth must be heavily guarded now that they know the poison is out there," Mirari said. "Would he be that bold? To attack the Council before taking down the rest of the region leaders?"

"The strongest regions have already been poisoned. He knows the other wussy leaders pose no threat."

"Your region still stands. Shiba hasn't been poisoned yet either."

"Yeah, well, since neither of us are sitting on our throne, he'll have to work extra hard to poison us."

Gaven, Mirari, and Lucan kept at it for hours, but they still couldn't decide where to place their bet on Laikos' next location.

The savory scent of roast meat caught Fangbane's attention, reminding him that the others would be waiting for him to feast. He left his beloved foyer and headed for the dining hall.

The tantalizing smells were thanks to Mirari. She was an excellent hand in the kitchen.

Fangbane wondered if he was expecting too much too soon from her. As far as her training went, she had surpassed expectations. But Fangbane felt that itself could be a problem. Her talent and skill helped her in her training, but real life was different from the controlled setting of a training ground. Mirari lacked the experience. Fangbane couldn't help but recall his failure as a warrior; the last time his father looked at him with love in his eyes.

The truth was that her skill and training were only part of his worry. The greatest unknown was her 'ability'. Whatever it was. He still had no idea what that special quality was. He could certainly sense her power – it was immense. But it was unfamiliar and he had no clue how to unlock it. He had seen her fire. But he was sure it was only a glimpse of what lay within this remarkable young woman. Maybe he could help her discover it, maybe not. She needed to gain control. Until she tamed it, she couldn't be trusted to use an ability so damn powerful. It made her dangerous.

In the dining hall, he saw Gaven making funny faces at his son in Mirari's lap. The door to the kitchen swung open, and Starlight greeted them with a platter of roast goat with onions and peppers. With baby Sarkan in her arms, Mirari followed the aroma, a blissful look on her face.

As tempting as the savory aroma was, Fangbane couldn't pass up a chance to smile and clown and act the complete fool to amuse his happy little son.

Gaven and Lucan didn't wait up. They dove straight for the goat, voraciously tucked into the vittles, as Mirari passed the baby over to Fangbane. Starlight reached her arms out, wanting to take Sarkan for herself.

"Darling, stop clowning and get something to eat." She reached for Sarkan, and told Mirari, "You too, girl. Put some meat on your—"

Gaven leaped to his feet, face twisted in agony. Lucan did the same, his hand covered his mouth as he coughed up the pieces of goat in his throat.

Fangbane froze with Sarkan still on his lap. He heard the chaos of pain and fear in both Gaven and Lucan's minds.

"Mirari, don't!" Fangbane warned just seconds before her hand touched a drumstick. Mirari quickly pulled back, knowing that every time Fangbane raised his voice, he was dead serious. She glanced over to Gaven and Lucan, who had both fallen weak to their knees.

Gaven's face had gone pale, almost as pale as Lucan. He could only hear Fangbane and Starlight's muffled voices, vision just as murky, as if he was being pulled under an icy sea. The tips of his fingers started to grow cold and numb.

"Your Honor!" Mirari was yelling, shaking Gaven's body, but not getting much of a response other than a few groans. She felt her own muscles starting to tighten the more Gaven suffered. She tried to stay strong for him, not letting any of those discomforts show on her face.

Mirari and Starlight were hunched over Gaven and Lucan's writhing bodies. The two men had no energy in their limbs, and on top of this disabling weakness, they were gasping for air. Starlight was already hard at work, measuring their vitals and taking note of their symptoms.

Fangbane looked over at the tray of food. It was clear what had happened.

"They've been poisoned."

"This... can't be." Starlight panicked. "I only took my eyes off the food for a second. There's no way it was tainted."

She took two of the precious vials of Kylah's antidote and poured the concoction into their mouths, careful to not spill a single drop. Immediately, Gaven and Lucan began to cough. The bitter antidote left a terrible burning sensation in their throats.

Mirari was frantic, unwilling to leave the men's side. "It

hasn't been three days. That means this is the weaker poison, right?"

Fangbane reached out with his mind, scanning the rest of the estate. A terrible certainty struck him. He could feel another heartbeat within the house, one that was strong and steady. It felt like someone was staring back at him, just waiting for Fangbane to get close to him, and then—

Fangbane broke the connection. For the first time in his life, he felt violated, his own power used against him. It had to be an empath.

"We're not alone…" Fangbane said, re-entering the dining hall, striding across the room, and reaching for a spear that was hidden in a drawer. "Take Sarkan, and go. We need to get out of here."

"Is it… the Blessed?" Mirari's voice trembled as she held her breath, unsure if they were being watched at that very moment.

Starlight looked at Gaven and Lucan, who were still too weak to stand. She was unwilling to leave, yet she knew that her duty as a mother came before her duty as a healer.

"Go with her!" Fangbane barked at Mirari. His own voice reminded him he was close to panic. He shook himself out of it, knowing he had to take charge. "Mirari, you need to escort her to the emergency rendezvous. You know where that is, right?"

"Of course, but what about—"

"We'll be fine," Gaven choked, finally able to understand what was happening around him. He said with a forced calm, "Five minutes, and we'll be right behind you."

Lucan nodded in agreement, still choking on the bitter medicine.

She gave in and got to her feet. Her arm was pulled back as Fangbane whispered one last message, "Draw your sword. I can't hear their thoughts, but I know we're being watched. I'm counting on you to get Starlight and Sarkan out of here. I'll take care of the intruder."

Mirari swallowed her nerves, grasped the hilt of her sword, and led the infant and his mother out of the room.

As soon as they were out of his sight, Fangbane turned back to Gaven and Lucan. "Get yourselves to safety. You can't fight in your condition."

"It'll take more than poison to bring us down," Gaven said, summoning false bravado. He dragged himself to sit up, struggling to catch his breath. He could feel a bit of energy returning to his limbs. In fact, he realized, it was the effect of his bond with Mirari which was helping him recover. Her energy glowed like a fire in his chest; his body relied on it as his only source of strength.

Fangbane ran into the kitchen, scouting for anything they could use to fight off the intruders. He only managed to grab a block of kitchen knives and a meat cleaver when the kitchen door slammed open.

"What are you going to do with that? Tenderize me?" said Gaven, staggering in from the dining hall with a flimsy spear in hand. Lucan was right behind, leaning heavily on the door with a sour look on his face.

"Where did you get—" Fangbane stopped mid-sentence as he figured out exactly where he got it.

"Pulled it off the wall."

"That was a display."

"I promise to wipe the blood off, then."

Lucan took the kitchen utensils and meat cleaver from Fangbane and sat against the wall to catch his breath. "We'll be right behind. In the meantime, I'll make sure nobody steals any sugar."

***

MIRARI CHASED AFTER STARLIGHT, but stopped as soon as they entered the foyer. Instead of heading toward the front door,

Starlight turned to the stairway and started moving up the wide, curving stairs.

That was the wrong way.

Mirari was just about to yell after Starlight when she saw the partial shadow of a man, hidden in a nook near the front door. As quietly as she could, she scampered up the stairs to catch up with Starlight.

"Did you see that man by the door?" Starlight rushed into the master bedroom, and beckoned for Mirari to follow. Mirari sprinted in and locked the door.

"Why do you think I ran upstairs?"

"Great, but… how are we going to get out of here?"

"I know a way," she said to Mirari, who was still clutching the sword. "Put that away, okay?"

Mirari sheathed the weapon as Starlight handed a sound asleep baby to her. It was hard to imagine him being in a peaceful state with such chaos unfolding around him.

"A perfect angel, isn't he?" Starlight pulled a soft blanket from the crib. "Here. He might get cold outside."

As Mirari bundled the child, she saw Starlight reaching for something under the bed. "What are you looking for? A diaper satchel?"

"Better," Starlight said, pulling out a backpack and slipping on the straps. "Water, food, money, rope, tarp, a dagger, first aid kit, lumastōne, and a good hunting knife. And diapers, of course."

"Wow…" Mirari said, impressed.

Starlight moved across the big room, and headed for the large walk-in closet. Mirari followed, stumbling over something; she was blind as a bat in here, until the lumastōne lit up. She saw Starlight slip open a hidden latch and heard a very slight squeak as Starlight pushed against the wall, opening the secret door with a creak.

"Fang thought his ideas might make him some enemies. He

likes to be prepared. C'mon, this way." She followed Starlight into a narrow hall, and around a corner. There it was – a steep, narrow set of stairs. Starlight looked at her, and held her arms out.

"Oh, right. Of course," Mirari said, handing the sleeping infant to his mother.

"It's not just my maternal instinct. You need your hands free." She stepped aside and nodded for Mirari to go past her. "You go first, and draw your sword already."

GLIDING SILENTLY THROUGH THE DARKNESS, Fangbane scanned every corner and shadow, hunting for the intruder. An uneasiness had come over him since he realized his ability to probe for the intruder's thoughts was diminished.

No, blocked off.

It was a vulnerable feeling, being reduced to the senses of an ordinary man. But he was at home in the darkness. He strained to focus on the sounds and scents around him. Instinct kicked in when he felt movement in the air, and he ducked as something shot out at him. The distinct clatter as it hit the wall told him it was a dagger.

He darted behind a stone pillar and took a split second glance around the corner. He couldn't see a thing. He hated the feeling of being stalked. Again, he tried scanning, but his probing was useless. He had long ago learned the hard way that he had to be more resourceful than simply relying on his empathic ability. He'd made that mistake as a child, and had paid dearly.

Behind him to his left, Fangbane sensed a difference in the air.

A subtle change, something… yes, there.

He caught the scent of stale breath, so faint it was nearly imperceptible. But he trusted it was real, and he lunged to snatch the dagger up off the ground. In a smooth motion, he wheeled and threw with all his might. He heard a thwack as it struck home, and a figure staggered from the black shadows, catching a hint of moonlight sneaking in from a window.

The dagger had found its mark, square in the intruder's chest. He listened as the man tried to draw a breath, and heard the gurgle of blood filling the punctured lung. The gasping shape took a stumbling step, then toppled over the edge of a couch.

Fangbane crept closer.

It was a young man, with scrawny limbs that indicated he never spent a day in his life doing hard labor. A person like that couldn't be an assassin.

But the worst part was that Fangbane still detected a heartbeat from somewhere else in his home. It was steady and even, with a hunter's cold control. There were more?

He noticed a dark object had fallen next to the man. He leaned in closer and picked it up, examining it in the pale shaft of light from outside. What he saw flooded him with fear.

It was a mask, just like his, and he immediately recognized its cool metallic interior made of cepha metals. Whoever had crafted this mask was aware that the metal was useful for amplifying psychic powers – abilities like his. In addition to the cepha metals, he could feel the faint power of hāstals inside this mask.

The hāstals must have been deflecting his ability. They could've been watching him for hours without his knowing. His blood ran cold, wondering how many more of these masked men were stalking through his house.

***

MIRARI HELD her blade at the ready, firm in her grip. She could see the latch to release the hidden door. She got ready to open it, pausing for Starlight to put away the lumastōne before they stepped into the unknown. Mirari let her ears take in every molecule of sound beyond that door.

But there was nothing. As she started to open the hidden passage door into the hall, she held her breath, and prepared to start slashing with that sword.

The hall was empty, quiet as a tomb. Mirari led the way, slipping between shadows, moving in fits and starts as they checked every corner. They paused at the entrance to a long corridor that seemed empty. They exchanged a silent nod and a second later took off running as hard as they could.

Fangbane's words clung to Mirari, and she found herself feeling hyper-vigilant, seeing every little nook and shadow as a possible threat. She gripped her sword tighter, ready to swing at the slightest provocation.

Mirari noticed movement from the corner of her eye. She stopped abruptly, Starlight nearly colliding into her. Mirari tightly gripped both her hands on the hilt of her sword, glaring at the figure in the shadows.

The man stepped out into the dimly lit hallway. He was tall and dressed in an ornate dark robe. He had two large, gleaming daggers in each hand, but it was his mask that caught her attention. It resembled Fangbane's in shape but was dark and ornamented with gilded etchings.

She felt a sudden overpowering flood of primal fear overcome her. Her sword nearly slipped from her hands as she felt its full burden. The figure approached.

"We need you to be brave, Mirari," Starlight said. Mirari took a deep breath, but her body continued to shiver.

"I've never killed someone before." Her hand was shaking uncontrollably as if she had become fearful of the sword she had carried for months.

"It's us or him."

Mirari tried to pace herself. She asked herself what Salathiel would've done. She knew he had killed before – she had witnessed it – and there had not been a hint of hesitation in his movement. She visualized his bravery and pushed down her fears.

"AAAH!" Mirari screamed at the top of her lungs, her voice echoing down the hall as she poured all her strength into her hands and took a swing at the masked man.

Caught by surprise, the man held up one of his daggers to block her attack, but her momentum was so powerful that it knocked the weapon out of his hand.

The man followed up immediately and lunged forward, swiping her with the other dagger. Mirari leaned back and twisted away in a spin. She reacted a split second too late as the blade grazed her arm.

Her every sense was on fire as she turned back to him. Taking a defensive posture with the point forward, she circled him carefully. The assassin remained calm, keeping his focus on her. He approached swiftly, his dagger missing by an inch. Mirari countered his attack and swung with both hands. Her blade knocked the dagger out of his hand; she followed with an aggressive kick to his head.

It sounded like a heavy pot hitting the stone as the mask spun away, the man now revealed as no more than a boy her age. He wasn't fazed. Weaponless, he charged straight at Mirari one last time. Taking advantage of the force, Mirari shoved her blade straight into his chest. Her sword glided through his body with ease. She stepped back and pulled out her sword, letting the lifeless body slump to the floor.

Footsteps caught her attention.

In the bright hallway, Fangbane paced toward them. He looked at the dead man hunched in front of Mirari, his blood creating a large stain over their marble floor.

Fangbane sighed with relief, knowing that they were safe and unharmed. He approached Starlight, placing a protective hand on Sarkan's head for a brief moment.

"Thank you, Mirari. Come. We have to leave. Now. There are more." He turned and took the lead.

"More men with masks? Are these all members of the Blessed?" Mirari hissed at him quietly as they neared the entrance hall, but Fangbane didn't answer her. Holding a hand up to stop them, he peered around the corner to make sure it was clear.

Mirari was nervous; Fangbane was never this cautious.

"Don't let their looks deceive you. The Blessed can be anyone. Nobles, peasants, fighters. You have to be careful, Mirari. I'm almost certain Laikos is here. I can sense him as if he's telling me to find him."

Mirari noticed that he shuddered slightly.

"We don't have a choice. If anyone comes at you with a blade, you must end them. If you find Laikos, be careful. Don't believe anything he says."

Fangbane held the door to the courtyard. As they moved through, he saw a glint of steel fly through the air. He stepped in front of Starlight, the dagger aimed at her back. Fangbane flicked his spear and struck the dagger, sending it spiraling into the night. He turned as Starlight looked back at him, her eyes reading the look on his face despite the mask.

With one quick nod, Fangbane slammed the door between them, separating himself from the rest.

Thud. Thud.

Two more daggers were nailed against the oak door.

Starlight recoiled as the tip of the blade stuck out on her side of the door. She paused only for a moment at the thought of Fangbane being alone with an unknown number of assassins, all equipped with technology designed to prevent him from using his ability.

Outside, the night breeze was chilly, but her heart was warm. In her chest, Starlight could feel Fangbane's confidence growing stronger. She was depending on their bond to let her know he will be alright. The best she could do for him was to transmit her support back to him through her heart.

"Will he be alright?" Mirari asked. Starlight nodded, nudging her to continue leading the way.

"We'll meet him there. Go."

CHAPTER THIRTY-THREE

Fangbane turned from the doorway, flaunting and spinning his spear around his body. He quickly scanned the room, searching for any sound from the enemy. Even though he couldn't hear their thoughts through the black fanged masks they wore, he could detect their malicious aura tainting the atmosphere around them.

Two… Three here. One in the next room. Two more waiting in the dining hall.

Fangbane took a deep breath, controlling the rhythm of his breathing in strict command of his own thoughts.

He was the darkness. He was the black hole to swallow his enemy.

One of the masked men stepped out from a nook, hurling two throwing stars in quick succession. Fangbane deflected them away with ease as he spun the spear in graceful arcs. He directed the flow of his mind through his hands, feet, and felt whole as three more shadows melded into view. All masked men, bearing daggers and swords, approached him in unison.

The man furthest to his left approached faster than the others and lunged with his pike. Fangbane spun left and swept the man's leg with his foot. Down he fell like a tree in a storm. His weapon landed in front of Fangbane, and he stepped hard on its shaft. The ax sprung up, striking the metal mask of the charging comrade who tried to avenge his friend. The impact sent a loud clang that echoed down the hall, followed by another discomforting plop of a heavy body landing on its back – another tree in the storm.

Fangbane seized the pike and drove it into the belly of the closest enemy. The others hesitated just enough for him to retreat to his favorite room. His feet were sure, high-stepping backward up the curving stairs, as he kept two at bay. The men were well trained – but they didn't know the territory, not in the darkness.

As two followed him, two others ran up the flight of stairs to cut him off on the balcony. Fangbane didn't stop, lunging forward and kicking the two intruders back down the steps. One fell in a daze, slumped on the stairway. The other tumbled hard, out of control, dead with his neck snapped by the time he reached the bottom.

The two men following him had reached the balcony now and were rushing to close in on Fangbane. He hopped onto the long curve of the banister and rode it swiftly to the bottom.

Fangbane landed with the finesse of an acrobat and saw the men scrambling down the stairs after him. The weapon of the dead man rested by his feet. He hefted the unfamiliar pike, and hurled it at one of them. It was an awkward, terrible throw, and missed badly, but it got stuck between the two banister posts and tripped both charging enemies. One tumbled ahead, falling on the point of Fangbane's spear, jammed between his ribs and through his heart. He tried to jerk it loose before the other got back on his feet.

The last man pulled a shuriken from his tunic and whipped it at Fangbane.

"Argh… Gods!" he cursed. Pain seared through his right

shoulder, as the throwing star struck him above his collar bone. He looked at the wound and pulled out the blade from his body.

Fangbane allowed himself only two deep breaths. Hot blood ran down his arm, and his shoulder burned with pain. Fangbane planted his foot on the dead man at his feet, desperately trying to yank his spear out from the body.

The attacker had his sword in hand now and was only four steps from Fangbane. With the spear still stuck in the body, Fangbane was now out of options. He could kick the man, but that would leave his body wide open. He thought about tackling him to the ground, but then the sword would have an express ticket to his chest.

A small object whirled into the assassin's skull from the side as if slicing a ripe melon. The object fell hard against the marble floor. Fangbane was sure it would leave a dent. Upon closer inspection, he realized it was a meat cleaver.

The door in the next room busted open and five more masked men charged in with swords raised high, battle cries filling their lungs.

Gaven ran out from under the balcony, the tip of his gleaming spear illuminating his enraged face. Their cries were quickly overshadowed by the mighty roar of the predator. A sweep of light slashed through the first assassin at the neck, giving him a merciful death.

The second man drew back his spear to throw at Gaven, hoping to silence the wild tiger. In a blink, Gaven's comrade stepped in front of him, his hand extended. The foyer lit up as sparks crackled from his finger, then struck forward. The bolt of electrical discharge that slammed into the assassin and the rest of the men behind him hit so hard that their feet never touched the ground until they hit the opposite wall, eighty feet across.

Gaven yanked Fangbane's spear from the body with ease and returned it to his owner. He took a closer look at his worn-out state. "You don't look so good."

"I can't possibly look as bad as you," Fangbane retorted. Saying this, he fainted, falling, out cold at Gaven's feet.

———

THE PRE-ARRANGED emergency meeting place was a glade deep in the woods behind the estate. It was well-hidden between two large ridges that stretched on for miles. Mirari scanned the clearing as Starlight watched their backs. Sarkan was awake and cranky now, struggling in Starlight's arms, and starting to whine. Not a full-scale tantrum yet, but an eruption was brewing. Mirari thought about offering to hold him but didn't dare. She would need her arms free if it came to a fight.

"Mirari… someone is out there."

Mirari followed Starlight's pointing finger, and saw a vague shape moving in the darkness. She could see the figure, a tall man, leading a magnificent gray stallion.

Her heart leaped with a jolt of alarm – and then, the fear vanished, and she felt a sudden calm soothe her like a gentle, warm wave. She shouldn't be calm.

Mirari recalled briefly seeing the man in Oban, but on his horse, he appeared to be an entirely different person. The handsome monk that once served under the Bishop now radiated under moonlight like a saint. She was entranced by the tresses that fell across his face, tumbling loosely down his elegant, lagoon-colored robes. Breathtaking. Incredibly attractive with his gorgeous hair free of that awful ponytail.

He was confident, a man of experience, resolve, one who walked without fear. A sword pommel gleamed in the moonlight, held by a belt of hammered gold links. The gold sparkled along with the dazzling bejeweled gold bracelet on his sinewy arm. A warm, delicious feeling stirred in her, a pleasurable sensation that brought a stimulating mixture of calm and excitement all at once.

"Come, child. There is nothing to fear."

Laikos' voice was like warm milk laced with caramel, and she wanted a taste of it. She felt the pull from him, but her feelings were trying to hold her back. Her soul was warning her, sending panic signals to her relaxed nerves. But her body couldn't resist the temptation. She took a tentative step forward.

"Don't listen to him." Mirari heard Starlight's faint warning, but she was entranced. No, enthralled. She rested her sword by her side, barely keeping hold of it, and took another step forward, then the next, until she had stepped clear off the shadowy treeling, revealing herself in the moonlit clearing.

The man looked up at the stars and hummed softly. He sounded like the chords of a heavenly chorus.

"Do you know the truth of the stars, young one?"

He looked so enraptured with the sky. She forced herself to resist answering, but she couldn't help sending her gaze to the shining wonder of the twinkling galaxies above.

"We all have our destinies, written in the heavens for all to see. All those with the vision to see it, that is. But only a tiny fraction have this rare ability, this divine sight. You are one of those, child. One who is Blessed. It is people like us who shall rule these lands."

His smile was silk sheets, fresh bread, hot baths, and his voice the babbling music of a brook, the song of larks. His head lowered from the firmament above, and his gaze bored deep into her eyes, penetrating her very soul. Mirari couldn't tear her eyes from his handsome face. His gray eyes gleamed at her and promised deep wisdom.

"Mirari, snap out of it!" She heard Starlight's faint voice once again, but the mother stayed under the shadow of a tree, afraid to let go of the little one.

Laikos paid no attention to her. His eyes were fixated on Mirari's.

Mirari found she could not move. Fear raced up her spine.

And she welcomed it – it was a feeling of her own. This was the man responsible for her Salathiel's death. She craved the power of her anger, longed for it to rise and give her back her own emotions.

But Laikos shoved her emotions back into icy waters until they grew numb.

"Ah, can't have you stirring up those nasty, rebellious feelings, now, can we?" He chuckled, but with admiration. "You have a strong will, young one. Yes, there is a great power within you." He reached a hand up to her heart, hovering in the air, and she felt a sudden pressure deep within her chest. "You have such a powerful spirit, your flame. But still, it is only in an infant state. I, Laikos, the loyal messenger to the Goddesses of Moranity, am here to bring you home. You belong with us, not with these privileged nobles."

Mirari marveled at his words, at the fleeting images of herself standing next to him, dressed in lavish gold with hundreds of people bowing at her awe-inspiring presence. His face softened, and she was flooded with a feeling of acceptance and love. She felt her resolve weaken even more as he drew closer.

No. That was his vision. Not hers.

Her eyes blinked rapidly, forcing her will to flicker back to reality. This dangerous dark soul of lies, he killed Salathiel. She dug deep to the core of her soul, to the certainty that this false trickster couldn't be trusted.

She unearthed the truth and spat it at him. "You are poisoning our leaders. You are filled with lies. I believe nothing you expel from your ugly, corrupt soul."

Laikos' countenance displayed pity. She felt tears as his own eyes became wet.

"Ah, child, what a sorrow it is. From birth, you have been mistreated. You have seen the selfish nature of nobles and leaders, and you understand what it's like to be powerless. People starve, fight over the fruits and rivers nobles hoard with greed. With your flame, you can help people in ways no one else can. In ways you know region leaders will not." He held out his hand. "Come. Join me. You will shine as the Goddess you are destined to become."

His power overcame her again, and she sank to her knees; sleepy and heavy. She struggled to think. But joining him was so tempting.

THUD!

A rock the size of an orange struck Laikos on his shoulder. He flinched, enraged, as his focus broke.

"Mirari!" screamed Starlight, already hefting another rock, ready to throw.

Laikos snapped his attention toward her. The momentary distraction released his mind control over Mirari.

Mirari's body surged to life with an overwhelming burst of power and will. She leaped back to her feet. She took a mighty swing, and nearly hacked off his arm.

Laikos frowned. His sword was in hand, but he didn't bother to use it.

Mirari felt thrilled to be back in control. She longed with a passion to kill this man, to chop his corruption into minced evil. Her strength and speed astounded her as she lunged and slashed at him.

Laikos simply turned, and focused his attention back on her. She stopped in her tracks. Profound sadness weighed her mind down like an anchor. Images of the Knights' corpses swam in pools of red. Her parents, those high and mighty Hales, glared down at her with disdain. Her brother, Salathiel, casting a shattered look over his shoulder as if she was a monster, the same look Gaven had given her before leaving their family forever. Waves of guilt racked her soul, tearing her asunder.

THUD!

Another stone smacked Laikos. The thoughts in Mirari's

mind dissipated like yesterday's chimney smoke. Laikos turned on Starlight. He was out of patience.

"Your wish for an early death shall be granted," he said, hurling his sword at her.

"Starlight!" Mirari screamed as she attempted to intervene.

But Starlight was faster than Mirari's sluggish reflexes. She dove, holding Sarkan's body tight to her chest, and twisting on the way down to land on her back, sparing him from being crushed. The rough landing jolted the fragile one awake, releasing the howling shriek only a baby can generate. The sword Laikos had thrown was lodged deep in a tree, wobbling like a vibrating tuning fork.

Mirari ran up to Starlight, checking for any wounds, and shrieking at Laikos, almost as loud as Sarkan. "I will never join you, never! You are the foul spawn of pure evil itself, and I will have no part of you!"

"It is not a choice, child. If you do not follow me, you will learn of your truth the hard way. Please, take my hand. I have taken the liberty to remove those pesky region leaders. All that's left is the Council. Nations will bow to you as to the will of Gods."

Dark shadows appeared from the treeline, masked men who seemed to materialize like an army of specters. They numbered more than Mirari could count. She was sure she could take them on – if she could summon her fire, that is. But that wasn't going to happen.

One of the masked men stumbled from the treeline, and collapsed, a gaping sword wound spouting arterial blood like a hose. Three more pitched forward, butchered like hogs with kitchen knives sticking out from their chest. Lucan leaped over the bodies. Gaven followed him, recovered well enough to slaughter the hapless cadre of killers Laikos had summoned. Fangbane staggered out behind them, taking a defensive position in front of his family.

A dozen more masked men fled the treeline, unwilling to be electrocuted by the man who could outrun them or chewed by the tiger's fanged teeth. The rest of the horde broke in a stampede. Laikos didn't want to waste the energy to rally the cowards. He spat on the ground in disappointment that barely felt like more than indifference. He didn't care. This was a minor skirmish. He had the weapon he needed to win the real war. So, he mounted his gray horse, and turned it around, ready for a temporary retreat.

Fangbane sighed in relief, thankful that the battle was over. He turned around and was even more relieved to see that the ladies and his son were unhurt. Starlight noticed he was barely able to stand, leaning on his spear for support, his shoulder a bloody mess, his whole side dripping with gore. He heard her gasp and smiled at her. "Barely a scratch, honey."

"I suppose you expect me to stitch up that mess?"

"Or you could just amputate. Whatever's easiest."

"I'll never get those bloodstains out. You should have taken off that tunic right away to let it soak."

Then, a chilling voice came at them, not a sound, just words in their heads.

You cannot avoid your fate.

CHAPTER THIRTY-FOUR

The night passed slowly for all of them. Starlight couldn't bear to lay Sarkan back into his crib, but spent the long hours until dawn with her precious child clutched snugly in her safe arms. Sleep did not come to her.

Fangbane, though his wounds healed rapidly after his wife's treatments, was beyond exhaustion. While he did lie comfortably, and his body was able to rest, it was a different story with his mind. A thousand plans and scenarios played themselves out, a thousand solutions to each one were weighed and considered.

How could the Knights stop an empath? How many followers does Laikos have? How many of his brave, fearless Knights would not survive?

Fangbane knocked on his comstōne twice as it pulsed in rainbow colors, hoping to reach Shiba. He may have called more times than necessary. When he finally answered, Fangbane told him about the attack.

"Are you all okay?" Hime's worried voice echoed from Fangbane's stone. Though Gaven, Mirari, and Lucan were also huddled in the room, they kept their heads lowered and said nothing.

"The poison's out of their system now, thankfully. Starlight is still a bit shaky, but Lucan's bringing reinforcements."

"I'll send some of my troops to the estate as well," Shiba offered. "Did you figure out his next move?"

Mirari spoke up, recalling the invasive words he whispered into her ear. "He said he was going to take down the Council."

"Now that we know he's still here in Avon, it'll take him a while to get to Valenia. If he finishes the poison today, then we might be able to outride him to the Hearth," Gaven said.

"Today…" Fangbane bit his lip. "Will the antidote be ready by then?"

"I'm working on it," Kylah said, having overheard their conversation. "But you should go to the Hearth first. We'll meet you there."

"We'll leave as soon as Lucan's reinforcements show up."

As Fangbane ended the connection, he turned to the silent fighters hunched over before him. They were all determined to stop Laikos, he read, but their confidence didn't eliminate all their fears.

Mirari's worries went beyond her own survival. Fangbane watched her conversation with Laikos play over and over again in her mind. He had invaded her mind and memories beyond discomfort, and claimed that her hidden power was a gift. Was he telling the truth? Or was he manipulating his words, hoping to use her fiery state as a weapon to create his new world?

"Nothing Laikos said can be believed," Gaven said, feeling the sinking feeling in his chest. He smiled, letting Mirari know that she wasn't fighting alone.

Mirari smiled back with gratitude. She had one brother to avenge, and another to defend. Laikos and his accursed *'Blessed'* had already taken the innocent life of Salathiel. They had nearly killed Gaven, and would certainly do their worst to finish the job. The sacred duty of her bond to him obligated her to do anything and everything to enable his survival, at all costs to herself, even death.

And there was the solemn oath to her fellow Knights, and her duty to protect all the innocent lives in every empire.

Finally, she had her duty to herself. Not merely to protect her own life and her personal interests. She had to become the person she was destined to be. She had a unique gift, an incredible power, and she was obligated to learn how to tame it, to use it for good. If their mission failed, if she failed – then Laikos would succeed. His terrifying prophecy about her fate – her preordained destiny – would become reality.

Shire arrived with a dozen servants riding on gallant mounts and carriages of armor. Lucan examined the goods, taking a handful of what appeared to be human-sized muddleberries on a stick and tossing them to the guards. These were anything but candy. They packed enough kore to electrocute anyone who came within its range. He directed the servants to position themselves and their wards across the estate. They were not strong fighters, but they would be enough to spook anyone who tried to infiltrate the property again.

A hundred more soldiers arrived and stationed themselves across the water's edge. They raised the flag bearing the crest of Avon to the height of their spears, ready to kill on order.

From his window, Fangbane watched the reinforcements surround his home, unwilling to wander away from the comstōne. Before he could check on the progress of the antidote, the Knights called first.

"It's done? That fast?" Fangbane beamed.

"Who do you think I am?" Kylah rattled a cardboard box that was now filled to the top with vials of her green concoction. Hime and Dorain were still bottling the last of them.

"We got Lucan's caravan of horses too," Neo said. "Shall we meet you at the Hearth?"

Fangbane heard their barn door creak. Directing his attention to the window to look at the stable, he saw that Mirari, Gaven, and Lucan had already saddled their horses and were ready to ride. His wife and newborn child were accompanied by Shire, who stood by their side, ready to send them off. She looked up at the window and telepathically told him she would be fine.

For a second, his heart melted, knowing that his dream, his vision for peace, wasn't just his own anymore. He knew that should anything happen to him, there would be others to carry on his mission. He stuck his head out the window and greeted his team.

"Let's go."

***

As the Knights reunited and made their way to the Hearth, Fangbane felt a stab of impending doom. The city was silent except for the sound of the hooves clattering on the cobbled streets.

Their worst fear was revealed as soon as they rounded the corner and the building came into view. Fangbane held up his hand for them to stop. A carpet of death lay before them. They were struck dumb at the ghastly sights of corpses littering the street all the way up the grand stairs of the Hearth.

Shiba was first to speak. "We're too late."

Gaven got down from his horse. "Shut your stupid gab hole. You don't know that." He was already stepping over the bodies, heading for the steps leading up to the Hearth with his spear drawn. In a split second, his kore traveled from his hand into his weapon, bursting into blue crystal light.

Dismounting, Fangbane ordered the Knights to follow. The air rang with the sound of steel being drawn. Passing his partner,

Neo grumbled, "You can stay here and order flowers for the funeral. I'm going in to fight for anyone still alive."

As all the others hurried toward the building, Shiba closed his eyes, and took in a deep breath. "Well, Mecate," he said quietly, "I guess you'd tell me there's always hope." Completing his muttered prayer to her, he hopped off his horse.

The Knights hop-scotched their way past the dead soldiers. Most of them lay without a wound, murdered with hardly a sword drawn.

"Wait!" Kylah shouted. "The airborne version of the poison works, obviously. It will be worse inside."

"The antidote?" Fangbane asked. "Can it be administered before we're infected?"

"I have something better." She pulled out a handful of green crystal charms that she made with the spare ingredients of the antidote. "Wear these around your neck, and the poison will not affect you."

Shiba cocked his head, skeptical as always. "That junk? It looks like you stole it from a blind sorceress. How's this supposed to protect us?"

"Anything is possible, except for the ignorant." She held one of the charms in his face. "Kamori powder. Acts as an antioxidant in concert with gamarite metals, charging an ionized field of—"

"In simple terms, Kylah," Gaven muttered.

"This will form a shield to repel the prions before they can enter your body."

"Why didn't you say so?" Shiba snatched a charm, dropping the chain around his neck. The rest of them did the same.

Before Kylah took her first steps onto the grand stairway leading up to the entrance, a large hand stopped her.

"You don't have to fight if you don't want to."

Kylah shook her head. "I caused this. I ran from it once, I

won't do it again." She revealed the inside of her cloak to him, pockets full of crystals ranging in every shape and color.

"By the Gods." Neo's jaw dropped. "You can use all those?"

Kylah gave him a wink. "I'm going to prove I'm the better spellcaster with or without the stones."

The huge bronze double doors at the top of the stairs flew open, a host of masked men pouring out, charging straight at them.

A sudden blast of wind tossed the first four enemies sideways. Fangbane saw Mirari, her hand raised, surprised herself at summoning enough kore. The other men continued to swarm down, engaging the Knights. Ice shards and arrows flew over their heads, landing perfect shots and sending the men tumbling down the stairs.

"We'll give you an opening," Hime called out. A large shield of ice formed in front of the princess with the young aegis by her side.

Fangbane charged through first. Mirari followed, along with Gaven and Shiba, heading into the building. The sea of masked men flooded the stairway before any other Knight could rush through.

More men waited in the grand vestibule. Gaven and Shiba lunged out first, desperate to claim the first kill. Gaven swiped in a fury faster than human eyes could follow. A single move – left, right, diagonal, all in perfect form – was all it took to take down his opponents. Gaven charged toward another man, but the scrawny soldier collapsed to the floor with a shuriken nailed to his neck before he could hack him. Gaven turned back to Shiba and fumed like a raging bull.

"Got to be faster than that, Kitten," Shiba mocked as he threw four more stars behind him without looking, each nailing a target perfectly. The hitmen hollered with agony as they melted to the ground.

"We have to find the Councilors," Fangbane shouted, leading

his three followers toward the curved stairway, where they ran into another dozen masked guards, ready to fight to death to keep them out.

THE REST of the force was still fighting the congestion outside.

Lucan pulled a knife with a golden hilt from his back pouch. With a click, it fanned open into four blades. Grasping onto the ring of gold, he threw the weapon into the crowd of masked men. It flew like a boomerang, clashing against masks and severing limbs until it made its way back to its owner.

Kylah was at the bottom of the stairway. A bloodied corpse fell in front of her, but she stayed focused on the azure crystal in her hands. The corpse was dragged away along with several live bodies with a single swipe of Neo's arm. He wrestled them as far away from Kylah as possible.

"Knights, hit the deck!" Kylah warned. Neo looked back and saw that the crystal in her hand was floating, twirling in a spherical reservoir of water between her palms. The other Knights were quick to respond, dropping low, seconds before a spiral of waves erupted from her hands like a tornado, pulsing forward then curving upward, sending a group of soaked men flying. "Lucan!"

He pointed to the sky as crackles of lightning scattered from his finger. "Clear!"

The bolt that sizzled forth swept through the ranks of masked men like a fire hose hitting bowling pins. Wisps of smoke rose from the fried defenders as their bodies rained from the sky. Stepping over the curled victims of electrocution, Kylah and the Knights dashed for the door, eager to catch up with the rest of the team.

BLOOD AND SCREAMS filled the air as they drove the masked men back.

Mirari kept her feet in sync with Gaven's, her movements mirroring his own grace. With their backs against each other, their weapons whirled and slashed, cutting through half a dozen swordsmen.

A wounded man grabbed her foot, pulling her down. She fell next to him, and he tried to put a dagger into her ribs. She caught his wrist just in time, but he was strong, and winning the struggle, pushing the dagger closer and closer as she tried to hold his arm back. Gaven turned around and tried to help his partner, but a hefty object, one larger than Neo, swept him off his feet. Man or animal, Gaven wasn't sure, but it had enough force to crush him against the nearest wall.

With her free hand, Mirari jerked the mask off the strangler's head. She could see his face; his eyes were vacant windows. She grasped him by the hair, and slammed him hard on the marble floor until his head lolled over unconscious, and he dropped his dagger.

Mirari quickly rose to her feet, desperate to help Gaven, only to be grabbed from behind by another masked killer, his arm wrapped around her neck in a chokehold. This time, she had no defense to break free, and she felt herself start to black out.

Twang!

Her assailant released her, trying to clutch at the arrow lodged in his neck. As the assailant dropped to the floor, Dorain gave her a wave.

Neo tackled the man twice his size, freeing Gaven from the crushed wall. The giant struggled against Neo's strength, rolling out of control as Neo tenderized his thick folds. With a strong kick, Neo catapulted the dough-like man toward one of Hime's sharp sculptures of ice. His body fell through it and molded into the shape of a perfect donut.

Kea flew gallantly ahead, pecking the heads of the masked

men. They flung their arms around, trying to shoo away the kestrel. Distracted by the cunning bird, the men were oblivious to the orange and white striped saberlion that pounced from the top of the stairway, landing on their bodies and shredding their limbs like paper with its arching fangs. Its roar sent a rumble through the corridor, daring for the next man to step forward. The two nearest men yelped and scattered for the exit.

"Pierce!" For once, Dorain was happy to see the intimidating beast. He looked up at the balcony. "That's my father's saberlion. They must be upstairs in the Grand Hall."

Shiba had already begun to make his way up the stairway when Fangbane saw a man draw back his arm, about to fling a shuriken star at him. He felt a memory twinge in his shoulder, but this time he was quick to hurl his spear, skewering the enemy before the shuriken found Shiba. Now without his spear, Fangbane was at the mercy of another swordsman on the attack.

Fangbane dodged once, twice, the blade barely missing him. But the marble floor was slippery with blood, and his feet slid from under him. He fell, helpless, as the masked swordsman raised his blade to strike.

His sword slipped away from his hand, carried off by a draft. The man looked up and found his sword lodged into the high ceiling. His head was gone with a single sweep of cobalt light. Mirari ran up the stairs with Gaven close behind. He hollered, "Point up your spear, you crazy old man!"

Fangbane scrambled back onto his feet, grabbed the nearest spear, and hurried up the stairway with the rest of them.

Dorain pounced up onto a pedestal. It was best to defend here, he thought, as he examined the wide foyer, satisfied with his vantage point. He did a double take when he saw the sculpture topping the tall block of marble – a naked Amazon, posed with one breast jutting forth, and her bow slung over the other shoulder, other breast missing. As interesting as that view was, Dorain extracted his focus from the lady, and began firing arrows rapidly, cutting down one masked man after another.

Hime waved to him from her own perch as she teleported onto a pedestal. Dorain chuckled at her choice of statuary – a graphically buff warrior holding a spear with a shaft as impressive as the one he stood on, anatomically correct and completely undressed. But Hime was not distracted, and conjured up a dozen sharp pointed shards of ice and shields around her body.

Lucan and Neo stood by Kylah as she removed the mask of one of the unconscious soldiers.

Kylah looked at the mask in her hand. She rubbed her fingers on the inside of the mask and examined the quality.

"Shit." Kylah dropped the mask and hurried up the stairs. Neo followed behind as they skipped over lifeless bodies.

"What is it?" he asked. "What's in the mask?"

"Cepha metals and empaths are like lightning on water. It amplifies psychic ability. Our masked leader isn't going to stand a chance!"

CHAPTER THIRTY-FIVE

Fangbane caught up with Gaven, Mirari, and Shiba as they rammed open the doors to the Grand Hall. The scene before them was as bad as they had expected.

Throughout the chamber, the bodies of royal guards lay bloody and twisted, along with corpses of masked men – a tangle of the dead, victims and murderers, the killers and the slain. The few that were still conscious coughed uncontrollably, growing weaker by the moment as they struggled against death's bony grip.

Tables were turned, papers scattered. Even the flags of the empires that hung high had now collapsed and dangled from the edge of their poles. Underneath the fallen flags laid Suzan and Tarek, slumped over their desks. It was unclear whether they were unconscious or dead.

Dareh and Novinha were crawling on the floor, barely able to move their slack and feeble limbs. The bow and sword in their hands signaled that they had put up a fight for as long as they could.

Adder laid by a stained window, curled forward as he coughed into his shirt to no end. In front of him stood a pillar with needles of ice blooming on one side. A few more pillars down the hall also had ice on them. The trail led to the last man standing – Laikos.

The sight of it sickened Fangbane.

But not as much as the sight of the simpering grin Laikos had stretched across his mouth. He stood, tall and prideful, at the opposite end of the chamber. His delight at his handiwork was evident. His pleasure at having the entire Council writhing at his feet put the Knights' blood to boil.

Gaven readied his mighty spear. To his side, Mirari lifted her sword, poised in a formal fighting stance. She tried not to be distracted by the rivulets of fresh blood, as they rolled down the blade, falling from the razor-sharp edge in fat drops.

Shiba moved first. He screamed a Minettan battle cry, charging from the side to distract Laikos. On the opposite end, his deadly shadow flowed silently toward the Blessed leader's back.

But just as the shadow was about to seize him, Laikos spun in a full circle. A blinding bright glow shone from his robe, casting a harsh light in every direction. This enchanted luminescence seemed to vaporize the shadow.

Laikos stopped, then reversed his spin, sending a wave of water rushing in every direction. Shiba was hit first. He resisted the force, holding his stance – but the water hardened into solid ice, and froze his body to the floor.

Suzan's head slowly lifted from the table, barely able to push herself up with her fragile arms. Weak but stubborn, Suzan summoned her last ounce of strength, her hand slithering for the whip on her belt, then lashing out at Laikos. A spark traveled down the whip, but he caught the snap of the end with his bare hand and extinguished it.

Gaven saw the opportunity and lunged forward. His spear crystalized with his kore even further, now a deadlier weapon with multiple sharp edges.

Tugging the whip loose, Laikos shot water balls with his other hand. The liquid engulfed Suzan, and upon impact, froze into ice and locked her in place.

Gaven was now in range to chop his blade into Laikos. He launched his spear just as another blast of water hit him, freezing him up to his chest. A disk of ice, no larger than a pocket mirror, formed between Laikos' hand and Gaven's spear. The spear nailed the disk perfectly in the center, but the ice did not crack in the slightest. The impact sent rippling waves of energy across the room, until the spear had no force left, and dropped helplessly like a tree branch.

The ice disk launched toward Fangbane, but Mirari stood in front of him, her adrenaline rushing through her veins as fast as the flying ringlet. Her eyes locked onto the disk as she raised her sword and took a swing at it. It ricocheted to the side, shattering the glass window above Adder's head.

"Ah, Sokal," Laikos greeted, enjoying the taste of chewing on that old name. "The lost son of Sarkan. You have arrived just in time."

Fangbane froze, despite the lack of ice on him.

Mirari looked at him, confused. "My Lord?" Fangbane slowly turned toward Mirari. Then without warning, he grabbed her neck, lifting her.

Mirari gasped, trying to catch a breath of air. She could tell from his stiff movement, an experience she faced herself, that he had no control over his actions. He was just a puppet with Laikos pulling the strings. She clawed at Fangbane's hand, urging him to let go, but she couldn't even utter a croak. Still, she struggled to scream, but his hand only gripped her throat tighter.

Gaven could only watch, desperate, tugging his head around trying to break free. He seethed with anger so hot he thought the ice trapping him would melt away.

He could feel his partner's panic rising in him. Her chest tried to heave, her mind screamed for air. Gaven felt it too. His face was red with the strain of trying to give her the power to break free.

He growled at Laikos. "Let us go, you bastard!"

"Bold words for someone so powerless." Laikos was not intimidated in the slightest. Instead, he was pleased with the suffering he could deal out like a deck of cards.

"I'll kill you. I'll kill you for this," Gaven fumed. "For the Althaean Siege, for Mirari's brother, for every person sacrificed for your selfish pleasure!"

"I am not the selfish one. You act on revenge. I act to better the lives of thousands. Leaders with blind arrogance like yours are the real poison for our empires."

"What a pompous crock of shit," Gaven said.

Laikos ignored Gaven and turned his attention back to Fangbane. He focused on his fellow empath and flashed a vision in his mind.

Fangbane was a terrified boy again, watching his father lying dead on the ground. His throat cut from ear to ear. A crowd of mourners appeared, wailing over his corpse. Sokal's attention shifted to the crowd. Among them, he spotted a familiar face – Aulus. The cadet stood staring, but his eyes were lifeless, his chin smeared with the blood he had coughed up, his tunic soaked with the blood flowing from the knife wound in his chest.

Fangbane let out a wrenching scream, horrified by Laikos invading his mind with such cruel and casual ease. Fangbane struggled to regain control of his body. He looked at Mirari, remorse crushing his soul as his helpless hand crushed her windpipe.

But she hadn't given up – she was a fighter, fiercely clutching at even a shred of life.

His profound sorrow deepened, along with the waves of terrible fear. Fear of hurting the ones closest to him, all because of his ability, and his stubborn vanity, his obsession with saving the world. Was he a fool?

"You were supposed to die that day, Sokal. Both you and your father. You defied the work of the Blessed. Yet, the Gods spared your lives." He turned his attention to Mirari. "They changed their minds all because of you. You were born, and the wheels of fate turned."

Mirari tried to shift her darkening gaze to Laikos. She couldn't make a sound, but even through her red-veined, bulging eyes, her menacing glare sent a clear message: *My destiny is not with you!*

"How amusing." Laikos chuckled. "I offered you the easy path. Now I give you the hard one. Sokal?" Fangbane tightened his grip on Mirari's neck. She struggled ferociously, knowing that her life would end if she did nothing.

"Don't... do this—" Fangbane struggled to regain his will. "Take me instead."

"You? You're nothing. A dandelion seed in a hurricane. It is Mirari who holds the future's key." He turned to her, patience at an end. "Join me, or I will command everyone in this building to cut into their own flesh until they beg to be killed." Laikos waited for her answer.

Mirari stared at Fangbane's silver helmet, now smeared with red prints. It was unsuited to his caring personality, and the mask didn't seem like it belonged to him anymore. She couldn't see his eyes, but she could tell they were filled with love. She needed to save him. She needed to save them all. She needed to stay alive.

If only she could summon it. Mirari tried to build up strength, rage, tension, whatever could help get her blood flowing. But nothing worked.

If it came, in control or not, she had faith that her flames would be on her side. The flame was a part of her, and she knew her place – a savior, not a destroyer. She embraced it as an extension of herself, pushing away her fears.

With full confidence, she shouted from her confined throat, "Only I... can write... my own fate."

Laikos reached out a hand and stroked her cheek, sending a thrill of adrenaline down her spine. Again, the seductive calm called to her. She felt her resolve start to melt. She held her soul by only a fingertip, and it was slipping away. His hold was so strong, and she had no fight left in her. She felt her body slacken, hanging limp from Fangbane's hand.

There was a flicker of movement to her left. The blonde spellcaster didn't conceal her presence at all, sprinting into the room and chucking two silver pearls at Laikos. He took one step back, letting the pearls fly past him and explode into the nearest pillar. A cloud of thin fog erupted upon impact.

Kylah planted her feet, holding a large yellow crystal, which crackled with electricity, as the fog brushed lightly over Laikos, disappearing into the air.

From his graceful hand, Laikos fired a round of water at the spellcaster. Neo stepped out from behind her with arms stretched wide to bring forth a barrier. The wave glided over the barrier like oil on vinegar, returning to the malicious monk. Laikos waved his hand hoping to pivot the flow of water, but nothing happened and it splattered over his now soaked robes.

Kylah uttered ancient words, summoning crackling bolts around her body through the crystal.

"Aten's power belongs to me!" She thrust the crystal forward, striking Laikos, and sending him flying.

He easily landed on his feet, dusting his vest off.

"Mirari, the mask! Remove it!" Kylah called out. But just as she did, a wave of water plowed into Kylah. Neo stepped in, trying to block the lashing waves, but couldn't stand fast against the force. They were enveloped, trapped within a sphere. The water was as tough as a thick bag of leather. It began shrinking, sucking the air, and restricting their movement. Kylah and Neo struggled to break out before the ball crushed them.

Mirari used the slight distraction to grab Fangbane's hand tightly. She rocked her body back and forth, swinging up momentum to lift her leg high enough. She kicked Fangbane on the side of his head. Fangbane recoiled, releasing his grip on her. The blow also knocked his helmet off and sent it lurching across the floor.

As she gasped for air, for the briefest of moments, she saw his face. A pale handsome face, slack and mindless, in a tight hood covering his head and ears.

The confusion in Fangbane's eyes lasted for a second before they lit with fury. He snatched a fallen spear and in the same continuous motion, hurled it at Laikos. This time the spear found a home in the right side of Laikos' chest, and he staggered backward. He tried to pull it out, but it was lodged firmly in his ribs, helpless as a pinned butterfly.

His concentration shattered, the ice trapping Kylah and Neo fell apart. In his panic, he lost control of his calm state, his silky face now fueled with the demonic eyes of a merciless killer. He focused every brain cell on surviving.

The air grew damp and cold as micro-droplets of water fogged the chamber, and started to form ice crystals in the air. The heavy ice trapping the others evaporated and reformed into sharp ice shards. Laikos oriented them at the Knights and attacked.

Fangbane barreled into Mirari and dragged her to cover behind an overturned table just in time. Spikes of ice quilled the wood.

Dragging Suzan's frail body with them, Gaven and Shiba crouched behind an overturned bench, while Neo cast his sturdy barrier around him and Kylah.

The icy air howled like an Arctic blizzard now. The noise was deafening. But not loud enough to drown out the Althaean battle cry as Gaven charged madly, his spear extended like a jousting lance.

Mirari saw what he was doing. She got to her feet and cried his name, yelled with her trembling hands stretched out, trying to pull apart a clear path. The air around him tore free of the blizzard and rolled out like a golden carpet to Laikos.

Laikos raised his hand and pointed right at Gaven's face, ready to shatter the annoying fighter into a thousand shards. But a shadow wrapped around Laikos' hand, pulling it to the side.

"Get him, Kitten!" Shiba rallied from behind the bench.

Kore trickled down from Gaven's hand and filled his spear. The shaft illuminated even brighter and the divine light drove into Laikos' chest.

"I'm a man who honors his word," Gaven growled. "Here's your express ticket to Inferna." He forced it in like a crooked screw twisting and grinding into tendons and bones, crunch after crunch.

Laikos grunted, looking at the gaping wound torn into his torso. In his face, Gaven could see a spooky acceptance. Laikos knew he would not live through this. But still… the scum smiled.

"This was my fate." Laikos sounded almost cheery. "All is happening as it was meant to be…" He raised his fading eyes to the ceiling, let out his last breath, as life left him.

The room stood still in cold silence as drizzles of ice crystals fell like merciful rain, cleansing the sweat and blood of the victorious fighters.

Fangbane slowly rose from behind the table, soaked in the refreshing dew. He saw Kylah already stepping up to the monk's corpse, unclipping the bracelet from his wrist and returning it to her hand. She smiled confidently, admiring the array of gems dangling on the bracelet.

A rush of footsteps pounded in the corridor, then the other Knights swarmed in.

Hime shook the box of vials from her pouch. "The antidotes! Hurry."

Dorain didn't hesitate. He snatched a handful of vials and ran over to a corner where the big striped cat whimpered over a slumped man. Dorain and the man were wearing practically identical coats, tailored feathered beauties from the Tribe of Aegises. The man, his father, couldn't speak, but his eyes followed Dorain as he poured the antidote down his throat. His body flinched and curled as he coughed his way back to life. Dorain watched with a pity that he never thought he would have for his father. He had always hated him, but he realized he wasn't ready to live without him.

Still coughing from the medicine, Dareh gave him a glance, then averted his eyes.

What an ungrateful prick. Dorain huffed, ready to turn away too. But before he could move an inch, Dareh pulled him down and squeezed him between his muscular arms. Dorain froze, stunned at the sudden affection. His anger began to dissipate and he felt his own arms rise, unable to resist the temptation of returning the hug.

Lucan gave a vial to Tarek while Hime cared for Suzan, gently tilting her head back to administer the antidote. Suzan coughed at the burn but instantly felt relief. She blinked wildly. The man hovering over her appeared to have no ears.

"Easy, easy. It's me." Fangbane calmed her. She couldn't help studying his face, unseen in all the years she'd known him. "What?" he said.

"Nothing. It's just… I always pictured you with a mustache."

Mirari handed him his mask, and he slipped it over his head. "I'll think about it."

Suzan chuckled to herself. "You look better with the bucket on your head." She turned to her fellow Councilors. One by one, they were starting to recover after drinking the antidote.

"This is unforgivable," Novinha scoffed, pulling herself up by the hilt of her sword. "Where did that monk obtain such a dangerous toxin?"

Kylah's heart skipped a beat, and her mouth fell open. But she swallowed her fear, ready to fess up. She had no intention of denying responsibility.

"It's an old family recipe from the Mora scripture." Fangbane spoke up before Kylah could say a word. "Typical crap from the Blessed, huh?"

"Did you say… the Blessed?" Adder's eyes widened. The Councilor had sprung up like a dandelion in a spring field, his youthful health to thank for being able to recover faster than the others. His eyes scanned the damage done to the room, counting the number of guards that fell before being able to draw their weapon. A grim realization fell upon him – they were not prepared for such an attack. He was certain there would be another attempt on their lives.

"All this time, we've been ignoring their threats," Tarek agreed. The celta who had always been neutral in the Council's affairs was putting his foot down for once. "There are more like him out there. We cannot ignore the Blessed any longer."

Adjusting his body to lie against a desk, Dareh was just glad to be alive. "Well done, Helmet. Couldn't have done it without you."

"You got that right." Fangbane taunted with pride, almost waiting for his medal of honor. Dareh rolled his eyes and turned to his conferees.

"I suppose we can re-evaluate our decision regarding the Knights," he gave in.

Hime handed Suzan her cane and helped her up. She limped closer to the rest of the Council, and in her husky voice, said, "Indeed, we have a lot to discuss."

One by one, lifeless bodies began to rise again. The room was filled with coughing guards, groaning at the bitter medicine being shoved down their throats.

Fangbane watched Shiba and Neo high-five each other. Mirari smiled at Gaven, who reciprocated with a tight hug. They had every right to celebrate. Fangbane fantasized about taking a long bath soak, indulging in bubbly wine once he returned home.

Pulling away from Mirari, Gaven cheered for Fangbane to

join them with a big smile on his face. "I thought I told you. Your spear is not a javelin. Stop throwing it, old man."

"Perhaps it's my turn for some training… if you're willing to stay with us, that is."

Gaven's face lit up as bright as his kore-filled spear. "It wouldn't hurt to stop by every once in a while."

Being around Fangbane was a bruise on his arm, a magnet for trouble. But the Knights were adventurous, daring, and a beautiful synchrony of what true teamwork looked like. They caused a kind of pain that nourished his thirst for adventure, and he looked forward to more.

With the Council occupied, Kylah leaned in closer to Fangbane and said, "Now I suppose you think I owe you for saving my head."

"Consider it paid. Without your antidote, we'd all be dead by now."

"Really? You're not going to use it as a bargaining chip to get me to join your cult?"

"I would, but I thought your lack of response to my letter meant—"

"I accept," she said, cutting him off. Her eyes briefly darted to Neo and the other cheery youths. "It's about time I step out of the shadows and reclaim honor to my name. Besides, I can see you're at least trying to do the right thing with this. A pretty half-assed job, but I think I can shape it up. Maybe."

Fangbane nodded. His face wasn't visible, but there was a smile underneath that mask.

It was more support than he could have ever dreamed of, a debt that he could never pay. But this dream of his that he had sought for most of his life was finally coming into form. And it wasn't over. No, it was far from it. This was only the beginning of their quest for justice.

A light chuckle escaped his mouth. His journey was woven with hundreds of serpentine stitches, more than he thought would be required to reach his goal. He began to wonder if he had truly lost his touch as a fortune teller, or if fate was now volatile, a force that could twist and challenge his predictions. It was more complex than he expected it to be, but he enjoyed it. The unpredictability, the challenge of defying the norm, it was… fascinating.

He was ready to face it all with his seven Knights, the Valiant Tiger, his wife, and newborn son, and all the new allies he had accumulated on this journey. The masked man reached out to shake Kylah's hand.

"Welcome to the Knights of the Alliance."

EPILOGUE

With my father's tainted sword sheathed by my side, I stepped out into the sunlight. I had to get out of that place before the smell of blood overwhelmed me. I tried to ignore the red fluid in my hair that had tangled and hardened, turning my focus to the warm breeze brushing against my skin. It was the perfect way to end the day.

Tribes from across Valenia were pouring in as fast as they could to help clean the mess Laikos left behind. The bodies were laid out on grand steps, the guards of the Council mingled with the slain invaders, now unmasked. Citizens from across the land helped to respectfully wrap the corpses in shrouds of gleaming white cotton. A delegation of holy men led by the High Priest moved through the ranks of dead men, performing sacred prayers for each of them.

On the other side of the Hearth, row after row of medical tents stretched to the end of the field. Hundreds of poison survivors were being treated with Kylah's antidote. To the side, the royal guards who were cured and able to walk again ate portions of the hot food dished up by volunteers. But most chewed without tasting, huddled in blankets to ward off the shock, their dull eyes lost in thousand-yard stares.

This is over, Sal. He won't hurt anyone else anymore.

I glanced at the lowering sun, watching the sky begin to change its blushing face, the streaks of ochre and tangerine highlights slashing across orange and shreds of purple breaking through.

"Hey." A hand smacked my shoulder. I'd felt this large, rigid hand on me many times. That tap, followed by a firm squeeze. It was Gaven. The squeeze meant he was proud. "Not used to the scent of blood yet, huh?"

"I'm still getting used to the stink of a certain partner in a workout." We stood in silence for a moment, staring at the rows of dead bodies. Then I had to say it. "People didn't have to die, not over something like this."

"On the contrary, things like this are exactly what people die for. They fight for what they believe in. That's the whole meaning of being a fighter."

"That's something you've always dreamed of, isn't it?"

"And something you've decided to join in on."

He was right. My new life, my new home. With luck, I wouldn't have to see too many more dead bodies. But I won't stand by and watch the innocent die. That was our purpose, I guess. At least, Lord Fangbane wanted it that way.

"The Council wants you, Kitten," Shiba called out from across the field.

Gaven pouted and began to head back inside, leaving me to deal with this fool. You'd think after a day of slaughter and mayhem, he would take a few hours off. No chance.

"So you finally got your sword stained. Congrats on losing your virginity."

"Piss off." I was in no mood to deal with his abuse. All that stabbing and chopping and what not. Everyone has their limit. I tried to walk away, but he just followed me.

"If you're going to stay with the Knights, you've got to toughen up. Can't let a little rough stuff get under your skin."

"Leave it alone, will you?"

"Aww. Are we feeling sensitive?"

"I'm giving you a chance to quit being an asshole."

"What?" I kept walking, but I knew that wasn't going to do it. "Beg your pardon, buttercup. Did you call me an asshole?"

I thought about Laikos. Sometimes you can't fight destiny. And if fate wanted to get in a tussle with you, why not get in the first lick?

I turned around, my eyes all soft and my voice on the verge of tears.

"Please, Shiba," I plead, trying to sound a little scared. "I don't want to do… THIS!"

He wasn't expecting it when I jammed my fist into his diaphragm, really driving it up under his ribs. I guess maybe I was still a little jacked on adrenaline because I don't think I've ever thrown such a sweet punch. Got the hip rotation behind it, full shoulder, real snap to it. Perfect focus on punching my fist right through him and out the other side.

And by the Holy Cave of Cheeses did I ever catch the bastard. It seemed to lift him off the ground, and somehow he was not just on his ass, he was about six feet away. I knocked so much wind out of him, he won't be able to blow out a candle for a week. His mouth was trying to move – I'm sure he just wanted to say something mean. But he couldn't even utter a whisper.

Then, I got a little concerned. He was gasping so bad I wondered if he got some of that poison in him. I was almost starting to feel bad. I offered my hand to help him up. He reached out, but his hand didn't have the strength to squeeze whipped cream. I grabbed his wrist in both hands and gave him a heave.

He was still trying to pull in a breath. Even so, he opened his mouth. I expected him to croak out some insult or other.

Nope. He just fell to his knees and puked like it was pledge night.

I wasn't just feeling bad anymore, I was feeling flat out like shit. I hunkered down beside him, patted him gently on his back.

"Easy. Take it slow. Little breaths. Baby bird breaths—"

He finally got enough air in him and said, "The fuck was that?"

"Karma?" I answered cheekily. "After all those bruises you gave me, it's about time you got one of your own."

He shook his head. "No. That's not—" he paused. I could barely hear him when he added, "I meant, your eyes."

I held back my tongue, wondering what he meant. "What about my eyes?"

"The glow?" He coughed and choked on his words. "When you… get… mad?" he said between gasps.

"My eyes glow?" What a crock. "You're punchy. Take a rest."

I gave him a light pat on the back and walked away. I still felt bad, but I knew he would recover eventually. More so, I just wanted to get out of there, out of sight. His words had made me uneasy, and I didn't want it to show.

Glowing eyes. Such a load of sour pig poop. Maybe it was a trick of the light from the amazing sunset; all kinds of colors. He must have seen a reflection. That's what.

I walked into the building. One of the healers was crouched over a bloody body, trying to bring back a heartbeat. Chest compressions. Mouth to mouth. Hime must have seen it and went over.

She greeted me with a quick wave and I said 'hi' back. The poor girl was still running around tending to the injured. Considering she had been in the grand fight, I thought she would get a break by now – the princess package in the executive suite. But there was not a hint of fatigue on her face, she looked like she could go on for hours.

Hime crouched down, looking over a patient. Dead. Hopeless. But the young healer kept giving him mouth to mouth.

"Charlene?" Hime said, very sweetly.

"He's going to make it," the girl insisted.

Hime put her tender, healing touch on the girl's shoulder. "Charlene, you've been at that for half an hour. I'm sorry, dear. But he's gone."

"I think he's…" She put her ear down, right next to his cold lips. "I think he might be breathing."

"Okay. Let's see." Hime reached into a first aid pack on her hip and took out a small hand mirror. She held it under the guy's nose and waited. Nothing happened. She waited ten more seconds.

It was obvious this guy had passed. Charlene tottered to her feet, and walked away, weeping.

Hime gave a sympathetic sigh. "Her first week. And look what she has to deal with. Poor thing."

But I was looking at that mirror. "Hime? You mind if I borrow that for a second?"

"Oh, sure. Of course." She handed the little mirror to me.

I'm not sure what she thought when I held it up to my eyes and stared into my own reflection. But I kept studying every detail, looking for… what? I don't know what I awaited. Maybe I was going nuts…

But there it was, for only the briefest of moments, my eyes shifted color to a deep magenta. And I swear, they had a weird light of their own inside them…

You might even call it a *glow*…

ACKNOWLEDGMENTS

First, I want to thank the fans who have kept me motivated since 2009, to never stop writing until my story was complete. I am honored that they have invited my characters into their world of imagination. Because of them, I knew I wanted to publish this story one day, but I didn't know if that day would be tomorrow or fifty years later.

This project became more than just about giving my characters an outlet to exist beyond my mind — it became a lifetime milestone. What started as a personal project ended up being a collaboration between family, friends, and devoted online strangers. As a first-time writer, I never could have imagined the immense support I have received.

A huge thank you to fellow authors and colleagues — some I haven't spoke to or reached out to in years — for the endless support during my writing endeavor.

Thank you to the true fighters, my beta readers, who slayed my imposter syndrome day after day.

Thank you to all the artists who contributed to twelve years of fanart and illustrations for my countless number of characters.

This book was not possible without the contributions of talented beta readers and editors from around the world:

Aanchal Jain, Lead Editor (India)
Rick Natkin, Editor (USA)
Nathanael Werdal, Editor (Canada)

Claire, Cover Designer (Australia)
Simona, Map Illustrator (Italy)
Amna, Graphic Designer (Pakistan)
Evan, Environmental Artist (Malaysia)

Every beta reader, including but not limited to:
Bridget (Canada), Viktoria (Bulgaria),
Kosha (India), Mawra (Pakistan), Anase (Nigeria)

And a big thanks to you, who decided to pick up this book and give it a chance. I hope the characters have found a place in your heart.

<h1 style="text-align:center">APPENDIX</h1>

FIGHTER CLASS – Fighters are trained in one of four styles:
  Aegis – bow users in touch with nature and animals.
  Celta – healers & spellcasters who are masters of ko*re*.
  Paragon – brawlers & warriors with close-combat weaponry.
  Umbra – mixed-weapon fighters with self-defense techniques.

HALE INVENTIONS – The Hale family discovered they could process raw crystals containing energy, known as hāstals, and enhanced them with kore to create new technology.
  <u>Aulāce</u> – indestructible shackles made with kore and alloys.
  <u>Aulōg</u> – a lock coded with one's aura. Used to secure doors.
  <u>Clōve</u> – a hāstal-sewn glove capable of communication.
  <u>Comstōne</u> – quartz geodes that direct sounds to other stones.
  <u>Kinastōne</u> – a barrel-shaped geode used to generate energy.
  <u>Kirinvā Stone</u> – a hāstal rumored to offer protection.
  <u>Kōnvoy</u> – a caravan that transports large shipping materials.
  <u>Lumastōne</u> – a glowing pebble that replaces candlelight.
  <u>Oriōn</u> – a cube that crafts a geometric replica of landscapes.
  <u>Renastōne</u> – palm-sized stones that amplify healing abilities.
  <u>Visōr</u> – a platform that mirrors images.

TERMINOLOGY – These jargons and commercial goods are unique to the land of the three empires.

Aster Spells – an advanced category of spells.

Aura – the spiritual energy unique to each individual.

Bitterworm – an invertebrate good for harvesting vegetables.

Buzzbean – a mixture of nuts and herbs used as tea.

Cepha Metal – a dense material that blocks psychic energy.

Cryphedeon – a disc-shaped herbal flower used for flavoring.

Featherpit – someone who wears feathers for fashion, directed at insulting Minettan culture.

Flatty/Flat-Faced – a derogatory word comparing two-faced Althaeans with the sides of a flat coin.

Galuchi Seeds – used as hunting bait to beckon wild animals.

Gotchen – a popular card game that often involves a wager.

Gritbear – a large omnivore with stocky legs and shaggy hair.

Iconel Alloys – materials used to improve durability.

Ilorinae – a territorial plant that can cause fainting spells.

Kamori Powder – pressed ash from the corpse of insects.

Kippin – a type of neutral tea that tastes like water.

Kore – affinity of elemental energy that one is born with.

Larmender – fortified wine made exclusively by House Tepis.

Lucifera Trees – tall and thin tropical trees with wide leaves.

Lorestone – a yellow sharpening stone.

Lumapetal – a herbal plant that grows in wet caves.

Mirithium – a common type of ore used to craft armor.

Muddleberry – a crimson-colored berry used to craft wine.

Norkfruit – a tropical citrus fruit with a purple skin.

Speedspike – plant seeds with a spiky surface.

Swine – a derogatory word used to describe Valenians, who live among nature and are bloated with wealth.

Talla – a symbol or drawing inked into skin.

Valkyrie – Obanian women who become fighters.

Yerna Hay – highly flammable grain crops grown in Valenia.

Zotweed – a mind-altering substance made of dried pedals.

RELIGIONS – It is a common belief that all life departs to either the spiritual world of Nagama or Inferna. If the Gods do not deem the soul worthy to join them in Nagama, they are sent to one of the seven flaming gates of Inferna.

Deity of Orism – Orists believe in one deity: Oris, the God of Judgment. He is primarily worshiped by Althaeans and celtas.

Deities of Quintism – Quintists, common among Minettans, worship only the five main Gods and Goddesses.

<u>Aten</u> – God of Elements
<u>Cordelia</u> – Goddess of War
<u>Sarkan</u> – God of Authority
<u>Taurin</u> – God of Land
<u>Urabe</u> – Goddess of the Sea

Deities of Plethorism – Plethorists acknowledge the existence of hundreds of Gods and Goddesses, but a tribe in Valenia will often choose to praise one or two deities. The following are only a fraction of all known deities:

<u>Accolade</u> – God of Reverence
<u>Candela</u> – Goddess of Purity
<u>Current</u> – God of Negotiation
<u>Cygnus</u> – Goddess of Fate
<u>Erel</u> – Goddess of Mercy
<u>Kanmor</u> – God of Wealth
<u>Lachess</u> – Goddess of Devotion
<u>Mersa</u> – Goddess of Fertility
<u>Mirari</u> – Goddess of Miracles
<u>Ophelia</u> – Goddess of Health
<u>Xerxes</u> – God of Power
<u>Verben</u> – God of Wisdom

Dear Reader,

I am honored that you have made it to this page.

If you enjoyed this read, then please leave
an honest review. Your support
means the world to me.

Love,
Stefanie

Can't wait for the next book? Be the first to
read it when you **become a VIP Member**.
Join today and get free desktop wallpapers.

www.StefanieChu.com/vip

THE STORY CONTINUES IN

ECHOES OF ENMITY
Prequel of the Alliance Series

Friendships are lost.
The trusted becomes traitor.

Follow Mirari's journey toward reuniting and confronting Gaven during the Althaean Siege.

Fall 2023
BIRTH OF RESILIENCE
Book 2 of the Alliance Series

Summer 2024
EDGE OF DIVERGENCE
Book 3 of the Alliance Series

STEFANIECHU.COM/ALLIANCE

ABOUT THE AUTHOR

Stefanie is often seen swooning over birds, applying lemon on everything, and torturing herself with bad films. She took advantage of her MBA studies to live in Asia and Europe, and can currently be spotted in her hometown in Northern California.

Learn more at STEFANIECHU.COM

 facebook.com/StefanieChu.Author
instagram.com/StefanieChu.Author